W9-CSI-104

IN HIGH PLACES

ARTHUR HAILEY

A DELL BOOK

Published by
Dell Publishing
a division of
Bantam Doubleday Dell Publishing Group, Inc.
666 Fifth Avenue
New York, New York 10103

ISBN: 0-440-14000-5

Reprinted by arrangement with Doubleday, New York, New York

Printed in the United States of America

Published simultaneously in Canada

April 1991

13 12 11 10 9 8 7 6 5 4

RAD

Contents

How are the mighty fallen in the midst of the battle! O Jonathan, thou wast slain in thy high places.

The Lament of David

One December 23

On the afternoon and early evening of December 23, three events occurred, seemingly unconnected and, in distance, three thousand miles apart. One was a telephone call, over closely guarded circuits, from the President of the United States to the Prime Minister of Canada; the conversation lasted almost an hour and was somber. The second event was an official reception at the Ottawa residence of Her Majesty's Governor General; the third, the berthing of a ship at Vancouver on the Canadian West coast.

The telephone call came first. It originated in the President's study of the White House and was taken by the Prime Minister in his East Block office on Parliament Hill.

Next was the berthing of the ship. It was the Motor Vessel *Vastervik*, 10,000 tons, Liberian registry, its master Captain Sigurd Jaabeck, a Norwegian. It made fast at La Pointe Pier, on the south and city side of Burrard Inlet Harbor at three o'clock.

Just an hour later in Ottawa where, because of a three-hour time difference it was already evening, the early reception guests began arriving at Government House. The reception was a smallish one: an annual pre-Christmas affair Their Excellencies gave cabinet members and their wives.

Only two of the party guests—the Prime Minister and his Secretary of State for External Affairs—had knowledge of the U.S. President's call. Not one of the guests had ever heard of the M. V. *Vastervik*, nor in the scheme of things was it likely that they would.

And yet, irrevocably and inextricably, the three occurrences were destined to intertwine, like planets and their nebulae whose orbits, in strange mysterious fashion, impinge and share a moment's scintillation.

1

Two The Prime Minister

The Ottawa night was crisp and cold, with clouding skies holding promise of snow before morning. The nation's capital—so the experts said—was in for a white Christmas.

In the rear of a black, chauffeur-driven Oldsmobile, Margaret Howden, wife of the Prime Minister of Canada, touched her husband's hand. "Jamie," she said, "you look tired."

The Right Honorable James McCallum Howden, P.C., LL.B., Q.C., M.P., had closed his eyes, relaxing in the car's warmth. Now he opened them. "Not really." He hated to admit to tiredness at any time. "Just unwinding a little. The past forty-eight hours . . ." He checked himself, glancing towards the chauffeur's broad back. The glass between was raised, but even so it paid to be cautious.

A light from outside touched the glass and he could see his own reflection: the heavy, hawklike face; eagle-beak nose and jutting chin.

Beside him, his wife said amusedly, "Stop looking at yourself or you'll develop . . . what's that psychiatry thing?"

"Narcissism." Her husband smiled, his heavy-lidded eyes crinkling. "But I've had it for years. In politics it's an occupational norm."

There was a pause, then they were serious again.

"Something's happened, hasn't it?" Margaret said softly. "Something important." She had turned towards him, her face troubled, and preoccupied as he was, he could perceive the classic shapeliness of her features. Margaret was still a lovely woman, he thought, and heads had always turned when they came into a room together.

"Yes," he acknowledged. For an instant he was tempted to confide in Margaret; to tell her everything that had occurred so swiftly, beginning with the secret telephone call from the White House, coming across the border two days earlier; the second call this afternoon. Then he decided: this was not the time.

Beside him Margaret said, "There have been so many things lately, and so few moments we've had alone."

2

"I know." He reached out and held her hand.

As if the gesture had unleashed words held back: "Is it worth it all? Haven't you done enough?" Margaret Howden spoke quickly, aware of the journey's shortness, knowing that it was a few minutes drive only between their own house and the Governor General's residence. In a minute or two more this moment of warmth and closeness would be gone. "We've been married forty-two years, Jamie, and most of that time I've had just a part of you. There isn't all that much of life that's left."

"It hasn't been easy for you, has it?" He spoke quietly, genuinely. Margaret's words had moved him.

"No; not always." There was a note of uncertainty. It was an entangled subject, something they spoke of rarely.

"There *will* be time, I promise you. If other things . . ." He stopped, remembering the imponderables about the future which the past two days had brought.

"What other things?"

"There's one more task. Perhaps the biggest I've had."

She withdrew her hand. "Why does it have to be you?"

It was impossible to answer. Even to Margaret, privy to so many of his thoughts, he could never mouth his innermost conviction: *because there is no one else; no other with my own stature, with intellect and foresight to make the great decisions soon to come.*

"Why you?" Margaret said again.

They had entered the grounds of Government House. Rubber crunched on gravel. In the darkness, park land rolled away on either side.

Momentarily he had a sharp sense of guilt about his relationship with Margaret. She had always accepted political life loyally, even though never enjoying it as he did himself. But he had long sensed her hope that one day he would abandon politics so that they could become closer again, as in the early years.

On the other hand he had been a good husband. There had been no other woman in his life . . . except for the one occasion years before: the love affair that had begun, and had lasted almost a year until he had ended it resolutely, before his marriage could be imperiled. But sometimes guilt nudged him there . . . nervousness, too, that Margaret should ever learn the truth.

"We'll talk tonight," he said placatingly. "When we get back."

The car stopped and the near-side door was opened. A Mountie in scarlet dress uniform saluted smartly as the Prime Minister and his wife alighted. James Howden smiled an acknowledgment, shook hands with the policeman, and introduced Margaret. It was the sort of thing Howden always did gracefully and without condescension. At the same time he was well aware that the Mountie would talk about the incident afterward, and it was surprising how far the ripples could extend from a simple gesture of that kind.

As they entered Government House an aide-de-camp—a youngish lieutenant of the Royal Canadian Navy—stepped smartly forward. The aide's gold-trimmed dress uniform looked uncomfortably tight; probably, Howden thought, the result of too much time at a desk in Ottawa and too little at sea. Officers had to wait their turn for sea duty now that the Navy was just a token force—in some ways a joke, though a costly one for taxpayers.

They were led from the high pillared entrance hall up a rich red-carpeted marble stairway, through a wide, tapestried corridor and into the Long Drawing Room where small receptions such as tonight's were usually held. A big, elongated, shoe-box shaped room, high ceilinged, with crossbeams plastered over, it had the intimacy of a hotel lobby, though with rather more comfort. So far, however, the invitingly grouped chairs and settees, upholstered in soft shades of turquoise and daffodil yellow, were unoccupied, the sixty or so guests standing, chatting in informal knots. From above their heads, a full-length portrait of the Queen stared haughtily across the room at window draperies, now drawn, of rich gold brocade. At the far end, festooned lights on a decorated Christmas tree flashed on and off. The buzz of conversation lessened perceptibly as the Prime Minister and his wife entered, Margaret Howden in a ball gown of pale mauve lace, above the gown her shoulders bare.

Still preceding, the naval lieutenant led the way directly to a point near a blazing log fire where the Governor General had been receiving. The aide announced: "The Prime Minister and Mrs. Howden."

His Excellency, the Right Honorable Air Marshal Sheldon Griffiths, V.C., D.F.C., R.C.A.F. (retired), Her Majesty's Governor General in the Dominion of Canada, extended his hand. "Good evening, Prime Minister." Then, inclining his head courteously, "Margaret."

Margaret Howden curtsied expertly, her smile including Natalie Griffiths at her husband's side.

"Good evening, Your Excellency," James Howden said. "You're looking extremely well."

The Governor General, silver-haired, ruddy, and militarily erect despite his years, was wearing faultless evening dress with a long impressive row of medals and decorations. He leaned forward confidentially. "I feel as if my damn tailplane's burning up." Gesturing to the fireplace, "Now you're here, let's move away from this inferno."

Together the four strolled through the room, the Governor General a courteous, friendly host.

"I saw your new Karsh portrait," he told Melissa Tayne, serene and gracious wife of Dr. Borden Tayne, the Health and Welfare Minister. "It's very beautiful and almost does you justice." Her husband, alongside, flushed with pleasure.

Next to them Daisy Cawston, lumpish, motherly, and not caring, burbled, "I've been trying to persuade my husband to sit for Karsh, Your Excellency, at least while Stuart has some hair left." Beside her, Stuart Cawston, Finance Minister, and known to friends and adversaries as "Smiling Stu," grinned good-naturedly.

Soberly the Governor General inspected Cawston's rapidly balding scalp. "Better take your wife's advice, old chap. Not much time left, I'd say." His tone robbed the words of any offense and there was a chorus of laughter in which the Finance Minister joined.

Now, as the viceregal group moved on, James Howden dropped back. He caught the eye of Arthur Lexington, the External Affairs Minister, several groups away with his wife Susan, and nodded imperceptibly. Casually Lexington excused himself and strolled over—a short cherubic figure in his late fifties whose easy-going, avuncular ways concealed one of the sharpest minds in international politics.

"Good evening, Prime Minister," Arthur Lexington said. Without changing his expression he lowered his voice. "Everything's teed."

"You've talked with Angry?" Howden asked crisply. His Excellency Philip B. Angrove, "Angry" to his friends, was the U.S. Ambassador to Canada.

Lexington nodded. He said softly, "Your meeting with the

President is set for January second. Washington, of course. That gives us ten days."

"We'll need all of it."

"I know."

"Have you discussed procedure?"

"Not in detail. There'll be a state banquet for you the first day—all the usual folderol—then the private meeting, just four of us, the following day. I suppose that's when we get down to business."

"How about an announcement?"

Lexington nodded warningly, and the Prime Minister followed his eyes. A manservant was approaching with a tray of drinks. Among them was a single glass of grape juice, the latter a beverage which James Howden—a teetotaler —was believed to favor. Noncommittally he accepted the drink.

As the manservant left, Lexington sipping rye and water, Aaron Gold, Postmaster General and only Jewish member of the Cabinet, joined them. "My feet are killing me," he announced. "Couldn't you drop a word to His Ex, Prime Minister—ask him for God's sake sit down, so the rest of us can get the weight off."

"Never known you in a hurry to get off your feet, Aaron." Arthur Lexington grinned. "Not judging by your speeches."

Stuart Cawston, near by, had overheard. He called across: "Why the tired feet, Aaron? Been delivering Christmas mail?"

"I should get humorists," the Postmaster General said gloomily, "when all I need is tenderness."

"It was my understanding you had that already," Howden said amusedly. The idiot counterpoint, he thought: comic dialogue on side-stage to Macbeth. Perhaps it was needed, though. The issues which had suddenly loomed ahead, touching the very existence of Canada, were formidable enough. How many in this room besides Lexington and himself had any idea . . . Now the others moved away.

Arthur Lexington said softly, "I talked to Angry about an announcement of the meeting and he called the State Department again. They say the President has asked there be no announcement for the time being. Their thinking seems to be that coming so soon after the Russian note, there might be some obvious implications."

"Can't see it'd do much harm," Howden said, his hawklike

features pensive. "It'll have to be announced soon. But if that's what he wants . . ."

Around them conversation swirled as glasses clinked. ". . . I took off fourteen pounds, then discovered this heavenly bakery. Now it's all back . . ." ". . . explained I didn't see the red light because I was hurrying to meet my husband who's a cabinet minister . . ." ". . . I'll say this for *Time;* even the distortions are interesting . . ." ". . . Really, Toronto people nowadays are insufferable; they've a kind of cultural indigestion . . ." ". . . So I told him, if we want stupid liquor laws, that's our business; anyway, just try using the telephone in London . . ." ". . . I think Tibetans are cute; there's a cave-man quality . . ." ". . . Haven't you noticed, the department stores are billing faster? One time you could count on two extra weeks . . ." ". . . We should have stopped Hitler at the Rhine and Khrushchev in Budapest . . ." ". . . Make no mistake: if men had to be pregnant, there'd be a lot less—thank you, a gin and tonic."

"When we do make the announcement," Lexington said, his voice still lowered, "we'll say the meeting is for trade talks."

"Yes," Howden agreed. "I suppose that's best."

"When will you tell the Cabinet?"

"I haven't decided. I thought perhaps the Defense Committee first. I'd like a few reactions." Howden smiled dourly. "Not everyone has your grasp of world affairs, Arthur."

"Well, I suppose I get certain advantages." Lexington paused, his homely face thoughtful, eyes questioning. "Even so, the idea will take a lot of getting used to."

"Yes," James Howden said. "I expect it will."

The two moved apart, the Prime Minister rejoining the viceregal group. His Excellency was offering a quiet word of condolence to a cabinet member whose father had died the week before. Now, moving on, he congratulated another whose daughter had won academic honors. The old man does it well, Howden thought—the right balance of affability and dignity; not too much of the one or the other.

James Howden found himself wondering just how long the cult of kings and queens and a royal representative would last in Canada. Eventually, of course, the country would cut itself loose from the British monarchy just as, years before, it had shed the yoke of rule by the British Parliament. The idea of royal occasions—quaint protocol, gilt coaches, court lackeys, and gold dinner services—was out of tune with the times, in North America especially. Already a good deal of ceremony associated with the throne seemed mildly funny, like a good-natured charade. When the day came, as it would, when people began to laugh out loud, then decay would have begun in earnest. Or perhaps, before that, some backstairs royal scandal would erupt and the crumbling come swiftly, in Britain as well as Canada.

The thought of royalty reminded him of a question he must raise tonight. The small entourage had paused, and now, easing the Governor General away from the others, Howden asked, "It's next month, sir, I believe, that you leave for England."

The "sir" was strictly for effect. In private, the two men had used first names for years.

"The eighth," the Governor General said. "Natalie's coerced me into going by sea from New York. Fine damn thing for an ex-Chief of Air Staff, isn't it?"

"You'll be seeing Her Majesty in London, of course," the Prime Minister said. "When you do, I wonder if you'd raise the question of the state visit here we've suggested for March. I think perhaps a few words from you might help towards a favorable decision."

The invitation to the Queen had been tendered several weeks earlier through the High Commissioner in London. It had been calculated—at least by James Howden and his senior party colleagues—as a maneuver before a late spring or early summer election, since a royal visit was usually a sure vote getter for the party in power. Now, with the developments of the past few days and the new and vital issues which the country would soon know about, it was doubly important.

"Yes, I'd heard the invitation had gone." The Governor General's tone held a hint of reservation. "Rather short notice, I'd say. They seem to like at least a year's warning at Buck House."

"I'm aware of that." Howden felt a momentary annoyance that Griffiths should presume to instruct him on a subject he was fully familiar with. "But sometimes these things can be arranged. I think it would be a good thing for the country, sir."

Despite the "sir" again, James Howden made it clear by inflection that he was issuing an order. And, he reflected, in some ways it would be close to that when received in London. The Court was fully conscious of Canada's position as the richest and most influential member of the shaky British Commonwealth, and if other commitments could be shuffled it was a virtual certainty that the Queen and her husband would come. Actually, he suspected the present delay in acceptance was probably merely for effect; but even so it was a precaution to use all the pressure he had.

"I'll pass on your sentiments, Prime Minister."

"Thank you." The exchange reminded Howden that he must begin to think about a successor to Sheldon Griffiths, whose twice-extended term of office was due to expire next year.

Across the hall from the Long Drawing Room a line had formed at the dining-room buffet. It was not surprising; the Government House chef, Alphonse Goubaux, was justly famed for his culinary skill. Once there had been a strong rumor that the U.S. President's wife was trying to lure Chef Goubaux from Ottawa to Washington. Until the report was quashed there had been all the makings of an international incident.

Howden felt Margaret touch his arm, and they moved with the others. "Natalie's boasting about the lobster in aspic; she claims it must be tasted to be believed."

"Tell me when I bite on it, dear," he said and smiled. It was an old joke between them. James Howden took scant interest in food and, unless reminded, sometimes missed meals entirely. At other times he ate with his mind preoccupied, and occasionally in the past, when Margaret had prepared special delicacies, he had consumed them with no idea afterwards what he had eaten. Early in their married life Margaret had been moved to anger and tears by her husband's disinterest in cooking, which she loved, but had long since switched to amused resignation.

Glancing at the well-stocked buffet, where an attentive waiter held two plates in readiness, Howden observed, "It looks impressive. What is it all?"

Pleased with the distinction of serving the Prime Minister, the waiter rattled off the name of each dish: beluga Malossol caviar, oysters Malpeque, *pâté maison*, lobster aspic, Winnipeg smoked gold-eye, *foie gras Mignonette*, cold roast prime ribs, galantine of capon, hickory-smoked turkey, Virginia ham.

"Thank you," Howden said. "Just give me a little beef, well done, and some salad."

As the man's face fell, Margaret whispered, "Jamie!" and the Prime Minister added hastily, "And also some of whatever it was my wife was recommending."

As they turned from the table the naval aide reappeared. "Excuse me, sir. His Excellency's compliments, and Miss Freedeman is telephoning you."

Howden put down his untouched plate. "Very well."

"Must you go now, Jamie?" There was annoyance in Margaret's tone.

He nodded. "Milly wouldn't call if it could wait."

"The call is put through to the library, sir." After bowing to Margaret the aide preceded him.

A few minutes later: "Milly," he said into the phone, "I made a promise that this would be important."

His personal secretary's soft contralto voice answered, "It is, I think."

Sometimes he liked to talk just for the sake of hearing Milly speak. He asked, "Where are you?"

"At the office; I came back. Brian is here with me. That's why I called."

He had an irrational flash of jealousy at the thought of Milly Freedeman alone with someone else . . . Milly who had shared with him, years before, the liaison he had remembered with a trace of guilt tonight. At the time their affair had been passionate and all-consuming, but when it ended, as, he had known from the beginning it must, both had resumed their separate lives as if closing and locking a door between two rooms which continued to adjoin. Neither had ever spoken of that singular, special time again. But occasionally, as at this moment, the sight or sound of Milly could thrill him anew, as if he were once again young and eager, the years falling away . . .

But afterward, always, nervousness would supervene: the nervousness of one who—in public life—could not afford to have the chink in his armor penetrated.

"All right, Milly," the Prime Minister instructed. "Let me talk to Brian."

There was a pause, and the sound of the telephone changing hands. Then a strong male voice declared crisply, "There's been a press leak in Washington, chief. A Canadian reporter down there has found out you're expected in town to meet the Big Wheel. We need a statement out of Ottawa. Otherwise, if the news comes from Washington, it could look as if you're being sent for."

Brian Richardson, the energetic forty-year-old director and national organizer of the party, seldom wasted words. His communications, spoken and written, still retained a flavor of the clear, crisp advertising copy he used to produce, first as a skilled copywriter, then as a top-flight agency executive. Nowadays, though, advertising was something he delegated to others, his principal duty being to advise James McCallum Howden on day-to-day problems in retaining public favor for the Government.

Howden inquired anxiously, "There's been no leak about the subject matter?"

"No," Richardson said. "All the taps are tight on that. It's just the fact of the meeting."

Appointed to his job soon after Howden's own accession to party leadership, Brian Richardson had already masterminded two victorious election campaigns and other successes in between. Shrewd, resourceful, with an encyclopedic mind and an organizing genius, he was one of the three or four men in the country whose calls were unquestioningly passed through the Prime Minister's private switchboard at any hour. He was also one of the most influential, and no Government decision of a major nature was ever taken without his knowledge or advice. Unlike most of Howden's ministers, who as yet were unaware of the forthcoming Washington meeting, or its purport, Richardson had been told at once.

And yet, outside a limited circle, the name of Brian Richardson was almost unknown, and on the rare occasions his picture appeared in newspapers it was always discreetly —in the second or third row of a political group.

"Our arrangement with the White House was no announcement for a few days," Howden said. "And then it'll be a cover statement that the talks are about trade and fiscal policy."

"Hell, chief, you can still have it that way," Richardson said. "The announcement will be a little sooner, that's all— like tomorrow morning."

"What's the alternative?"

"Speculation all over the lot, including the subjects we want to avoid. What one joe found out today others can learn tomorrow." The party director went on crisply. "At the moment only one reporter has the story that you're planning a trip—Newton of the Toronto *Express*. He's a smart cookie, called his publisher first and the publisher called me."

James Howden nodded. The *Express* was a strong Government supporter, at times almost a party organ. There had been exchange of favors before.

"I can hold up the story for twelve, maybe fourteen hours," Richardson continued. "After that it's a risk. Can't External Affairs get off the pot with a statement by then?"

With his free hand the Prime Minister rubbed his long, birdlike nose. Then he said decisively, "I'll tell them to." The words would presage a busy night for Arthur Lexington and his senior officials. They would have to work through the U.S. Embassy and with Washington, of course, but the White House would go along, once it was known that the press was on to something; they were conditioned to that kind of situation down there. Besides, a plausible cover statement was as essential to the President as it was to himself. The real issues behind their meeting in ten days' time were too delicate for public chewing at this moment.

"While we're talking," Richardson said, "is there anything new on the Queen's visit?"

"No, but I talked to Shel Griffiths a few minutes ago. He'll see what he can do in London."

"I hope it works." The party director sounded doubtful. "The old boy's always so damn correct. Did you tell him to give the lady a real hard push?"

"Not quite in those words." Howden smiled. "But that was the gist of my suggestion."

A chuckle down the line. "As long as she comes, anyway. It could help us a lot next year, what with all the other things."

About to hang up, a thought occurred to Howden. "Brian."

"Yes."

"Try to drop in over the holiday."

"Thanks. I will."

"How about your wife?"

Richardson answered cheerfully, "I guess you'll have to settle for me solo."

"I don't mean to pry." James Howden hesitated, aware that Milly was hearing half the conversation. "Are things no better?"

"Eloise and I live in a state of armed neutrality," Richardson answered matter-of-factly. "But it has advantages."

Howden could guess the kind of advantages Richardson meant, and once more he had an irrational jealousy at the thought of the party director and Milly alone together. Aloud, he said, "I'm sorry."

"It's surprising what you can get used to," Richardson said. "At least Eloise and I know where we stand, and that's separately. Anything else, chief?"

"No," Howden said, "nothing else. I'll go and talk to Arthur now."

He returned from the library to the Long Drawing Room, the hum of conversation moving out to meet him. The atmosphere was freer now; drinks and supper, which was almost over, had contributed to an air of relaxation. He avoided several groups whose members looked up expectantly as he passed, smiling and moving on.

Arthur Lexington was standing on the fringe of a laughing cluster of people watching the Finance Minister, Stuart Cawston, do minor conjuring tricks—a pastime with which, once in a while, he relieved the tedium during breaks in cabinet meetings. "Watch this dollar," Cawston was saying. "I shall now make it disappear."

"Hell!" someone said predictably, "that's no trick; you do it all the time." The Governor General, among the small audience, joined in the mild laughter.

The Prime Minister touched Lexington's arm and for the second time took the External Affairs Minister aside. He explained the purport of what the party director had said and the need for a press announcement before morning. Typically, Lexington asked no unnecessary questions. Nodding his agreement, "I'll call at the embassy and talk to Angry," he said, "then start some of my own people working." He chuckled. "Always gives me a sense of importance to keep others out of bed."

"Now then you two! No affairs of state tonight." It was Natalie Griffiths. She touched their shoulders lightly.

Arthur Lexington turned, beaming. "Not even an itsy-bitsy world crisis?"

"Not even that. Besides, I've a crisis in the kitchen. That's much more important." The Governor General's wife moved toward her husband. She said in a distressed whisper, not meant to be overheard but carrying clearly to those near by, "Of all things, Sheldon, we've no cognac."

"That's impossible!"

"Shush! I don't know how it happened, but it has."

"We'll have to get an emergency supply."

"Charles has phoned the air force mess. They're rushing some over."

"My God!" There was a plaintiveness to His Excellency's voice. "Can't we ever entertain without something going wrong?"

Arthur Lexington murmured, "I suppose I must drink my coffee neat." He glanced at the fresh glass of grape juice which a few minutes earlier had been brought to James Howden. "You don't have to worry. They've probably gallons of that."

The Governor General was muttering angrily, "I'll have someone's scalp for this."

"Now, Sheldon"—still the whispers, host and hostess oblivious of their amused audience—"it's just one of those things, and you know how careful one has to be with the help."

"Blast the help!"

Natalie Griffiths said patiently, "I thought you ought to know. But let me deal with it, dear."

"Oh, very well." His Excellency smiled—a mixture of resignation and affection—and together they returned to their original place by the fire.

"*Sic transit gloria.* The voice which launched a thousand airplanes may not now rebuke the scullery maid." It had been said with an edge and a shade too loudly. The Prime Minister frowned.

The speaker was Harvey Warrender, Minister of Citizenship and Immigration. He stood beside them now, a tall, pudgily built figure with thinning hair and a bass, booming voice. His manner was habitually didactic—a hangover, perhaps, from the years he had spent as a college professor, before entering politics.

"Steady, Harvey," Arthur Lexington said. "That's royalty you're treading on."

"Sometimes," Warrender responded, his voice lower, "I resent reminders that brass hats invariably survive."

There was an uncomfortable silence. The reference was well understood. The Warrenders' only son, a young air force officer, had been killed heroically in action during World War II. The father's pride in his son had been lasting, as had his grief.

Several replies to his remark about brass hats might easily have been made. The Governor General had fought bravely in two wars, and the Victoria Cross was not awarded lightly . . . Death and sacrifice in war observed no boundaries of rank or age . . .

It seemed best to say nothing.

"Well, on with the motley," Arthur Lexington said brightly. "Excuse me, Prime Minister; Harvey." He nodded, then crossed the room to rejoin his wife.

"Why is it," Warrender said, "that to some people certain subjects are embarrassing? Or is there a cut-off date for remembrance?"

"I think it's mainly a question of the time and place." James Howden had no desire to pursue the subject. He sometimes wished he could dispense with Harvey Warrender as a member of the Government, but there were compelling reasons he could not.

Seeking to change the subject, the Prime Minister said, "Harvey, I've been wanting to talk about your department." He was remiss, he supposed, in using a social occasion for so much official business. But of late many subjects he should have dealt with at his desk had had to stand aside for more urgent business. Immigration was one.

"Is it praise or blame you are about to tender me?" Harvey Warrender's question had a touch of belligerence. Plainly the drink he was holding was not his first.

Howden was reminded of a conversation a few days ago when he and the party director had been discussing current political problems. Brian Richardson had said: "The Immigration Department has gotten us a consistently bad press, and unfortunately it's one of the few issues that electors can understand. You can fool around with tariffs and the bank rate all you want, and the votes it will affect are negligible. But let the papers get one picture of a mother and child being deported—like that case last month—and that's when the party needs to worry."

Momentarily, Howden experienced a sense of anger at having to consider trivia when—particularly now—bigger and vital issues demanded so much of his mind. Then he reflected that the need to mix homely things with great affairs had always been a politician's lot. Often it was a key to power—never to lose sight of small events amid the big. And immigration was a subject which always disturbed him. It had so many facets, hedged around with political pitfalls as well as advantages. The difficult thing was to be certain which were which.

Canada was still a promised land for many, and likely to remain so; therefore any Government must handle its population inlet valves with extreme caution. Too many immigrants from one source, too few from another, could be sufficient to change the balance of power within a generation. In a way, the Prime Minister thought, we have our own *apartheid* policy, though fortunately the barriers of race and color are set up discreetly and put into effect beyond our borders, in Canadian embassies and consulates overseas. And definite as they are, at home we can pretend they do not exist.

Some people in the country, he knew, wanted more immigration, others less. The "more" group included idealists who would fling the doors wide to all comers, and employers, who favored a bigger labor force. Opposition to immigration usually came from labor unions, given to crying "unemployment" each time immigration was discussed, and failing to recognize that unemployment, in some degree at least, was a necessary economic fact of life. On this side also were the Anglo-Saxon and Protestant segments—in surprising numbers—who objected to "too many foreigners," particularly if the immigrants happened to be Catholic. Often it was necessary for the Government to walk a tightrope to avoid alienating one side or the other.

He decided this was a moment to be blunt. "Your department has been getting a bad press, Harvey, and I think a good deal of it is your own fault. I want you to take a tighter hold of things and stop letting your officials have so much of their own way. Replace a few if you have to, even at the top; we can't fire civil servants but we've plenty of shelves to put them on. And for God's sake keep those controversial immigration cases out of the papers! The one last month, for example—the woman and child."

"That woman had been running a brothel in Hong Kong," Harvey Warrender said. "And she had V.D."

"Perhaps that isn't a good example. But there've been plenty of others, and when these sensitive cases come up you make the Government look like some heartless ogre, which harms us all."

The Prime Minister had spoken quietly but intensely, his strong eyes riveting the other man.

"Obviously," Warrender said, "my question is answered. Praise is not the order of the day."

James Howden said sharply, "It isn't a question of praise or blame. It's a matter of good political judgment."

"And your political judgment has always been better than mine, Jim. Isn't that so?" Warrender's eyes squinted upward. "Otherwise I might be leader of the party instead of you."

Howden made no reply. The liquor in the other man was obviously taking hold. Now Warrender said, "What my officials are doing is administering the law as it stands. I happen to think they're performing a good job. If you don't like it, why don't we get together and amend the Immigration Act?"

He had made a mistake, the Prime Minister decided, in choosing this time and place to talk. Seeking to end the conversation, he said, "We can't do that. There's too much else in our legislative program."

"Balls!"

It was like a whipcrack in the room. There was a second's silence. Heads turned. The Prime Minister saw the Governor General glance in their direction. Then conversation resumed, but Howden could sense that others were listening.

"You're afraid of immigration," Warrender said. "We're all afraid—the way every other Government has been. That's why we won't admit a few things honestly, even among ourselves."

Stuart Cawston, who had finished his conjuring tricks a moment or two earlier, strolled with seeming casualness to join them. "Harvey," the Finance Minister said cheerfully, "you're making an ass of yourself."

"Take care of him, Stu," the Prime Minister said. He could feel his anger growing; if he continued to handle this himself there was a danger he would lose his temper, always volatile, which could only make the situation worse. Moving away, he joined Margaret and another group.

But he could still hear Warrender, this time addressing Cawston.

"When it comes to immigration I tell you we Canadians are

a bunch of hypocrites. Our immigration policy—the policy that I administer, my friend—has to say one thing and mean another."

"Tell me later," Stuart Cawston said. He was still trying to smile, but barely succeeding.

"I'll tell you now!" Harvey Warrender had gripped the Finance Minister's arm firmly. "There are two things this country needs if it's to go on expanding and everybody in this room knows it. One is a good big pool of unemployed for industry to draw on, and the other is a continued Anglo-Saxon majority. But do we ever admit it in public? No!"

The Minister of Citizenship and Immigration paused, glared around him, then plowed on. "Both those things need carefully balanced immigration. We have to let immigrants come in, because when industry expands the manpower should be ready and waiting—not next week, or next month, or next year, but at the moment the factories need it. But open the gates of immigration too wide or too often, or both, and what happens? The population goes out of balance. And it wouldn't take too many generations of those kind of mistakes before you'd have the House of Commons debating in Italian and a Chinaman running Government House."

This time there were several comments of disapproval from the other guests to whom Warrender's voice had become increasingly audible. Moreover the Governor General had quite plainly heard the last remark and the Prime Minister saw him beckon an aide. Harvey Warrender's wife, a pale, fragile woman, had moved uncertainly toward her husband and taken his arm. But he ignored her.

Dr. Borden Tayne, the Health and Welfare Minister and a former college boxing champion who towered above them all, said in a stage whisper, "For Christ's sake, knock it off!" He had joined Cawston at Warrender's side.

A voice murmured urgently, "Get him out of here!"

Another answered, "He can't go. Nobody can leave until the Governor General does."

Unabashed, Harvey Warrender was continuing.

"When you're talking about immigration," he declared loudly, "I tell you the public wants sentiment, not facts. Facts are uncomfortable. People like to think of their country as holding the door open for the poor and suffering. It makes them feel noble. Only thing is, they'd just as soon the poor and suffering keep well out of sight when they get here, and not track lice in the suburbs or muddy up the prissy new churches. No siree, the public in this country doesn't want wide-open immigration. What's more, it knows the Government will never allow it, so there's no real risk in hollering for it. That way, everybody can be righteous and safe at the same time."

In a separate compartment of his mind the Prime Minister acknowledged that everything Harvey had said made sound sense but impractical politics.

"What started all this?" one of the women asked.

Harvey Warrender heard the remark and answered. "It started because I was told to change the way I'm running my department. But I'd remind you I'm enforcing the Immigration Act—the law." He looked at the phalanx of male figures now around him. "And I'll go on enforcing the law until you bastards agree to change it."

Somebody said, "Perhaps you won't have a department tomorrow, chum."

One of the aides—an air force flight lieutenant this time—appeared at the Prime Minister's side. He announced quietly, "His Excellency asked me to tell you, sir, that he is withdrawing."

James Howden glanced toward the outer doorway. The Governor General was smilingly shaking hands with a few of the guests. With Margaret beside him, the Prime Minister moved across. The others melted away.

"I hope you won't mind our retiring early," the Governor General said. "Natalie and I are a little tired."

"I do apologize," Howden began.

"Don't, my dear fellow. Best if I don't see anything." The Governor General smiled warmly. "A most happy Christmas to you Prime Minister. And to you, Margaret my dear."

With quiet, firm dignity, preceded by an aide as the woman guests curtsied and their husbands bowed, their Excellencies withdrew.

2

In the car returning from Government House, Margaret asked, "After what happened tonight, won't Harvey Warrender have to resign?"

"I don't know, dear," James Howden said thoughtfully. "He may not want to."

"Can't you force him?"

He wondered what Margaret would say if he answered truthfully: *No, I can't force Harvey Warrender to resign. And the reason is that somewhere in this city—in a safety deposit box, perhaps—there is a scrap of paper with some handwriting—my own. And if produced and made public, it might just well be an obituary—or a suicide note from James McCallum Howden.*

Instead he answered, "Harvey has a big following in the party, you know."

"But surely a following wouldn't excuse what happened tonight."

He made no answer.

He had never told Margaret about the convention, about the deal that he and Harvey had made nine years ago over the party leadership; the hard-driven deal, with the two of them alone in the small theatrical dressing room while outside in the big Toronto auditorium their rival factions cheered, awaiting the balloting which had been unaccountably delayed—unaccountably, that is, except to the two chief opponents dealing their cards, face up, behind the scenes.

Nine years. James Howden's thoughts went back . . .

. . . They would win the next election. Everyone in the party knew it. There was eagerness, a smell of victory, a sense of things to come.

The party had convened to elect a new leader. It was a virtual certainty that whoever was elected would become Prime Minister within a year. It was a prize and an opportunity which James McCallum Howden had dreamed of all his political life.

The choice lay between himself and Harvey Warrender. Warrender led the party's intellectuals. He had strong support among the rank and file. James Howden was a middle-of-the-roader. Their strength was approximately equal.

Outside in the meeting hall there was noise and cheering.

"I'm willing to withdraw," Harvey said. "On terms."

James Howden asked, "What terms?"

"First—a cabinet post of my own choosing, for as long as we're in power."

"You can have anything except External Affairs or Health." Howden had no intention of creating an ogre to compete with himself. External Affairs could keep a man permanently in the headlines. The Health Department disbursed family allowances to the populace and its minister rode high in public favor.

"I'd accept that," Harvey Warrender said, "providing you agree to the other."

The delegates outside were getting restless. Through the closed door they could hear feet stomping, impatient shouts.

"Tell me your second condition," Howden said.

"When we're in office," Harvey said slowly, "there'll be a lot of changes. Take television. The country's growing and there's room for more stations. We've already said we'll reorganize the Board of Broadcast Governors. We can load it with our own people, and a few others who'll go along." He stopped.

"Go on," Howden said.

"I want the TV franchise for ————." He named a city —the country's most prosperous industrial center. "In my nephew's name."

James Howden whistled softly. If it were done, it would be patronage on a grand scale. The TV franchise was a plum of plums. Already there were many favor seekers—big money interests among them—jostling in line.

"It's worth two million dollars," Howden said.

"I know." Harvey Warrender seemed a little flushed. "But I'm thinking of my old age. They don't pay college professors a fortune, and I've never saved any money in politics."

"If it were traced back . . ."

"It won't be traceable," Harvey said. "I'll see to that. My name won't appear anywhere. They can suspect all they want, but it won't be traceable."

Howden shook his head in doubt. Outside there was another burst of noise—catcalls now, and some ironic singing.

"I'll make you a promise, Jim," Harvey Warrender said. "If I go down—for this or anything else—I'll take the blame alone and I won't involve you. But if you fire me, or fail to support me on an honest issue, I'll take you too."

"You couldn't prove . . ."

"I want it in writing," Harvey said. He gestured toward the hall. "Before we go out there. Otherwise we'll let it go to a vote."

It would be a close thing. They both knew it. James Howden envisaged the cup he had coveted slipping away.

"I'll do it," he said. "Give me something to write on."

Harvey had passed him a convention program and he had scribbled the words on the back—words which could destroy him utterly if they were ever used.

"Don't worry," Harvey said, pocketing the card. "It will be safe. And when we're both out of politics I'll give it back to you."

They had gone outside then—Harvey Warrender to make a speech renouncing the leadership—one of the finest of his political life—and James Howden to be elected, cheered, and chaired through the hall . . .

The bargain struck had been kept on both sides even though, over the years, as James Howden's prestige had risen, Harvey Warrender's had steadily declined. Nowadays it was hard to remember that Warrender had once been a serious contender for the party leadership; certainly he was nowhere in line of succession now. But that sort of thing happened so often in politics; once a man was eclipsed in a contest for power, his stature, it seemed, grew less as time went on.

Their car had turned out of Government House grounds, heading west toward the Prime Minister's residence at 24 Sussex Drive.

"I've sometimes thought," Margaret said half to herself, "that Harvey Warrender is just a little mad."

That was the trouble, Howden thought; Harvey *was* a little mad. That was why there was no assurance that he might not produce that hastily written agreement of nine years earlier even though, in doing so, he would destroy himself.

What were Harvey's own feelings about that long-ago deal, Howden wondered. As far as he knew, Harvey Warrender had always been honest in politics until that time. Since then, Harvey's nephew had had his TV franchise and, if rumor were true, had made a fortune. So had Harvey, presumably; his standard of living now was far beyond the means of a cabinet minister, though fortunately he had been discreet and not indulged in sudden changes.

At the time the franchise was awarded there had been plenty of criticism and innuendo. But nothing had ever been

proven and the Howden government, newly elected with a
big majority in the House of Commons, had steam-rollered
its critics, and eventually—as he had known from the first
would happen—people had grown tired of the subject and
it dropped out of sight.

But was Harvey remembering? And suffering a little, with
a stirring of uneasy conscience? And trying, perhaps, in
some warped and twisted way to make amends?

There had been a strange thing about Harvey lately—an
almost obsessive concern with doing the "right" thing and
hewing to the line of law, even in trifling ways. On several
occasions recently there had been argument at Cabinet—
Harvey objecting because some proposed action had overtones of political expediency; Harvey arguing that every fine-
print clause in every law must be scrupulously observed.
When that happened James Howden had thought little about
the incidents, dismissing them as passing eccentricity. But
now, remembering Harvey's alcoholic insistence tonight that
immigration law must be administered exactly as laid down,
he began to wonder.

"Jamie, dear," Margaret said, "Harvey Warrender doesn't
have some hold over you, does he?"

"Of course not!" Then, wondering if he had been a shade
too emphatic, "It's just that I don't want to be rushed into
a hasty decision. We'll see what reaction there is tomorrow.
After all, it was just our own people who were there."

He felt Margaret's eyes upon him and wondered if she
knew that he had lied.

3

They entered the big stone mansion—official residence of
the Prime Minister for his term of office—by the awning-
shielded main front door. Inside, Yarrow, the steward, met
them and took their coats. He announced, "The American
Ambassador has been trying to reach you, sir. The embassy
called twice and stated the matter was urgent."

James Howden nodded. Probably Washington had learned
of the press leak too. If so, it would make Arthur Lexington's assignment that much easier. "Wait for five minutes,"
he instructed, "then let the switchboard know I'm home."

"We'll have coffee in the drawing room, Mr. Yarrow,"

Margaret said. "And some sandwiches, please, for Mr. Howden; he missed the buffet." She stopped in the main-hall powder room to arrange her hair.

James Howden had gone ahead, through the series of hallways to the third hall, with its big french doors overlooking the river and the Gatineau Hills beyond. It was a sight which always enraptured him and even at night, oriented by distant pin-point lights, he could visualize it: the wide, windflecked Ottawa River; the same river which the adventurer Etienne Brûlé had navigated three centuries and a half before; and afterwards Champlain; and later the missionaries and traders, plying their legendary route westward to the Great Lakes and the fur-rich North. And beyond the river lay the distant Quebec shore line, storied and historic, witness to many changes: much that had come, and much that would one day end.

In Ottawa, James Howden always thought, it was difficult not to have a sense of history. Especially now that the city —once beautiful and then commercially despoiled—was fast becoming green again: tree-thronged and laced with manicured parkways, thanks to the National Capital Commission. True the government buildings were largely characterless, bearing the stamp of what a critic had called "the limp hand of bureaucratic art." But even so there was a natural ruggedness about them, and given time, with natural beauty restored, Ottawa might one day equal Washington as a capital and perhaps surpass it.

Behind him beneath the wide, curved staircase, one of two gilt telephones on an Adam side table chimed softly twice. It was the American Ambassador.

"Hullo, Angry," James Howden said. "I hear that your people let the cat out."

The Hon. Phillip Angrove's Bostonian drawl came back. "I know, Prime Minister, and I'm damned apologetic. Fortunately, though, it's only the cat's head and we still have a firm grip on the body."

"I'm relieved to hear it," Howden said. "But we must have a joint statement, you know. Arthur's on his way . . ."

"He's right here with me now," the ambassador rejoined. "As soon as we've downed a couple we'll get on with it, sir. Do you want to approve the statement yourself?"

"No," Howden said. "I'll leave it to you and Arthur."

They talked for a few minutes more, then the Prime Minister replaced the gilt telephone.

Margaret had gone ahead into the big comfortable living room with its chintz-covered sofas, Empire armchairs, and muted gray drapes. A log fire was burning brightly. She had put on a Kostelanetz recording of Tchaikovsky which played softly. It was the Howdens' favorite kind of music; the heavier classics seldom appealed to them. A few minutes later a maid brought in coffee with a piled plate of sandwiches. At a gesture from Margaret the girl offered the sandwiches to Howden and he took one absently.

When the maid had gone he untied his white tie, loosened the stiff collar, then joined Margaret by the fire. He sank gratefully into a deep overstuffed chair, hooked a footstool nearer, and lifted both feet onto it. With a deep sigh: "This is the life," he said. "You, me . . . no one else . . ." He lowered his chin and out of habit stroked the tip of his nose.

Margaret smiled faintly. "We should try it more often, Jamie."

"We will; we really will," he said earnestly. Then, his tone changing, "I've some news. We'll be going to Washington quite soon. I thought you'd like to know."

Pouring from a Sheffield coffee service his wife looked up. "It's rather sudden, isn't it?"

"Yes," he answered. "But some pretty important things have come up. I have to talk with the President."

"Well," Margaret said, "fortunately I've a new dress." She paused thoughtfully. "Now I must buy some shoes and I'll need a matching bag; gloves too." A worried look crossed her face. "There'll be time, won't there?"

"Just about," he said, then laughed at the incongruity.

Margaret said decisively, "I'll go to Montreal for a day's shopping right after the holiday. You can always get so much more there than in Ottawa. By the way, how are we for money?"

He frowned. "It isn't too good; we're overdrawn at the bank. We shall have to cash some more bonds, I expect."

"Again?" Margaret seemed worried. "We haven't many left."

"No. But you go ahead." He regarded his wife affectionately. "One shopping trip won't make all that difference."

"Well . . . if you're sure."

"I'm sure."

But the only thing he was really sure of, Howden thought, was that no one would sue the Prime Minister for slow payment. Shortage of money for their personal needs was a constant source of worry. The Howdens had no private means beyond modest savings from his time in law practice, and it was characteristic of Canada—a national small-mindedness persisting in many places—that the country paid its leaders meanly.

There was biting irony, Howden had often thought, in the fact that a Canadian Prime Minister, guiding his nation's destiny, received less in salary and allowances than a U.S. congressman. He had no official car, providing his own from an inadequate allowance, and even provision of a house was something comparatively new. As recently as 1950 the then Prime Minister, Louis St. Laurent, had been obliged to live in a two-room apartment, so small that Madame St. Laurent had stored the family preserves under her bed. Moreover, after a lifetime of parliamentary service, the most an ex-Prime Minister could expect to receive on retirement was three thousand dollars a year from a contributory pension scheme. One result for the nation in the past had been that Prime Ministers tended to cling to office in old age. Others retired to penury and the charity of friends. Cabinet Ministers and M.P.s fared even less well. It's a remarkable thing, Howden thought, that so many of us stay honest. In a remote way he sympathized a little with Harvey Warrender for what he had done.

"You'd have done better to marry a businessman," he told Margaret. "Second vice presidents have more cash for spending."

"I suppose there've been other compensations." Margaret smiled.

Thank God, he thought, we have had a good marriage. Political life could bleed you of so many things in return for power—sentiment, illusions, integrity even—and without the warmth of a woman close to him a man could become a hollow shell. He brushed aside the thought of Milly Freedeman, though with a sense of nervousness he had experienced earlier on.

"I was thinking the other day," he said, "about that time your father found us. Do you remember?"

"Of course. Women always remember those things. I thought it was you who'd forgotten."

It had been forty-two years before in the western foothills city of Medicine Hat, himself twenty-two—the product of an orphanage school and now a new-hatched lawyer without clients or immediate prospects. Margaret had been eighteen, the eldest of seven girls, all daughters of a cattle auctioneer who, outside his work, was a dour, uncommunicative man. By the standards of those days Margaret's family had been well-to-do, compared with James Howden's penury at the end of his schooling.

On a Sunday evening before church the two of them had somehow secured the parlor to themselves. They were embracing with mounting passion, and Margaret partly in dishabille when her father had entered in search of his prayer book. He had made no comment at the time beyond a muttered "Excuse me," but later in the evening, at the head of the family supper table, had looked sternly down its length and addressed James Howden.

"Young man," he had said, his large placid wife and the other daughters watching interestedly, "in my line of work when a man spreads his fingers around an udder, it indicates a more than passing interest in the cow."

"Sir," James Howden had said, with the aplomb which was to serve him well in later years, "I would like to marry your eldest daughter."

The auctioneer's hand had slammed upon the loaded supper table. "Gone!" Then, with unusual verbosity and glancing down the table, "One down, by the Lord Harry! and six to go."

They had been married several weeks later. Afterwards it had been the auctioneer, now long dead, who had helped his son-in-law first to establish a law practice and later to enter politics.

There had been children, though he and Margaret rarely saw them nowadays, with the two girls married and in England, and their youngest, James McCallum Howden, Jr., heading an oil-drilling team in the Far East. But the influence of having had children lasted, and that was important.

The fire had burned low and he threw on a fresh birch log. The bark caught with a crackle and burst into flame. Sitting beside Margaret he watched the flames engulf the log.

Margaret asked quietly, "What will you and the President be talking about?"

"There'll be an announcement in the morning. It'll say talks on trade and fiscal policy."

"But is it really about that?"

"No," he said, "it isn't."

"What, then?"

He had trusted Margaret before with information about government business. A man—any man—had to have someone he could confide in.

"It'll be mostly about defense. There's a new world crisis coming and before it does, the United States may be taking over a lot of things which, until now, we've done for ourselves."

"Military things?"

He nodded.

Margaret said slowly, "Then they'd be in control of our Army . . . all the rest?"

"Yes, dear," he said, "it looks as if they may."

His wife's forehead creased in concentration. "If it happened, Canada couldn't have its own foreign policy any more, could we?"

"Not very effectively, I'm afraid." He sighed. "We've been moving towards this—for a long time."

There was a silence, then Margaret asked: "Will it mean the end of us, Jamie—as an independent country?"

"Not while I'm Prime Minister," he answered firmly. "And not if I can plan the way I want." His voice sharpened as conviction took hold. "If our negotiations with Washington are handled properly; if the right decisions are made over the next year or two; if we're strong ourselves, but realistic; if there's foresight and integrity on both sides; if there's all of that, then it can be a new beginning. In the end we can be stronger, not weaker. We can amount to more in the world, not less." He felt Margaret's hand on his arm and laughed. "I'm sorry; was I making a speech?"

"You were beginning to. Do eat another sandwich, Jamie. More coffee?" He nodded.

Pouring, Margaret said quietly, "Do you really think there's going to be a war?"

Before answering he stretched his long body, eased more comfortably in the chair, and crossed his feet on the footstool. "Yes," he said quietly, "I'm sure there will be. But

I think there's a good chance it can be delayed a little longer—a year, two years, perhaps even three."

"Why does it have to be that way? Why?" For the first time there was emotion in his wife's voice. "Especially now, when everyone knows it means annihilation for the whole world."

"No," James Howden said, speaking slowly, "it doesn't have to mean annihilaton. That's a current fallacy."

There was a silence between them, then he went on, choosing his words with care. "You understand, dear that outside this room, if I were asked the question you just put to me, my answer would have to be no? I would have to say that war is not inevitable, because each time you admit the inevitability it's like adding an extra little squeeze to a trigger that's already cocked."

Margaret had put the coffee cup in front of him. Now she said, "Then surely it's better not to admit it—even to yourself. Isn't it best to keep on hoping?"

"If I were just an ordinary citizen," her husband answered, "I think I'd delude myself that way. I suppose it wouldn't be hard to do—without a knowledge of what was going on at the heart of things. But a head of government can't afford the luxury of delusion; not if he's to serve the people who've trusted him—as he should."

He stirred his coffee, sipped without tasting, then put it down.

"War is inevitable sooner or later," James Howden said slowly, "because it's always been inevitable. It always will be, too, just as long as human beings are capable of quarreling and anger, no matter over what. You see, any war is just a little man's quarrel magnified a million times. And to abolish war you'd need to abolish every last vestige of human vanity, envy, and unkindness. It can't be done."

"But if all that's true," Margaret protested, "then there's nothing worth while, nothing at all."

Her husband shook his head. "That isn't so. Survival is worth while, because survival means living, and living is an adventure." He turned, eyes searching his wife's face. "It's been an adventure with us. You wouldn't want to change it?"

"No," Margaret Howden said, "I don't suppose I would."

His voice was stronger now. "Oh, I know what's said about a nuclear war—that it would wipe out everything and extinguish all life. But when you think of it, there have been forecasts of doom about every weapon from the breech-loading cannon to the airplane bomb. Did you know that when the machine gun was invented somebody calculated that two hundred machine guns firing for a thousand days would kill the whole world's population?"

Margaret shook her head. Howden went on, not pausing.

"The human race has survived other perils that logically it shouldn't have: the Ice Age and the Flood are two that we know of. A nuclear war would be a mess and, if I could, I suppose I'd give my life to prevent it. But every war is a mess, though none of us dies more than once, and maybe it would be an easier way to go than some of the older means —like an arrow through the eye or being nailed to a cross.

"We'd set civilization back, though. No one can argue that, and maybe we'd be in the Dark Ages again, if there's a darker one than this. We'd lose the knack of a lot of living, I expect—including how to explode atoms, which might not be a bad thing for a while.

"But annihilation, no! I won't believe in it! Something will survive, come crawling from the ruins, and try again. And that's the worst way it could be, Margaret. I believe that our side—the free part of the world—can do better. If we do the right things now and use the time we have."

With the last words James Howden had risen. He crossed the room and turned.

Looking at him, Margaret said softly, "You're going to use it, aren't you—the time we have left?"

"Yes," he said, "I am." His expression softened. "Perhaps I shouldn't have told you all this. Has it upset you very much?"

"It's made me sad. The world, mankind—whatever name you give to it—we have so much and we're going to squander it all." A pause, then gently: "But you wanted to tell someone."

He nodded. "There aren't many people I can talk with freely."

"Then I'm glad you told me." Out of habit, Margaret moved the coffee things together. "It's getting late. Don't you think we should go up?"

He shook his head. "Not yet. But you go: I'll follow later."

Partway to the door Margaret paused. On a Sheraton games table was a pile of papers and press clippings sent over from

Howden's parliamentary office earlier in the day. She picked up a slim booklet, turning it over.

"You don't really read this sort of thing, Jamie, do you?"

There was a title on the cover—*Stargazer*. Around it were the zodiac signs of astrology.

"Good God, no!" Her husband colored slightly. "Well, occasionally I glance at it—just for amusement."

"But the old lady who used to send these to you—she died, didn't she?"

"I expect someone keeps on sending them." Howden's voice had a trace of irritability. "It's hard to get off any mailing list once you're on."

"But this is a subscription copy," Margaret persisted. "Look—it's been renewed; you can tell from the date on the label."

"Really, Margaret, how do I know how and when and where it's been renewed? Have you any idea how much mail comes addressed to me in the course of a day? I don't check it all. I don't even see it all. Maybe this is something which someone in the office did without telling me. If it bothers you I'll have it stopped tomorrow."

Margaret said calmly, "There's no need to be testy, and it doesn't bother me. I was just curious, and even if you do read it, why make such a fuss? Perhaps it'll tell you how to deal with Henry Warrender." She put the book down. "You're sure you won't come to bed now?"

"I'm sure. I've a lot of planning to do, and not much time."

It was an old experience. "Good night, dear," she said.

Climbing the broad, curving staircase, Margaret wondered how many times in her married life she had spent solitary evenings or gone to bed this way, alone. It was as well, perhaps, that she had never counted them. In recent years, especially, it had become a pattern for James Howden to stay up late, brooding on politics or affairs of state, and usually when he came to bed Margaret was asleep and seldom woke. It was not the sexual intimacies of bed she missed, she told herself with feminine frankness; those, in any case, had become channeled and organized years before. But companionship at close of day was a warmth a woman cherished. There have been good things about our marriage, Margaret thought, but there has been aloneness too.

The talk of war had left her with a sense of unaccustomed sadness. Inevitability of war, she supposed, was something which men accepted but women never would. Men made war; not women, save with small exceptions. Why? Was it because women were born to pain and suffering, but men must make their own? Suddenly she had a yearning for her children; not to comfort them, but to be comforted. Tears filled her eyes and a temptation seized her to return downstairs; to ask that for just one night, at the hour of sleep, she need not be alone.

Then she told herself: I'm being silly. Jamie would be kind, but he would never understand.

4

Briefly after his wife's departure James Howden remained before the fire—a glowing red, the earlier flames diminished —allowing his thoughts to drift along. What Margaret had said was true; talking had been a relief, and some of the things said tonight had been spoken aloud for the first time. But now he must make specific plans, not only for the Washington talks, but for his approach to the country afterwards.

The first essential, of course, was to retain power for himself; it was as if destiny beckoned him. But would others see it the same way? He hoped they would, but it was best to be sure. That was why, even at this time, he must chart a careful, guarded course in domestic politics. For the country's sake, an election victory for his own party in the next few months was vital.

As if in relief for a switch to smaller issues, his mind returned to the incident tonight involving Harvey Warrender. It was the kind of thing which must not occur again. He must have a showdown with Harvey, he decided, preferably tomorrow. One thing he was determined about—there would be no more embarrassment for the Government from the Department of Citizenship and Immigration.

The music had stopped and he crossed to the hi-fi to put on another record. He chose a Mantovani selection called "Gems Forever." On the way back he picked up the magazine which Margaret had commented on.

What he had told Margaret had been perfectly true. There *was* a mass of mail came into his office and this was a trifling fragment only. Of course, many papers and magazines never reached him, except when there was some reference to himself, or a photograph. But for years now Milly Freedeman had put this particular one among a small selection. He was not aware that he had ever asked her to, but neither had he objected. He supposed, too, that Milly had automatically renewed the subscription whenever it ran out.

Naturally, the whole subject was nonsense—astrology, the occult, and its associated hocus-pocus—but it was interesting to see how gullible others could be. That was solely the basis for his own interest, though it had seemed difficult, somehow, to explain to Margaret.

It had started years before in Medicine Hat when he was becoming established in law and just beginning a political career. He had accepted a free legal-aid case, one of a good many he handled in those days, and the accused had been a white-haired, motherly woman charged with shoplifting. She was so obviously guilty and had a long record of similar offenses that there seemed nothing to do but admit the facts and plead for leniency. But the old lady, a Mrs. Ada Zeeder, had argued otherwise, her main concern being that the court hearing should be postponed for a week. He had asked why.

She had told him, "Because the magistrate won't convict me then, silly." Pressed further, she had explained, "I'm a child born under Sagittarius, dear. Next week is a strong week for all Sagittarians. You'll see."

To humor the old woman he had had the case stood over and later entered a plea of not guilty. To his great surprise, and following the flimsiest of defenses, a normally tough magistrate had dismissed the charge.

After that day in court he had never seen old Mrs. Zeeder again, but for years until her death she had written him regularly with advice about his career based on the fact that he, too, she had discovered, was a child of Sagittarius. He had read the letters but paid scant attention, except amusedly, though once or twice had been startled by predictions which seemed to have come true. Later still, the old woman had entered a subscription in his name to the astrology magazine and when her letters finally stopped the copies continued to come.

Casually he opened the pages to a section headed "Your Individual Horoscope—December 15 to 30." For every day of the two weeks there was a paragraph of advice to the birth-date conscious. Turning to the Sagittarius section for tomorrow, the twenty-fourth, he read:

An important day for decisions and a good opportunity to turn events in your favor. Your ability to persuade others will be most marked and therefore progress which can be accomplished now should not be put off till later. A time of meeting. But beware the small cloud no larger than a man's hand.

It was absurd coincidence, he told himself. Besides, looked at intelligently, the words were vague and could be applied to any circumstance. But he *did* have decisions to make, and he *had* been considering a meeting of the cabinet Defense Committee for tomorrow, and it *would* be necessary for him to persuade others. He speculated on what could be meant by the cloud no larger than a man's hand. Something to do with Harvey Warrender, perhaps. Then he stopped himself. This was ridiculous. He put down the book, dismissing it.

He had been reminded of one thing, though: the Defense Committee. Perhaps, after all, the meeting should be held tomorrow, Christmas Eve notwithstanding. The announcement about Washington would be out and he would have to gain support in Cabinet by persuading others to his own opinions. He began to plan what he would tell the committee. His thoughts raced on.

It was two hours before he retired to bed. Margaret was already sleeping, and he undressed without waking her, setting a small bedside alarm for 6 A.M.

At first he slept soundly, but towards morning his rest was disturbed by an odd recurring dream—a series of clouds, which rose from the smallness of hands into somber, storm-like shapes.

Three The M. V. *Vastervik*

On the Canadian West coast—2300 miles from Ottawa as the jets fly—the Motor Vessel *Vastervik* docked, between showers, on December 23.

The wind in Vancouver harbor was wintry and gusting. The harbor pilot, who had boarded the ship half an hour earlier, had ordered out three shackles of anchor chain and now the *Vastervik* was berthing gently, its big hook dragging like a brake on the silt-layered, rock-free bottom. The tug ahead of the ship gave one short blast and a heaving line snaked shoreward, others following.

Ten minutes later, at 3 P.M. local time, the ship was secure and its anchor recovered.

La Pointe Pier, at which the ship had moored, was one of several projecting, fingerlike, from the busy, building-crowded shore line. Around the new arrival, and at adjoining piers, other ships were loading or discharging freight. Cargo slings rose swiftly and were lowered. Box cars shunted fussily on dockside rail spurs while lift trucks squirreled back and forth from ships to warehouses. From a berth near by a squat gray freighter eased out toward open water, a tug and line boat fore and aft.

A group of three men approached the *Vastervik* purposefully. They walked in step, competently skirting obstacles and working parties. Two of the men wore uniforms. One was a customs officer, the other from Canadian Immigration. The third man was in civilian clothes.

"Damn!" the customs man said. "It's raining again."

"Come aboard our ship," said the civilian, grinning. He was the shipping-company agent. "It'll be dryer there."

"I wouldn't count on it," the immigration officer said. He had a stern face and spoke unsmilingly. "Some of these tubs of yours are wetter inside than out. How you keep them floating is a mystery to me."

A rusty iron gangway was being lowered from the *Vastervik*.

Looking up at the ship's side, the company agent said, "Sometimes I wonder myself. Oh well, I suppose it'll hold three more." He swung himself onto the gangway, the others following.

2

In his cabin immediately beneath the bridge, Captain Sigurd Jaabeck, big-boned, stolid, and with a weathered seaman's face, shuffled papers he would need for port clearance of his cargo and crew. Before docking the captain had changed from his usual sweater and dungarees to a double-breasted blue suit, but still had on the old-fashioned carpet slippers he wore most of the time on board.

It was good, Captain Jaabeck thought, that they had berthed

in daylight and tonight could eat ashore. It would be a
relief to escape the fertilizer smell. The captain wrinkled
his nose distastefully at the all-pervading odor, suggestive of
a combination of wet sulphur and decaying cabbage. For
days it had been seeping up from the cargo in number three
hold, to be circulated impartially through the ship by the hot-
air blowers. It was heartening, he thought, that the *Vastervik's*
next cargo would be Canadian lumber, sawmill fresh.

Now, the documents in his hand, he moved out onto the
upper deck.

In the crew's living quarters aft, Stubby Gates, able-bodied
seaman, ambled across the small square mess hall which
also served as a day rest room. He joined another figure
standing silently, gazing through a porthole.

Gates was a London Cockney. He had the scarred, disar-
ranged face of a fighter, stocky build and long dangling arms
which made him apish. He was the strongest man on the
ship and also, unless provoked, the gentlest.

The other man was young and small of stature. He had a
round, strong-featured countenance, deep-set eyes and black
hair grown over-long. In appearance he looked little more than
a boy.

Stubby Gates asked, "Wotcher thinkin' about, Henri?"

For a moment the other continued to look out as if he had
not heard. His expression held a strange wistfulness, his eyes
seeming fixed on the city skyline, with its tall, clean buildings,
visible beyond the dockside. The sound of traffic carried
clearly across the water and through the open port. Then,
abruptly, the young man shrugged and turned.

"I think of nothing." He spoke with a thick, throaty—
though not unpleasing—accent. English came hard to him.

"We'll be in port for a week." Stubby Gates said. "Ever bin
to Vancouver before?"

The young man, whose name was Henri Duval, shook his
head.

"I bin 'ere three times," Gates said. "There's better places
to get orf a ship. But the grub's good an' you can always
pick up a woman quick." He glanced sideways at Duval.
"Think they'll let you go ashore this time, matey?"

The young man answered moodily, dejection in his voice.
The words were hard to understand but Stubby Gates was
able to make them out. "Sometime," Henri Duval said,
"I think I never get ashore again."

3

Captain Jaabeck met the three men as they came aboard. He shook hands with the company agent, who introduced the customs and immigration officers. The two officials—all business now—nodded politely to the captain but did not shake hands.

"Is your crew mustered, Captain?" the immigration man asked.

Captain Jaabeck nodded. "Follow me, please."

The routine was familiar and no instructions had been needed to bring the crew to the officers' dining room amidships. They were lining up outside while the ship's officers waited within the room.

Stubby Gates nudged Henri Duval as the group, led by the captain, passed by. "Those are the government blokes," Gates murmured. "They'll say if you can go ashore."

Henri Duval turned to the older man. "I make good try," he said softly. There was a boyish enthusiasm in his heavily accented voice, the earlier depression banished. "I try to work. Maybe get stay."

"That's the stuff, Henri," Stubby Gates said cheerfully. "Never say die!"

Inside the dining room a table and chair had been set up for the immigration officer. He sat at it, inspecting the typewritten crew list which the captain had handed him. Across the room the customs man leafed through a cargo manifest.

"Thirty officers and crew, and one stowaway," the immigration man announced. "Is that correct, Captain?"

"Yes." Captain Jaabeck nodded.

"Where did you pick up the stowaway?"

"In Beirut. His name is Duval," the captain said. "He has been with us a long time. Too long."

The immigration man's expression did not change.

"I'll take the officers first." He beckoned the first officer who came forward, offering a Swedish passport.

After the officers, the crew filed in from outside. Each examination was brief. Name, nationality, place of birth, a few perfunctory questions. Afterward, each man moved across for questioning by Customs.

Duval was last. For him the immigration man's questions were less perfunctory. He answered them carefully, with an earnestness, in halting English. Some of the seamen, Stubby Gates among them, had hung back, listening.

Yes, his name was Henri Duval. Yes, he was a stowaway on the ship. Yes, he had boarded at Beirut, Lebanon. No, he was not a citizen of Lebanon. No, he had no passport. He had never had a passport. Nor a certificate of birth. Nor any document. Yes, he knew his birthplace. It was French Somaliland. His mother had been French, his father English. His mother was dead, his father he had never known. No, he had no means to prove that what he said was true. Yes, he had been refused entry to French Somaliland. No, officials there had not believed his story. Yes, he had been refused a landing at other ports. There were many ports. He could not remember them all. Yes, he was sure he had no papers. Of any kind.

It was a repetition of other questioning in other places. As it continued the hope which had dawned briefly on the young man's face faded into despondency. But at the end he tried once more.

"I work," he pleaded, the eyes searching the immigration man's face for a glimmer of response. "Please—I work good. Work in Canada." He pronounced the last name awkwardly, as if he had learned it, but not well enough.

The immigration man shook his head negatively. "Not here, you won't." He addressed Captain Jaabeck. "I'll issue a detaining order against this stowaway, Captain. It will be your responsibility that he doesn't go ashore."

"We'll take care of that," the shipping agent said.

The immigration man nodded. "The rest of the crew are clear."

Those who remained had begun to leave when Stubby Gates spoke up.

"Can I 'ave a word wi' you, guv?"

Surprised, the immigration man said, "Yes."

There was a pause at the doorway and one or two men edged back inside.

"It's abaht young Henri 'ere."

"What about him?" There was an edge to the immigration man's voice.

"Well, seein' as it's Christmas in a couple o' days, an' we'll be in port, some of us thought maybe we could take Henri ashore, jist for one night."

The immigration man said sharply, "I just got through saying he has to stay on the ship."

Stubby Gates's voice rose. "I know all about that. But jist for five bleeding minutes couldn't you forget your bloody red tape?" He had not intended to become heated but he had a sailor's contempt for shorebound officialdom.

"That'll be enough of that!" The immigration officer spoke harshly, his eyes glowering.

Captain Jaabeck moved forward. The seamen in the room tensed.

"It may be enough for you, you stuck-up sod," Stubby Gates said belligerently. "But when a bloke 'asn't bin orf a ship in near two years, and it's bloody Christmas . . ."

"Gates," the captain said quietly. "That will be all."

There was a silence. The immigration man had gone red-faced and then subsided. Now he was looking doubtfully at Stubby Gates. "Are you trying to tell me," he said, "that this man Duval hasn't been ashore in two years?"

"It is not quite two years," Captain Jaabeck interjected quietly. He spoke English clearly with only a trace of his native Norwegian tongue. "Since this young man boarded my ship as a stowaway twenty months ago, no country has permitted him to land. In every port, everywhere, I am told the same thing: He has no passport, no papers. Therefore he cannot leave us. He is ours." The captain raised his big sea-man's hands, fingers outspread, in a gesture of interrogation. "What am I to do—feed his body to the fishes because no country will have him?"

The tension had gone. Stubby Gates had moved back, silent, in deference to the captain.

The immigration man—no sharpness now—said doubtfully, "He claims to be French—born in French Somaliland."

"This is true," the captain agreed. "Unfortunately the French, too, demand papers and this man has none. He swears to me he has never had papers and I believe it so. He is truthful and a good worker. This much one learns in twenty months."

Henri Duval had followed the exchange, his eyes moving hopefully from one face to the next. Now they returned to the immigration officer.

"I'm sorry. He can't land in Canada." The immigration man seemed troubled. Despite the outward sternness, he was not a harsh man and sometimes wished the regulations of his job were less exact. Half apologetically, he added, "I'm afraid there's nothing I can do, Captain."

"Not even one night ashore?" It was Stubby Gates, still trying with Cockney persistence.

"Not even one night." The answer had a quiet finality. "I'll make out the detaining order now."

It was an hour since docking and, outside the ship, dusk was closing in.

4

A few minutes after 11.00 P.M. Vancouver time, some two hours after the Prime Minister had retired to bed in Ottawa, a taxi drew up, in pouring rain, at the dark deserted entry to La Pointe Pier.

Two men got out of the cab. One was a reporter, the other a photographer from the Vancouver *Post*.

The reporter, Dan Orliffe, a comfortable bulky man in his late thirties, had a ruddy, broad-cheeked face and a relaxed manner which made him seem, sometimes, more like an amiable farmer than a successful and occasionally ruthless newsman. In contrast, the photographer, Wally de Vere, was a lean six-footer who moved with quick nervous movements and affected a veneer of perpetual pessimism.

As the cab backed away, Dan Orliffe looked around him, holding his coat collar tightly closed as token protection from the wind and rain. At first the sudden withdrawal of the taxi's headlights had made it hard to see. Surrounding where they stood were dim, wraithlike shapes and patches of deeper blackness with, ahead, a gleam of water. Silent, deserted buildings loomed vaguely, their outlines blurring into gloom. Then, slowly, eyes adjusting to the darkness, nearer shadows crept into focus and he could see they were standing on a wide cement ramp built parallel with the shore line.

Behind, the way the cab had brought them, were the towering cylinders of a grain elevator and darkened dockside sheds. Near by, piles of ship's cargo, tarpaulin-covered, dotted the ramp and, from the ramp, two docks extended outward, armlike above the water. On both sides of each dock, ships were moored and a few lights, dimly burning, showed that altogether there were five. But nowhere was there any sign of people or movement.

De Vere had shouldered his camera and equipment. Now he motioned in the direction of the ships. "Which one is it?" he asked.

Dan Orliffe used a pocket flashlight to consult a note which the night city editor had handed him half an hour earlier following a phoned-in tip. "We want the *Vastervik*," he said. "Could be any of these, I guess." He turned to the right and the photographer followed. Already in the minute or two since leaving the cab their raincoats were streaming wet. Dan could feel his trouser legs becoming sodden and a trickle of water flowed uncomfortably beneath his collar.

"What they need here," De Vere complained, "is a doll in an information booth." They picked their way cautiously through a litter of broken packing cases and oil drums. "Who is this character we're looking for, anyway?"

"Name's Henri Duval," Dan said. "According to the desk, he's a man without a country and nobody'll let him off the ship."

The photographer nodded sagely. "Sob story, eh? I get it— Christmas Eve and no-room-at-the-inn stuff."

"It's an angle," Dan acknowledged. "Maybe you should write it."

"Not me," De Vere said. "When we get through here I'm getting in the dryer with the prints. Besides, I'll lay you ten against five the guy's a phony."

Dan shook his head. "Nothing doing. You might win."

They were halfway along the right-hand dock now, stepping carefully beside a line of railway freight cars. Fifty feet below, in blackness, water glistened and the rain splashed audibly on a sullen harbor swell.

At the first ship they craned upward to read the name. It was in Russian.

"Come on," Dan said. "Not here."

"It'll be the last one," the photographer predicted. "It always is."

But it was the next. The name *Vastervik* stood out on the flared bow high above. And below it, rusted, rotting plates.

"Does this bucket of bolts really float?" De Vere's voice was incredulous. "Or is somebody kidding?"

They had clambered up a ramshackle gangway and were standing on what appeared to be the vessel's main deck.

Viewed from the dockside, even in darkness, the *Vastervik* had seemed a haggard ship. Now, at close quarters, the signs of age and accumulated neglect were even more startling. Faded paintwork had great patches of rust extending over superstructure, doors, and bulkheads. Elsewhere the last remnants of paint hung down in peeled strips. From a solitary light bulb above the gangway a layer of grime was visible on the deck under their feet and near by were several open boxes of what appeared to be garbage. A short distance forward a steel ventilator had corroded and broken from its housing. Probably unrepairable, it had been lashed uselessly to the deck.

Dan sniffed.

"Yeah," the photographer said. "I'm receiving too."

The fertilizer stench was drifting out from the ship's interior.

"Let's try in here," Dan said. He opened a steel door directly ahead and moved down a narrow passageway.

After a few yards there was a fork two ways. To the right was a series of cabin doors—obviously officers' quarters. Dan turned left, heading for a doorway a short distance along, from which light was streaming. It turned out to be a galley.

Stubby Gates, wearing greasy coveralls, was seated at a table reading a girlie magazine.

"Ullo, matey," he said, " 'Oo are you?"

"I'm from the Vancouver *Post*," Dan told him. "I'm looking for a man called Henri Duval."

Opening his mouth in a wide grin, the seaman exposed a row of darkly stained teeth. "Young Henri was 'ere earlier on, but 'e retired to 'is private cabin."

"Do you think we could wake him?" Dan said. "Or maybe we should see the captain."

Gates shook his head. "Best leave the skipper alone. 'E's touchy about bein' woke up in port. But I reckon I can roust out Henri for you." He glanced toward De Vere. " 'Oo's this bloke?"

"He's going to take pictures."

The seaman stood up, stuffing the girlie magazine into his coveralls. "All right, gents," he said. "Follow me."

They went down two companionways and forward in the ship. In a gloomy passageway, lighted by a solitary low-power bulb, Stubby Gates banged on a door, turned a key, and opened it. Reaching inside he switched on a light.

"Show a leg, Henri," he announced. " 'Ere's a couple of gents to see yer." He stood back, beckoning Dan.

Moving to the doorway Dan saw a small figure sitting up sleepily in a metal bunk. Then he looked at the scene behind.

My God! he thought. Does a man live here?

It was a metal box—a cube approximately six feet square. Long ago the walls had been painted a drab ocher but now much of the paint had gone, with rust replacing it. Both paint and rust were covered with a film of moisture, disturbed only where heavier water droplets coursed downward. Occupying the length of one wall and most of the width inside was the single metal bunk. Above it was a small shelf about a foot long and six inches wide. Below the bunk was an iron pail. And that was all.

There was no window or porthole, only a vent of sorts near the top of one wall.

And the air was foul.

Henri Duval rubbed his eyes and peered at the group outside. Dan Orliffe was surprised how young the stowaway seemed. He had a round, not unpleasing, face, well-proportioned features, and dark deep-set eyes. He was wearing a singlet, a flannel shirt, unbuttoned, and rough denim pants. Beneath the clothing his body seemed sturdy.

"Bon soir, Monsieur Duval," Dan said. *"Excusez-nous de troubler votre sommeil, mais nous venons de la presse et nous savons que vous avez une histoire intéressante à nous raconter.*

The stowaway shook his head slowly.

"It won't do no good talking French," Stubby Gates interjected. "Henri don't understand it. Seems like 'e got 'is languages mixed up when 'e was a nipper. Best try 'im in English, but take it slow."

"All right." Turning back to the stowaway, Dan said carefully, "I am from the Vancouver *Post.* A newspaper. We would like to know about you. Do you understand?"

There was a pause. Dan tried again. "I want to talk with you. Then I will write about you."

"Why you write?" The words—the first Duval had spoken —held a mixture of surprise and suspicion.

Dan said patiently, "Perhaps I can help you. You want to get off this ship?"

"You help me leave ship? Get job? Live Canada?" The words were mouthed awkwardly, but with unmistakable eagerness.

Dan shook his head. "No, I can't do that. But many people

will read what I write. Perhaps someone who will read can help you."

Stubby Gates put in: "Wotcher got ter lose, Henri? It can't do no 'arm; might even do yer a bit o' good."

Henri Duval appeared to be considering.

Watching him closely, it occurred to Dan that whatever his background, the young stowaway possessed an instinctive, unobtrusive dignity.

Now he nodded. "Ho-kay," he said simply.

"Tell you what, Henri," Stubby Gates said. "You go an' wash up, an' me an' these people'll go up an' wait for you in the galley."

The young man nodded and eased himself from the bunk.

As they moved away, De Vere said softly, "Poor little bastard."

"Is he always locked in?" Dan asked.

"Just at night when we're in port," Stubby Gates said. "Captain's orders."

"Why?"

"It's to make sure 'e don't take orf. The captain's responsible for 'im, see?" The seaman paused at the top of a companionway. "It ain't as bad for 'im, 'ere, though, as in the States. When we was in Frisco they 'ad 'im 'andcuffed to 'is bunk."

They reached the galley and went inside.

"How about a cuppa tea?" Stubby Gates asked.

"All right," Dan said. "Thanks."

The seaman produced three mugs and crossed to an enamel teapot which was standing on a hot plate. He poured a strong dark brew to which milk had already been added. Putting the mugs on the galley table he motioned the others to sit down.

"I expect, being on a ship like this," Dan said, "you get to meet all kinds of people."

"You said it, matey." The seaman grinned. "All shapes 'n' colors 'n' sizes. Some queer ones, too." He glanced knowingly at the others.

"What's *your* opinion about Henri Duval?" Dan asked.

Stubby Gates took a deep swig from his own mug before answering.

" 'E's a decent little fellow. Most of us like 'im. 'E works when we ask 'im to, though a stowaway don't have to. That's the law o' the sea," he added knowledgeably.

"Were you in the crew when he stowed aboard?" Dan asked.

"You betcher! We fahnd 'im when we was two days out o' Beirut. Thin as a ruddy broomstick, 'e was. I reckon the poor bastard was starvin' before 'e come on the ship."

De Vere had tasted his tea and put it down.

"Bloody awful, ain't it?" their host said cheerfully. "It tastes o' zinc concentrate. We picked up an 'old full of it in Chile. Bleedin' stuff gits in everything—yer 'air, yer eyes, even the tea."

"Thanks," the photographer said. "Now I'll be able to tell them at the hospital."

Ten minutes later Henri Duval came to the galley. In the meantime he had washed, combed his hair, and shaved. Over his shirt he wore a blue seaman's jersey. All his clothing was old but clean. A tear in the trousers, Dan noted, had been neatly darned.

"Come and sit down, Henri," Stubby Gates said. He filled a fourth mug and placed it before the stowaway, who smiled his thanks. It was the first time he had smiled in the presence of the two newsmen, and it lighted his face, making him seem more boyish even than before.

Dan began the questioning simply. "How old are you?"

There was the slightest of pauses, then Duval said, "I twenty-three."

"Where were you born?"

"I born on ship."

"What was the name of the ship?"

"I not know."

"Then how do you know you were born on a ship?"

Again a pause. "I not understand."

Patiently, Dan repeated the question. This time Duval nodded understanding. He said, "My mother tell me."

"What nationality was your mother?"

"She French."

"Where is your mother now?"

"She die."

"When did she die?"

"Long time back—Addis Ababa."

"Who was your father?" Dan asked.

"I not know him."

"Did your mother tell you about him?"

"He English. A seaman. I never see."

"You never heard his name?"

A negative headshake.

"Did you have any brothers or sisters?"

"No brother, sister."

"When did your mother die?"

"Excuse—I not know."

Reframing the question, Dan asked, "Do you know how old you were when your mother died?"

"I six year old."

"Afterwards, who looked after you?"

"I take care myself."

"Did you ever go to school?"

"No school."

"Can you read or write?"

"I write name—Henri Duval."

"But nothing else?"

"I write name," Duval insisted. "I show."

Dan pushed a sheet of copy paper and a pencil across the table. Slowly and in a wavering, childish hand the stowaway signed his name. It was decipherable but only just.

Dan gestured around him. "Why did you stow aboard this ship?"

Duval shrugged. "I try find country." He struggled for words, then added, "Lebanon not good."

"Why not good?" Involuntarily Dan used the young stow-away's abbreviated English.

"I not citizen. If police find—I go jail."

"How did you get to Lebanon?"

"I on ship."

"What ship was that?"

"Italian ship. Excuse—I not remember name."

"Were you a passenger on the Italian ship?"

"I stowaway. I on ship one year. Try get off. No one want."

Stubby Gates put in, "As far as I can figure it, 'e was on this Eyetalian tramp, see? They was jist goin' back and forth rahnd the Middle East. So 'e 'ops it at Beirut an' gits on this one. Git it?"

"I get it," Dan said. Then, to Duval, "What did you do before you were on the Italian ship?"

"I go with men, camels. They give me food. I work. We go Somaliland, Ethiopia, Egypt." He pronounced the names awk-

wardly, making a back-and-fourth movement with his hand.
"When I small boy, crossing border not matter, no one care.
Then when I bigger, they stop—no one want."

"And that was when you stowed on the Italian ship?"
Dan asked. "Right?"

The young man nodded assent.

Dan asked, "Do you have any passport, papers, anything
to prove where your mother came from?"

"No paper."

"Do you belong to any country?"

"No country."

"Do you want a country?"

Duval looked puzzled.

"I mean," Dan said slowly, "you want to get off this ship.
You told me that."

A vigorous nod, assenting.

"Then you want to have a country—a place to live?"

"I work," Duval insisted. "I work good."

Once more, thoughtfully, Dan Orliffe surveyed the young
stowaway. Was his tale of homeless wandering true? Was he,
in fact, a castoff, a misborn whom no one claimed or wanted?
Was he a man without a country? Or was it all a fabrication,
an artful texture of lies and half-truths calculated to elicit
sympathy?

The youthful stowaway looked guileless enough. But was he
really?

The eyes seemed appealing, but somewhere within them was
a veil of inscrutability. Was there a hint of cunning behind it,
or was imagination playing tricks?

Dan Orliffe hesitated. Whatever he wrote would, he knew,
be hashed over and checked out by the *Post's* rival afternoon
paper, the Vancouver *Colonist*.

With no immediate deadline, it was up to himself how
much time he took in getting the story. He decided to give
his doubts a thorough workout.

"Henri," he asked the stowaway, "do you trust me?"

For an instant the earlier suspicion returned to the young
man's eyes. Then abruptly he nodded.

"I trust," he said simply.

"All right," Dan said. "I think perhaps I *can* help. But
I want to know everything about you, right back from the
beginning." He glanced toward where De Vere was assem-

bling his camera flash equipment. "We'll take some photographs first, then we'll talk. And don't skip anything, and don't hurry because this is going to take a long time."

5

Henri Duval was still tiredly awake in the galley of the *Vastervik*.

The man from the newspaper had a tongue with many questions.

It was a puzzle at times, the young stowaway thought, to be certain what he wished. The man asked much, expecting plain words in return. And each answer made was written down quickly upon the sheets of paper before them at the table. It was as if Duval himself were being drawn out through the hurrying pencil point, his life that was past placed carefully in order. And yet, about so much of his life, there was nothing of order, only disconnected pieces. And so many things were hard to tell in plain words—this man's words—or even to remember in just the way they happened.

If only he had learned to read and write, to use pencil and paper for storing things from the mind, as this man and others like him did. Then he, too—Henri Duval—could preserve thoughts and the memory of things past. And not everything would have to stay in his brain, as on a shelf, hoping it would not become lost in forgetfulness, as some of the things he searched for now, it seemed, had done.

His mother had spoken once of schooling. She herself had been taught as a child to read and write. But that was long ago, and his mother had died before any schooling for himself could be begun. After that there was no one else to care what, or whether, he learned.

He frowned, his young face creased, groping for recollection; trying to answer the questions; to remember, remember, remember . . .

First there had been the ship. His mother had told him of it and it was on the ship that he had been born. They had sailed from Djibouti, in French Somaliland, the day before his birth and he believed that his mother had once told him where the ship was bound, but he had long since forgotten. And if she had ever said what flag the ship flew, that was forgotten too.

The birth had been hard and there was no doctor. His mother became weak and fevered and the ship's captain had turned his vessel, putting back into Djibouti. At the port, mother and child had been taken to a hospital for the poor. They had had little money, then or later.

Henri remembered his mother as comforting and gentle. His impression was that she was beautiful, but perhaps this was only fancy because the memory of how she looked had faded in his mind and now, when he thought of her, her face was in shadow, with features vague. But she had given him love; that much he was sure of, and he remembered because it was the only love he had ever known.

The early years were disjointed fragments in his mind. He knew that his mother had worked, when she could, to keep them in food, though at times there had been none. He had no recollection of the kind of work his mother had done, though he believed at one time she had been a dancer. The two of them had moved around a good deal—from French Somaliland into Ethiopia, first to Addis Ababa, then Massawa. Two or three times they had made the Djibouti-Addis Ababa trek.

At the beginning they had lived, though meagerly, among other French nationals. Later, as they had become poorer still, the native quarter was all the home they knew. Then, when Henri Duval was six, his mother died.

After his mother's death his memories were mixed again. For a time—it was hard to be sure how long—he had lived in the streets, begging for food and sleeping at night in whatever hole or corner he could find. He had never gone to the authorities; it had not occurred to him to do so, for among the circle he moved in the police were looked on as enemies, not friends.

Then an elderly Somali, living alone in a hovel in the native quarter, had taken him in and provided shelter of a sort. The arrangement had lasted five years and then, for some reason, the old man left and Henri Duval was alone once more.

This time he drifted from Ethiopia across into British Somaliland, getting work where he could, and for another four years he was variously a shepherd's helper, a goatherd and a boat boy, eking out a precarious day-to-day existence with wages seldom more than food and shelter.

Then and later, crossing international borders had been

simple. There were so many families with children on the
move that officials at border points seldom bothered with the
children individually. At such moments he would merely at-
tach himself to a family and pass unnoticed through the
guards. In time he became adept at it. Even in his late
teens his small stature continued to make this possible.
Until, at twenty, after traveling with some Arab nomads, he
was stopped for the first time and turned back at the borders
of French Somaliland.

Two truths were now revealed to Henri Duval. One: his
days of slipping across borders with groups of children
were over. Second: French Somaliland, which until this moment he had regarded as his own country, was closed to
him. The first thing he had already suspected; the second
came as a profound shock.

Fatefully, inevitably, he had encountered one of the funda-
mentals of modern society: that without documentation—
the all-important fragments of paper, the very least of which
is a certificate of birth—man is nothing, officially non-existent, and belonging nowhere on the territorially divided
earth.

If men and women of learning have, at times, found the
proposition hard to accept, to Henri Duval—without schooling of any kind and forced through his years of childhood
to live like an unloved scavenger—it had come with shatter-
ing impact. The Arab nomads moved on, leaving Duval
behind in Ethiopia, where he now knew he had no right to
be either, and for a day and a night he sat huddled near the
border crossing point at Hadele Gubo . . .

. . . There was a fold of bleached and weathered rock.
In its shelter the twenty-year-old youth—still a child in
many ways—stayed unmoving and alone. Directly ahead
were the arid, boulder-studded plains of the Somalilands,
bleak in moonlight and barren in the bright noon sun. And
across the plains, sinuously winding like a dun-colored ser-
pent, was the dust-blown roadway to Djibouti—the final
tenuous thread between Henri Duval and his past, between
his childhood and his manhood, between his body, undocu-
mented except by its living presence, and the sun-baked
coastal city whose fish-smelling alleyways and salt-encrusted
wharves he had thought of as his birthplace and his
only home.

Suddenly, the desert ahead seemed familiar and inviting ground. And like a creature drawn by some primeval instinct to the place of its birth and mother love, so he longed to return to Djibouti, but now it was out of reach, as so much else was out of reach and would remain so for always.

Then, thirst and hunger at last stirring him, he rose. He turned from the forbidden country, heading north, because he had to head somewhere, toward Eritrea and the Red Sea . . .

The journey into Eritrea, west coast territory of Ethiopia, was one that he remembered clearly. He remembered, too, that on this journey he first began to steal systematically. Previously he had stolen food, but only in desperation when begging or work had failed. Now he no longer sought work and lived by thievery alone. He still stole food whenever there was an opportunity, and also goods or trinkets which could be sold for small amounts. What little money he got seemed to disappear at once, but always in back of his mind was the thought of accumulating enough to buy a passage on a ship—to some place where he could belong and could begin life again.

In time he had come to Massawa, port of coral and gateway from Ethiopia to the Red Sea.

It was in Massawa that retribution for stealing came close to overtaking him. Mingling in the crowd near a fishmonger's stall, he had purloined a fish, but the keen-eyed merchant had observed and given chase. Several others in the crowd, including a policeman, had joined in and within seconds Henri Duval was being pursued by what, to his youthful frightened ears, sounded like an angry mob. At a desperately fevered pace he had led them around Massawa's coral buildings and through tortuous back streets of the native quarter. Finally, having gained enough headway to reach the docks, he had hidden himself amid bales of ship's cargo waiting loading. From a peephole he had watched his pursuers search, then eventually give up and go away.

But the experience had shaken him and he resolved to quit Ethiopia by any means he could. In front of his hiding place a freighter was moored and after nightfall he crept aboard, stowing in a dark locker which he stumbled into from a lower deck. The vessel sailed next morning. Two hours later he was discovered and brought before the captain.

The ship was an antiquated Italian coal burner, plying leakily between the Gulf of Aden and the eastern Mediterranean.

The languid Italian captain boredly scraped dirt from beneath his finger nails as Henri Duval stood, trembling, before him.

After several minutes had passed the captain asked a sharp question in Italian. There was no response. He tried English, then French, but without result. Duval had long forgotten the little French he had learned from his mother and his speech was now a polyglot hodgepodge of Arabic, Somali, and Amharic, interspersed with stray words from Ethiopia's seventy languages and twice as many dialects.

Finding he could not communicate, the captain shrugged indifferently. Stowaways were no novelty on the ship and the captain, unhampered by tiresome scruples about maritime law, ordered Duval put to work. His intention was to dump the stowaway at the next port of call.

What the captain had not foreseen, however, was that Henri Duval, a man without a country, would be firmly rejected by immigration officials at every port of call, including Massawa, to which the ship returned several months later.

With the increasing time that Duval spent aboard, the captain's anger increased in ratio until, after ten months had gone by, he called his bosun into conference. Between them they devised a plan—which the bosun obligingly explained to Duval through an interpreter—whereby the stowaway's life was to be made so untenable that sooner or later he would be glad to jump ship. And eventually, after something like two months of overwork, beatings and semistarvation, that was precisely what he did.

Duval recalled in sharp detail the night he had slipped silently down the gangway of the Italian ship. It was in Beirut, Lebanon—the tiny buffer state between Syria and Israel where, the legend says, St. George once slew his dragon.

He had left, as he had come, in darkness; and departure was easy because he had nothing to take and no possessions except the ragged clothes he wore. Once disembarked, he had at first scurried through the dockyard, intending to head

for town. But the glimpse of a uniform in a lighted area
ahead had unnerved him and sent him darting back, seeking
shelter in the shadows. More reconnaissance showed that
the dockyard was fenced and patrolled. He felt himself
trembling; he was twenty-one, weak from hunger, incredibly
alone and desperately afraid.

As he moved, another shadow loomed. It was a ship.

At first he thought he had returned to the Italian freighter
and his immediate impulse was to steal back on board.
Better the misery he knew than the prison he envisaged
waiting if police arrested him. Then he saw that the shadow
was not the Italian ship but a larger one and he had scuttled
aboard it like a rat up a rope. It was the *Vastervik*, a fact
he was to learn two days later and twenty miles at sea when
starvation conquered fear and drove him, quaking, out of
hiding.

Captain Sigurd Jaabeck of the *Vastervik* was very different
from his Italian counterpart. A slow-speaking, gray-haired
Norwegian, he was a firm man, but just, who respected both
the precepts of his Bible and the laws of the sea. Captain
Jaabeck explained sternly but carefully to Henri Duval that a
stowaway was not compelled to work but could do so voluntarily, although without pay. In any case, whether working
or not, he would receive the same rations as the ship's crew.
Duval chose to work.

Like the Italian shipmaster, Captain Jaabeck fully intended
to dispose of his stowaway at the first port of call. But unlike the Italian—after learning that there was to be no
quick disposal of Duval—the thought of ill-treatment did
not occur to him.

And so for twenty months Henri Duval remained aboard
while the *Vastervik* mooched, cargo questing, over half the
oceans of the world. They jogged with tramplike monotony
through the Mediterranean, the Atlantic and Pacific. They
touched North Africa, Northern Europe, Southern Europe,
England, South America, the United States, and Canada.
And everywhere the petition of Henri Duval to land and
remain was met with an emphatic no. The reason, when port
officials bothered to give it, was always the same—the stowaway had no papers, no identity, no country, and no rights.

And then, after a while, when the *Vastervik* had settled
down to accepting Duval as a permanency, the young stowaway had become something of a ship's pet.

The *Vastervik's* crew was an international miscellany which included Poles, Scandinavians, Lascars, a Chinese, an Armenian, and several English seamen of whom Stubby Gates was the accepted leader. It was the latter group which had adopted Duval and made his life, if not pleasant, at least as tolerable as crowded conditions in the ship allowed. They had helped him in speaking English, and now, although his accent was thick and phrasing awkward, at least with patience on both sides he could make himself understood.

It was one of the few genuine kindnesses that Henri Duval had ever experienced, and he responded much as an eager puppy dog responds to approval from its master. Nowadays he did personal jobs for the crew, helped the officers' steward, and ran shipboard errands. In return the men brought gifts of cigarettes and candy from their trips ashore and occasionally Captain Jaabeck provided small sums of money which other seamen spent on Duval's behalf. But with it all, the stowaway was still a captive and the *Vastervik*, once a refuge, had become his prison.

Thus Henri Duval, whose only home was the sea, had come to the gates of Canada on the eve of Christmas.

6

The interrogation had taken almost two hours. Partway through, Dan Orliffe had repeated some of his earlier questions in different terms, seeking to trip the young stowaway into an admission or inconsistency. But the ruse failed. Except for misunderstandings of language, which were cleared up as they went along, the basic story stayed the same.

Near the end, after a leading question phrased with deliberate inaccuracy, Duval had not answered. Instead he had turned his dark eyes upon his interrogator.

"You trick me. You think I lie," the stowaway said, and again the newspaperman was aware of the same unconscious dignity he had noted earlier.

Ashamed at having his own trickery exposed, Dan Orliffe had said, "I was just checking. I won't do it again." And they had gone on to something else.

Now, back at his beat-up desk in the cramped, cluttered newsroom of the Vancouver *Post* Dan spread out his notes and reached for a sheaf of copy paper. Shuffling in carbons, he called across to the night city editor, Ed Benedict, at the city desk.

"Ed, it's a good story. How many words can you handle?"

The night city editor considered. Then he called back. "Hold it down to a thousand."

Pulling his chair closer to the typewriter, Dan nodded. It would do. He would have liked more but, assembled tautly, a thousand words could say a great deal.

He began to type.

Four Ottawa, Christmas Eve

At 6.15 A.M. on Christmas Eve Milly Freedeman was awakened by the telephone's insistent ringing in her apartment in the fashionable Tiffany Building on Ottawa Driveway. Slipping a robe of faded yellow terrycloth over silk pajamas, she groped with her feet for the old, heel-trodden moccasins she had kicked off the night before. Unable to locate them, the Prime Minister's personal secretary padded barefoot into the adjoining living room and snapped on a light.

Even this early, and viewed through sleepy eyes, the room which the light revealed seemed as inviting and comfortable as always. It was a far cry, Milly knew, from the chic bachelor-girl apartments so often featured in the glossy magazines. But it was a place she loved to come home to every evening, usually tired, and sinking at first into the down cushions of the big overstuffed chesterfield—the one which had given the movers so much trouble when she had brought it here from her parents' home in Toronto.

The old chesterfield had been re-covered since then, in Milly's favorite shade of green, and was flanked now by the two armchairs she had bought at an auction sale outside Ottawa—a little threadbare, but wonderfully comfortable. She kept deciding that someday soon she must have autumn-colored chintz covers made for the chairs. The covers would go well with the apartment's walls and woodwork, painted in a warm mushroom shade. She had done the painting herself one weekend, inviting a couple of friends in for a scratch dinner, then cajoling them into helping her finish.

On the far side of the living room was an old rocking chair, one that she was absurdly sentimental about because she had rocked in it, daydreaming, as a child. And beside the rocking chair, on a tooled-leather coffee table for which she had paid an outrageously high price, was the telephone.

Settling into the chair with a preliminary rock, Milly lifted the receiver. The caller was James Howden.

"Morning, Milly," the Prime Minister said briskly. "I'd like a cabinet Defense Committee meeting at eleven o'clock." He made no reference to the earliness of the call, nor did Milly expect it. She had long ago grown used to her employer's addiction to early rising.

"Eleven this morning?" With her free hand Milly hugged the robe around her. It was cold in the apartment from a window she had left slightly open the night before.

"That's right," Howden said.

"There'll be some complaining," Milly pointed out. "It's Christmas Eve."

"I hadn't forgotten. But this is too important to stand over."

When she had hung up she checked the time from the tiny leather traveling clock which stood beside the telephone and resisted a temptation to return to bed. Instead she closed the open window, then crossed to the tiny kitchenette and put on coffee. After that, returning to the living room, she switched on a portable radio. The coffee was beginning to perk when the 6.30 radio news carried the official announcement of the Prime Minister's forthcoming talks in Washington.

Half an hour later, still in pajamas, but this time with the old moccasins on her feet, she began to call the five committee members at their homes.

The Minister of External Affairs was first. Arthur Lexington responded cheerfully, "Sure thing, Milly. I've been at meetings all night, what's another more or less? By the way, did you hear the announcement?"

"Yes," Milly said. "It was just on the radio."

"Fancy a trip to Washington?"

"All I ever get to see on trips," Milly said, "is the keyboard of a typewriter."

"You must come on one of mine," Lexington said. "Never need a typewriter. All my speeches are on the backs of cigarette packets."

Milly said, "They sound better than most that aren't."

"That's because I never worry." The External Affairs Minister chuckled. "I start with the assumption that nothing I say can make the situation worse."

She laughed.

"I must go now," Lexington said, "it's a big occasion in our house—I'm having breakfast with my children. They want to see how much I've changed since last time I was home."

She smiled as she wondered just what breakfast would be like this morning in the Lexington household. Bordering on bedlam probably. Susan Lexington, who had been her husband's secretary years before, was a notoriously poor housekeeper, but the family always seemed close-knit when doing things together while the Minister was home in Ottawa. Thinking of Susan Lexington, Milly was reminded of something she had once been told: different secretaries go different ways; some get laid and married, others old and harried. So far, she thought, I've half a point each way. I'm not old, or married either.

She might have been married, of course, if her life had been less oriented to the life of James McCallum Howden . . .

A dozen years or so ago, when Howden had been merely a back-bench M.P., though a forceful, rising figure in the party, Milly, his young, part-time secretary, had fallen blindly and blissfully in love with him to the point where she longed for each new day and the delight of their physical closeness. She had been in her twenties then, away from her home in Toronto for the first time, and Ottawa had proved a virile and exciting world.

It seemed even more virile on the night that James Howden, having guessed her feelings, had made love to her for the first time. Even now, ten years later, she remembered the way it had been: early evening; the House of Commons adjourned for dinner; herself sorting letters in Howden's parliamentary office when he had come in quietly. Without speaking he had locked the door and, taking Milly by the shoulders, turned her towards him. Both knew that the other M.P. who shared the office with Howden was away from Ottawa.

He kissed her and she responded ardently, without pretense or reserve, and later he had taken her to the leather office couch. Her awakening, bursting passion and a total lack of inhibition surprised even herself.

It was the beginning of a time equaled in joy by no other part of Milly's life, before or since. Day after day, week after week, their clandestine meetings were contrived, excuses minted, minutes snatched . . . At times their affair took on the pattern of a game of skill. At other moments it seemed as if life and love were geared for their devouring.

Milly's adoration of James Howden was deep and consuming. She was less certain of his feelings for her, even though he frequently declared them to be identical with her own. But she closed her mind to doubts, choosing to accept gratefully the here-and-now which circumstance had brought. Someday soon, she knew, there would be a point of no return either for the Howdens' marriage or for James Howden and herself. On the eventual outcome she cherished hope, dimly, but with scant illusion.

And yet, at one point—almost a year after their affair began—the hope seemed stronger.

It had been close to the time of the convention at which the party leadership would be decided, and one night James Howden had told her, "I've been thinking of giving up politics and asking Margaret for a divorce." After the first excitement, Milly had asked—what of the convention which would decide whether Howden or Harvey Warrender would win the leadership which both men sought.

"Yes," he said. He had stroked his eagle-beak nose thoughtfully, his heavy face somber. "I've thought about that. If Harvey wins I'm getting out."

She had watched the convention breathlessly, not daring to think of the thing she wanted most: a Warrender victory. For if Warrender won, her own future would be assured. But if Warrander lost and James Howden won, Milly sensed that her love affair inevitably must end. The personal life of a party leader soon to become Prime Minister must be impeccable and beyond any breath of scandal.

At the end of the first convention day the odds favored Warrender. But then, for a reason Milly never understood, Harvey Warrender withdrew and Howden won.

A week later, in the parliamentary office where it had begun, the romance between the two of them was ended.

"It has to be this way, Milly darling," James Howden had said. "There isn't any other."

Milly had been tempted to reply that there was another way, but she knew it would be time and effort wasted. James Howden was riding high. There had been intense excitement ever since his election to the party leadership, and even now, though his emotion was genuine, there was a sense of impatience behind it, as if to clear out the past so the future might move in.

"Shall you stay on, Milly?" he had asked.

"No," she said, "I don't think I could."

He had nodded understandingly. "I can't say I blame you. If you ever change your mind . . ."

"I won't," she said, but six months later she had. After a Bermuda holiday and another job which bored her, she had gone back and had remained. The return, at first, had been difficult and a sense of what-might-have-been was never far away. But sadness and private tears had never soured into embitterment and, in the end, love had turned to generous loyalty.

Sometimes Milly wondered if Margaret Howden had ever known of that almost-year and the intensity of feeling of her husband's secretary; women had an intuition for that kind of thing which men lacked. But if so, Margaret had wisely said nothing, either then or since.

Now, her mind pivoting to the present, Milly made her next call.

It was to Stuart Cawston, whose wife answered drowsily with the information that the Finance Minister was in the shower. Milly passed on a message, which was relayed, and she heard Smiling Stu acknowledge with a shouted, "Tell Milly I'll be there."

Adrian Nesbitson, Minister of Defense, was next on her list and she had to wait several minutes before the old man's shuffling footsteps reached the phone. When she told him about the meeting he said resignedly, "If that's what the chief wants, Miss Freedeman, I'll have to be there, I suppose. Too bad, I'd say, it couldn't have waited until after the holiday."

Milly made sympathetic noises, despite her awareness that the presence or absence of Adrian Nesbitson would make little difference to anything decided at this morning's meeting. Something else she knew, which Nesbitson did not, was that James Howden planned several cabinet changes in

the new year and among the people to go would be the
present Minister of Defense.

Nowadays, Milly thought, it seemed strange to remember
that General Nesbitson had once been an heroic figure in
the nation—a legendary, much-decorated veteran of World
War II, with a reputation for daring, if not imagination.
It was Adrian Nesbitson who had once led an armored attack against panzers, standing in an open jeep, his personal
bagpiper perched, playing, on the seat behind. And as much
as generals are ever loved, Nesbitson had been loved by the
men who served him.

But after the war, Nesbitson the civilian would have
amounted to nothing had it not been that James Howden
wanted someone well-known but administratively weak in
the Defense slot. Howden's objective had been to have the
appearance of possessing a stalwart Defense Minister but
actually to control the portfolio closely himself.

That part of the plan had worked out well enough—too
well, at times. Adrian Nesbitson, the gallant soldier, had
proved entirely out of his depth in an era of missiles and
nuclear power and only too willing to do exactly as told
without the nuisance of argument. Unfortunately he had
not always grasped the briefings of his own officials, and,
lately, before press and public, had assumed the appearance of a tired and harassed Colonel Blimp.

Talking with the old man depressed Milly and she replenished her coffee and went to the bathroom to freshen
up before making the remaining two calls. Pausing, before
going back, she looked at herself in the long bathroom mirror under the bright fluorescent light. She saw a tall, attractive woman, still young if you used the word tolerantly,
full-bosomed; also a bit hippy, she thought critically. But
she had good bones, a strong, well-shaped face with high
classic cheekbones, and thickish eyebrows which she tweezed
spasmodically when she thought of it. Eyes were big,
sparkling, gray-green and wide in her face. A straight nose,
broad at the end, was set over full, sensuous lips. Dark
brown hair cut very short: Milly looked at it critically,
wondering if it was time for cutting again. She disliked
beauty salons and preferred to wash, set, and brush her
own hair into shape. To do this, though, it had to be cut well
and, it seemed, much too frequently.

Short hair had one big advantage, though—you could run your hands through it, and Milly often did. James Howden had liked doing that too, just as he had liked the old yellow robe she still wore. For the twentieth time she decided she must get rid of it soon.

Returned to the apartment living room, she made her two remaining calls. One was to Lucien Perrault, Minister of Defense Production, who was openly annoyed at being called so early, and Milly was as snippy in return as she reasoned she could get away with. Afterwards she was a little sorry about that, remembering that someone or other had once described the right to be disagreeable in the early morning as the sixth human freedom, and most times Perrault—who wore the mantle of French Canadian leadership in Canada—treated her courteously enough.

The final call was to Douglas Martening, Clerk of the Privy Council, and procedural Solon at all cabinet meetings. With Martening, Milly was more respectful than with the others. Ministers might come and go, but the Clerk of the Privy Council, while in office, was the senior civil servant in Ottawa. He also had a reputation for aloofness and most times when Milly spoke to him gave the impression of scarcely being aware of her. But today, unusually, he was gloomily chatty.

"It will be a long meeting, I suppose. Probably go right on over into Christmas Day."

"It wouldn't surprise me, sir," Milly said. Then tentatively, "But if it does I could always send out for turkey sandwiches."

Martening grunted, then again surprisingly came back, "It isn't sandwiches I need, Miss Freedeman. Just some other kind of work where a fellow gets a little home life now and then."

Afterwards Milly reflected: was disenchantment infectious? Could the great Mr. Martening be about to join the parade of senior civil servants who had left the ranks of government for higher-paying industrial jobs? The question made her wonder about herself. Was this a time for departure; a time for change before it became too late for change?

She was still wondering four hours later as the members of the cabinet Defense Committee began to assemble in the

Prime Minister's office suite on Parliament Hill. Dressed in a smartly tailored gray suit with a white blouse, Milly ushered them in.

General Nesbitson had been last to arrive, his balding, pudgy figure wrapped in a heavy overcoat and scarf. Helping him off with them, Milly had been shocked to see how unwell the old man appeared and now, as if to confirm the opinion, he suddenly began a coughing spell into his handkerchief.

Milly poured some ice water from a carafe and held it out. The old warrior sipped it, nodding gratefully. After an interval and more coughing, he managed to gasp, "Excuse me—this blasted catarrh. Always get it when I have to stay the winter in Ottawa. Used to take a winter holiday down south. Can't get away now, with so many important things going on."

Next year, maybe, Milly thought.

"A Merry Christmas, Adrian." Stuart Cawston had joined them, his amiably ugly features beaming, as usual, like an illuminated sign.

Lucien Perrault spoke from behind him. "And such a one to be wishing it, whose taxes pierce our souls like daggers." Jauntily handsome, with a shock of black curls, bristling mustache, and a humorous eye, Perrault was as fluent in English as in French. At times—though not now—his manner betrayed a touch of hauteur, reminder of his seigneurial ancestors. At thirty-eight, and the youngest member of Cabinet, his influence was actually much stronger than indicated by the comparatively minor office he held. But the Defense Production Ministry had been Perrault's own choosing, and since it was one of the three patronage ministries (the others, Public Works and Transport), by ensuring that plum contracts went to the party's financial supporters, his influence in the party hierarchy was considerable.

"You shouldn't have your soul so near your bank account, Lucien," the Finance Minister rejoined. "In any case I'm Santa Claus to you fellows. You and Adrian here are the ones who buy the expensive toys."

"But they explode with such a remarkable bang," Lucien Perrault said. "Moreover, my friend, in Defense Production we create much work and employment which bring you more taxes than ever."

"There's an economic theory tied in there somewhere," Cawston said. "Too bad I've never understood it."

The office intercom buzzed and Milly answered. Metallically James Howden's voice announced, "The meeting will be in the Privy Council chamber. I'll be there in a moment."

Milly saw the Finance Minister's eyebrows rise with mild surprise. Most small policy meetings aside from the full Cabinet usually took place informally in the Prime Minister's office. But obediently the group filed out into the corridor toward the Privy Council chamber a few yards away.

As Milly closed her office door behind Perrault, the last to leave, the Bourdon Bell of the Peace Tower carillon was chiming eleven.

Unusually, she found herself wondering what to do. There was plenty of accumulated work, but on Christmas Eve she felt disinclined to begin anything new. All of the seasonal things—routine Christmas telegrams to the Queen, Commonwealth Prime Ministers, and heads of friendly governments—had been prepared and typed yesterday for early dispatch today. Anything else, she decided, could wait until after the holiday.

Her earrings were being bothersome and she slipped them off. They were pearl, like small round buttons. She had never been fond of jewelry and knew it did nothing for her. The one thing she had learned—jewelry or not—was that she was attractive to men, though she had never quite known why . . .

The phone on her desk buzzed and she answered it. It was Brian Richardson.

"Milly," the party director said, "has the defense meeting started?"

"They just went in."

"Goddam!" Richardson sounded out of breath, as if he had been hurrying. Abruptly he asked, "Did the chief say anything to you about the blow-up last night?"

"What blow-up?"

"Obviously he didn't. There was practically a fist fight at the G.G.'s. Harvey Warrender blew his cork—dipped generously in alcohol, I gather."

Shocked, Milly said, "At Government House? The reception?"

"That's the word around town."

"But why Mr. Waddender?"

"I'm curious too," Richardson admitted. "I've a notion it might have been because of something I said the other day."

"What?"

"About immigration. Warrender's department has been getting us a stinking bad press. I asked the chief to lay some law down."

Milly smiled. "Perhaps he laid it down too heavily."

"It ain't funny, kid. Brawling between cabinet ministers doesn't win elections. I'd better talk to the chief as soon as he's free, Milly. And there's another thing you can warn him about: unless Harvey Warrender pulls his finger out fast we're heading for more immigration trouble on the West coast. I know there's a lot sizzling right now, but this is important too."

"What kind of trouble?"

"I had a call from one of my people out there this morning," Richardson said. "It seems the Vancouver *Post* has broken a story about a jerk stowaway who claims he isn't getting a fair deal from Immigration. My man says some goddam writer is sobbing all over page one. It's exactly the kind of case I've been warning everybody about."

"*Is* he getting a fair deal—the stowaway?"

"For Christ sake, who cares?" The party director's voice rattled sharply in the receiver. "All I want is for him to quit being news. If the only way to shut the papers up is by letting the bastard in, then let's admit him and have done with it."

"My!" Milly said. "You *are* in a forceful mood."

"If I am," Richardson snapped back, "it's because sometimes I get downright weary of stupid hicks like Warrender who make political farts and then look for me to clear up the mess."

"Apart from the vulgarity," Milly said lightly, "isn't that a mixed metaphor?" She found the rough edge to Brian Richardson's tongue and character refreshing after the professional smoothness and spoken clichés of most politicians she met. Perhaps it was this, Milly thought, which had made her think more warmly of Richardson of late—more so, in fact, than she had ever intended.

The feeling had begun six months earlier when the party director had begun to ask her out on dates. At first, uncertain whether she liked him or not, Milly had accepted out of curiosity. But later the curiosity had turned to liking and, on the evening a month or so ago which had ended in her apartment, to physical attraction.

Milly's sexual appetite was healthy enough but not enormous, which was sometimes, she thought, just as well. She had known a number of men since her feverish year with James Howden, but the occasions ending in her bedroom had been few and far between, reserved only for those for whom Milly felt genuine affection. She had never taken the view, as some did, that romping into bed should be a thank-you-for-the-evening gesture, and perhaps it was this hard-to-get quality which attracted men as much as her casual, sensual charm. But in any case the night with Richardson, which ended surprisingly as it had, did little to satisfy her and merely demonstrated that Brian Richardson's roughness extended to more than his tongue. Afterwards she thought of it as a mistake . . .

They had had no other meeting since and, in the meantime, Milly had resolved firmly that she would not fall in love, for a second time, with a married man.

Now Richardson's voice on the telephone said, "If they were all as smart as you, doll, my life would be a dream. Some of these people think public relations is sexual intercourse between the masses. Anyway, have the chief call me as soon as his meeting's over, eh? I'll wait in the office."

"Will do."

"And Milly."

"Yes."

"How would it be if I dropped around this evening? Say sevenish?"

There was a silence. Then Milly said doubtfully, "I don't know."

"What don't you know?" Richardson's voice held a matter-of-factness; the tone of one not intending to be put off. "Had you planned anything?"

"No," Milly said, "but . . ." She hesitated. "Isn't it a tradition to spend Christmas Eve at home?"

Richardson laughed, though the laugh had a hollowness. "If that's all that worries you—forget it. I can assure you Eloise has made her own arrangements for Christmas Eve and they don't include me. In fact she'd be grateful to you for making sure I can't intrude."

Still Milly hesitated, remembering her own decision. But

now . . . she wavered; it might be a long while . . . Stalling for time she said, "Is all this wise? Switchboards have ears."

"Then let's not give 'em too much to flap about," Richardson said crisply. "Seven o'clock?"

Half-unwillingly, "All right," Milly said, and hung up. Out of habit, after phoning, she replaced her earrings.

For a moment or two she remained by the desk, one hand touching the telephone as if a thread of contact still remained. Then, her expression pensive, she moved over to the high arched window overlooking the front courtyard of the Parliament Buildings.

Since she had come in earlier, the sky had darkened and it had begun to snow. Now, in thick white flakes, the snow was blanketing the nation's capital. From the window she could see the heart of it: the Peace Tower, sheer and lean against the leaden sky, gauntly surmounting the House of Commons and Senate; the square gothic towers of the West Block and, behind, the Confederation Building, hunched hugely like some somber fortress; the colonnaded Rideau Club nudging the white sandstone U.S. Embassy; and Wellington Street in front, its traffic—as of habit—snarled. At times, it could be a stern, gray scene—symbolic, Milly sometimes thought, of the Canadian climate and character. Now, in the clothing of winter, its hardness and angularity were already blurring into softness. The forecasters had been right, she thought. Ottawa was in for a white Christmas.

Her earrings still hurt. For the second time she took them off.

2

Serious-faced, James Howden entered the high-ceilinged, beige-carpeted Privy Council chamber. The others—Cawston, Lexington, Nesbitson, Perrault, and Martening—were already seated near the head of the big oval table with its twenty-four carved-oak and red-leather chairs, scene of most decisions affecting Canadian history since Confederation. Off to one side, at a smaller table, a shorthand writer had appeared —a small, self-effacing man with pince-nez, an open notebook, and a row of sharpened pencils.

At the approach of the Prime Minister the five already in the room made to rise, but Howden waved them down, moving to the tall-backed, thronelike chair at the table's head. "Smoke if you wish," he said. Then pushing back the chair, he remained standing, and for a moment silent. When he began, his tone was business-like.

"I ordered our meeting to be held in this chamber, gentlemen, for one purpose: as a reminder of the oaths of secrecy which all of you took on becoming Privy Councillors. What is to be said here is of utmost secrecy, and must remain so until the proper moment, even among our closest colleagues." James Howden paused, glancing at the official reporter. "I believe it might be best if we dispensed with a stenographic record."

"Excuse me, Prime Minister." It was Douglas Martening, his intellectual's face owlish behind big horn-rimmed spectacles. As always the Clerk of the Privy Council was respectful but definite. "I think it might be better if we had recorded minutes. It avoids any disagreement subsequently about who said exactly what."

Faces at the center table turned toward the shorthand writer, who was carefully recording the discussion concerning his own presence. Martening added, "The minutes will be safeguarded, and Mr. McQuillan, as you know, has been trusted with many secrets in the past."

"Yes, indeed." James Howden's response was cordial with a touch of his public presence. "Mr. McQuillan is an old friend." With a slight flush the subject of their discussion looked up, catching the Prime Minister's eye.

"Very well," Howden conceded, "let the meeting be recorded, but in view of the occasion I must remind the reporter of the applicability of the Official Secrets Act. I imagine you're familiar with the act, McQuillan?"

"Yes, sir." Conscientiously the reporter recorded the query and his own response.

His glance ranging over the others, Howden brought his thoughts into focus. Last night's preparation had shown him clearly the sequence of steps he must follow in advance of the Washington meeting. One essential, to be achieved early on, was persuasion of others in Cabinet to his own views, and that was why he had brought this small group together first. If he could obtain agreement here, he would then have a hard core of support which could influence the remaining ministers to give him their endorsement.

James Howden hoped that the five men facing him would share his views and see the issues and alternatives clearly.

It could be disastrous if the fulminations of lesser brains than his own resulted in needless delay.

"There can no longer be any doubt," the Prime Minister said, "of Russia's immediate intention. If there were ever any doubt, events these past few months have surely dispelled it. Last week's alliance between the Kremlin and Japan; before that, the Communist coups in India and Egypt and now the satellite regimes; our further concessions on Berlin; the Moscow-Peking axis with its threats to Australasia; the increase in missile bases aimed at North America—all these admit to only one equation. The Soviet program of world domination is moving to its climax, not in fifty years or twenty even, as we once comfortably supposed, but now, in our generation and within this decade.

"Naturally, Russia would prefer its victory without recourse to war. But it is equally plain that the gamble of war may be undertaken if the West holds out and the Kremlin's objectives can be reached in no other way."

There was a reluctant murmur of assent. Now he continued. "Russian strategy has never been afraid of casualties. Historically their regard for human life is notably less than our own and they are prepared not to be afraid now. Many people, of course—in this country and elsewhere—will continue to have hope, just as there was hope that someday Hitler would stop gobbling Europe of his own accord. I do not criticize hope; it is a sentiment to be cherished. But here among us we cannot afford its luxury and must plan, unequivocally, for our defense and for survival."

As he spoke, James Howden was remembering his words to Margaret of the night before. What was it he had said? *Survival is worth while, because survival means living, and living is an adventure.* He hoped it would be true, in the future as well as now.

He went on, "What I have said, of course, is not news. Nor is it news that in some degree our defenses have been integrated with those of the United States. But what will be news is that within the past forty-eight hours a proposal has been made, directly to me by the U.S. President, for a measure of integration as far-reaching as it is dramatic."

Swiftly, perceptibly there was a sharpening of interest around the table.

"Before I tell you of the nature of the proposal," Howden said, speaking carefully, "there is some other ground I wish

to be covered." He turned to the External Affairs Minister.
"Arthur, shortly before we came in here, I asked for your
assessment of present world relations. I'd like you to repeat
your answer."

"Very well, Prime Minister." Arthur Lexington laid down
a cigarette lighter he had been turning over in his hand. His
cherubic face was unusually solemn. Glancing to left and
right in turn, he said evenly, "In my opinion, international
tension at this moment is more serious and dangerous than
at any other time since 1939."

The calm, precise words had honed an edge of tension.
Lucien Perrault said softly, "Are things really that bad?"

"Yes," Lexington responded, "I'm convinced they are. I
agree it's difficult to accept, because we've been poised on a
needle point so long that we're used to crisis as a daily habit.
But eventually there comes a point beyond crisis. I think
we're close to it now."

Stuart Cawston said lugubriously, "Things must have been
easier fifty years ago. At least the threats of war were
spaced at decent intervals."

"Yes." There was tiredness in Lexington's voice. "I suppose
they were."

"Then a new war . . ." It was Perrault's question. He left
it unfinished.

"My own opinion," Arthur Lexington said, "is that despite
the present situation we shall not have war for a year. It
could be longer. As a precaution, however, I have warned
my ambassadors to be ready to burn their papers."

"That's for the old kind of war," Cawston said. "With all
your diplomatic doodads." He produced a tobacco pouch
and a pipe, which he began to fill.

Lexington shrugged. He gave a faint smile. "Perhaps."

For a calculated interval James Howden had relaxed his
dominance of the group. Now, as if gathering reins, he resumed it.

"My own views," the Prime Minister said firmly, "are
identical with those of Arthur. So identical, that I have
ordered immediate partial occupancy of the government's
emergency quarters. Your own departments will receive
secret memoranda on the subject within the next few days."
At the audible gasp which followed, Howden added severely,
"Better too much too early than too little too late."

Without waiting for comment he continued, "What I have

to say next is not new, but we must remind ourselves of our own position when a third world war begins."

He surveyed the others through the haze of smoke which was beginning to fill the room. "In the state of affairs today, Canada can neither wage war—at least, as an independent country—nor can we remain neutral. We have not the capacity for the first, nor the geography for the second. I offer this, not as opinion, but as a fact of life."

The eyes around the table were fixed steadfastly upon his own. So far, he observed, there had been no gesture of dissension. But that could come later. "Our own defenses," Howden said, "have been, and are, of a token nature only. And it is no secret that the United States budget for Canadian defense, though not high as defense budgets go, is greater by far than the total of our own."

Adrian Nesbitson spoke for the first time. "But it isn't philanthropy," the old man said gruffly. "The Americans will defend Canada because they've got to, to defend themselves. We're under no compulsion to be grateful."

"There is never any compulsion about gratitude," James Howden responded sharply. "Though I will admit at times to thanking Providence that honorable friends, not enemies, adjoin our borders."

"Hear, hear!" It was Lucien Perrault, his teeth clamped on a cigar pointed jauntily upward. Now he put down the cigar and clapped his paw of a hand on the shoulders of Adrian Nesbitson next to him. "Never mind, old friend, I will be grateful for the two of us."

The interjection, and its source, had surprised Howden. Traditionally he had assumed that the greatest opposition to his own immediate plans would come from French Canada, whose spokesman was Lucien Perrault: French Canada, with its ancient fear of encroachment; its deep-rooted, historic mistrust of alien influence and ties. Could he have misjudged? Perhaps not; it was early yet to tell. But for the first time he wondered.

"Let me remind you of some facts." Once again, Howden's voice was firm and commanding. "We are all familiar with the possible effects of a nuclear war. After such a war, survival will depend on food, and food production. The nation whose food-producing areas have become contaminated by radioactive fallout will already have lost the battle for survival."

"More than food would be wiped out," Stuart Cawston said. His customary smile was absent.

"But food production is the single thing that matters most." Howden's voice rose. "The cities can be blasted to rubble, and a good many will be. But if, afterwards, there's clean land, uncontaminated; land to grow food, then whoever is left can come out of the rubble and begin again. Food and the land to grow it in—that's what will really count. We came from the land and we'll go back to it. That's the way survival lies! The only way!"

On a wall of the Privy Council chamber a map of North America had been hung. James Howden crossed to it, the heads of the others turning with him. "The government of the United States," he said, "is well aware that food areas must be protected first. Their plan, at all costs, is to safeguard their own." His hand raced across the map. "The dairy lands—northern New York, Wisconsin, Minnesota; the mixed farming of Pennsylvania; the wheat belt—the Dakotas and Montana; Iowa corn; Wyoming livestock; the specialty crops —Idaho, northern Utah, and to the south; and all the rest." Howden's arm dropped. "These will be protected first, the cities secondarily."

"With no provision for Canadian land," Lucien Perrault said softly.

"You're wrong," James Howden said. "There *is* provision for Canadian land. It's reserved for the battleground."

Again he turned to the map. With the index finger of his right hand he stubbed a series of points directly to the south of Canada, moving inward from the Atlantic seaboard. "Here is the line of United States missile sites—the launching sites for defensive and intercontinental missiles—with which the U.S. will protect its food-producing areas. You know them as well as I know them, as well as every junior in Russian Intelligence knows them."

Arthur Lexington murmured softly, "Buffalo, Plattsburg, Presque Isle . . ."

"Exactly," Howden said. "These points represent the spearhead of American defense and, as such, they will form the first prime target of a Soviet attack. If that attack—by Russian missiles—is repelled by interception, the intercept will occur directly over Canada." Dramatically he swept the palm of his hand across the Canadian segment of the map. "There is the battleground! There, in the scheme of things now, is

where war will be fought." Eyes followed where the
hand had moved. Its path of travel had been a broad swathe
north of the border, bisecting the grain-growing West and
the East's industrial heartland. In its path were the cities—
Winnipeg, Fort William, Hamilton, Toronto, Montreal, the
smaller communities in between. "Fallout will be heaviest
here," Howden said. "In the first days of war we could expect our cities to go and our food areas to become poisoned
and useless."

Outside, the Peace Tower carillon announced the quarter-
hour. Within the room only Adrian Nesbitson's heavy breathing broke the silence, and the rustle of paper as the official
reporter turned a page of his notebook. Howden wondered
what the man was thinking, if he was thinking; and if he
was, unless conditioned in advance, could any mind grasp
truly the portent of what was being said? For that matter
could any of them really understand, until it happened, the
sequence of events to come?

The basic pattern, of course, was appallingly simple. Unless there were an accident of some sort, or a false warning,
the Russians almost certainly would be the first to fire. When
they did, the trajectory of their missiles would lie directly
over Canada. If the joint warning systems worked efficiently,
the American command would have several minutes warning
of attack—time enough to launch their own defensive, short-
range missiles. The initial series of intercepts would occur, at
best guess, somewhere north of the Great Lakes, in southern
Ontario and Quebec. The American short-range weapons
would not have nuclear warheads, but the Soviet missiles
would be nuclear-armed and contact-fused. Therefore the result of each successful intercept would be a hydrogen blast
which would make the atom bombing of Hiroshima squiblike
and archaic by comparison. And beneath each blast—it was
too much to hope that there would be merely one or two,
Howden thought—would be five thousand square miles of
devastation and radioactivity.

Swiftly, in terse crisp sentences, he transposed the picture
into words. "As you must see," he concluded, "the possibilities of our survival as a functioning nation are not extraordinary."

Again the silence. This time Stuart Cawston broke it,
speaking softly, "I've known all this. I suppose we all have.

And yet one never truly faces . . . you put things off; other things distract . . . perhaps because we want them to . . ."

"We've all been guilty of that," Howden said. "The point is: can we face it now?"

"There is an 'unless' in what you have said, is there not?" This time Lucien Perrault, his deep eyes searching.

"Yes," Howden acknowledged. "There is an 'unless.' " He glanced at the others, then faced Perrault squarely. His voice was strong. "All that I have described will occur inevitably unless we choose, without delay, to merge our nationhood and sovereignty with the nationhood of the United States."

Reaction came swiftly.

Adrian Nesbitson was struggling to his feet. "Never! Never! Never!" His face brick-red, the old man sputtered angrily.

Cawston's expression was shocked. "The country would throw us out!"

Douglas Martening, startled into response, said, "Prime Minister, have you seriously . . ." The sentence was never finished.

"Silence!" The hamlike fist of Lucien Perrault smashed down upon the table. Startled, the other voices stopped. Nesbitson subsided. Below his black locks, Perrault's face scowled. Well, Howden thought, I've lost Perrault and with him goes any hope I had of national unity. Now Quebec—French Canada—would stand alone. It had before. Quebec was a rock—sharp-edged, immovable—on which other Governments had foundered in the past.

He could carry the others today, or most of them; that much he still believed. Anglo-Saxon logic in the end would see what had to be seen, and afterwards English-speaking Canada alone might still provide the strength he needed. But division would be deep, with bitterness and strife, and scars which would never heal. He waited for Lucien Perrault to walk out.

Instead, Perrault said, "I wish to hear the rest." He added darkly: "Without the chattering of crows."

Again James Howden wondered. But he wasted no time.

"There is one proposal which, in event of war, could change our situation. That proposal is perfectly simple. It is the movement of United States missile bases—ICBM and short-range missiles—to our own Canadian North. If it were done, a good deal of radioactive fallout which I have spoken of would occur over uninhabited land."

"But there are still the winds!" Cawston said.

"Yes," Howden acknowledged. "If winds were from the north, there is a degree of fallout we would not escape. But remember that no country will come unscathed through a nuclear war. The best we can hope for is reduction of its worst effect."

Adrian Nesbitson protested, "We have already co-operated . . ."

Howden cut the aging Defense Minister short. "What we have done are half-measures, quarter-measures, temporizing! If war came tomorrow our puny preparations would be insignificant!" His voice rose. "We are vulnerable and virtually undefended, and we should be overwhelmed and overrun as Belgium was overrun in the great wars of Europe. At best we should be captured and subjugated. At worst we should become a nuclear battleground, our nation destroyed utterly and our land laid waste for centuries to come. And yet this need not be. The time is short. But if we are swift, honest and above all realistic, we can survive, endure, and perhaps beyond find greatness as we have not dreamed of."

The Prime Minister stopped, his own words stirring him. Momentarily he had a sense of breathlessness, of excitement at his own leadership, at the looming pattern of great events to come. Perhaps, he thought, this was the way Winston Churchill felt when he had impelled others to destiny and greatness. For a moment he considered the parallel between Churchill and himself. Was it so obscure? Others, he supposed, might fail to see it now, though later they might not.

"I have spoken of a proposal, made to me forty-eight hours ago, by the President of the United States." James Howden paused. Then, clearly and with deliberation: "The proposal is for a solemn Act of Union between our two countries. Its terms would include total assumption of Canadian defense by the United States; disbandment of the Canadian armed forces and their immediate recruitment by the U.S. forces under a joint Oath of Allegiance; the opening of all Canadian territory as part of the maneuvering arena of the U.S. military; and—most important—the transfer, with every possible speed, of all missile-launching bases to the Far North of Canada."

"My God!" Cawston said. "My God!"

"One moment," Howden said. "That is not quite all. The Act of Union, as proposed, would provide also for customs union and the joint conduct of foreign affairs. But outside those areas, and the others I have named specifically, our national entity and independence would remain."

He moved forward, bringing his hands from behind and placing their finger tips upon the oval table. Speaking for the first time with emotion he said, "It is, as you will see at once a proposal both awesome and drastic. But I may tell you that I have weighed it carefully, envisaging consequences, and, in my opinion, it is our only possible course if we are to emerge, as a nation, from a war to come."

"But why *this* way?" Stuart Cawston's voice was strained. The Finance Minister had never seemed more troubled or perplexed. It was as if an old, established world were crumbling about him. Well, Howden thought, it's crumbling for all of us. Worlds had a way of doing that, even though each man thought his own world was secure.

"Because there is no other way and no other time!" Howden rapped out the words like the crackle of machine guns. "Because preparation is vital and we have three hundred days and perhaps—God willing—a little more, but not much more. Because action must be sweeping! Because the time for timidity has gone! Because until now, in every council of joint defense, the specter of national pride has haunted us and paralyzed decision, and it will haunt and paralyze us still if we attempt more compromise and patching! You ask me—why this way? I tell you again—there is no other!"

Now, quietly, in his best mediator's voice, Arthur Lexington spoke. "The thing, I imagine, most people would want to know is whether we could remain a nation under such a covenant or if we would be merely an American satellite—a sort of unregistered fifty-first state. Once our control of foreign policy was surrendered, as would happen of course whether we spelled it out or not, a good deal would need to be taken on trust."

"In the unlikely event that such an agreement were ever ratified," Lucien Perrault said slowly, his dark brooding eyes fixed upon Howden, "it would, of course, have a specific term."

"The period suggested is twenty-five years," the Prime Minister said. "There would, however, be a clause that the Act of Union could be dissolved by mutual agreement, though not by one country acting alone. As to the point about taking a good deal on trust—yes, we would certainly have to do that. The question is: where would you prefer your trust to be—in a vain hope that war may not occur, or in the pledged word of a neighbor and ally whose concept of international ethics is somewhat as our own."

"But the country!" Cawston said. "Could you ever convince the country?"

"Yes," Howden responded. "I believe we could." He proceeded to tell them why: the approach he had devised; the opposition to be expected; the election on the issue which they must fight and win. The talk moved on. An hour passed, two hours, two and a half. Coffee had been brought in, but except for a brief moment discussion had not stopped. The paper napkins with the coffee had a design of holly, Howden noticed. It seemed a strange reminder—that Christmas was only hours away. The birthday of Christ. What he taught us was so simple, Howden thought: that love is the only worthwhile emotion—a teaching sane and logical, whether you believed in Christ the Son of God, or Jesus, a saintly mortal man. But the human animal had never believed in love—pure love—and never really would. He had corrupted the word of Christ with prejudice, and his churches had obfuscated it; and so we are here, Howden thought, doing what we are on Christmas Eve.

Stuart Cawston was refilling his pipe for what was probably the tenth time. Perrault had run out of cigars and was smoking Douglas Martening's cigarettes. Arthur Lexington —like the Prime Minister a non-smoker—had opened a window behind them for a while, but later had shut it because of the draft. A pall of smoke hung over the oval table, and, like the smoke, a sense of unreality. What was happening, it seemed, was impossible; it could not be true. And yet, slowly, James Howden could feel reality taking hold, conviction settling on the others as it had settled upon himself.

Lexington was with him; to the External Affairs Minister none of this was new. Cawston was wavering. Adrian Nesbitson had been mostly silent, but the old man didn't count. Douglas Martening had seemed shocked at first, but after all he was a civil servant and eventually would do as he was told. Lucien Perrault remained—his opposition to be expected, but so far undeclared.

The Clerk of the Privy Council said, "There would be

several constitutional problems, Prime Minister." His voice was disapproving, but mildly so, as if objecting to some minor procedural change.

"Then we will solve them," Howden said decisively. "I, for one, do not propose to accept annihilation because certain courses are closed off in the rule book."

"Quebec," Cawston said. "We'd never carry Quebec."

The moment had come.

James Howden said quietly, "I will admit that the thought had already occurred to me."

Slowly the eyes of the others swung round to Lucien Perrault—Perrault, the chosen; the idol and spokesman of French Canada. As others had before him—Laurier, Lapointe, St. Laurent—he alone in two elections past had swung the strength of Quebec behind the Howden government. And behind Perrault were three hundred years of history; New France, Champlain, the Royal Government of Louis XIV, the British conquest—and French Canadians' hatred of their conquerors. Hatred had gone in time, but mistrust—two-sided—had never vanished. Twice, in twentieth-century wars involving Canada, their disputations had divided the country. Compromise and moderation had salvaged uneasy unity. But now . . .

"There would appear no need to speak," Perrault said dourly. "It seems that you, my colleagues, have a pipeline to my mind."

"It's hard to ignore facts," Cawston said. "Or history either."

"History," Perrault said softly, then slammed down his hand. The table shook. His voice boomed angrily. "Has no one told you that history moves; that minds progress and change; that divisions do not last forever? Or have you slept—slept while better minds matured?"

The change in the room was electric. The startling words had come like a thunderclap.

"How do you consider us—we of Quebec?" Perrault raged. "Forever as peasants, fools, illiterates? Are we unknowing; blind and oblivious to a changing world? No, my friends, we are saner than you, and less bemused by what is past. If this *must* be done, it will be done with anguish. But anguish is not new to French Canada; or realism either."

"Well," Stuart Cawston said quietly, "you can never tell which way the cat will jump."

It was all that was needed. Tension, as if by magic, dissolved in a howl of laughter. Chairs scraped back. Perrault, tears of mirth streaming, cuffed Cawstor vigorously across the shoulders. We are a strange people, Howden thought: an unpredictable admixture of mediocrity and genius, with now and then a flash of greatness.

"Perhaps it will be the end of me." Lucien Perrault shrugged, a Gallic gesture of indifference. "But I will support the Prime Minister, and perhaps I can persuade others." It was a masterpiece of understatement and Howden felt a surging gratitude.

Adrian Nesbitson alone had remained silent in the last exchange. Now, his voice surprisingly strong, the Defense Minister said, "If that's the way you feel, why stop at half-measures? Why not sell out to the United States completely?" Simultaneously five heads had turned toward him.

The old man flushed but continued doggedly, "I say we should maintain our independence—at whatever cost."

"To the point, no doubt, of repelling a nuclear invasion," James Howden said icily. Coming after Perrault, Nesbitson's words had seemed like a dismal, chilling shower. Now, with controlled anger, Howden added, "Or perhaps the Defense Minister has some means of doing so that we have not yet heard about."

Bitterly, in his mind, Howden reminded himself that this was a sample of the unseeing, obtuse stupidity he would have to face in the weeks immediately ahead. For an instant he pictured the other Nesbitsons still to come: the cardboard warriors with aged, faded pennants, a Blimplike cavalcade marching blindly to oblivion. It was ironic, he reflected, that he must expend his own intellect in convincing fools like Nesbitson of the need to save themselves.

There was an uneasy silence. It was no secret in Cabinet that lately the Prime Minister had been dissatisfied with his Minister of Defense.

Now Howden continued, his hawklike face bleak, pointedly addressing his words to Adrian Nesbitson. "In the past this Government has been amply concerned with maintenance of our national independence. And my own feeling in that area has been demonstrated time and time again." There was a murmur of assent. "The personal decision I have now reached has not been easy and I think I may say it has required a modicum of courage. The easy way is the reckless way, which some might think of as courage but, in the end, would be the greater cowardice." At the word "cowardice" General Nesbitson flushed crimson, but the Prime Minister had not finished. "There is one more thing. Whatever our discussions in the weeks ahead, I shall not expect to encounter, among members of this Government, political gutter phrases like 'selling out to the United States.' "

Howden had always ridden his Cabinet hard, tongue-lashing ministers at times, and not always in private. But never before had his anger been quite this pointed.

Uncomfortably the others watched Adrian Nesbitson.

At first it seemed as if the old warrior might strike back. He had moved forward in his chair, his face suffused angrily. He started to speak. Then, suddenly, like a worn mainspring run down, he visibly subsided, becoming once again the old man, insecure and floundering among problems far removed from his own experience. Muttering something about, "Perhaps misunderstood . . . unfortunate phrase," he receded into his seat, plainly wishing the focus of attention to move on from himself.

As if in sympathy, Stuart Cawston said hastily, "Customs union would have a large attraction from our point of view since we would have most to gain." As the others turned to him, the Finance Minister paused, his astute mind plainly assessing possibilities. Now he continued, "But any agreement should go considerably further than that. After all, it's their own defense as well as ours that the Americans are buying. There must be guarantees for manufacturing here, enlargement of our industries . . ."

"Our demands will not be light and I intend to make that clear in Washington," Howden said. "In whatever time is left we must strengthen our economy so that after a war we can emerge stronger than either of the principal contenders."

Cawston said softly, "It could work that way. In the end it really could."

"There is something else," Howden said. "Another demand —the biggest of all—that I intend to make."

There was a silence which Lucien Perrault broke. "We are listening attentively, Prime Minister. You spoke of another demand."

Arthur Lexington was toying with a pencil, his expression thoughtful.

He dare not tell them, Howden decided. At least, not yet.

The concept was too big, too bold, and in a way preposterous. He remembered Lexington's reaction yesterday during their private talk, when the Prime Minister had revealed his thoughts. The External Affairs Minister had demurred: "The Americans would never agree. Never." And James Howden had answered slowly, "If they were desperate enough, I think they might."

Now, determinedly, he faced the others. "I cannot tell you," he said decisively, "except that if the demand is met it will be the greatest achievement for Canada in this century. Beyond that, until after the White House meeting, you must trust me." Raising his voice he said commandingly, "You have trusted me before. I demand your trust again."

Slowly, around the table, there was a succession of nods. Watching, Howden felt the beginning of a new exultation. They were with him, he knew. By persuasion, logic, and force of leadership he had carried the argument here and gained support. It had been the first test, and what he had done once could be done elsewhere.

Only Adrian Nesbitson remained unmoving and silent, eyes downcast, his lined face somber. Glancing down the table Howden felt a resurgence of anger. Even though Nesbitson might be a fool, as Minister of Defense his token support was necessary. Then the anger subsided. The old man could be disposed of quickly, and once dismissed would be bothersome no more.

Five Senator Richard Deveraux

The Vancouver *Post*, a newspaper not given to decorous pussyfooting, had accorded full human-interest treatment to Dan Orliffe's report on the would-be immigrant, Henri Duval. The story ran at the top left on page one through all Christmas Eve editions, taking second place only to a day-old sex slaying which led the paper. A four-column head proclaimed:

Homeless Ocean Waif
Faces Bleak, Lone Yule

Below, also across four columns, and forty lines deep, was a closeup picture of the young stowaway, his back to a ship's boat. Unusually for a press photograph, the camera had caught a depth of expression which coarse newsprint etching had not entirely lost; it combined a suggestion of yearning and something close to innocence.

The effect of story and picture was such that the managing editor scribbled upon a proof copy, "Good, let's keep this hot," and sent it to the city desk. The city editor, phoning Dan Orliffe at home, said, "Try to find a forward angle for Thursday, Dan, and see what you can get out of the Immigration people besides bull. Looks like this thing may rouse a lot of interest."

Locally the interest began at a high point and sustained itself over the Christmas holiday. Across the city and its environs the *Vastervik's* stowaway was a major topic of conversation in homes, clubs, and bars. Some who discussed the young man's plight were moved to pity; others angrily referred to "damned officialdom" and "bureaucratic inhumanity." Thirty-seven phone calls, beginning an hour after publication, commended the *Post* for its initiative in bringing the matter to public attention. As usual on such occasions, all calls were carefully logged so that, afterwards, advertisers could be shown just how much impact there had been from a typical *Post* newsbeat.

There were other signs. Five local disc jockeys referred sympathetically to the item on the air, one of their number dedicating a platter of "Silent Night" to Henri Duval "in case our friend from the seven seas is tuned to Vancouver's most listened-to station." In Chinatown, amid applause, a night-club stripper dedicated her next uncovering to "that lonely little guy on the ship." And in pulpits, at least eight Christmas sermons had been hastily revised to include a topical reference to the "stranger that is within thy gates."

Fifteen people were sufficiently moved to compose letters to the editor, fourteen of which were subsequently printed. The fifteenth, largely incoherent, exposed the incident as part of an infiltration plot from outer space, with Duval a Martian agent. Apart from the last, most letter writers were agreed that something should be done by somebody, but were not clear as to what or by whom.

A handful did practical things. A Salvation Army officer and a Catholic priest made notes to visit Henri Duval and subsequently did. The mink-weighted widow of a one-time gold prospector personally gift-wrapped a parcel of food and cigarettes and dispatched it, via her uniformed chauffeur and white Cadillac, to the *Vastervik*. As an afterthought she also sent a bottle of her late husband's favorite whisky. At first the chauffeur had considered stealing this but, en route, discovering it to be of a kind much inferior to the brand he favored himself, he rewrapped the bottle and delivered it as instructed.

An electrical-appliance dealer, desperately harried by impending bankruptcy, took a new portable radio from his stock and, without quite knowing why, addressed the carton to Duval and delivered it to the ship's side. An age-bent railroad pensioner, eking out his years on a monthly sum which would have been just adequate if the cost of living had stayed at 1940 levels, put two dollars in an envelope and mailed it to the *Post* for transmission to the stowaway. A group of bus drivers, reading the *Post* report before going on duty, passed around a uniform cap and collected seven dollars and thirty cents. The cap owner took it to Duval in person on Christmas morning.

The ripples went beyond Vancouver.

The first news story appeared in the *Post's* Mainland edition at 10 A.M., December 24. By 10.10 Canadian Press wire service had rewritten and condensed the item, then fed it out to press and radio stations in the West. Another wire carried the news to Eastern papers, and CP in Toronto rerouted it to AP and Reuters in New York. The American agencies, news-starved over the Christmas holiday, capsuled the piece some more and fanned it out across the world.

The Johannesburg *Star* gave the item an inch and the Stockholm *Europa Press* a quarter of a column. The London *Daily Mail* allowed four lines and the *Times of India* delivered itself of an editorial. The Melbourne *Herald* used a paragraph, as did the Buenos Aires *La Prensa*. In Moscow, *Pravda* quoted the incident as an example of "capitalist hypocrisy."

In New York the U. N. Peruvian delegate learned of the story and resolved to ask the General Assembly if something couldn't be done. In Washington the British Ambassador heard the report and frowned.

The news got to Ottawa by early afternoon in time for the late editions of the capital's two evening newspapers. The *Citizen* front-paged the CP dispatch and tagged it:

Man Minus Country
Pleads 'Let Me In'

More sedately, the *Journal* ran the item on page three under
the head:

Ship's Stowaway
Asks Entry Here

Brian Richardson, who had been brooding about the problem which the party would face when the secret Washington
proposals eventually became known, read both papers in his
sparsely furnished Sparks Street office. The party director
was a big, athletically built man with blue eyes, sandy hair,
and ruddy cheeks. His expression, most times, conveyed an
amused skepticism, but he could be quick to anger and there
was a sense of latent power about him. Now his heavy,
broad-shouldered figure was slumped into a tilted chair, both
feet planted upon a cluttered desk, a pipe clenched between
his teeth. The office was lonely and silent. His second in command, as well as the assistants, researchers, and office workers who formed the sizable staff of party headquarters, had
gone home, some laden with Christmas parcels, several
hours earlier.

Having gone through the two newspapers thoroughly, he
returned to the stowaway item. Long experience had given
Richardson a sensitive nose for political trouble and it was
reacting now. Compared with the bigger issues pending, he
knew that the matter was unimportant; all the same, it was
the kind of thing the public was likely to seize on. He sighed;
there were times when vexations seemed endless. He had
still not heard from the Prime Minister since his own call
to Milly earlier in the day. Uneasily putting the newspapers
aside, he refilled his pipe and settled down once more to
wait.

2

Less than a quarter-mile from Brian Richardson, within
the sacrosanct cloister of the Rideau Club on Wellington
Street, Senator Richard Deveraux, who was killing time before a scheduled jet flight to Vancouver, also read both
papers, then rested his cigar in an ash tray and smilingly

tore the stowaway item out. Unlike Richardson, who hoped fervently that the case would not embarrass the Government, the Senator—chairman of the Opposition party organization—was happily confident that it would.

Senator Deveraux had purloined the news item in the Rideau Club's reading room—a square, lofty chamber overlooking Parliament Hill, and guarded at its doorway by a stern bronze bust of Queen Victoria. To the aging Senator, both the reading room and the club itself were an old familiar habitat.

The Rideau Club of Ottawa (as its members sometimes point out) is so exclusive and discreet that not even its name appears outside the building. A pedestrian passing by would never know what place it was unless he were told, and, if curious, he might take it for a private, though somewhat seedy, mansion.

Within the club, above a pillared entrance hall and broad divided stairway, the atmosphere is just as rarefied. There is no rule about silence, but most times of the day a sepulchral hush prevails and newer members tend to speak in whispers.

Membership of the Rideau Club, though non-partisan, is made up largely of Ottawa's political elite—cabinet ministers, judges, senators, diplomats, military chiefs of staff, top civil servants, a handful of trusted journalists, and the few ordinary Members of Parliament who can afford the stiff fees. But despite the non-partisan policy a good deal of political business is transacted. In fact, some of the larger decisions affecting Canada's development have been shaped, over brandy and cigars, by Rideau Club cronies, relaxed in the club's deep red-leather armchairs, as Senator Deveraux was relaxing now.

In his mid-seventies Richard Borden Deveraux was an imposing figure—tall, straight-backed, with clear eyes and a healthy robustness which had come from a lifetime entirely without exercise. His paunch was sufficient for distinction but not for ridicule. His manner was an amiable mixture of bluffness and bulldozing which produced results but rarely gave offense. He talked at length and gave the impression of listening not at all, though, in fact, there was little that he missed. He had prestige, influence and enormous wealth founded upon a western Canada logging empire bequeathed by an earlier Deveraux.

Now, rising from his chair, the Senator proceeded, cigar

jutting ahead, to one of two unobtrusive telephones—direct exchange lines—in the rear of the club. He dialed two numbers before reaching the man he wanted. On the second call he located the Hon. Bonar Deitz, leader of the parliamentary Opposition. Deitz was in his Center Block office.

"Bonar, my boy," Senator Deveraux announced, "I'm delighted, if surprised on Christmas Eve, to find you applying yourself so assiduously."

"I've been writing letters," the voice of Deitz said shortly. "I'm going home now."

"Splendid!" The Senator boomed. "Will you stop in at the club on the way? Something has arisen and we need to get together."

There was the beginning of a protest from the other end of the line which the Senator cut off. "Now, my boy, that's not the attitude at all—not if you want our side to win elections and make you Prime Minister instead of that bag of wind James Howden. And you *do* want to be Prime Minister, don't you?" The Senator's voice took on a caressing note. "Well, you will be, Bonar boy, never fear. Don't be long now. I'm waiting."

Chuckling, the Senator padded to a chair in the club's main lounge, his canny mind already at work on methods of turning the news item he had read to the Opposition party's advantage. Soon there was a cloud of cigar smoke above him as he indulged his favorite mental exercise.

Richard Deveraux had never been a statesman, either young or elder, or even a serious legislator. His chosen field was political manipulation and he had practiced it all his life. He enjoyed the exercise of semi-anonymous power. Within his party he had held few elective offices (his current tenure as organization chairman was a belated exception), yet in party affairs he had wielded authority as few others before him. There had been nothing sinister about this. It was based simply upon two factors—a natural political astuteness which in the past had made his advice eagerly sought, plus the judicious use of money.

In time, and during one of his own party's periods in power, these dual activities had brought Richard Deveraux the ultimate reward bestowed among the party faithful—a lifetime appointment to the Canadian Senate, whose members were once accurately described by one of their own as "the highest class of pensioners in Canada."

Like most of his elderly Senate brethren, Senator Deveraux rarely attended the few perfunctory debates which the upper chamber held as proof of its existence, and only on two occasions had he ever risen to speak. The first was to propose additional reserved parking for Senators on Parliament Hill, the second to complain that the Senate ventilating system was producing draughts. Both pleas resulted in action which, as Senator Deveraux was wont to observe dryly, "is more than you can say for the majority of Senate speeches."

It was ten minutes since the phone call and the Leader of the Opposition had not yet appeared. But he knew that eventually Bonar Deitz would come, and meanwhile the Senator closed his eyes to doze. Almost at once—age and a heavy lunch taking their toll—he was asleep.

3

The Center Block of Parliament was deserted and silent as the Hon. Bonar Deitz closed the heavy oaken door of his parliamentary office, Room 407S, behind him. His light footsteps on the marble floor echoed sharply through the long corridor, the sound bouncing forward and down from its vaulted Gothic arches and Tyndall limestone walls. He had stayed, handwriting some personal notes, longer than he had intended and now going to the Rideau Club to meet Senator Deveraux would make him even later. But he supposed he had better see what the old boy wanted.

Not bothering to wait for an elevator, he used the square marble staircase leading down to the main-floor front corridor. It was two flights only and he trod the stairs quickly, his long bony frame moving in short jerky movements like a tightly wound toy soldier. A thin, delicate hand touched the brass stair rail lightly.

A stranger seeing Bonar Deitz for the first time might have taken him for a scholar—which, in fact, he was—but not for a political leader. Leaders, traditionally, have robustness and authority, and externally Deitz had neither. Nor did his triangular, gaunt face—an unfriendly cartoonist had once drawn him with an almond head on a string-bean body— have any of the physical handsomeness which attracts votes to some politicians irrespective of anything they say or do.

And yet he had a surprising following in the country— among discriminating people, some said, who could detect

qualities in Deitz finer and deeper than those of his major
political opponent James McCallum Howden. Nevertheless in
the last election Howden and his party had beaten Deitz
resoundingly.

As he entered Confederation Hall, the vaulted outer lobby
with its soaring columns of dark polished syenite, a uniformed attendant was talking with a young man—he looked
like a teen-ager—in tan slacks and a Grenfell jacket. Their
voices carried clearly.

"Sorry," the attendant said. "I don't make the rules, son."

"I realize that, but couldn't you make just this one exception?" The boy's accent was American; if not from the
Deep South, then close to it. "I've two days, is all. My folks
start back . . ."

Involuntarily Bonar Deitz stopped. It was none of his business, but something about the boy . . . He asked, "Is there a
problem?"

"The young man wants to see the House, Mr. Deitz,"
the attendant said. "I've explained it isn't possible, being the
holiday . . ."

"I'm at Chattanooga U., sir," the boy said. "Majoring in
constitutional history. I figured while I was here . . ."

Deitz glanced at his watch. "If we're very quick I'll show
you. Come with me." Nodding to the attendant, he turned
around the way he had come.

"Boy, this is great!" The lanky sophomore walked beside
him, taking long easy strides. "This is really swell."

"If you're studying constitutional history," Deitz said,
"you'll understand the difference between our Canadian
system of government and yours."

The boy nodded. "I think I do, most of it. The biggest
difference is that we elect a President, but your Prime Minister isn't elected."

"He isn't elected as Prime Minister," Deitz said. "To sit in
the House of Commons, though, he must seek election as a
Member of Parliament, the same way as all the other members. After an election the leader of the majority party becomes Prime Minister and then forms a ministry from among
his own followers."

Continuing, he explained, "The Canadian system is a parliamentary monarchy with a single, unbroken line of authority all the way upward from the ordinary voter, through
the Government, to the Crown. Your system is a divided

authority with separation of powers—the President has some, Congress others."

"Checks and balances," the boy said. "Only sometimes there are so many checks, nothing gets done."

Bonar Deitz smiled. "I won't comment on that. We might upset foreign relations."

They had come to the House of Commons lobby. Bonar Deitz opened one of the heavy double doors and led the way onto the floor of the House. They stopped, the deep silence—almost physically felt—enfolding them. Only a few lights were burning and, beyond their range, the soaring galleries and the chamber's outer edges blurred into darkness.

"When the House is sitting it's a good deal livelier," Deitz said dryly.

"I'm glad I saw it this way," the boy said softly. "It's . . . it's sort of hallowed."

Deitz smiled. "It has very old traditions." They moved forward and he explained how the Prime Minister and the Leader of the Opposition—himself—faced each other daily across the floor of the House. "You see," he said, "we think directness has a lot of advantages. With our kind of government the Executive is accountable to Parliament immediately for everything it does."

The boy looked curiously at his guide. "If your party had elected more people, sir, then you'd be Prime Minister instead of leading the Opposition."

Bonar Deitz nodded. "Yes, I would."

With unembarrassed frankness the boy asked, "Do you think you'll ever make it?"

"Now and then," Deitz said wryly, "I get to wondering that myself."

He had intended to take only a few minutes. But he found himself liking the boy and, by the time they had finished talking, much longer had elapsed. Once again, Deitz thought, he had allowed himself to be sidetracked. It happened frequently. He wondered sometimes if that were the real reason he had not been more successful in politics. Others whom he knew—James Howden was one—saw a straight, undeviating line and followed it. Deitz never did, politically or any other way.

He was an hour later than he had expected in reaching the Rideau Club. Hanging up his coat he remembered ruefully that he had promised his wife he would spend most of today at home.

In the lounge upstairs Senator Deveraux, still asleep, was snoring in gentle undulations.

"Senator!" Bonar Deitz said softly. "Senator!"

The old man opened his eyes, taking a moment to focus them. "Dear me." He eased upright from the depths of the big chair. "I appear to have dropped off."

"I expect you thought you were in the Senate," Bonar Deitz said. He lowered himself angularly, like a collapsible spindle, into an adjoining seat.

Senator Deveraux chuckled. "If that were so, you would have wakened me less easily." Shifting around, he reached into a pocket and produced the newspaper item he had torn out earlier. "Read this, my boy."

Deitz adjusted his rimless glasses and read carefully. While he did so the Senator trimmed a new cigar and lit it.

Looking up Deitz said mildly, "I have two questions, Senator."

"Ask away, my boy."

"My first question is—since I am now sixty-two years old, do you conceivably think you could stop calling me 'my boy'?"

The Senator chuckled. "That's half the trouble with you young fellows—you want to become old men before your time. Don't worry; age will creep up soon enough. Now, my boy, what's your second question?"

Bonar Deitz sighed. He knew better than to argue with the older man, who he suspected was baiting him. Instead he lighted a cigarette and asked, "What about this chap in Vancouver—Henri Duval? Is there something you know?"

Senator Deveraux waved his cigar in a gesture of dismissal. "I know nothing whatever. Except that the moment I learned of this unfortunate young man and his unheeded plea to enter our country, I said to myself: here is an opportunity for some ordure stirring which will embarrass our opponents."

Several others had come into the room, greeting Deitz and Senator Deveraux as they passed. The Senator lowered his voice conspiratorially. "You've heard what occurred at Government House last night? A fight!—among members of the Cabinet."

Bonar Deitz nodded.

"Under the very nose, mind you, of the duly appointed representative of our gracious sovereign."

"These things happen," Deitz said. "I remember once when our people had a shindig . . ."

"Please!" Senator Deveraux seemed shocked. "You're committing a cardinal political sin, my boy. You're trying to be *fair*."

"Look," Bonar Deitz said, "I promised my wife . . ."

"I'll be brief." Maneuvering the cigar to the left side of his mouth the Senator brought his hands together, checking off points upon his pudgy fingers. "Point one: we know that our opponents have dissension in their midst, as witness the disgraceful occurrence of last night. Point two: from what my informants tell me, the spark which touched off the explosion concerned immigration and Harvey Warrender—that egghead with the addled yolk. Are you with me so far?"

Bonar Deitz nodded. "I'm listening."

"Very well. Point three: in the matter of immigration, the individual cases which have come to public attention lately —what we might call the sentimental cases have been handled with appalling disregard . . . appalling from our opponents' point of view, of course, not ours . . . appalling disregard of practical politics and the impact of these cases upon the public conscience. Do you agree?"

Again a nod. "I agree."

"Splendid!" Senator Deveraux beamed. "Now we come to point four. It seems equally likely that our inhabile Minister of Immigration will deal with this unfortunate young man, Duval, with the same blundering ineptness as the rest. At any rate, we hope so."

Bonar Deitz smiled.

"Therefore"—the Senator's voice was still lowered—"therefore, I say, let us—the Opposition party—espouse this young man's cause. Let us turn this thing into a public issue, striking a blow against the unyielding Howden government. Let us . . ."

"I get the point," Bonar Deitz said. "Let's pick up a few votes too. It's not a bad idea."

The Leader of the Opposition regarded Senator Deveraux thoughtfully through his glasses. It was true, he told himself, the Senator was becoming senile in some ways, but all the same, when you ignored the tiresome Micawberisms, the old

SENATOR RICHARD DEVERAUX   91

man still possessed a remarkable political astuteness. Aloud
Deitz said, "What I'm more concerned about is this morning's announcement of this meeting in Washington between
Howden and the President. They say it's for trade talks but
I've a feeling there's something bigger involved. My idea
was to demand a fuller explanation of what they plan to discuss."

"I urge upon you not to do it." Senator Deveraux shook
his head severely. "It could gain us nothing in public sympathy and you may appear petulant in certain eyes. Why
begrudge even Howden the occasional little junket to touch
the hem in the White House? It's one of the prerogatives of
office. You'll do it yourself someday."

"If it's really for trade talks," Bonar Deitz said slowly,
"why at this particular time? There's no urgent issue; nothing
new that's in dispute."

"Exactly!" The Senator's voice held a note of triumph. "So
what better time—when everything in his own kennel is quiet
—for Howden to make himself a headline or two and get
photographed in bigger company. No, my boy, you'll do no
good attacking there. Besides, if it's trade they're going to
talk about, who cares outside a few importers and exporters?"

"I care," Bonar Deitz responded, "and so should everybody."

"Ah! but what people should do and really do are different
things. It's average voters we have to think about, and average
voters don't understand international trade and, what's more,
don't want to. What they care about is issues they can understand—human issues which stir their emotions; that they can
weep for or cheer about; something like this lost and lonely
young man, Henri Duval, who so badly needs a friend. Will
you be his friend, my boy?"

"Well," Bonar Deitz said thoughtfully, "maybe you have
something."

He paused, considering. Old man Deveraux was right
about one thing: the Opposition did need a good popular
issue with which to clobber the Government, because lately
there had been all too few.

There was another thing. Bonar Deitz was acutely aware
that recently there had been growing criticism of himself
among his own supporters. He was too mild, they said, in
his attacks, as Opposition Leader, upon the Government.
Well, perhaps his critics were right; he had been mild at

times and he supposed it was the result of being able, always, to see the other fellow's point of view. In the cut and thrust of politics such reasonableness could be a handicap.

But a clear-cut human-rights issue—if this turned out to be one; and it looked as if it might—well, that would be different. He could fight hard, hitting the Government in its tender underbelly and perhaps, that way, his own record would be evened out. Even more important, it would be the kind of fight which newspapers and the public could grasp and applaud.

But would it help his own party at the next election? That was the real test, and particularly for himself. He remembered the question which the boy had asked this afternoon: "Do you think you'll ever make it?" The real answer was that the next campaign would decide one way or the other. Bonar Deitz had led the Opposition through one election which had brought defeat. A second defeat would spell the end of his own tenure as Leader and his ambition to become Prime Minister.

Would it help to have the kind of fight which the Senator was suggesting? Yes, he decided, it very likely would.

"Thank you, Senator," Bonar Deitz said. "I think your suggestion is sound. If it can be done, we'll make this man Duval an issue and there are a lot of other things about immigration we can hit at the same time."

"Now you're talking." The Senator beamed.

"There'll have to be some precautions," Deitz said. He glanced at the others in the lounge, making sure he could not be overheard. "We must be certain that this fellow in Vancouver is what he purports to be, and of good character. That's clear, isn't it?"

"Naturally, my boy. Naturally."

"How do you suggest we begin?"

"The first thing is to secure a lawyer for this young man," Senator Deveraux said. "I'll take care of that myself in Vancouver tomorrow. After that there'll be legal steps during which, we trust, the Immigration Department will behave with its usual blundering heartlessness. And then . . . well, the rest will be up to you."

The Opposition Leader nodded approval. "That sounds all right. There's one thing about the lawyer, though."

"I'll get the right man—someone we can rely on. You may be sure of that."

"It might be wise if the lawyer isn't one of our own party." Bonar Deitz spoke slowly, thinking aloud. "That way, when we come into the picture it won't look too much like a setup. In fact, the lawyer really shouldn't belong to any party."

"A well-taken point. There is a problem, however, that most of our lawyers support one party or another."

"Not all lawyers do," Bonar Deitz said carefully. "Not all the new ones, for instance. Those just in practice, fresh from law school."

"Brilliant!" A slow grin spread over Senator Deveraux's face. "That's it my boy! We will find an innocent." His grin widened. "A little lamb whom we shall lead."

4

It was still snowing, though wetly, when Brian Richardson, his scarf wound tightly, overshoes snug, and topcoat collar upturned, left the office on Sparks Street for the short walk to Parliament Hill. The Prime Minister had finally called him and said, "You'd better come up. There's a lot I want to talk about." Now, taking long plunging strides through the crowds of Christmas Eve shoppers, Richardson shivered at the cold which seemed intensified by dusk settling grayly over the city.

Richardson disliked winter and Christmas with equal impartiality—the first through a built-in physical craving for warmth, the second because of an agnosticism which he was convinced most others shared but would not admit. He had once told James Howden, "Christmas is ten times phonier than any politics you ever saw, but nobody dare say so. All they'll tell you is 'Christmas is too commercialized.' Hell!— the commercial bit is the only part that makes sense."

Some of the commercial bit impinged on Richardson's consciousness now as he passed store fronts, most lighted garishly, with their inevitable Christmas themes. He grinned at a combination of signs he had noticed earlier. In the window of an appliance showroom a bright green panel blazoned in neoned misquotation, PEACE ON EARTH GOODWILL TOWARD MEN. Below, a second sign, equally bright, read: ENJOY IT NOW—PAY LATER.

Aside from a few gifts—including one for Milly Freedeman, which he must buy before this evening—Brian Richardson was glad there was no part he would have to act out in the Christmas scheme of things. Like James Howden, for instance, who would be obliged to turn out for church tomorrow morning, as he did most Sundays, even though his religious beliefs were about as non-existent as Richardson's own.

Once, years before, when Richardson had worked as an advertising account executive, a major industrial client had underwritten a "go to church" campaign which Richardson had handled. At one point the client had suggested pointedly that Richardson, too, should follow the advice in his own clever advertising copy and become a church attender. He had gone; the industrial end of the account was too important to take chances with. But he had been secretly relieved when the agency later lost the account and that particular client no longer had to be appeased.

That was one of the reasons he enjoyed his work so greatly nowadays. There were no clients for him to appease, and any appeasement needed was handled by others at Richardson's direction. Nor, because he was out of the public eye, was there any front that had to be maintained; that kind of thing was politicians' business. Far from worrying about appearances, the party director had a duty to remain obscure, and behind the obscurity he could live pretty much as he pleased.

That was one reason he had been less concerned than Milly Freedeman about a possible eavesdropper when they had made their date for tonight, though perhaps, he thought, out of consideration he should be more discreet another time. If there were another time.

Come to think of it, that was something to consider and perhaps after tonight it would be wise to ring down the curtain on the incident with Milly. Love 'em and leave 'em, he thought. After all, there were always plenty of women whose company—in and out of bed—a well-organized male could enjoy.

He liked Milly, of course; she had a personal warmth and depth of character which appealed to him, and she hadn't been bad—though a bit inhibited—the one time they had made love. All the same, if the two of them went on meeting there was always the danger of emotional involvement—not for himself, because he intended to avoid that sort of thing for a long time to come. But Milly might be hurt—women were apt to become serious about what men thought of as casual love-making—and it was something he preferred not to happen.

A plain-featured girl in Salvation Army uniform jingled a handbell in his face. Beside her on a stand was a glass jar of coins, mostly pennies and small silver. "Spare something, sir. It's Christmas cheer for the needy." The girl's voice was shrill, as if worn thin; her face glowed redly from the cold. Richardson reached into a pocket and his fingers found a bill among loose change. It was ten dollars and on impulse he dropped it into the glass jar.

"God be with you, and bless your family," the girl said.

Richardson grinned. Explaining, he thought, would spoil the picture; explaining that there never had been a family, with children, the way he had once pictured in what he thought of now as stickily sentimental moments. Better not to explain that he and his wife Eloise had a working arrangement whereby each went his own way, pursuing his separate interests but preserving the shell of their marriage to the extent that they shared accommodation, had meals together sometimes, and occasionally, if conditions happened to be right, slaked their sexual appetites by the polite use of each other's bodies.

Beyond that there was nothing else, nothing left, not even the once bitter arguments they used to have. He and Eloise never argued nowadays, having accepted the gulf between them as too wide even for their differences to bridge. And lately, as other interests had become dominant—his work for the party principally—the rest had seemed to matter less and less.

Some people might wonder why they bothered retaining their marriage at all, since divorce in Canada (except in two provinces) was relatively easy, entailing merely some mild perjury which the courts went along with. The truth was that both he and Eloise were freer married than they would have been unattached. As things stood now, each of them could have affairs, and did. But if an affair became complicated, the fact of an existing marriage was a convenient "out." Moreover, their own experience had convinced them both that a second marriage for either was no more likely to be successful than the first.

He quickened his steps, anxious to be out of the snow and cold. Entering the silent, deserted East Block, he went up by the stairs and into the Prime Minister's office suite.

Milly Freedeman, wearing a coral woolen topcoat and fur-trimmed snow boots with high heels, was peering into a mirror to adjust a white mink cloche hat. "I've been told to go home." She glanced around, smiling. "You can go in; though if it's anything like the Defense Committee you're in for a long session."

"It can't be too long," Richardson said. "I've a later appointment."

"Perhaps you should cancel it." Milly had turned. The hat was in place; it was the finest, most practical, and attractive winter headgear, he thought. Her face was glowing and her large gray-green eyes sparkled.

"Like hell I will," Richardson said. His eyes, moving over her, were frankly admiring. Then he warned himself of the decision he had made about tonight.

5

When he had finished talking, James Howden pushed his chair back tiredly. Opposite, on the visitors' side of the old-fashioned four-legged desk at which a succession of Prime Ministers had worked, Brian Richardson sat silently meditative, his alert mind indexing and absorbing facts he had just been given. Though he had known broadly of the Washington proposals, this was his first detailed briefing. Howden had told him, too, of the Defense Committee's reaction. Now the party director's thoughts, like veins and arteries of a human body, were branching out busily, assessing credits and debits, implications and eventualities, actions and counteractions, all with practiced skill. Details would be filled in later; many details. What was needed now was a broad plan of strategy —a plan, Richardson knew, more critically important than any other he had yet devised. For if he failed it would mean defeat for the party and perhaps more than defeat, eclipse.

"There's another thing," James Howden said. He had risen and was standing by the window, looking down on Parliament Hill. "Adrian Nesbitson must go."

"No!" Emphatically Richardson shook his head. "Later maybe, but not now. If you drop Nesbitson, no matter what reason we give, it'll look like a cabinet split. It's the worst thing that could happen."

"I was afraid you'd think that," Howden said. "The trouble is, he's completely useless. But I suppose we can manage, if we have to."

"Apart from that, can you keep him in line?"

"I think so." The Prime Minister massaged his long, curved nose. "I believe there's something he might want. I can use it to bargain."

"I'd go easy on the bargaining," Richardson said doubtfully. "Don't forget the old boy has a reputation for straightness."

"I'll remember your advice." Howden smiled. "Do you have any more?"

"Yes," the party director said crisply, "quite a lot. But first let's talk about a timetable. I agree that for something this big there'll have to be a mandate from the country." He mused. "In a lot of ways a fall election would be our best chance."

"We can't wait that long," Howden said decisively. "It'll have to be spring."

"Exactly when?"

"I'd thought of dissolving Parliament right after the Queen's visit, then the election could be in May."

Richardson nodded. "It might work."

"It *has* to work."

"What's your plan after the Washington meeting?"

The Prime Minister considered. "I think an announcement to the House in, say, three weeks from now."

The party director grinned. "That'll be when the fireworks start."

"Yes, I expect it will." Howden smiled faintly. "It will also give the country time to get used to the idea of the Act of Union before the election."

"It sure will help a lot if we can get the Queen over," Richardson said. "That way she'd be here between the announcement and the election."

"That was my thought, too," Howden agreed. "She'll be a symbol of what we're retaining, and it should convince people—on both sides of the border—that we've no intention of losing our national identity."

"I take it there'll be no signing of any agreement until after the election."

"No. It will have to be understood that the election is the

real decision. But we'll do our negotiating beforehand so there will be no time lost afterward. Time is the thing that matters most."

"It always does," Richardson said. He paused, then continued thoughtfully, "So it's three weeks before the whole thing is out in the open, then fourteen weeks to the election. It isn't long but there could be advantages—getting everything over before any splits become too wide." His voice became more businesslike. "All right, here's what I think."

Howden had returned from the window to his chair. Tilting it back, he placed his finger tips together and prepared to listen.

"Everything," Brian Richardson said deliberately, "—and I really mean everything—depends upon a single thing: trust. There must be absolute trust and confidence in one individual—you. And it must exist right across the country and down through every level. Without that kind of trust we'll lose; with it, we can win." He paused, thinking deeply, then continued. "The Act of Union . . . by the way, I think we must find another name . . . but the kind of union you're proposing isn't outrageous. After all, we've been moving towards it for half a century or more, and in some ways we'd be insane to turn it down. But the Opposition will do their best to make it seem outrageous and I guess you can hardly blame them. For the first time in years they'll have a real live issue to get their teeth into, and Deitz and company will make the most of it. They'll hurl words like 'betrayal' and 'sellout' and they'll call you Judas."

"I've been called names before, and I'm here, aren't I?"

"The trick is to stay." Richardson's expression was unsmiling. "What must be done is consolidate your image so clearly in the public mind that people will trust you absolutely, and have confidence that whatever you recommend is for their own good."

"Are we so far removed from that now?"

"Complacency isn't going to help either of us," Richardson snapped, and the Prime Minister flushed but made no comment. The party director went on, "our latest private polls show that the Government—and you—have slipped four per cent in popularity since this time last year, and you personally are weakest in the West. Fortunately it's a minor change, but still a trend. We can change the trend, though, if it's worked at hard—and fast."

"What's your suggestion?"

"I'll have a long list of them—the day after tomorrow. Mostly, though, it will mean getting out of here"—Richardson waved a hand around the office—"and moving about the country—speaking engagements, press coverage, television time where we can get it. And it must start soon—immediately you're back from Washington."

"You're not forgetting that Parliament reconvenes in less than two weeks."

"I'm not forgetting. Some days you'll have to be two places at once." Richardson permitted himself a grin. "I hope you haven't lost that old knack of sleeping in airplanes."

"You envisage, then, that part of this tour should take place before the announcement in the House."

"Yes. We can arrange it if we work fast. As far as we can, I'd like to condition the country to expect what's coming, and that's where your speeches will be important. I think we should hire some new men to write them—really top people who can make you sound like Churchill, Roosevelt, and Billy Graham rolled together."

"All right. Is that all?"

"It's all for now," Richardson said. "Oh, except for one thing—a nuisance item, I'm afraid, amongst all this. We've an immigration hassle in Vancouver."

Irritably Howden said, "Again!"

"There's a ship's stowaway who hasn't got a country and wants to come in. It looks as if the press has taken his case up and it ought to be settled quickly." He related the details which had appeared in the afternoon papers.

Briefly Howden was tempted to brush the matter side. There were limits, after all, to the number of things a Prime Minister could become involved in personally, and with so much else . . . Then he was reminded of his intention to have a showdown with Harvey Warrender . . . his own awareness that small issues could sometimes become important. But still he hesitated.

"I talked to Harvey Warrender last night."

"Yes," Richardson said dryly. "I heard about it."

"I want to be fair." Howden was still debating in his own mind. "Some of what Harvey said last night made sense—about not letting people into the country. That particular case you told me about—the woman who was deported. I understand she'd been running a brothel in Hong Kong and she had V.D."

"But the newspapers wouldn't print that, even if we leaked it," Richardson said irritably. "All that people see is a mother and baby being thrown out by the big bully of a Government. The Opposition made the most of it in the House, didn't they? You needed overshoes to wade through the tears."

The Prime Minister smiled.

"That's why we should settle this Vancouver thing pronto," the party director insisted.

"But surely you wouldn't admit undesirables—like that woman, for instance—as immigrants."

"Why not?" Richardson argued, "if it means avoiding bad publicity? It can be done quietly by order in council. After all, there were twelve hundred special admissions last year, mostly to oblige our own M.P.s. You can be sure there were some maggots among the lot, so what difference do a few more make?"

The figure of twelve hundred surprised Howden. It was not news, of course, that the immigration laws of Canada were frequently bent, and the bending process was a form of patronage accepted by all political parties. But the extent surprised him. He asked, "Was it really that many?"

"A few more, actually," Richardson said. He added dryly, "Fortunately the department lumps twenty to fifty immigrants under each order, and nobody adds the total."

There was a pause, then the Prime Minister said mildly, "Harvey and his deputy apparently think we should enforce the Immigration Act."

"If you weren't the Queen's first minister," Richardson responded, "I'd be tempted to reply with a short, succinct word."

James Howden frowned. Sometimes, he thought, Richardson went a little far.

Oblivious to the disapproval, the party director continued, "Every government in the past fifty years has used the Immigration Act to help its own party members, so why should we suddenly stop? It doesn't make political sense."

No, Howden thought, it didn't make sense. He reached for a telephone. "All right," he told Richardson, "we'll do it your way. I'll have Harvey Warrender in now." He instructed the government operator, "Get Mr. Warrender. He'll probably be at home." With a hand cupped over the mouthpiece he asked,

"Apart from what we've talked about, is there anything else you think I should tell him?"

Richardson grinned. "You could try suggesting that he keep both feet on the ground. That way he might not put one in his mouth so often."

"If I tell Harvey that," Howden said, "he'll probably quote Plato at me."

"In that case you could come back with Menander: *He is raised the higher that he may fall the heavier.*"

The Prime Minister's eyebrows went up. There were things about Brian Richardson which constantly surprised him.

The operator came on the line and Howden listened, then replaced the phone. "The Warrenders are away for the holiday—at their cottage in the Laurentians, and there isn't a phone."

Richardson said curiously, "You give Harvey Warrender a lot of leeway, don't you:—more than some of the others."

"Not this time," James Howden said. After their discussion his mind was quite made up. "I'll have him up here the day after tomorrow and this Vancouver case will not boil over. I guarantee it."

6

It was seven-thirty when Brian Richardson arrived at Milly Freedeman's apartment and he carried two packages, one containing an ounce of Guerlain, a perfume he knew Milly liked, the other twenty-six ounces of gin.

The perfume pleased Milly. About the gin she was less certain, though she took it to the kitchenette to mix drinks.

Waiting in the softly lighted living room, Richardson watched from one of the two deep armchairs. He stretched his feet luxuriously across the beige broadloom—the single large-expense item Milly had indulged in when decorating the apartment—then said approvingly, "You know, a lot of the stuff you've got in here, Milly, other people would throw out. But the way you've put it together, this is the coziest hangout I know."

"I assume that's a compliment." In the kitchenette Milly turned, smiling. "Anyway, I'm glad you like it."

"Sure I like it. Who wouldn't?" Mentally Brian Richardson was contrasting the apartment with his own, which Eloise had remodeled just over a year ago. They had ivory walls, with off-white broadloom, Swedish walnut furniture and tailored curtains of pale peacock blue. He had long grown indifferent to it all, and the effect no longer offended him. But he recalled the bitter fight there had been with Eloise when on being confronted with the bill he had protestingly described it as "the President's suite in a whorehouse."

Milly, he thought, would always know how to make a place warm and personal . . . a little untidy, books piled on tables, some place a man could relax.

Milly had turned away again. He watched her thoughtfully.

Before his arrival she had changed out of the suit which she had worn earlier into orange slacks and a plain black sweater, relieved only by a triple strand of pearls. The effect, Richardson thought, was simple and physically exciting.

As she returned to the living room he found himself admiring her gracefulness. There was a rhythm and economy about each of Milly's movements and she seldom wasted a gesture.

"Milly," he said, "you're an astonishing girl."

She brought their drinks across the room, ice clinking. He was aware of slim legs and firm thighs under the slacks; again the unself-conscious rhythm of movement . . . like a young, long-legged race horse, he thought absurdly.

"Astonishing in what way?" Milly asked. She handed him his glass and their fingers touched.

"Well," he said, "without the filmy negligee routine, pants and all, you're the sexiest thing on two legs."

He put down the glass she had given him, stood up, and kissed her. After a moment she eased herself gently free and turned away.

"Brian," Milly said, "is this any good?"

Nine years ago she had known what love meant, and afterwards the intolerable anguish of loss. She supposed she was not in love with Brian Richardson, as she had been with James Howden, but there was a warmth and tenderness; and there could be more, she knew, if time and circumstance allowed. But she suspected they would not allow. Richardson was married . . . he was practical; and in the end it would mean, once more, breaking . . . parting . . .

Richardson asked, "Is *what* any good, Milly?"

She said levelly, "I think you know."

"Yes, I know." He had returned to his drink. He held the glass against the light, inspected it, then put it down.

She wanted love, Milly thought. Her body ached for it. But suddenly the need for more than physical love overwhelmed her . . . There must be some permanence. Or must there? Once, when she had loved James Howden, she had been willing to settle for less.

Brian Richardson said slowly, "I guess I could kid you with a lot of words, Milly. But we're both grown up; I didn't think you'd want it."

"No," she answered. "I don't want to be kidded. But I don't want to be an animal, either. There ought to be something more."

He responded harshly, "For some people there isn't any more. Not if they're honest with themselves."

A moment after, he wondered why he had said it: an excess of truthfulness perhaps, or merely self-pity, an emotion he despised in others. But he had not expected the effect upon Milly. Her eyes glistened with tears.

"Milly," he said, "I'm sorry."

She shook her head and he went to her. Taking out a handkerchief, he gently wiped her eyes and the rivulets beneath.

"Listen," he said, "I shouldn't have said that."

"It's all right," Milly said. "I was just being womanly, I suppose."

Oh God, she thought, what's happening to me—the self-reliant Millicent Freedeman . . . crying like an adolescent. What does this man mean to me? Why can't I take something of this kind in my stride as I've done before.

His arms went around her. "I want you, Milly," he said softly. "I don't know any other way to say it, except I want you."

He lifted her head again and kissed her. This time she responded. After a while he began easing her sweater upward.

Hesitancy assailed her. "No Brian! Please no!" But she made no effort to pull away. As he fondled her, desire grew stronger. Now, she knew, she cared. Afterwards, there would be loneliness again; the sense of loss. But now . . . now . . . eyes closed, her body trembled . . . now.

"All right." Her voice was husky.

The light switch snapped in the silence. As it did, faintly

from outside came the high-pitched whine of airplane jet engines high over the city. The sound came closer, then receded as the night flight to Vancouver—Senator Deveraux among its passengers—turned westward, climbing swiftly through the darkness.

"Be gentle, Brian," Milly whispered. "This time . . . please be gentle."

Six Alan Maitland

In Vancouver on Christmas morning Alan Maitland slept late, and when he awoke there was a furry taste in his mouth from the drinks he had had at his law partner's home the night before. Yawning and scratching the top of his crew-cut head which itched, he remembered they had killed a couple of bottles between the three of them—himself, Tom Lewis, and Tom's wife Lillian. It was an extravagance, really, since neither he nor Tom had money to spare for that kind of thing, especially now that Lillian was pregnant and Tom was having trouble keeping up his mortgage payments on the tiny house he had bought six months ago in North Vancouver. Then Alan thought: Oh, what the hell, and rolling his athlete's six-foot length out of bed, padded barefoot to the bathroom.

Returning, he put on old flannel trousers and a faded college T shirt. Then he mixed instant coffee, made toast, and scraped on some honey from a jar. To eat, he sat on the bed which occupied most of the available space in the cramped bachelor apartment on Gilford Street near English Bay. Later the bed could be made to disappear into the wall like a retracted landing gear, but Alan seldom hurried this, preferring to meet the day gradually, as he always had since discovering long ago he could do most things best by easing into them slowly.

He was wondering if he should bother frying some bacon when his phone rang. It was Tom Lewis.

"Listen, you lunkhead," Tom said. "How come you never told me about your high society friends?"

"A guy doesn't like to boast. The Vanderbilts and me . . ."

Alan swallowed a piece of half-chewed toast. "What high society friends?"

"Senator Deveraux, for one. *The* Richard Deveraux. He wants you up at his house—today; chop, chop."

"You're crazy!"

"Crazy, my eye! I just had a call from G. K. Bryant—of Culliner, Bryant, Mortimer, Lane and Roberts, otherwise known as 'we the people.' They do most of old Deveraux's legal work, it seems, but this time the Senator has asked for you specifically."

"How could he?" Alan was skeptical. "Somebody's made a mistake; got a name wrong obviously."

"Listen, junior," Tom said, "if nature endowed you with above-average stupidity, try not to add to it. The man they want is Alan Maitland of the thriving young law firm—at least, it would be if we had a couple of clients—of Lewis and Maitland. That's you, isn't it?"

"Sure, but . . ."

"Now why a man like Senator Deveraux should want Maitland when he can get Lewis, who was a year ahead of Maitland in law school, and considerably smarter, as this conversation demonstrates, is beyond me, but . . ."

"Wait a minute," Alan interjected. "You did say Deveraux."

"Not more than six times which, I admit, is not enough for penetration . . ."

"There was a Sharon Deveraux in my last year of college. We met a few times, went on a date once, though I haven't seen her since. Maybe she . . ."

"Maybe she did; maybe she didn't. All I know is that Senator Deveraux, on this clear and sunny Christmas morning, is waiting for one Alan Maitland."

"I'll go," Alan said. "Maybe there's a present for me under his tree."

"Here's the address," Tom said, and, when Alan had written it down, "I shall pray for you. I might even call our office landlord and get him to pray too; after all, his rent depends upon it."

"Tell him I'll do my best."

"There was never a doubt," Tom said. "Good luck."

2

Senator Deveraux—not surprisingly, Alan Maitland thought—lived on South West Marine Drive.

Alan knew the Drive well, by reputation and through occasional contact during his days in college. High above downtown Vancouver, facing southward across the North Arm of the widening Fraser River towards pastoral Lulu Island, the area was a social mecca and seat of much accumulated wealth. The view from most points along the Drive was remarkable, on clear days extending as far as the U.S. border and the State of Washington. It was also, Alan knew, a symbolic view, since most who lived there had either attained social eminence or were born to it. A second symbolism was in the great, patterned log booms, moored in the river below or towed majestically by tugs to sawmills. Logging and lumber founded the fortune of the Province of British Columbia and even now sustained it largely.

Alan Maitland caught a glimpse of the Fraser River at the same time that he located Senator Deveraux's house. The Senator, Alan decided, must possess one of the best views along the entire shore line.

It was sunny, clear, and crisp as he drove toward the big Tudor-style mansion. The house was shielded from questing eyes of passers-by by a tall cedar hedge and set well back from the road, with a curving driveway presided over at its entrance by twin gargoyles on double wrought-iron gates. A shining Chrysler Imperial was in the driveway and Alan Maitland parked his elderly, paint-faded Chev behind it. He walked to the massive, studded front door set in a baronial portico and rang the bell. Presently a butler opened it.

"Good morning," Alan said; "my name is Maitland."

"Please come in, sir." The butler was a frail, white-haired man who moved as if his feet hurt. He preceded Alan through a short tiled corridor into a large open entrance hall. At the entry to the hallway a slim, slight figure appeared.

It was Sharon Deveraux and she was as he recalled her—not beautiful but petite, elfin almost, her face longish and with deep humorous eyes. Her hair was different, Alan noticed. It was raven black and she used to wear it long; now it was done in a pixie cut and becoming, he thought.

"Hullo," Alan said. "I hear you could use a lawyer."

"At the moment," Sharon said promptly, "we'd prefer a plumber. The toilet in Granddaddy's bathroom won't stop running."

There was something else he was reminded of—a dimple in her left cheek which came and went when she smiled, as she was doing now.

"This particular lawyer," Alan said, "does plumbing on the side. Things haven't been too brisk around the law books lately."

Sharon laughed. "Then I'm glad I remembered you." The butler took his coat and Alan looked curiously around him.

The house, inside and out, bespoke wealth and substance. They had stopped in a large open entrance hall, its walls of polished linen-fold paneling, its ceiling Renaissance, above a gleaming pegged-oak floor. In a massive Tudor fireplace, flanked by fluted pilasters, a log fire burned brightly, and near the fireplace an arrangement of red and yellow roses graced an Elizabethan refectory table. On a colorful Kerman rug a dignified Yorkshire armchair faced a Knoll sofa, and opposite, on the far side of the hall, crewel embroidery hangings framed oriel windows.

"Granddaddy got back from Ottawa last night," Sharon said, rejoining him, "and at breakfast was talking about wanting a young Abe Lincoln. So I said there was someone I used to know called Alan Maitland who was going to be a lawyer and had all sorts of ideals . . . do you still have them, by the way?"

"I guess so," Alan said, a shade uncomfortably. He reflected that he must have sounded off to this girl more than he remembered. "Anyway, thanks for thinking of me." It was warm in the house and he wriggled his neck inside the starched white shirt he had put on under his one good charcoal-gray suit.

"Let's go in the drawing room," Sharon said. "Granddaddy will be here soon." He followed her across the hall. She opened a door and sunlight streamed through.

The room they came into was larger than the hallway, but brighter and less formidable, Alan thought. It was furnished in Chippendale and Sheraton, with light Persian rugs, the walls damask-covered and ornamented with gilt and crystal sconces. There were some original oils—Degas, Cézanne, and a more modern Lawren Harris. A large decorated Christ-

mas tree occupied one corner of the room, next to a Stein-
way piano. Leaded casement windows, closed now, led to a
flagstoned terrace.

"Grandaddy, I take it, is Senator Deveraux," Alan said.

"Oh yes, I forgot you wouldn't know." Sharon motioned
him to a Chippendale settee and sat down opposite. "My
parents are divorced, you see. Nowadays Daddy lives in Europe—Switzerland, most of the time—then Mummy got
married again and went to Argentina, so I live here." She
said it unself-consciously and with no trace of bitterness.

"Well, well, well! So this is the young man." A voice
boomed from the doorway where Senator Deveraux stood,
white hair brushed, his cutaway morning suit faultlessly
pressed. There was a small red rose in his lapel and as he
entered he was rubbing his hands together.

Sharon performed the introductions.

"I do apologize, Mr. Maitland," the Senator said courteously, "for bringing you here on Christmas Day. I trust it
was not inconvenient."

"No, sir," Alan said.

"Good. Then before our business, perhaps you'll join us
in a glass of sherry."

"Thank you."

There were glasses and a crystal decanter on a mahogany
table. As Sharon poured sherry, Alan ventured, "You have
a beautiful home, Senator."

"I'm delighted you think so, my boy." The old man
seemed genuinely pleased. "All my life I've taken a pleasure
in surrounding myself with exquisite things."

"Granddaddy has quite a reputation as a collector," Sharon said. She had brought the glasses to them. "The only
trouble is, sometimes it's like living in a museum."

"The young scoff at antiquity, or pretend to." Senator
Deveraux smiled indulgently at his granddaughter. "But I
have hopes for Sharon. She and I arranged this room together."

"It's an impressive result," Alan said.

"I will admit to believing that is true." The Senator's eyes
roved around him fondly. "We have a few rather special
things here. This, for instance—a splendid example from the
Tang Dynasty." His fingers reached out, gently caressing a
superb pottery horse and rider, delicately colored. The piece
stood alone on a marble-topped taboret. "Twenty-six hun-

dred years ago this was designed by a master craftsman in a civilization more enlightened, perhaps, than our own today."

"It *is* beautiful," Alan said. He thought: there must be a fortune in this single room. He reflected on the contrast between these surroundings and Tom Lewis's boxlike two-bed-roomed bungalow in which he had spent the evening before.

"But now to business." The Senator's tone had become brisk and businesslike. The three of them sat down.

"I apologize, my boy, as I said, for the suddenness of this call. There is, however, a matter which excites my concern and sympathy and, I think, brooks no delay." His interest, Senator Deveraux explained, was in the ship's stow-away, Henri Duval—"that unfortunate young man, homeless and without a country, who stands outside our gates plead-ing, in the name of humanity, to enter."

"Yes," Alan said. "I read about it last night. I remember thinking there wasn't much could be done."

Sharon, who had been listening carefully asked, "Why not?"

"Mostly," Alan answered, "because the Canadian Immigra-tion Act is quite definite about who can come in and who can't."

"But according to the newspaper," Sharon protested, "he won't even be given a public hearing."

"Yes, my boy, what about that, eh?" The Senator cocked an inquiring eyebrow. "Where is our vaunted freedom when a man—any man—cannot have his day in court?"

"Don't misunderstand me," Alan said. "I'm not defending the way things are. As a matter of fact, we studied the Im-migration Act in law school and I think there's a lot wrong. But I'm talking about the law the way it stands. If it's a question of changing it, that's more in your line, Senator."

Senator Deveraux sighed. "It's hard, hard, with a govern-ment as inflexible as the one in office. But tell me, do you really believe there is nothing can be done for this unfor-tunate young man—in a legal sense, I mean?"

Alan hesitated. "It's an off-the-cuff opinion, of course."

"Naturally."

"Well, assuming the facts to be reasonably true as the newspaper had them, this man Duval has no rights at all. Before he could get a hearing in court—even if it would do any good, which I doubt—he would have to be officially landed in the country and, the way things are, that seems unlikely." Alan glanced at Sharon. "What I expect will happen is that the ship will sail and Duval with it—the way he came."

"Perhaps, perhaps." The Senator mused, his eyes on a Cézanne landscape on the wall facing him. "And yet occasionally there are loopholes in the law."

"Very often." Alan nodded agreement. "I said it was just an off-the-cuff opinion."

"So you did, my boy." The Senator had withdrawn his eyes from the painting and was businesslike again. "That's why I want you to probe into this whole affair more deeply to see what loophole, if any, exists. In short, it is my wish that you act as counsel for this unfortunate young man."

"But supposing he . . ."

Senator Deveraux raised an admonitory hand. "I entreat you: hear me out. It is my intention to pay legal fees and any expenses you may incur. In return I shall ask only that my own part in the affair be kept confidential."

Alan shifted uncertainly on the settee. This moment, he knew, could be important, to himself as well as others. The case itself might come to nothing, but if handled properly it could mean connections for the future, leading to other cases later on. When he had come here this morning he had not known what to expect; now that he did, he supposed he should be pleased. And yet, uneasily, there was a stirring of doubt. He suspected there was more below the surface than the older man had revealed. He was aware of Sharon's eyes upon him.

Abruptly Alan asked, "Why, Senator?"

"Why what, my boy?"

"Why do you want your part in this kept secret?"

Momentarily the Senator seemed nonplused, then brightened. "There is a text in the good book. I believe it reads: 'When thou doest alms, let not thy left hand know what thy right hand doeth.' "

It was dramatically done. But something had clicked in Alan Maitland's brain. He asked quietly, "Alms, sir, or politics?"

The Senator's brows came down. "I'm afraid I don't follow you."

Well, Alan thought, here we go; here's where you blow the deal and lose the first big client you almost had. He said deliberately, "Immigration right now is a top political issue. This particular case has already been in the papers and could stir up a lot of trouble for the Government. Isn't that what you had in mind, Senator—just using this man on the ship as a kind of pawn? Isn't that why you wanted me—someone young and green instead of your regular law firm, who'd be identified with you? I'm sorry, sir, but that's not the way I plan to practice law."

He had spoken more strongly than he intended at first, but indignation had got the better of him. He wondered how he would explain to his partner Tom Lewis and whether Tom would have done the same thing. He suspected not; Tom had more sense than to throw away a fee quixotically.

He was conscious of a rumbling sound. Surprised, he became aware that Senator Deveraux was chuckling.

"Young and green, I think you said, my boy." The Senator paused, chuckling again, his waistline heaving gently. "Well, you may be young, but certainly not green. What's your opinion, Sharon?"

"I'd say you got caught out, Granddaddy." Alan was aware that Sharon was looking at him with respect.

"And so I did, my dear; indeed I did. This is a smart young man you have found."

Somehow, Alan realized, the situation had changed, though he was not sure in which way. The only thing he was certain of was that Senator Deveraux was a man of many facets.

"Very well; so all our cards are face up on the table." The Senator's tone had changed subtly; it was less ponderous, more as if directed to an equal. "Let us suppose that everything you allege is true. Is this young man on the ship still not entitled to legal help? Is he to be denied an aiding hand because the motives of an individual, to wit, myself, happen to be mixed? If you were drowning, my boy, would you care if the one who swam to save you did so because he considered you might be of use to him alive?"

"No," Alan said, "I don't suppose I would."

"What, then, is the difference?—if there is a difference." Senator Deveraux leaned forward in his chair. "Allow me to ask you something. You believe, I assume, in the correction of injustice."

"Of course."

"Of course." The Senator nodded sagely. "Let us consider, then, this young man on the ship. He has no legal rights, we are told. He is not a Canadian, or a bona fide immigrant, nor even a transient who has landed and will leave soon. In the law's eyes he is not even present. Therefore, even though he may wish to appeal to the law—to plead in court for admittance to this or any other country—he cannot do so. Is that correct?"

"I wouldn't put it quite in those terms," Alan said, "but in substance that's correct."

"In other words, yes."

Alan smiled wryly. "Yes."

"And yet supposing tonight, on the ship in Vancouver Harbor, this same man committed murder or arson. What would happen to him?"

Alan nodded. He could see the question's point. "He'd be taken ashore and tried."

"Exactly, my boy. And if guilty he would be punished, and never mind his status or the lack of it. So that way, you see, the law can reach Henri Duval, even though he cannot reach the law."

It was a neatly packaged argument. Not surprisingly, Alan reflected, the old man had a smooth debater's skill.

But skillful or not, the point he made was sound. Why should the law work only one way—against a man and not for him? And even though Senator Deveraux's motives were political, nothing changed the essential fact he had pointed out: that an individual, present in the community, was being denied a basic human right.

Alan pondered. What could the law do for the man on the ship? Anything or nothing? And if nothing—why?

Alan Maitland had no callow illusions about the law. New as he was in its service, he was aware that justice was neither automatic nor impartial, and that sometimes injustice triumphed over right. He knew that social status had a good deal to do with crime and punishment, and that the well-heeled who could afford to make use of all the law's processes were less likely to suffer direly for sinning than those, less wealthy, who could not. The law's slowness, he was sure, at times denied the innocent their rights, and some who deserved redress failed to seek it because of the high cost of a day in court. And at the other end of the scale were the case-loaded magistrates' courts, dispensing pressure-cooker justice, often without proper care for the rights of an accused.

He had come to know of these things in much the same
way that all students and young lawyers gradually and inevitably became informed of them. At times they pained him
deeply, as they pained many of his elder colleagues whose
idealism had not rubbed off through their years at the bar.

But with all the law's faults it had one great virtue. It
was there. It existed. Its greatest merit was its availability.

Existence of the law was an acknowledgment that equality
of human rights was a worth-while goal. As to its defects, in
time reform would come; it always had, though it lagged
behind the need. Meanwhile, to the humblest and greatest—
if they chose—the courtroom door was always open as, beyond it, were the chambers of appeal.

Except, it seemed, to a man named Henri Duval.

Alan was aware of the Senator watching him expectantly.
Sharon's face had the slightest of frowns.

"Senator Deveraux," Alan said, "if I were to take this
case—assuming the man on the ship is willing to be represented—he himself would be my client. Is that true?"

"I suppose you could put it that way."

Alan smiled. "In other words—yes."

The Senator threw back his head, guffawing. "I'm beginning to like you, my boy. Please proceed."

"Even though you were in the background, Senator," Alan
said carefully, "any action taken on my client's behalf would
be decided solely by my client and myself without consultation with any third party."

The older man regarded Alan shrewdly. "Don't you consider that he who pays the piper . . ."

"No, sir; not in this instance. If I have a client, I want to
do what's best for him, not what's the cagiest thing politically."

The Senator's smile had gone and now his voice held a
distinct coolness. "I might remind you that this is an opportunity which many young lawyers would be glad to accept."

Alan stood up. "Then I suggest you look in the yellow
pages, sir." He turned to Sharon. "I'm sorry if I've let you
down."

"Just a moment!" It was the Senator. He had risen also
and faced Alan directly. Now he boomed, "I want to tell
you, my boy, that I consider you impatient, impertinent, un-
grateful—and I accept your terms."

They shook hands on the agreement then, and afterwards Alan declined an invitation from the Senator to remain for lunch. "I'd better get down to the ship today," he said. "There may not be too much time because of sailing."

Sharon showed him to the door. Pulling on his coat, he was aware of her closeness and a faint perfume.

A little awkwardly he said, "It was good seeing you, Sharon."

She smiled. "I thought so too." Once more the dimple came and went. "And even though you won't report to Granddaddy, do come to see us again."

"The thing that puzzles me," Alan said cheerfully, "is how I stayed away so long."

3

The previous night's rain had left pools of water on the dockside, and Alan Maitland skirted them warily, occasionally glancing upward and ahead at the line of ships silhouetted drearily against a gray low-stratus sky. A one-armed watchman with a mongrel dog—the only person he had encountered in the silent, deserted dockyard—had directed him here and now, reading the names on the moored vessels, he could see the *Vastervik*, second down the line.

A thin column of smoke, dissipated by the wind as quickly as it climbed, was the sole sign of life aboard. Around the ship the sounds were faint: a lapping of water and the creak of wood somewhere below; and above, the melancholy cry of heron gulls in flight. Harbor sounds are lonely sounds, Alan thought, and wondered in how many other harbors the man he had come to see had heard them also.

He wondered too what kind of a person the stowaway Henri Duval would prove to be. It was true the newspaper story had portrayed him sympathetically, but newspapers so often were off base in what they published. More than likely, Alan thought, the man was the worst kind of ocean drifter whom no one wanted, and with good reason.

He reached the ship's iron gangway and swung onto it from the dock. By the time he had climbed to the top his hands were stained with rust.

Across the entry to the deck a chain barred the way. Hanging from the chain was a piece of plywood, crudely lettered.

NO ADMISSION
WITHOUT SHIP'S BUSINESS
By order
S. Jaabeck, Master.

Alan unhooked the chain and stepped beyond it. He had
gone a few feet toward a steel doorway when a voice hailed
him.

"You see the notice! No more reporters!"

Alan turned. The man approaching along the deck was in
his mid-thirties, tall and wiry. He wore a rumpled brown suit
and had a stubble of beard. His accent, by its slurred *r*'s, was
Scandinavian.

"I'm not a reporter," Alan said. "I'd like to see the captain."

"The captain is busy. I am third officer." The tall man
gave a catarrhal cough, cleared his throat, and spat neatly
over the side.

"That's a nasty cold you have," Alan said.

"Ach! It is this country of yours—damp and chill. In
my home, Sweden, it is cold too, but the air sharp like a
knife. Why do you wish the captain?"

"I'm a lawyer," Alan said. "I came to see if I could help
this stowaway of yours, Henri Duval."

"Duval! Duval! Suddenly it is all Duval; he becomes the
most important thing here. Well, you will not help him.
We are—how is it said?—stuck? He will be with us until the
ship sinks." The tall man grinned sardonically. "Look around
you; it will not be long."

Alan surveyed the rust and peeling paintwork. He sniffed;
the decaying cabbage smell was strong. "Yes," he said, "I
see what you mean."

"Well," the tall man said. "Perhaps, since you are not a
reporter, the captain will see you." He beckoned. "Come! As
a Christmas gift I shall take you to him."

The captain's cabin was suffocatingly hot. Its owner evidently liked it that way because both portholes onto the outside deck, Alan noticed, were clamped tightly shut. The air
was also thick with the smoke from strong tobacco.

Captain Jaabeck, in shirt sleeves and old-fashioned carpet
slippers, rose from a leather chair as Alan came in. He had

been reading a book—a heavy volume—which he put down.

"It was good of you to see me," Alan said. "My name is Maitland."

"And I am Sigurd Jaabeck." The captain extended a gnarled, hairy hand. "My third officer says you are a lawyer."

"That's right," Alan acknowledged. "I read about your stowaway and came to see if I could help."

"Sit down, please." The captain indicated a chair and resumed his own. In contrast to the rest of the ship, Alan noticed, the cabin was comfortable and clean, its woodwork and brass gleaming. There was mahogany paneling on three sides, with green leather chairs, a small dining table, and a polished roll-top desk. A curtained doorway led to what was presumably a bedroom. Alan's eyes moved round, then settled curiously on the book the captain had put down.

"It is Dostoevsky," Captain Jaabeck said. *"Crime and Punishment."*

"You're reading it in the original Russian," Alan said, surprised.

"Very slowly, I fear," the captain said. "Russian is a language I do not read well." He picked up a pipe from an ash tray, knocked out the bowl, and began to refill it. "Dostoevsky believes there is always justice in the end."

"Don't you?"

"Sometimes one cannot wait so long. Especially when young."

"Like Henri Duval?"

The captain pondered, sucking at his pipe. "What can you hope to do? He is a nobody. He does not exist."

"Perhaps nothing," Alan said. "All the same, I'd like to talk with him. People have become interested, and some would like to help him if they could."

Captain Jaabeck regarded Alan quizzically. "Will this interest last? Or is my young stowaway what you call a nine days' wonder?"

"If he is," Alan said, "there are seven days left."

Again the captain paused before responding. Then he said carefully, "You understand it is my duty to be rid of this man. Stowaways cost money to feed and there is little enough money nowadays in running a ship. Profits are low, the owners say, and therefore we must use economy. You have already seen the condition of the ship."

"I understand that, Captain."

"But this young man has been with me for twenty months. In that time one forms, shall we say, opinions, even attachments." The voice was slow and ponderous. "The boy has not had a good life; perhaps he will never have one, and I suppose it is no affair of mine. And yet I would not like to see his hopes raised, then destroyed cruelly."

"I can only tell you again," Alan said, "that there are people who would like to see him given a chance here. It may not be possible, but if no one tries we shall never know."

"That is true." The captain nodded. "Very well, Mr. Maitland, I will send for Duval and you may talk here. Would you like to be alone?"

"No," Alan said. "I'd prefer it if you stayed."

Henri Duval stood in the doorway nervously. His eyes took in Alan Maitland, then darted to Captain Jaabeck.

The captain motioned Duval inside. "You need not be afraid. This gentleman, Mr. Maitland, is a lawyer. He has come to help you."

"I read about you yesterday," Alan said, smiling. He offered his hand and the stowaway took it uncertainly. Alan noticed that he was younger even than the newspaper picture had made him seem, and that his deep-set eyes held an uneasy wariness. He was wearing denims and a darned seaman's jersey.

"It was good, what was written. Yes?" The stowaway asked the question anxiously.

"It was very good," Alan said. "I came to find out how much of it was true."

"It all true! I tell truth!" The expression was injured, as if an accusation had been hurled. Alan thought: I must choose my words more carefully.

"I'm sure you do," he said placatingly. "What I meant was whether the newspaper had got everything right."

"I not understand." Duval shook his head, his expression still hurt.

"Let's forget it for the moment," Alan said. He had made a bad start, it seemed. Now he went on, "The captain told you I am a lawyer. If you would like me to, I will represent you and try to bring your case before the courts of our country."

Henri Duval glanced from Alan to the captain. "I have not money. I cannot pay lawyer."

"There would be nothing to pay," Alan said

"Then who pay?" Again the wariness.

"Someone else will pay."

The captain interjected, "Is there any reason you cannot tell him who, Mr. Maitland?"

"Yes," Alan said. "My instructions are not to reveal the person's name. I can only tell you it is someone who is sympathetic and would like to help."

"There are sometimes good people," the captain said. Apparently satisfied, he nodded reassuringly to Duval.

Remembering Senator Deveraux and the Senator's motives, Alan had a momentary qualm of conscience. He stilled it, reminding himself of the terms he had insisted on.

"If I stay, I work," Henri Duval insisted, "I earn money. I pay back all."

"Well," Alan said, "I expect you could do that if you wanted."

"I pay back." The young man's face mirrored eagerness. For the moment mistrust had gone.

"I have to tell you, of course," Alan said, "there may be nothing I can do. You understand that?"

Duval appeared puzzled. The captain explained, "Mr. Maitland will do his best. But perhaps the Immigration will say no . . . as before."

Duval nodded slowly. "I understand."

"One thing occurs to me, Captain Jaabeck," Alan said. "Have you, since coming here, taken Henri to the Immigration Department and asked for an official hearing of his application to land?"

"An immigration officer was aboard my ship . . ."

"No," Alan insisted, "I mean apart from that. Have you taken him to the Immigration Building and demanded an official inquiry?"

"What is the good?" The captain shrugged. "It is always one answer. Besides, in port there is so little time and I have many attentions for the ship. Today is the Christmas holiday. That is why I read Dostoevsky."

"In other words," Alan said mildly, "you haven't taken him and asked for a full inquiry because you've been too busy. Is that it?" He was careful to keep his voice casual, even though a half-formed idea was taking shape in his mind.

"That is so," Captain Jaabeck said. "Of course, if any good might come . . ."

"Let's leave that now," Alan said. His thought had been vague and fleeting and might come to nothing. In any case he needed time to read the immigration statutes thoroughly. Abruptly he switched the subject.

"Henri," he told Duval, "what I'd like to do now is go over all the things that have happened to you as far back as you can recall. I know that some of it was in the newspapers but there may have been things which were left out, and others you've thought of since. Why don't you begin at the beginning? What's the first thing you remember?"

"My mother," Duval said.

"What do you remember most about her?"

"She kind to me," Duval said simply. "After she die, no one kind again—until this ship."

Captain Jaabeck had risen and turned away, his back to Alan and Duval. He was slowly refilling his pipe.

"Tell me about your mother, Henri," Alan said; "what she was like, what she used to talk about, what you did together."

"My mother beautiful, I think. When I a little boy she hold me; I listen and she sing." The young stowaway spoke slowly, carefully, as if the past were something fragile, to be handled gently lest it disappear. "Other time she say: someday we go on ship and find new home. We to go together . . ." Haltingly at some moments, with more confidence at others, he talked on.

His mother, he believed, had been the daughter of a French family which had returned to France before his own birth. Why she had no connection with her parents could only be guessed at. Perhaps it had something to do with his father who (so his mother said) had lived with her briefly in Djibouti then, leaving her, had returned to sea.

Essentially it was the same story which had been told to Dan Orliffe two days before. Throughout Alan listened carefully, prompting where necessary and interjecting a question or retracing where there seemed confusion. But most of the time he watched the face of Henri Duval. It was a convincing face which lighted or mirrored distress as incidents were relived in its owner's mind. There were moments of anguish too, and a point where tears glistened as the young stowaway described his mother's death. If this were a witness in court, Alan told himself, I would believe what he says.

As a final question he asked, "Why do you want to come here? Why Canada?" This time it's sure to be a phony answer, Alan thought; he'll probably say it's a wonderful country and he always wanted to live here.

Henri Duval considered carefully. Then he said, "All others say no. Canada last place I try. If not here, I think no home for Henri Duval, ever."

"Well," Alan said, "I guess I got an honest answer."

He found himself strangely moved and it was an emotion he had not expected. He had come with skepticism, prepared if necessary to go through legal motions, though not expecting to succeed. But now he wanted more. He wanted to do something for Henri Duval in a positive sense; to remove him from the ship and offer him the chance to build a life for himself in a way which fate had denied him until now.

But could it be done? Was there a loophole somewhere, somehow, in immigration law through which this man could be brought in? Perhaps there was, but if so there was no time to lose in finding it.

During the last part of the interview Captain Jaabeck had come and gone several times. Now he was back in the cabin and Alan asked, "How long will your ship remain in Vancouver?"

"It was to have been five days. Unfortunately there are engine repairs and now it will be two weeks, perhaps three."

Alan nodded. Two or three weeks was little enough, but better than five days. "If I'm to represent Duval," he said, "I must have written instructions from him."

"Then you will have to put down what is needed," Captain Jaabeck said. "He can write his name, but that is all."

Alan took out a notebook from his pocket. He thought for a moment, then wrote:

I, Henri Duval, am at present being detained on the Motor Vessel *Vastervik* at La Pointe Pier, Vancouver, B.C. I hereby make application for permission to be landed at the above port of entry and I have retained Alan Maitland of the firm of Lewis and Maitland to act as counsel for me in all matters pertaining to this application.

The captain listened carefully as Alan read the words aloud, then nodded. "That is good," he told Duval. "If Mr. Maitland is to help, you must put your name to what he has written."

Using a pen which the captain supplied, Henri Duval slowly and awkwardly signed the notebook page in a childish, sprawling hand. Alan watched impatiently. His one thought now was to get away from the ship and examine more thoroughly the fleeting idea which had occurred to him earlier. He had a sense of mounting excitement. Of course, what he had in mind would be a long shot. But it was the kind of long shot which might, just might, succeed.

Seven The Hon. Harvey Warrender

The brief respite of Christmas had sped by as if it had never been.

On Christmas Day the Howdens had gone to early Communion and, after returning home, received guests until lunchtime—mostly official callers and a few family friends. In the afternoon the Lexingtons had driven over, and the Prime Minister and Arthur Lexington spent two hours closeted privately, discussing arrangements for Washington. Later, Margaret and James Howden talked by transatlantic telephone to their daughters, sons-in-law, and grandchildren in London, who were spending Christmas together. By the time everyone had spoken to everyone else it was a lengthy call and, glancing at his watch at one point, James Howden was glad that his wealthy industrialist son-in-law, and not himself, would receive the bill. Later still, the Howdens dined quietly by themselves and afterward the Prime Minister worked alone in his study while Margaret watched a movie on television. It was the sad, gentle James Hilton story *Goodbye, Mr. Chips,* and Margaret was reminded nostalgically that she and her husband had seen it together in the 1930s, but now the star, Robert Donat, and its author were long dead, and nowadays the Howdens no longer went to movies . . . At 11.30, after saying good night, Margaret went to bed, while James Howden continued to work until 1 A.M.

Milly Freedeman's Christmas Day had been less arduous, but also less interesting. She had wakened late and, after some mental indecision, went to a church service but not Communion. In the afternoon she took a taxi to the home of a former girl friend from Toronto, now married and living in Ottawa, who had invited Milly for Christmas dinner. There were several small children in the household, who became trying after a while and, later still, boredom set in at the inevitable talk of child management, domestic help, and the cost of living. Once more—as she had on other occasions—Milly realized she was not fooling herself in believing that scenes of so-called domestic bliss held no charm for her. She preferred her own comfortable apartment, independence, and the work and responsibility she enjoyed. Then she thought: maybe I'm just getting old and sour, but all the same it was a relief when it became time to go. Her friend's husband drove her home and, on the way, made tentative advances which Milly rejected firmly.

Throughout the day she had thought a good deal about Brian Richardson, wondering what he was doing and if he would telephone. When he failed to call, her disappointment was intense.

Common sense warned Milly against deeper emotional involvement. She reminded herself of Richardson's marriage, the unlikelihood of anything permanent between the two of them, her own vulnerability . . . But still the image persisted, daydreams ousting reason, an echo of softly whispered words: *I want you, Milly. I don't know any other way to say it, except I want you* . . . And in the end it was this thought which became, deliciously and dreamily, her last remembrance of the waking day.

Brian Richardson had a hard-working Christmas Day. He had left Milly's apartment in the early morning and, after four hours of sleep, his alarm clock wakened him. Eloise, he noticed, had not come in overnight, a fact occasioning no surprise. After fixing breakfast for himself he had driven to party headquarters on Sparks Street, where he remained through most of the day, working on details of the general campaign plan he had discussed with the Prime Minister. Since only a janitor and himself were in the building and there were no interruptions, he accomplished a great deal and eventually returned to his own still empty apartment with a sense of satisfaction. Once or twice, earlier on, he had been surprised to find himself distracted by remembering Milly the way she had been the night before. Twice he was tempted to telephone her, but a sense of caution warned him against it. After all, the whole thing was just a passing affair, not to be

taken with too much seriousness. In the evening he had read
for a while and went to bed early.

And now Christmas had gone.

It was 11 A.M. December 26.

2

"Mr. Warrender is available if you'd like him this morning,"
Milly Freedeman announced. She had slipped into the Prime
Minister's inner office with a coffee tray as his executive assistant left. The executive assistant, an earnest, ambitious
young man of independent means named Elliot Prowse, had
been coming and going all morning, receiving instructions
and reporting their outcome to James Howden in between a
steady stream of other callers with appointments. A good
deal of the activity, Milly knew, had to do with the forthcoming Washington talks.

"Why should I want Warrender?" A trifle irritably, James
Howden looked up from a folder over which he had been
poring—one of a series on his desk, prominently marked TOP
SECRET and relating to intercontinental defense. Military matters had never interested James Howden overwhelmingly and,
even now, he had to compel concentration in himself in order
to absorb facts. Occasionally it saddened him that there was
so little time nowadays he could devote to social welfare matters, which were once his ruling interest in politics.

Pouring coffee from an aluminum vacuum jug, Milly answered equably, "I understand you called Mr. Warrender the
day before the holiday, and he was away." She added the
customary four lumps of sugar and generous cream, then
placed the cup carefully on the Prime Minister's blotter with
a small plate of chocolate cookies beside it.

James Howden put down the folder, took a cookie, and bit
into it. He said approvingly, "These are better than the last
lot. More chocolate."

Milly smiled. If Howden had been less preoccupied he
might have noticed that she seemed unusually radiant this
morning, as well as attractively dressed in a brown tweed
suit flecked with blue, and a soft blue blouse.

"I remember—I did call," the Prime Minister said after a
pause. "There was some sort of immigration trouble in Vancouver." He added hopefully, "Perhaps it's cleared itself up
by now."

"I'm afraid not," Milly told him. "Mr. Richardson phoned this morning with a reminder." She consulted a notebook. "He asked me to tell you it's a very live issue in the West, and the Eastern newspapers are becoming interested." She failed to say that Brian Richardson had also added warmly and personally, "You're a pretty wonderful person, Milly. I've been thinking about it, and we'll talk again soon."

James Howden sighed. "I suppose I'd better see Harvey Warrender. You'll have to fit him in somehow; ten minutes should be enough."

"All right," Milly said. "I'll make it this morning."

Sipping coffee, Howden asked, "Is there much of a backlog outside?"

Milly shook her head. "Nothing that won't keep for a while. I've passed on a few urgent things to Mr. Prowse."

"Good." The Prime Minister nodded approvingly. "Do that as much as you can, Milly, these next few weeks."

Sometimes, even now, he had a strange nostalgic feeling about Milly, even though physical desire had evaporated long since. He sometimes wondered how it could all have happened . . . the affair between them; his own intensity of feeling at the time. There had been the loneliness, of course, which back-bench M.P.s always suffered in Ottawa; the sense of emptiness, with so little to do to fill the long hours when the House was sitting. And, at the time, Margaret had been away a good deal . . . But it all seemed something distant, far away.

"There is one thing and I hate to bother you with it." Milly hesitated. "There's a letter from the bank. Another reminder that you're overdrawn."

Switching his thoughts back, Howden said gloomily, "I was afraid there would be soon." As he had when Margaret brought up the subject three days ago, he found himself resentful of the need to deal with something like this at such a time. It was his own fault in a way, he supposed. He knew that he had only to let word leak out among a few of the party's rich supporters and generous American friends, and gifts of money would come in quietly and amply, without strings attached. Other Prime Ministers before him had done the same thing, but Howden had always declined, principally as a matter of pride. His life, he reasoned, had begun with charity in the orphanage and he rejected the idea that after a lifetime's achievement he should become dependent on charity again.

He recalled Margaret's concern about the speed with which their modest savings were disappearing. "You'd better call the Montreal Trust," he instructed. "Find out if Mr. Maddox can come to see me for a talk."

"I thought you might want him, so I checked," Milly answered. "The only time you're free is late tomorrow afternoon and he'll come then."

Howden nodded assent. He was always grateful for Milly's efficient shortcuts.

He had finished the coffee—he liked it near-scalding as well as sweet and creamy—and Milly refilled his cup. Tilting back his padded leather chair, he relaxed consciously, enjoying one of the few unpressured moments of the day. Ten minutes from now he would become intense and preoccupied once more, setting a work pace which his staff found hard to equal. Milly knew this, and over the years had learned to be relaxed herself in these time-out periods, something she knew James Howden liked. Now he said easily, "Did you read the transcript?"

"Of the Defense Committee?"

Taking another chocolate cookie, Howden nodded.

"Yes," Milly said. "I read it."

"What did you think?"

Milly considered. For all the question's casualness she knew an honest answer was expected. James Howden had once told her complainingly, "Half the time I try to find out what people are thinking, they don't tell me the truth; only what they believe I'd like to hear."

"I wondered what we'd have left, as Canadians," Milly said. "If it happens—the Act of Union, I mean—I can't see our going back to the way things were before."

"No," Howden said, "I can't either."

"Well, then, wouldn't it be just the beginning of a swallowing-up process? Until we're part of the United States. Until all our independence has gone." Even as she asked the question, Milly wondered: would it matter if it were true? What was independence, really, except an illusion which people talked about? No one was truly independent, or ever could be, and the same was true of nations. She wondered how Brian Richardson would feel; she would have liked to talk to him about it now.

"Possibly we *shall* be swallowed, or appear to be for a while," Howden said slowly. "It's also possible that after a war it might prove the other way around." He paused, his long face brooding, then went on. "Wars have a way of changing things, you know, Milly; of exhausting nations and reducing empires, and sometimes those who think they've won a war have really lost. Rome discovered that; so did a lot of others in their time: the Philistines, Greece, Spain, France, Britain. The same thing could happen to Russia or the United States; perhaps to both in the end, leaving Canada strongest." He stopped, then added: "A mistake people make sometimes is to assume that the great changes of history always occur in other lifetimes than their own."

There was another thought too, unexpressed, in Howden's mind. A Canadian Prime Minister might easily have more influence in a joint relationship than under total independence. He could become an intermediary, with authority and power which could be fostered and enlarged. And in the end—if Howden himself were the one to wield it—the authority could be used for his own country's good. The important thing, the key to power, would be never to let the final thread of Canadian independence go.

"I realize it's important moving the missile bases north," Milly said, "and I know what you said about saving the food-producing land from fallout. But we're really heading directly into war; that's what it means, doesn't it?"

Should he confide his own conviction about war's inevitability and the need to prepare for it in terms of survival? Howden decided not. It was an issue on which he would have to hedge publicly and he might as well practice now.

"We're choosing sides, Milly," he said carefully, "and we're doing it while the choice can still mean something. In a way, believing what we believe, it's the only choice we could ever make. But there's a temptation to put it off; to avoid a decision; to sit on our hands hoping unpalatable truths will go away." He shook his head. "But not any more."

Tentatively she asked, "Won't it be hard—convincing people?"

Fleetingly the Prime Minister smiled. "I expect so. It may even make things somewhat hectic around this place."

"In that case," Milly said, "I shall try to reduce them to order." With the words, she felt a surge of affection and admiration for this man whom, over the years, she had seen achieve so much and now proposed to shoulder so much more. It was not the old, urgent feeling she had once experienced, but, in a deeper way, she wanted to protect and shield him. Satisfyingly, she had a sense of being needed.

James Howden said quietly, "You've always reduced things to order, Milly. It's meant a great deal to me." He put down the coffee cup—a signal the time-out period was over.

Forty-five minutes and three appointments later Milly ushered in the Hon. Harvey Warrender.

"Sit down, please." Howden's voice was cool.

The Minister of Citizenship and Immigration eased his tall, bulging figure into the seat facing the desk. He shifted uncomfortably.

"Look, Jim," he said with an attempt at heartiness, "if you've called me in to tell me I made a fool of myself the other night, let me say it first. I did, and I'm damn sorry."

"Unfortunately," Howden said acidly, "it's somewhat late to be sorry. And aside from that, if you choose to behave like the town drunk, a Governor General's reception is scarcely the place to begin. I assume you're aware that the whole story was around Ottawa next day." He noted with disapproval that the suit the other man wore was in need of pressing.

Warrender avoided the Prime Minister's glowering eyes above the beaklike nose. He waved a hand self-deprecatingly. "I know, I know."

"I'd be entirely justified in demanding your resignation."

"I hope you won't do that, Prime Minister. I sincerely hope you won't." Harvey Warrender had leaned forward, the movement revealing beads of sweat on the balding surface of his head. Was there an implied threat in the phrasing and tone, Howden wondered? It was hard to be sure. "If I may add a thought," Warrender said softly, smiling—he had regained some of his usual confidence—"it is *graviora quaedam sunt remedia periculis*, or freely translated from Virgil, 'Some remedies are worse than the dangers.' "

"There is also a line some place about the braying of an ass." Howden snapped back angrily; the other man's classical quotations invariably annoyed him. Now the Prime Minister continued tightlipped, "I was about to say that I had decided to take no action beyond a warning. I suggest you don't provoke me into changing my mind."

Warrender flushed, then shrugged. He murmured softly, "The rest is silence."

"The reason, principally, for calling you in is to talk about this latest immigration case in Vancouver. It appears to be the same kind of troublesome situation I insisted we avoid."

"Aha!" Harvey Warrender's eyes gleamed with aroused interest. "I've had a full report on that, Prime Minister, and I can tell you all about it."

"I don't want to be told," James Howden said impatiently. "It's your job to run your own department and in any event I've more important things." His eyes strayed to the open folders on intercontinental defense; he was anxious to get back to them. "What I want is for the case to be settled and out of the newspapers."

Warrender's eyebrows went up. "Aren't you being contradictory? In one breath you tell me to run my own department, then in the next to settle a case . . ."

Howden cut in angrily, "I'm telling you to follow Government policy—*my* policy: which is to avoid contentious immigration cases, particularly at this time, with an election next year and"—he hesitated—"other things coming up. We went into all that the other night." Then bitingly: "Or perhaps you don't remember."

"I wasn't all that drunk!" Now the anger was Harvey Warrender's. "I told you then what I thought of our so-called immigration policy, and it still goes. Either we get ourselves some new, honest immigration laws which admit what we're doing, and what every government before us . . ."

"Admit what?"

James Howden had risen and was standing behind the desk. Looking up at him Harvey Warrender said softly, intensely, "Admit we have a policy of discrimination; and why not—it's our own country, isn't it? Admit we have a color bar and race quotas, and we ban Negroes and Orientals, and that's the way it's always been, and why should we change it? Admit we want Anglo-Saxons and we need a pool of unemployed. Let's admit there's a strict quota for Italians and all the rest, and we keep an eye on the Roman Catholic percentage. Let's quit being fakers. Let's write an honest Immigration Act that spells things out the way they are. Let's quit having one face at the United Nations, hobnobbing with the coloreds, and another face at home . . ."

"Are you insane?" Incredulously, half-whispering, James Howden mouthed the question. His eyes were on Warrender. Of course, he thought, he had been given a clue: what had been said at the Government House reception . . . but he had assumed the effect of liquor . . . Then he remembered Margaret's words: *I've sometimes thought that Harvey is just a little mad.*

Harvey Warrender breathed heavily; his nostrils quivered. "No," he answered, "I'm not insane; just tired of damned hypocrisy."

"Honesty is fine," Howden said. His anger had dissipated now. "But that kind is political suicide."

"How do we know when nobody's tried it? How do we know people wouldn't like to be told what they already know?"

Quietly James Howden asked, "What's your alternative?"

"You mean if we don't write a new Immigration Act?"

"Yes."

"Then I'll enforce the one we have right down the line," Harvey Warrender said firmly. "I'll enforce it without exception or camouflage or back-door devices to keep unpleasant things out of the press. Maybe that'll show it up for what it is."

"In that case," James Howden said evenly, "I'd like your resignation."

The two men faced each other. "Oh no," Harvey Warrender said softly, "oh, no."

There was a silence.

"I suggest you be explicit," James Howden said. "You've something on your mind?"

"I think you know."

The Prime Minister's face was set, his eyes unyielding. "'Explicit' was the word I used."

"Very well, if that's what you wish." Harvey Warrender had resumed his seat. Now, conversationally, as if discussing routine business, he said, "We made an agreement."

"That was a long time ago."

"The agreement had no term to it."

"Nevertheless it's been fulfilled."

Harvey Warrender shook his head obstinately. "The agreement had no term." Fumbling in an inside pocket he pulled out a folded paper and tossed it on the Prime Minister's desk. "Read for yourself and see."

Reaching out, Howden felt his hand tremble. If this were the original, the only copy . . . It was a photostat.

For a moment his control left him. "You fool!"

"Why?" The other's face was bland.

"You had a photostat . . ."

"No one knew what was being copied. Besides I stood there all the time, beside the machine."

"Photostats have negatives."

"I have the negative," Warrender said calmly. "I kept it in case I ever need more copies. The original is safe too." He gestured. "Why don't you read it? That's what we were talking about."

Howden lowered his head and the words came up at him. They were simple, to the point, and in his own handwriting.

1. H. Warrender withdraws from leadership, will support J. Howden.
2. H. Warrender's nephew (H.O'B) to have —— TV franchise.
3. H. Warrender in Howden Cabinet—to choose own portfolio (except Ext. Affairs or Health.) J.H. not to dismiss H.W. except for indiscretion, scandal. In latter event H.W. takes full respon., not involving J.H.

Then there was the date—nine years ago—and the scribbled initials of them both.

Harvey Warrender said quietly, "You see—just as I said, the agreement has no term."

"Harvey," the Prime Minister said slowly, "is it any good appealing to you? We've been friends . . ." His mind reeled. One copy, in a single reporter's hands, would be an instrument of execution. There could be no explaining, no maneuver, no political survival, only exposure, disgrace . . . His hands were sweating.

The other man shook his head. Howden was conscious of a wall . . . unreasoning, impregnable. He tried again. "There's been the pound of flesh, Harvey; that and more. What now?"

"I'll tell you!" Warrender leaned near the desk, his voice a fierce, intense whisper. "Let me stay; let me do something worth while to balance out. Maybe if we rewrite our immigration law and do it honestly—spelling out things the way we really do them—maybe then people will stir their consciences and want to change. Maybe the way we do things *should* be changed; perhaps it's change that's needed in the end. But we can't begin without being honest first."

Perplexed, Howden shook his head. "You're not making sense. I don't understand."

"Then let me try to explain. You talked of a pound of flesh. Do you think I care about that part? Do you think I wouldn't go back and unmake that agreement of ours if it could be done? I tell you there've been nights, and plenty of them, when I've lain awake until the daylight came, loathing myself and the day I made it."

"Why, Harvey?" Perhaps if they could talk this out it might help . . . anything might help . . .

"I sold out, didn't I?" Warrender spoke emotionally now. "Sold out for a mess of potage that wasn't worth the price. And I've wished a thousand times since that we could be in that convention hall again and I'd take my chances against you—the way they were."

Howden said gently, "I think I'd still have won, Harvey." Momentarily he felt a deep compassion. Our sins revisit us, he thought—in one form or another, according to ourselves.

"I'm not so sure," Warrender said slowly. His eyes came up. "I've never been quite sure, Jim, that I couldn't have been here at this desk instead of you."

So that was it, Howden thought: much as he had imagined, with an extra ingredient added. Conscience plus dreams of glory thwarted. It made a formidable combination. Warily he asked, "Aren't you being inconsistent? In one breath you say you loathe the agreement we made, and yet you insist on hewing to its terms."

"It's the good part that I want to salvage, and if I let you send me out I'm finished. That's why I'm holding on." Harvey Warrender took out a handkerchief and wiped his head, which was perspiring freely. There was a pause, then he said more softly, "Sometimes I think it might be better if we were exposed. We're both frauds—you and me. Perhaps that's a way of setting the record straight."

This was dangerous. "No," Howden said quickly, "there are better methods, believe me." One thing he was sure of now: Harvey Warrender was mentally unstable. He must be led; coaxed, if necessary, like a child.

"Very well," James Howden said, "we'll forget the talk of resignation."

"And the Immigration Act?"

"The act remains the way it is," Howden said firmly. There was a limit to compromise, even here. "What's more, I want something done about that situation in Vancouver."

"I'll act by the law," Warrender said. "I'll look at it again; I promise you that. But by the law—exactly."

Howden sighed. It would have to do. He nodded, signifying the interview was at an end.

When Warrender had gone he sat silently, weighing this new untimely problem thrust upon him. It would be a mistake, he decided, to minimize the threat to his own security. Warrender's temperament had always been mercurial; now the instability was magnified.

Briefly he wondered how he could have done the thing he had . . . committed himself recklessly to paper when legal training and experience should have warned him of the danger. But ambition did strange things to a man, made him take risks, supreme risks sometimes, and others had done it too. Viewed across the years it seemed wild and unreasoning. And yet, at the time, with ambition driving, lacking a foreknowledge of things to come . . .

The safest thing, he supposed, was to leave Harvey Warrender alone, at least for the time being. The wild talk of rewriting legislation posed no immediate problem. In any case it was not likely to find favor with Harvey's own deputy minister, and senior civil servants had a way of delaying measures they disagreed with. Nor could legislation be brought in without cabinet consent, though a direct clash between Harvey Warrender and others in Cabinet must be avoided.

So what it really came down to was doing nothing and hoping for the best—the old political panacea. Brian Richardson would not be pleased, of course; obviously the party director had expected swift, firm action, but it would be impossible to explain to Richardson why nothing could be done. In the same way, the Vancouver situation would have to simmer, with Howden himself obliged to back up Harvey Warrender in whatever ruling the Immigration Department made. Well, that part was unfortunate, but at least it was a small issue entailing the kind of minor-key criticism which the Government had ridden out before, and no doubt they could survive it again.

The essential thing to remember, James Howden thought, was that preservation of his own leadership came first. So much depended on it, so much of the present and the future. He owed it to others to retain power. There was no one else at this moment who could replace him adequately.

Milly Freedeman came in softly. "Lunch?" she queried in her low contralto voice. "Would you like it here?"

"No," he answered. "I feel like a change of scene."

Ten minutes later, in a well-cut black overcoat and Eden homburg, the Prime Minister strode briskly from the East Block towards the Peace Tower doorway and the Parliamentary Restaurant. It was a clear, cold day, the crisp air invigorating, with roadways and sidewalks—snow heaped at their edges—drying in the sun. He had a sense of well-being, and acknowledged cordially the respectful greetings of those he passed and the snapped salutes of R.C.M.P. guards. Already the Warrender incident had receded in his mind; there were so many other things of greater import.

Milly Freedeman, as she did most days, had coffee and a sandwich sent in. Afterwards she went into the Prime Minister's office taking a sheaf of memoranda from which she had pruned nonurgent matters that could wait. She left the papers in an "in" tray on the desk. Its surface was untidily paper-strewn but Milly made no attempt to clear it, aware that in the middle of the day James Howden preferred to find things as he had left them. A plain, single sheet of paper, however, caught her eye. Turning it over curiously she saw it was a photostat.

It took two readings for the full meaning to sink in. When it had, Milly found herself trembling at the awful significance of the paper she held. It explained many things which over the years she had never understood: the convention . . . the Howden victory . . . her own loss.

The paper could also, she knew, spell the end of two political careers.

Why was it here? Obviously it had been discussed . . . today . . . in the meeting between the Prime Minister and Harvey Warrender. But why? What could either gain? And where was the original? . . . Her thoughts were racing. The questions frightened her. She wished she had left the paper unturned; that she had never known. And yet . . .

Suddenly, she experienced a fierce surge of anger against James Howden. How could he have done it? When there had been so much between them; when they could have shared happiness, a future together, if only he had lost the leadership . . . lost at the convention. She asked herself emotionally: Why didn't he play it fair? . . . at least leave her a chance to win? But she knew there had never been a chance . . .

Then, almost as suddenly as before, the anger was gone and sorrow and compassion took its place. What Howden had done, Milly knew, had been done because he had to. The need for power, for vanquished rivals, for political success . . . these had been all-consuming. Beside them, a personal life . . . even love . . . had counted for nothing. It had always been true: there had never been a chance . . .

But there were practical things to think of.

Milly stopped, willing herself to think calmly. Plainly there was a threat to the Prime Minister and perhaps to others. But James Howden was all that mattered to herself . . . there was a sense of the past returning. And only this morning, she remembered she had resolved to protect and shield him. But how could she . . . using this knowledge . . . knowledge she was certain that no one else possessed, probably not even Margaret Howden. Yes, in this she had at last become closer to James Howden even than his wife.

There was no immediate thing to do. But perhaps an opportunity might come. Sometimes blackmail could be turned against blackmail. The thought was vague, ephemeral . . . like groping in the dark. But if it happened . . . if an opportunity came . . . she must be able to substantiate what she knew.

Milly glanced at her watch. She knew Howden's habits well. It would be another half hour before he returned. No one else was in the outer office.

Acting on impulse she took the photostat to the copying machine outside. Working quickly, her heart beating at a footfall which approached, then passed, she put the photostat through. The copy which came out—a reproduction of a reproduction—was of poor quality and blurred, but clear enough to read, and the handwriting unmistakable. Hastily she folded the extra copy and crammed it to the bottom of her bag. She returned the photostat, face down, as she had found it.

Later in the afternoon James Howden turned the single sheet over and blanched. He had forgotten it was there. If he had left it overnight . . . He glanced at the outside door. Milly? No; it was a long-standing rule that his desk was never disturbed at midday. He took the photostat into the toilet adjoining his office. Shredding the paper into tiny pieces, he flushed them down, watching until all had gone.

3

Harvey Warrender reclined comfortably, a slight smile on his face, in the chauffeur-driven pool car which returned him to the Ministry of Citizenship and Immigration on Elgin Street. Alighting from the car, he entered the boxlike brown brick building, breasting a tide of office workers headed outward in a hasty lunchtime exit. He rode an elevator to the fifth floor and entered his own office suite through a direct door. Then, throwing overcoat, scarf, and hat carelessly over a chair, he crossed to his desk and pressed the intercom switch connecting him directly to the department's deputy minister.

"Mr. Hess," Harvey Warrender said, "if you're free, could you come in, please."

There was an equally polite acknowledgment, after which he waited. It always took a few minutes for the deputy minister to arrive; his office, though on the same floor, was some distance away, perhaps as a reminder that the administrative head of a ministry should not be sent for lightly or too often.

Harvey Warrender paced the room's deep broadloom slowly and thoughtfully. He still had a sense of elation from his encounter with the Prime Minister. Without any question, he thought, he had come off best, turning what could have been a reverse, or worse, into a clear-cut victory for himself. Moreover, the relationship between the two of them had now been clearly and sharply redefined.

Succeeding the elation came a glow of satisfaction and possession. This was where he belonged: in authority; if not at the pinnacle, then at least in a secondary throne of power. A well-upholstered throne, too, he reflected, glancing around with satisfaction, as he often did. The personal office suite of the Minister of Immigration was the most lavish in Ottwa, having been designed and furnished at large expense by a female predecessor—one of the few women in Canada ever to hold cabinet rank. On taking office himself, he had left the place as he found it—the deep gray carpet, pale gray drapes, a comfortable mixture of English period furniture—and visitors were invariably impressed. It was so very different from the chilly college cubbyhole in which he had toiled unrewardingly years before and, despite the stirrings of conscience he had confessed to James Howden, he had to admit it would be hard to relinquish the bodily comforts which rank and financial success provided.

The thought of Howden reminded him of his own promise to re-examine the tiresome Vancouver affair and to act precisely by existing law. And he would keep the promise. He was determined there should be no blundering or error in that direction for which Howden or others could blame him later.

A tap at the door, and his own secretary ushered in the deputy minister, Claude Hess, a portly career civil servant who dressed like a prosperous undertaker and sometimes had the pontifical manner to match.

"Good morning, Mr. Minister," Hess said. As always, the deputy managed to combine a judicious mixture of respect and familiarity, though somehow conveying that he had seen elected ministers come and go, and would still be exercising his own power when the present incumbent had moved on.

"I was with the P.M.," Warrender said. "On the carpet." He had formed the habit of speaking frankly to Hess, having found it paid off in the shrewd advice he often got in return. On this basis, and partly because Harvey Warrender had been Immigration Minister through two terms of the Government, their relationship worked well.

The deputy's face assumed a commiserating expression. "I see," he said. He had, of course, already received through the higher civil-service grapevine a detailed description of the brawl at Government House, but discreetly refrained from mentioning it.

"One of his beefs," Harvey said, "was about this Vancouver business. Some people it seems don't like our keeping to the rules."

The deputy minister sighed audibly. He had grown used to retreats and back-door dodges by which immigration laws were subverted to political ends. But the Minister's next remark surprised him.

"I told the P.M. we wouldn't back down," Warrender said.

"Either that or we revise the Immigration Act and do what we have to do above board."

The deputy asked tentatively, "And Mr. Howden . . ."

"We've a free hand," Warrender said shortly. "I've agreed to review the case, but after that we handle it our way."

"That's very good news." Hess put down a file he had been carrying and the two men lowered themselves into facing chairs. Not for the first time the pudgy deputy speculated on the relationship between his own Minister and the Rt. Hon. James McCallum Howden. Obviously some kind of special rapport existed, since Harvey Warrender had always seemed to have an unusual degree of freedom, compared with other members of the Cabinet. It was a circumstance, though, not to be quarreled with and had made possible the translation of some of the deputy minister's own policies into reality. Outsiders, Claude Hess reflected, sometimes thought that policy was the sole prerogative of elected representatives. But to a surprising degree the process of government consisted of elected representatives putting into law the ideas of an elite corps of deputy ministers.

Pursing his lips, Hess said thoughtfully, "I hope you weren't serious about revising the Immigration Act, Mr. Minister. On the whole it's good law."

"Naturally you'd think so," Warrender said shortly. "You wrote it in the first place."

"Well, I must admit to a certain parental fondness . . ."

"I don't agree with all your ideas about population," Harvey Warrender said. "You know that, don't you?"

The deputy smiled. "In the course of our relationship I have gathered something of the kind. But, if I may say so, you are, at the same time, a realist."

"If you mean I don't want Canada swamped by Chinese and Negroes, you're right," Warrender said tersely. He went on, more slowly, "All the same though, I sometimes wonder. We're sitting on four million square miles of some of the richest real estate in the world, we're underpopulated, underdeveloped; and the earth is teeming with people, seeking sanctuary, a new home . . ."

"Nothing would be solved," Hess said primly, "by opening our doors wide to all comers."

"Not for us, perhaps, but what about the rest of the world —the wars which may happen again if there isn't an outlet for population expansion somewhere?"

"It would be a high price to pay, I think, for eventualities which may never occur." Claude Hess folded one leg over another, adjusting the crease in his faultlessly tailored trousers. "I take the view, Mr. Minister—as you are aware, of course—that Canada's influence in world affairs can be far greater as we are, with our present balance of population, than by allowing ourselves to be overrun by less desirable races."

"In other words," Harvey Warrender said softly, "let's hang on to the privileges we were lucky enough to be born to."

The deputy smiled faintly. "As I said a moment ago, we are both realists."

"Well, maybe you're right." Harvey Warrender drummed his fingers on the desk. "There are some things I've never really made up my mind about, and that's one. But one thing I am sure of, is that the people of this country are responsible for our immigration laws, and they should be made to realize it, and they'll never realize it while we shift and waver. That's why we'll enforce the act right down the line—no matter which way it reads as long as I'm sitting in this chair."

"Bravo!" The pudgy deputy mouthed the word softly. He was smiling.

There was a pause between them in which Harvey Warrender's eyes moved up to a point above the deputy's head. Without turning, Hess knew what it was the Minister saw: a portrait in oils of a young man, in Royal Canadian Air Force uniform. It had been painted from a photograph after the death in action of Harvey Warrender's son. Many times before in this room Claude Hess had seen the father's eyes straying to the picture, and sometimes they had spoken of it.

Now Warrender said, as if recognizing the other's awareness, "I often think about my son, you know."

Hess nodded slowly. It was not a new opening and sometimes he sidestepped it. Today he decided to reply.

"I never had a son," Hess said. "Just daughters. We've a good relationship, but I've always thought there must be something special between a father and son."

"There is," Harvey Warrender said. "There is, and it never quite dies—not for me, anyway." He went on, his voice warming. "I think so many times of what my son Howard could have been. He was a splendid boy, always with the finest courage. That was his outstanding feature—courage; and in the end he died heroically. I've often told myself I've that to be proud of."

The deputy wondered if heroism were the kind of thing he would remember a son of his own by. But the Minister had said much the same thing before, to others as well as himself, seeming unaware of repetition. Sometimes Harvey Warrender would describe in graphic detail the blazing air battle in which his son had died until it was hard to be sure where sorrow ended and hero worship began. At times there had been comments around Ottawa on the subject, though most of them charitable. Grief did strange things, Claude Hess thought, even sometimes producing a parody of grief. He was glad when his superior's tone became more business-like.

"All right," Warrender said, "let's talk about this Vancouver thing. One thing I want to be sure of is that we're absolutely in the clear legally. That's important."

"Yes, I know." Hess nodded sagely, then touched the file he had brought in. "I've gone over the reports again, sir, and I'm sure there's nothing you need worry about. Only one thing concerns me a little."

"The publicity?"

"No; I think you'll have to expect that." Actually the publicity *had* bothered Hess, who had been convinced that political pressure would cause the Government to back down on enforcement of the Immigration Act, as had happened many times before. Apparently, though, he had been wrong. Now he continued, "What I was thinking is that we don't have a senior man in Vancouver right now. Williamson, our district superintendent, is on sick leave and it may be several months before he's back, if at all."

"Yes," Warrender said. He lit a cigarette, offering one to the deputy minister, who accepted it. "I remember now."

"In the ordinary way I wouldn't get concerned; but if the pressure builds up, as it may, I'd like to have someone out there I can rely on personally, and who can handle the press."

"I presume you've something in mind."

"Yes." Hess had been thinking quickly. The decision to stand firm had pleased him. Warrender was eccentric at times, but Hess believed in loyalty, and now he must protect his Minister's position in every way possible. He said thoughtfully, "I could shuffle some responsibilities here and relieve one of my deputy directors. Then he could take charge in Vancouver—ostensibly until we know about Williamson, but actually to handle this specific case."

"I agree." Warrender nodded vigorously. "Who do you think should go?"

The deputy minister exhaled cigarette smoke. He was smiling slightly. "Kramer," he said slowly. "With your approval, sir, I'll send Edgar Kramer."

4

In her apartment, restlessly, Milly Freedeman reviewed once more the events of the day. Why had she copied the photostat? What could she do with it, if anything? Where did her loyalty really lie?

She wished there could be an end to the conniving and maneuvers in which she was obliged to share. As she had a day or two before, she considered leaving politics, abandoning James Howden, and beginning something new. She wondered if somewhere, anywhere, among any group of people, there was a sanctuary where intrigue never happened. On the whole, she doubted it.

The telephone's ringing was an interruption.

"Milly," Brian Richardson's voice said briskly, "Raoul Lemieux—he's a deputy in Trade and Commerce and a friend of mine—is starting a party. We're both invited. How about it?"

Milly's heart leapt. She asked impulsively, "Will it be gay?"

The party director chuckled. "Raoul's parties usually get that way."

"Noisy?"

"Last time," Richardson said, "the neighbors called the police."

"Does he have music? Can we dance?"

"There's a stack of records; at Raoul's, anything goes."

"I'll come," Milly said. "Oh, please; I'll come."

"I'll pick you up in half an hour." His voice sounded amused.

She said impetuously, "Thank you, Brian; thank you."

"You can thank me later." There was a click as the line went dead.

She knew just the dress that she would wear; it was crimson chiffon, a low-cut neck. Excitedly, with a feeling of release, she kicked her shoes across the living room.

Eight Edgar Kramer

In the thirty-six hours during which Edgar S. Kramer had been in Vancouver, he had come to two conclusions. First, he had decided there was no problem in the West Coast Headquarters of the Department of Citizenship and Immigration which he could not handle with ease. Second, he was dismally aware that a personal and embarrassing physical disability was steadily becoming worse.

In a square, functionally furnished office on the second story of the department's water-front Immigration Building, Edgar Kramer mentally debated both matters.

Kramer was a gray-eyed, spare man in his late forties, with wavy brown hair parted in the middle, rimless glasses, and an agile logician's mind which had already taken him a long way, from a modest beginning, in government service. He was industrious, undeviatingly honest, and impartial in administering official regulations to the letter. He disliked sentiment, inefficiency, and disrespect for rules and order. A colleague had once observed that, "Edgar would cut off his own mother's pension if there was a comma out of place in the application." While exaggerated, the charge held a basis of truth, though it could equally well be said that Kramer would help his greatest enemy unstintingly if the regulations of his job required it.

He was married, without children, to a plain woman who ordered their home with a kind of colorless efficiency. She was already apartment hunting in sections of the city which she had decided were respectable and therefore suited to her husband's government position.

In the higher civil service Edgar S. Kramer had become one of a few marked men, picked out—largely through ability, and partly by a knack of getting noticed—for advancement to higher things. In the Department of Immigration he was looked on as a dependable trouble shooter and it was a safe prediction that within a few years, allowing for promotions and retirements, he would be eligible for appointment as deputy minister.

Fully aware of this favored position, and also exceedingly ambitious, Edgar Kramer sought constantly to safeguard and improve it. He had been delighted by the assignment to take charge temporarily in Vancouver, especially since learning that the Minister himself had approved his selection and would be watching results. For this reason alone, the personal problem which currently plagued him could not have been more untimely.

Stated simply, the problem was this: Edgar Kramer was obliged to urinate with annoying and humiliating frequency.

The urologist to whom his private physician had sent him a few weeks earlier had summed up the situation. "You are suffering from prostatism, Mr. Kramer, and before it gets better it will have to get worse." The specialist had described the distressing symptoms: frequent daytime urination, a weakened stream and, at night, nocturia—the need to relieve himself, interrupting sleep and leaving him tired and irritable next day.

He had asked how long it must go on, and the urologist had said sympathetically, "I'm afraid you must expect another two or three years until you reach the point where surgery is practical. When that happens we'll do a resection which should make things more comfortable."

It had been small consolation. Even more depressing was the thought that his superiors should learn he had contracted, prematurely, an old man's disease. After all his efforts—the years of work and application, with reward finally in sight—he dreaded what such knowledge might do.

Trying to forget for a while, he returned to several ruled sheets of paper spread over the desk before him. On them, in a neat, precise hand, he had tabulated actions taken so far since his arrival in Vancouver, and those planned next. On the whole he had found the district headquarters well run and in good order. A few procedures, though, needed revision, including some tightening of discipline, and there was one other change he had made already.

It had occurred yesterday at lunchtime when he had sampled the meal distributed to prisoners in detention cells —the captured illegal entrants, dejectedly awaiting deportation overseas. To his annoyance, the food, though palatable, was neither hot nor of the same quality as served to himself earlier in the staff cafeteria. The fact that some of the deportees were living better than at any other time in their lives, and others might possibly be starving a few weeks hence, mattered not at all. Regulations on the treatment of prisoners were specific, and Edgar Kramer had sent for the senior cook, who proved to be a huge man, towering over the slight, spare superintendent. Kramer—never impressed by other people's size—had administered a sharply severe reprimand and from now on, he was sure, any food for prisoners would be carefully prepared, and hot when they received it.

Now he began considering discipline. There had been some unpunctuality this morning in the general offices and he had noticed, too, a certain slackness in appearance of the uniformed officers. A careful dresser himself—his dark pinstriped suits were always well-pressed, with a folded white handkerchief in the breast pocket—he expected subordinates to maintain a similar standard. He began a notation, then uncomfortably became aware of the need, once again, to relieve himself. A glance at his watch revealed that it was barely fifty minutes since the last time. He decided he would *not* . . . he would force himself to wait . . . He tried concentrating. Then, after a moment, sighing dispiritedly, he rose and left the office.

When he returned, the young stenographer who was serving as his secretary for the time being, was waiting in his office. Kramer wondered if the girl had noticed how many times he had been in and out, even though he had used a direct door to the corridor. Of course, he could always make excuses that he was going somewhere in the building . . . It might be necessary to do that soon . . . He must devise ways of escaping notice.

"There's a gentleman to see you, Mr. Kramer," the girl announced. "A Mr. Alan Maitland; he says he's a lawyer."

"All right," Kramer said. He took off his rimless glasses to wipe them. "Bring him in, please."

Alan Maitland had walked the half-mile from his office to the water front and his cheeks were flushed and ruddy from the cold wind outside. He wore no hat, only a light topcoat which he shrugged off as he entered. In one hand he carried a brief case.

"Good morning, Mr. Kramer," Alan said. "It was good of you to see me without an appointment."

"I'm a public servant, Mr. Maitland," Kramer said in his precise, punctilious voice. With a polite, formal smile he gestured Alan to a chair and sat down at the desk himself. "My office door is always open—within reason. What can I do for you?"

"Perhaps your secretary told you," Alan said, "I'm a lawyer."

Kramer nodded. "Yes." A young and inexperienced one, he thought. Edgar Kramer had seen many lawyers in his time and crossed swords with a few. Most had not impressed him.

"I read about your assignment here a couple of days ago and decided to wait until you arrived." Alan was aware of feeling his way carefully, not wanting to antagonize this small man facing him, whose good will could be important. He had intended, at first, to approach the Immigration Department on behalf of Henri Duval as soon as possible following Christmas. But then, after he had spent an entire day reading immigration law and legal precedents, the evening papers of the twenty-sixth had carried a brief announcement that the Department of Immigration had named a new head to its Vancouver district. After talking it over with his partner Tom Lewis, who had also made a few discreet inquiries, they had decided—even at the loss of several precious days —to wait for the new appointee.

"Well, I've arrived. So perhaps you'll tell me why you waited." Kramer creased his face into a smile. If he could help this novice lawyer, he decided—provided the youngster proved co-operative with the department—he would certainly do so.

"I'm here on behalf of a client," Alan said carefully. "His name is Henri Duval and at present he is being detained on a ship, the M. V. *Vastervik*. I would like to show you my authority to act on his behalf." Unzippering the brief case he produced a single sheet of paper—a typed copy of the retainer which the stowaway had signed at their first interview—and placed it on the desk.

Kramer read the paper carefully, then put it down. At the mention of the name Henri Duval he had frowned slightly. Now, a trifle warily, he inquired, "If I may ask, Mr. Maitland, how long have you known your client?"

It was an unusual question, but Alan decided not to be resentful. In any case, Kramer seemed friendly enough. "I've known my client three days," he answered cheerfully. "As a matter of fact, I first read about him in the newspapers."

"I see." Edgar Kramer brought the tips of his fingers together above the desk. It was a favorite gesture whenever he was thinking or mentally marking time. He had, of course, obtained a full report of the Duval incident immediately on arrival. The deputy minister, Claude Hess, had told him of the Minister's concern that the case should be handled with absolute correctness, and Kramer was satisfied that that had already been done. In fact, he had answered questions from the Vancouver newspapers to that effect the previous day.

"Perhaps you didn't see the newspaper articles." Alan reopened his brief case and reached inside.

"Don't bother, please." Kramer decided he would be friendly but firm. "I did see one of them. But we don't rely on newspapers here. You see"—he smiled thinly—"I have access to official files, which we consider somewhat more important."

"There can't be much of a file on Henri Duval," Alan said. "As far as I can make out, no one officially has done much inquiring."

"You're quite right, Mr. Maitland. There's been very little done because the position is perfectly clear. This person on the ship has no status, no documents, and apparently no citizenship of any country. Therefore, as far as the department is concerned, there is no possibility even of considering him as an immigrant."

"This person, as you call him," Alan said, "has some pretty unusual reasons for having no citizenship. If you read the press report, you must know that."

"I am aware there have been certain statements in print." Again the thin smile. "But when you have had as much experience as me, you will learn that newspaper stories and the true facts are sometimes at variance."

"I don't believe everything I read either." Alan found the on-and-off smile and the other man's attitude beginning to annoy him. "All that I'm asking—and that's really the reason I'm here—is that you investigate the matter a little more."

"And what I'm telling you is that any further investigation is pointless." This time there was a distinct coolness in Edgar Kramer's tone. He was conscious of an irritability, perhaps from tiredness—he had had to get up several times last night and was far from being rested on waking this morning. Now he continued, "The individual concerned has no legal rights in this country, nor is he likely to have any."

"He's a human being," Alan persisted. "Doesn't that count for anything?"

"There are many human beings in the world, and some are less fortunate than others. My business is to deal with those who come within the provisions of the Immigration Act, and Duval does not." This young lawyer, Kramer thought, was definitely *not* co-operative.

"I am asking," Alan said, "for a formal hearing into my client's immigration status."

"And I," Edgar Kramer said firmly, "am refusing it."

The two eyed each other with the beginnings of dislike. Alan Maitland had the impression of facing a wall of impregnable smugness. Edgar Kramer saw a brash youthfulness and disrespect of authority. He was also bothered by a new urge to urinate. It was ridiculous, of course . . . so soon. But he had noticed that mental excitability sometimes had that effect. He willed himself to ignore it. He must hold out . . . not give way . . .

"Couldn't we be reasonable about this?" Alan wondered if perhaps he had been too brusque; it was an occasional fault he tried to guard against. Now he asked—he hoped persuasively—"Would you do me the favor of seeing this man yourself, Mr. Kramer? I think you might be impressed."

The other shook his head. "Whether I was impressed or not would be entirely beside the point. My business is to administer the law as it stands. I do not make the law or approve exceptions to it."

"But you can make recommendations."

Yes, Edgar Kramer thought, he could. But he had no intention of doing so, particularly in this case with its sentimental overtones. And as for personally interviewing some would-be immigrant, his own status nowadays put him a long way above that.

There had been a time, of course, when he had done a good deal of that kind of interviewing—overseas, after the war, in the shattered countries of Europe . . . selecting immigrants for Canada, and rejecting others in much the same way (he had once heard someone say) that one selected the best dogs from a pound. Those had been the days when men and women would sell their souls, and sometimes did, for an immigrant visa, and there had been many temptations for immigration officers, to which a few succumbed. But he himself had never wavered and, although not caring greatly for the work—he preferred administration to people—he had done it well.

He had been known as a tough official, guarding his country's interests carefully, approving only immigrants of the highest standard. He had often been proud to think of the good people . . . alert, industrious, medically fit . . . whom he had allowed in.

Rejecting those who were substandard, for whatever reason, had never disturbed him, as it sometimes disturbed others.

His thoughts were interrupted.

"I'm not asking for admittance of my client as an immigrant—not yet, anyway," Alan Maitland said. "All that I'm seeking is the very first stage—an immigration hearing away from the ship."

Despite his earlier determination to ignore it, Edgar Kramer could feel the pressure on his bladder growing. He was also angered at the assumption he might fall for an old and elementary lawyer's trick. He answered sharply, "I'm perfectly aware what you're asking for, Mr. Maitland. You're asking the department to recognize this man officially, and then reject him officially, so that afterwards you can begin legal steps. Then, when you're going through all the procedures of appeal—as slowly, as possible, no doubt—the ship will sail, with your so-called client left here. Isn't that the sort of thing you had in mind?"

"To tell you the truth," Alan said, "it was." He grinned. The strategy was one which he and Tom Lewis had planned together. But now that it was in the open there seemed no point in denying it.

"Exactly!" Kramer snapped. "You were prepared to indulge in cheap legal trickery!" He ignored the friendly grin as well as an inner voice which cautioned him he was handling this badly.

"Just for the record," Alan Maitland said quietly, "I don't happen to agree that it was either cheap or trickery. However, I've just one question. Why did you refer to my 'so-called client'?"

It was too much. The gnawing physical discomfort, the anxiety of weeks, and nights of accumulated tiredness, combined to produce a retort which at any other time Edgar

Kramer, tactful and trained in diplomacy, would never have considered making. He was also acutely aware of the youthful, glowing health of the young man who faced him. He observed acidly, "The answer should be perfectly obvious, just as it is obvious to me that you have accepted this absurd and hopeless case for one purpose only—the publicity and attention you expect to gain from it."

For the span of several seconds there was silence in the small square room.

Alan Maitland felt a flush of blood suffuse his face angrily. For an insane instant he considered reaching across the desk to strike the older man.

The charge had been utterly false. Far from courting publicity, he had already discussed with Tom Lewis how it could be avoided, since both had been convinced that too much press attention might hamper legal action on Henri Duval's behalf. This was one reason he had come quietly to the Department of Immigration. He had been prepared to suggest that no statement to the press should be issued for the time being . . .

His eyes met Edgar Kramer's. The civil servant's had a fierce, oddly pleading intensity.

"Thank you, Mr. Kramer," Alan said slowly. Standing, he picked up his topcoat, tucked the brief case under an arm. "Thank you very much for suggesting what I now intend to do."

2

For three days after the Christmas holiday the Vancouver *Post* had kept the story of Henri Duval—the man without a country—alive in its news pages. To a lesser extent, so had the other two papers in the city—the rival afternoon *Colonist* and the more sedate morning *Globe*—though with hints of skepticism, since the *Post* had uncovered the incident first.

But now the story was about to die.

"We've run the gamut, Dan, and all we've got is a lot of interest but no action. So let's forget it until the ship leaves in a few days, then you can do a nostalgic piece about the sad little guy sailing into the sunset."

It was 7.45 A.M. in the *Post* newsroom. The speaker was Charles Woolfendt, day city editor, his listener Dan Orliffe. Arranging the day's assignments, Woolfendt, scholarly and quiet spoken but with a mind which, some said, worked like an IBM machine, had beckoned Dan over to the city desk.

"Whatever you say, Chuck." Orliffe shrugged. "All the same, I wish we could give it one more day."

Woolfendt regarded the other searchingly. He respected Orliffe's judgment as a seasoned hand, but there were other problems to be weighed. Today a new local story was in progress which would lead the afternoon edition and for which he needed several more reporters. A woman hiker had disappeared on Mount Seymour, just outside the city, and an intensive search had failed to locate her. All three newspapers were covering the search closely, and there was growing suspicion of foul play by the woman's husband. The managing editor had already sent Woolfendt a note this morning which read: "Did Daisy fall or was she pushed? If alive, let's get to her before her old man." Dan Orliffe, Woolfendt reflected, would be a good man to have on the mountain.

"If we could be sure of something important happening on the stowaway story, I'd go along," Woolfendt said. "But I don't mean just another angle."

"I know," Dan agreed. "It needs some fresh human interest with impact. I wish I could guarantee it."

"If you could, I'd give you the extra day," Woolfendt said. "Otherwise I can use you on this search deal."

"Go ahead," Dan countered. He knew that Woolfendt, for whom he had worked a long time, was sounding him out. "You're the boss, but the other could still be a better story."

Around them, as others of the day shift came in, the newsroom was coming to life. The assistant managing editor moved into his place beside the city desk. Across at the main news desk, copy had begun to flow through the slot to Composing and Makeup three floors below. Already there was a subdued, steady tempo which would rise to a succession of peaks as the day's deadlines came and went.

"I'm disappointed too," the city editor said thoughtfully. "I really thought there'd be more happen to that stowaway of yours than has." He ticked off points on his fingers. "We've covered the man himself, the ship, public reaction, the Immigration people—no dice; we've made overseas checks—no results; we've wired the U.N.—they'll look into it, but God knows when, and meanwhile I've a paper to get out. What else?"

"I was hoping," Dan said, "that somebody who mattered might come forward to help him."

A hurrying copy boy put ink-wet proofs of early closed pages on the city desk.

Woolfendt paused. Behind the domed forehead his incisive mind clicked pros and cons. Then, decisively, "All right," he announced, "I'll give you another twenty-four hours. That means one clear day to find a guy on a white horse."

"Thanks, Stu." Dan Orliffe grinned, turning away. Over his shoulder he called, "It would have been cold on that mountain."

With nothing specific in mind he had gone home then for a late breakfast with his wife Nancy and afterwards driven Patty, their six-year-old daughter, to school. By the time he returned downtown and had parked outside the Immigration Building it was close to ten o'clock.

He had no special reason for coming here, having interviewed Edgar Kramer the day before and gained nothing beyond a colorless official statement. But it seemed a logical place to start.

"I'm looking for a man on a white horse," he told the young girl who was doing duty as Edgar Kramer's secretary.

"He went that way," she said pointing. "Right through to the padded cell."

"I've often wondered," Dan observed, "how it is that girls nowadays can be sexy and yet so intelligent."

"My hormones have a high I.Q.," she told him. "And my husband taught me a lot of answers."

Dan sighed.

"If we're through with the comic dialogue," the girl said, "you're a newspaper reporter, and you'd like to see Mr. Kramer, but right now he's busy."

"I didn't think you'd remember me."

"I didn't," the girl said pertly. "It's just that you can pick reporters out. They're usually a little gone."

"This one hasn't yet," Dan said. "In fact, if you don't mind, I'll wait."

The girl smiled. "It won't be long, from the sound of it." She nodded towards the closed door of Edgar Kramer's office.

Dan could hear raised, sharp voices. His acute hearing

caught the word "Duval." A few minutes later Alan Maitland strode out, his face flushed.

Dan Orliffe caught up with him at the building's main doorway. "Excuse me," he said. "I wonder if we have a mutual
interest."

"It's unlikely," Alan snapped. He made no attempt to stop.
Fierce anger surged through him—a delayed reaction from
his earlier calm.

"Take it easy." Walking alongside, Dan inclined his head
toward the building they had now left. "I'm not one of them.
Just a newspaperman." He introduced himself.

Alan Maitland halted on the sidewalk. "Sorry." He took a
deep breath, then grinned sheepishly. "I was ready to blow
up, and you happened to be handy."

"Any time," Dan said. Mentally he had already taken in
the brief case and a U.B.C. tie. "This is my day for long
shots. Could you perhaps be a lawyer?"

"Could and am."

"Representing one Henri Duval?"

"Yes."

"Could we talk somewhere?"

Alan Maitland hesitated. Edgar Kramer had accused him
of seeking publicity, and Alan's own angry retort had been
to the effect that now he would. But a lawyer's instinct for
avoiding statements to the press was hard to shake off.

"Off the record," Dan Orliffe said quietly, "things aren't
going too well, are they?"

Alan made a wry grimace. "Equally off the record, they
couldn't be worse."

"In that case," Orliffe said, "what have you—or Duval—
got to lose?"

"Nothing, I suppose," Alan said slowly. It was true enough,
he thought; there was nothing to lose and maybe something
could be gained. "All right," he said. "Let's go for coffee."

"I had a feeling this was going to be a good day," Dan
Orliffe said contentedly. "By the way, where did you tether
your horse?"

"Horse?" Alan looked puzzled. "I walked here."

"Take no notice," Dan said. "Sometimes I get whimsical.
Let's use my car."

An hour later, over a fourth cup of coffee, Alan Maitland
commented, "You've asked a lot of questions about me, but
surely Duval is more important."

Dan Orliffe shook his head emphatically. "Not today. Today you're the story." He glanced at his watch. "Just one more question, then I must get writing."

"Go ahead."

"Don't get me wrong," Dan said. "But why is it that with all the big names and legal talent in a city like Vancouver, you're the only one who's come forward to help this little guy?"

"To tell you the truth," Alan answered, "I was wondering that myself."

3

The Vancouver *Post* building was a drab brick pile with offices in front, printing plant at the rear, and the editorial tower rising stubbily above both like a brief, disjointed thumb. Ten minutes after leaving Alan Maitland, Dan Orliffe parked his Ford station wagon in the employees' lot across the street and headed inside. He took the tower elevator and, in the now-bustling newsroom, settled down at an empty desk to write.

The lead came easily.

An angry young Vancouver lawyer is preparing, like David, to assault Goliath.

He is Alan Maitland, 25, Vancouver-born graduate of U.B.C. law school.

His Goliath is the Government of Canada—specifically the Immigration Department.

Department officials adamantly refuse to heed the "let me in" pleas of Henri Duval, the youthful "man without a country," now a shipboard prisoner in Vancouver harbor.

Alan Maitland now is legal counsel for Henri Duval. The friendless wanderer had almost abandoned hope of getting legal help, but Maitland volunteered his services. The offer was gratefully accepted.

Dan typed the word "more" and shouted, "Copy!" He ripped out the sheet which a copy boy yanked from his hand and delivered to the city desk.

Automatically he checked the time. It was 12.17, sixteen minutes to the Mainland edition closing. The Mainland was the day's principal deadline—the home-delivery edition with the longest press run. What he wrote would be read tonight in thousands of homes . . . warm, comfortable homes, their occupants secure . . .

Post readers will recall that this newspaper was the first to reveal the tragic plight of Henri Duval who—through a quirk of fate—has no nationality. Almost two years ago, in desperation, he stowed aboard ship. Since then, country after country has refused to let him in.

England jailed Duval while his ship was in port. The U.S. had him chained. Canada does neither, pretending instead that he does not exist.

"Let's have another take, Dan!" It was Stu Woolfendt, urgently from the city desk. Again a copy boy. He snatched the page from the typewriter as another went in.

Is there a chance that young Henri Duval might be admitted here? Can legal measures help him?

Older, cooler heads have said no. The Government and Immigration Minister, they claim, have powers which it is useless to challenge.

Alan Maitland disagrees. "My client is being denied a basic human right," he said today, "and I intend to fight for it."

He wrote three more paragraphs of Maitland quotes on Henri Duval. They were crisp and to the point.

"Keep it coming, Dan!" It was the city editor again and now, beside Woolfendt, the managing editor had appeared also. The mountain search story had proved disappointing—the missing woman found alive, no foul play, and her husband vindicated. Tragedy made livelier news than happy endings.

Dan Orliffe typed steadily, his mind framing sentences, fingers nimbly following.

Whether Alan Maitland succeeds or fails in his objective, there will be a race against time. Duval's ship, the Vastervik—an ocean-going tramp which may never come here again—is due to sail in two weeks or less. The ship would have gone already, but repairs detained it.

More background next. He filled it in, recapping events. Now the assistant city editor at his elbow. "Dan, did you get a picture of Maitland?"

"No time." He answered without looking up. "But he played football for U.B.C. Try Sports."

"Right!"

12.23. Ten minutes left.

"The first thing we are seeking is an official hearing into Henri Duval's case," Maitland told the *Post*. "I have asked for such a hearing as a matter of simple justice. But it has been refused flatly and, in my opinion, the Immigration Department is acting as if Canada were a police state."

Next, some background on Maitland . . . Then—in fairness—a restatement of the Immigration Department's stand, as expressed by Edgar Kramer the day before . . . Back to Maitland—a quote in rebuttal, then a description of Maitland himself.

On the keyboard Dan Orliffe could visualize the young lawyer's face, grimly set, as it had been this morning when he strode from Kramer's office.

He is an impressive young man, this Alan Maitland. When he talks his eyes gleam, his chin juts forward with determination. You get the feeling he is the sort of individual you would like to have on your side.

Perhaps, tonight, in his lonely locked cabin aboard ship, Henri Duval has much the same feeling.

12.29. Time was crowding him now; a few more facts, another quote, and it would have to do. He would expand the story for the final edition, but what he had written here was what most people would read.

"All right," the managing editor instructed the group around him near the city desk. "We'll still lead with finding the woman, but keep it short and run Orliffe's story top left alongside."

"Sports had a cut of Maitland," the assistant city editor reported. "Head and shoulders, one column. It's three years old, but not bad. I sent it down."

"Get a better picture for the final," the managing editor commanded. "Send a photog to Maitland's office and let's get some law books in the background."

"I already did," the assistant responded crisply. He was a lean, brash youth, at times almost offensively alert. "And I figured you'd want law books, so I said so."

"Christ!" the managing editor snorted. "You ambitious bastards wear me down. How'm I gonna give orders around here if you birds think of everything first?" Grumblingly he retreated to his office as the Mainland edition closed.

A few minutes later, before copies of the *Post* had reached the street, the gist of Dan Orliffe's report was on the national CP wire.

4

Alan Maitland, in the late morning, was unaware of the extent to which his name would shortly become known.

Leaving Dan Orliffe, he had returned to the modest office on the fringe of the downtown business district which he and Tom Lewis shared. Located over a block of stores and an Italian restaurant from which the odor of pizza and spaghetti frequently wafted up, it consisted of two glass-paneled cubicles with a tiny waiting room holding two chairs and a stenographer's desk. Three mornings a week the latter was occupied by a grandmotherly widow who, for a modest sum, did the small amount of typing necessary.

At the moment Tom Lewis was at the outside desk, his short chunky figure hunched over the second-hand Underwood they had bought cheaply a few months earlier. "I'm drafting my will," he said cheerfully, looking up. "I've decided to leave my brain to science."

Alan slipped off his coat and hung it in his own cubicle. "Be sure to send yourself a bill and remember I'm entitled to half."

"Why not sue me, just for practice?" Tom Lewis swung away from the typewriter. "How'd you make out?"

"Negatively." Tersely Alan related the substance of his interview at Immigration headquarters.

Tom stroked his chin thoughtfully. "This man Kramer is no lame-brain. Not if he saw through the delay gambit."

"I guess the idea wasn't all that original," Alan said ruefully. "Other people have probably tried it."

"In law," Tom said, "there are no original ideas. Only endless mutations of old ones. Well, what now? Is it Plan Two?"

"Don't dignify it as a plan. It's the longest long shot, and we both know it."

"But you'll give it a whirl?"

"Yes, I will." Alan nodded slowly. "Even if for no other reason than to displease Mr. Smugly-Smiling Kramer." He added softly, "Oh, how I'd love to beat that bastard in court!"

"That's the attitude!" Tom Lewis grinned. "Nothing leavens life like a little good-natured hatred." He wrinkled his nose and sniffed. "Man alive!—do you dig that spaghetti sauce?"

"I smell it," Alan said. "And if you go on eating that stuff at lunchtime just because we work near it, you'll be a fat pig in two years."

"It's part of my plan to stop just short of that," Tom announced. "What I really want is oversize jowls and three chins, like lawyers in the movies. It'll impress clients no end."

The outer door opened without benefit of knocking and a cigar came in, followed by a sharp-chinned stocky man, wearing a suede windbreaker and battered fedora, tilted back. He carried a camera, with a leather satchel over one shoulder. Speaking around the cigar he asked, "Whicha you guys is Maitland?"

"I am," Alan said.

"Wanta pitcher, gotta rushit, needit fora final." The photographer began putting his equipment together. "Backup againsta law books, Maitland."

"Pardon me for asking," Tom inquired. "But what the hell *is* this?"

"Oh yes," Alan said. "I was about to tell you. I spilled the beans, and I guess you could call it Plan Three."

5

Captain Jaabeck was sitting down to lunch when Alan Maitland was shown into the master's cabin aboard the *Vastervik*. As on the previous occasion, the cabin was orderly and comfortable, its mahogany paneling polished and brasswork gleaming. A small square table had been moved out from one wall, and on a white linen cloth with gleaming silverware a place was set for one, at which Captain Jaabeck was serving himself from a large open dish of what appeared to be shredded green vegetables. As Alan came in he put down the servers and stood up courteously. Today he was wearing a brown serge suit but still the old-fashioned carpet slippers.

"I beg your pardon," Alan said. "I didn't know you were at lunch."

"Please, I do not mind, Mr. Maitland." Captain Jaabeck gestured Alan to a green leather armchair and resumed his own seat at the table. "If you have not yourself had lunch . . ."

"I did, thank you." Alan had declined Tom Lewis's suggestion of midday spaghetti, settling instead for a hastily consumed sandwich and milk en route to the ship.

"It is perhaps as well." The captain gestured to the central dish. "A young man such as you might find a vegetarian meal unsatisfying."

Surprised, Alan said, "You're a vegetarian, Captain?"

"For many years. Some think it a . . ." He stopped. "What is the English word?"

"A fad," Alan said, then wished he had spoken less quickly.

Captain Jaabeck smiled. "That is what is sometimes said. But untruly. You do not mind, if I continue . . ."

"Oh, yes, please do."

The captain munched several forkfuls of the mixture steadily. Then, pausing, "The vegetarian belief, I expect you know, Mr. Maitland, is older than Christianity."

"No," Alan said, "I didn't."

The captain nodded. "By many centuries. The true follower holds that life is sacred. Therefore all living creatures should have the right to enjoy it without fear."

"Do you believe that yourself?"

"Yes, Mr. Maitland, I do." The captain helped himself once more. He appeared to consider. "The entire matter, you see, is very simple. Mankind will never live in peace until we overcome the savagery existing within us all. It is this savagery which causes us to kill other creatures, which we eat, and the same savage instinct propels us into quarrels, wars, and perhaps, in the end, our own destruction."

"It's an interesting theory," Alan said. He found himself being constantly surprised by this Norwegian shipmaster. He began to see why Henri Duval had received more kindness aboard the *Vastervik* than anywhere else.

"As you say, a theory." The captain selected a date from several on a side plate. "But, alas, it holds a flaw like all theories."

Alan asked curiously, "What kind of a flaw?"

"It is a fact, scientists now inform us, that plant life, too, has a form of understanding and feeling." Captain Jaabeck chewed on the date, then wiped his fingers and mouth fastidiously with a linen napkin. "A machine exists, I am told, Mr. Maitland, so sensitive it can hear the death screams of a peach when plucked and skinned. Thus, in the end, perhaps, the vegetarian achieves nothing, being as cruel to the defenseless cabbage as the meat eater to the cow and pig." The captain smiled, and Alan wondered if his leg were being gently pulled.

More briskly the captain said, "Now, Mr. Maitland, what can we do?"

"There are one or two points I'd like to talk over," Alan told him. "But I wonder if my client could be present."

"Certainly." Captain Jaabeck crossed the cabin to a wall telephone, depressed a button, and spoke briskly. Returning, he said dryly, "I am told that your client is helping to scour our bilges. But he will come."

A few minutes later there was a hesitant knock and Henri Duval entered. He was in grease-stained coveralls and a strong odor of fuel oil clung to him. There were black grease marks on his face, extending into his hair, which was matted and disordered. He stood diffidently, youthful, both hands clasped around a knitted woolen cap.

"Good day, Henri," Alan said.

The young stowaway smiled uncertainly. He glanced self-consciously at his filthy clothing.

"Do not be nervous," the captain instructed him, "nor ashamed of the signs of honest work." He added, for Alan's benefit, "Sometimes, I fear, advantage is taken of Henri's good nature by giving him tasks which others do not choose. But he does them willingly and well."

At the words, the subject of them grinned broadly. "First I clean ship," he announced. "Then Henri Duval. Both most dirty."

Alan laughed.

The captain smiled somberly. "What is said of my ship is, alas, true. There is so little money spent, so small a crew. But as for our young friend, I would not wish his lifetime to be used in cleaning it. Perhaps you have some news, Mr. Maitland."

"Not news exactly," Alan replied. "Except that the Im-

migration Department has refused to grant an official hearing
of Henri's case."

"Ach!" Captain Jaabeck raised his hands impatiently.
"Then, once more, there is nothing can be done." Henri
Duval's eyes, which had brightened, dimmed.

"I wouldn't say that entirely," Alan said. "In fact there's
one point I want to discuss with you, Captain, and it's why
I wished my client to be present."

"Yes?"

Alan was aware of the eyes of the other two intently upon
him. He considered carefully the words he must use next.
There was a question to be put and a specific answer he
hoped to get. The right answer from Captain Jaabeck would
open the way to what Tom Lewis had called Plan Two. But
the words and response must be the captain's own.

"When I was here previously," Alan said carefully, "I
asked if, as master of this ship, you would take Henri Duval
to Immigration headquarters and demand a hearing into his
application to land. Your answer at that time was no, and
the reasons given"—Alan consulted a note he had made—
"were that you were too busy and you thought it would do
no good."

"It is true," the captain said. "I remember talking of that."

As he spoke, Duval's eyes turned inquiringly from one to
the other.

"I'm going to ask you again, Captain," Alan said quietly,
"if you will take my client Henri Duval from this ship to the
Immigration Department and there demand a formal hearing."

Alan held his breath. What he wanted was the same answer once more. If the captain again said no, even casually
and for whatever reason, then technically it would mean
Duval was being kept a prisoner aboard ship . . . a ship in
Canadian waters, subject to Canadian law. And just conceivably—based on Alan's own affidavit to that effect—a
judge might grant a writ of habeas corpus . . . a direction to
bring the prisoner to court. It was a hairsbreadth point of
law . . . the long shot he and Tom had talked of. But its
launching depended on obtaining the right answer now,
so that the affidavit could be truly sworn.

The captain appeared puzzled. "But surely you have just
told me that Immigration has said no."

Alan made no response. Instead he eyed the captain

steadily. He was tempted to explain, to ask for the words he wanted. But to do so would be a breach of legal ethics. True, it was a fine distinction, but it was there and Alan was acutely aware of it. He could only hope that the other's astute mind . . .

"Well . . ." Captain Jaabeck hesitated. "Perhaps you are right, and everything should be attempted once. Perhaps, after all, I must find time . . ."

It was going wrong. This was not what he wanted. The captain's reasonableness was effectively sealing off the only legal opening . . . a door, slightly ajar, was closing. Alan tightened his lips, revealing disappointment in his face.

"It is not what you wished? And yet you asked." Again puzzlement in the captain's voice.

Alan faced him squarely. He said, with deliberate formality, "Captain Jaabeck, my request remains. But I must advise you that if you disregard it I reserve the right, in my client's interest, to continue with whatever legal steps may then be necessary."

A slow smile spread over the captain's face. "Yes," he said. "Now I understand. You must do things by certain means because that is the law's way."

"And my request, Captain?"

Captain Jaabeck shook his head. He said solemnly, "I regret I cannot comply. There is much business for the ship to be done in port, and I have no time to waste on worthless stowaways."

Until now Henri Duval's brow had been furrowed in concentration, although obviously he had understood very little of what was being said. But with the captain's last remark his expression became suddenly surprised and hurt. It was almost, Alan thought, as if a child, abruptly and inexplicably, had been disowned by a parent. Once more he was tempted to explain but decided he had already gone far enough. Holding out his hand, he told Henri Duval, "I'm doing everything I can. I'll come to see you again soon."

"You may go." The captain addressed the young stowaway sternly. "Back to the bilges!—and do your work well."

Unhappily, eyes downcast, Duval went out.

"You see," Captain Jaabeck said quietly, "I am a cruel man too." He took out his pipe and began to fill it. "I do not understand exactly what it is you require, Mr. Maitland. But I trust there is nothing I have missed."

"No, Captain." Alan was smiling. "To tell you the truth, I don't think there's much you miss at all."

6

Near the end of the dock a white MG convertible was parked, its top raised. As Alan Maitland approached from the *Vastervik*, his collar turned up against the cold damp wind coming off the water, Sharon Deveraux opened the driver's door.

"Hullo," she said. "I called at your office and Mr. Lewis said to come here and wait."

"Sometimes," Alan responded cheerfully, "old Tom shows real horse sense."

Sharon smiled, the dimple appearing. She was hatless, with a pale beige coat and gloves to match. "Get in," she instructed, "and I'll drive you wherever."

He went around the other side and eased his length gingerly into the tiny two-seater. On the second attempt he made it. "Not bad," Sharon said approvingly. "Granddaddy tried it once, but we never got his second leg in."

"I," Alan said, "am not only younger, but also more flexible than Granddaddy."

In three swift movements Sharon turned the car around and they moved off, jolting rapidly over the dockside road. The MG's interior was small and snug. Their shoulders touched and he was conscious of the same perfume he had noticed last time they met.

"About being flexible," Sharon said, "the other day I was beginning to wonder. Where to?"

"Back to the office, I guess. There's some swearing I have to do."

"Why not here? I know most of the words."

He grinned. "Let's not go through the dumb-brunette routine. I know better."

She turned her head. Her lips were red, full, and slightly parted in a humorous bow. He was conscious again of the petite elfin quality.

"All right, so it's some sort of legal thing." She returned her eyes to the road. They took a corner sharply and he was jolted against her. The contact was pleasant.

"It's an affidavit," he told her.

"If it doesn't offend your stuffy old rules to tell me,"

Sharon said, "how is it all going? The man on the ship, I mean."

"I'm not sure yet," Alan said seriously. "The Immigration people turned us down, but we expected that."

"And then?"

"Something happened today . . . just now. It might turn out that there's a chance—just a remote one—we can get the case into court."

"Would that help?"

"It might not, of course." Sharon's question was one he had already asked himself. But with this kind of problem you could take only one step at a time and hope for the best after that.

"Why do you want to go into court if it might not help?" They swung through traffic, accelerating to beat a light already changed to amber. In the intersecting street, brakes squealed. "Did you see that bus?" Sharon said. "I thought it was going to hit us." They made a sharp turn, left then right, around a halted milk truck, barely missing its driver. "You were talking about getting into court."

"There are different ways," Alan said, swallowing, "and different kinds of courts. Could we go a little slower?"

Obligingly Sharon slowed from forty to thirty-five. "Tell me about the court."

"You can never know in advance just what's going to come out in evidence," Alan said. "Sometimes there are things you'd never get to hear of otherwise. Points of law, too. And in this case there's another reason."

"Go on," Sharon urged. "It's exciting." Their speed, Alan noticed, had crept up again to forty.

"Well," he explained, "whatever we do, we've nothing to lose. And the longer we keep things stirred up, the better chance there is that the Government will change its mind and give Henri the chance to be an immigrant."

"I don't know if Granddaddy would like that," Sharon said thoughtfully. "He hopes to make it a big political issue, and if the Government gave in there wouldn't be anything left to argue about."

"Frankly," Alan said, "I don't give a damn what Granddaddy wants. I'm more interested in what I can do for Henri."

There was a silence. Then Sharon said, "You called him by his first name—twice. Do you like him?"

"Yes, I do," Alan said. He found he was speaking with conviction. "He's a nice little guy who's had it rough all his life. I don't think he'll ever be president of anything, or amount to very much, but I'd like to see him get a decent break. If he does, it'll be the first he's ever had."

Sharon glanced sideways at Alan's profile then returned her eyes to the road. After a moment she asked, "Do you know something?"

"No. Tell me."

"If I were ever in trouble," she said, "you're the one, Alan, I'd like to have help me."

"We're in trouble now," he said. "Will you let me drive?"

Their tires squealed. The MG slid to a halt. "Why?" Sharon asked innocently. "We're here."

The mixed odor of pizza and spaghetti sauce was unmistakable.

Within the office Tom Lewis was reading the Mainland edition of the Vancouver *Post*. He put down the paper as they came in. "The Law Society will disbar you, of course," he announced. "After a public unfrocking, no doubt, in Stanley Park. You *did* know the rules about advertising?"

"Let me see," Alan said. He took the paper. "I just said what I thought. At the time I was a bit peeved."

"That," Tom said, "comes through with remarkable clarity."

"My God!" Alan had the front page spread out, Sharon beside him. "I didn't think it would be like this."

"It's been on the radio, too," Tom informed him.

"But I thought it would be mostly Duval . . ."

"To be perfectly honest," Tom said, "I am bright chartreuse with envy. Somehow, without even trying, you seem to have corralled the outstanding case, a hero's publicity, and now, it seems . . ."

"Oh, I forgot," Alan interjected. "This is Sharon Deveraux."

"I know," Tom said. "I was just getting to her."

Sharon's eyes sparkled with amusement. "After all, Mr. Lewis, you *are* mentioned in the newspaper. It says quite distinctly Lewis and Maitland."

"For that crumb, I shall be eternally grateful." Tom put on his coat. "Oh, by the way, I'm off to see a new client. He has a fish store and, I gather, a problem about his lease. Unfortunately he has no one to mind the store so I must go to the fish. You wouldn't like a nice cod cutlet for supper?"

"Not tonight, thanks." Alan shook his head. "I'm planning to take Sharon out."

"Yes," Tom said. "I somehow thought you would."

When they were alone, "I'll have to work on the affidavit," Alan observed. "It has to be ready, so I can appear before a judge tomorrow."

"Could I help?" Sharon asked. She smiled at him, the dimple coming and going. "I can type too."

"Come with me," Alan said. He took her by the hand into his glass-paneled cubicle.

Nine General Adrian Nesbitson

The entire Cabinet, with the exception of three ministers who were away from Ottawa, had come to Uplands Airport to witness the departure of the Prime Minister's party for Washington. This was not unusual. Early in his regime James Howden had allowed it to be known that he liked to be seen off and met, not merely by one or two of his ministers, but by the entire group. And this applied, not just on special occasions, but to all his journeys in and out of the capital.

Among cabinet members the process had become known familiarly as "the line-up." Occasionally there was mild grumbling and, once, word of it had reached James Howden's ears. But his own attitude—defined to Brian Richardson, who had reported the complaints—was that the occasions were a demonstration of party and Government solidarity, and the party director agreed. Not mentioned by the Prime Minister was a boyhood memory he sometimes even now recalled.

Long ago, young James Howden had journeyed from his orphanage school to Edmonton, three hundred and fifty miles distant, where he was to write examinations for entry to the University of Alberta. He had been provided with a return train ticket and set off alone. Three days later, brimming with a success he desperately needed to share, he had returned—to an empty railway station, with no one to meet him. In the end, carrying his cardboard suitcase, he had had to walk to the orphanage three miles out of town, his first flush of excitement evaporating along the way. Ever after, he had shrunk from beginning or ending a journey alone.

There would be no aloneness today. Others, in addition to the Cabinet, had come to the airport, and from the rear seat of the chauffeur-driven Oldsmobile, with Margaret beside him, James Howden observed the chiefs of staff—Army, Navy, and Air Force, in uniform, with aides—as well as the Mayor of Ottawa, the R.C.M.P. Commissioner, several chairmen of Government boards, and discreetly in rear, His Excellency Phillip B. Angrove, U.S. Ambassador. In a separate group were the inevitable cluster of reporters and photographers and, with them, Brian Richardson and Milly Freedeman.

"Good heavens!" Margaret whispered. "You'd think we were going to China as missionaries."

"I know," he answered. "It's a nuisance, but people seem to expect this sort of thing."

"Don't be silly," Margaret said softly. Her hand touched his. "You love it all, and there's no reason you shouldn't."

The limousine swung in a wide arc across the airport ramp, halting smoothly near the V.I.P. *Vanguard*, its fuselage gleaming in the morning sunshine, the R.C.A.F. crew drawn up at attention alongside. An R.C.M.P. constable opened the car door and Margaret alighted, James Howden following. The military and police snapped to salutes and the Prime Minister raised the new pearl-gray Homburg which Margaret had brought him back from her shopping trip in Montreal. There was an air of expectancy among those waiting, he thought; or perhaps it was the sharp, cold wind sweeping across the airport runways which made faces seem tense. He wondered about secrecy—whether it had been preserved, or if there had been leakage, with hints of the true importance of today's journey.

Stuart Cawston stepped forward, beaming. Smiling Stu, as the senior member of Cabinet, would be Acting Prime Minister in Howden's absence. "Greetings, sir—and Margaret," the Finance Minister said. Then, as they shook hands, "We are, as you see, a sizable cheering section."

"Where are the massed bands?" Margaret asked irreverently. "It seems the only thing missing."

"It's supposed to be a secret," Cawston answered lightly, "but we flew them ahead to Washington disguised as U.S. Marines. So if you see any, assume they're ours." He touched the Prime Minister's arm. His face becoming serious, he asked, "Is there any further word—proof or disproof?"

James Howden shook his head. There was no need for explanations; the question was one which the world had been asking ever since, forty-eight hours earlier, Moscow had trumpeted the destruction of a U.S. nuclear submarine, the *Defiant*, in the East Siberian Sea. According to the Russian claim—which Washington had since denied—the submarine had encroached on Soviet territorial waters. The incident had brought to an apparent peak mounting world tensions of the past several weeks.

"There can't possibly be any proof, not now," Howden said softly. The welcoming group waited as he spoke earnestly to Cawston. "I believe it's a calculated act of provocation and we should resist any temptation to retaliate. I intend to urge that on the White House because we still need time—as much as we can get."

"I agree," Cawston said quietly.

"I've ruled against any statement or protest ourselves," the Prime Minister said, "and you must understand there's to be none unless Arthur and I decide in Washington, and in that case it'll be from there. Is that clear?"

"Quite clear," Cawston said. "Frankly I'm glad it's you and Arthur, and not me."

They returned to the waiting group and James Howden began to shake hands. At the same time the other three cabinet members who would accompany him on the flight—Arthur Lexington, Adrian Nesbitson, and Styles Bracken of Trade and Commerce—fell in behind.

Adrian Nesbitson looked a good deal healthier, Howden thought, than the last time they had met. The old warrior, pink cheeked and tightly cocooned in woolen scarf, fur hat, and heavy overcoat, had a touch of his parade-ground manner and was obviously enjoying the occasion, as he did all ceremonial. They must talk during the flight, Howden realized; there had been no opportunity since the Defense Committee meeting and it was essential, somehow, to bring the old man into line. Even though Nesbitson would not participate directly in the Presidential talks, there must be no apparent dissension within the Canadian group.

Behind Nesbitson, Arthur Lexington wore the casual air becoming an External Affairs Minister to whom travel anywhere in the world was routine business. Seemingly unbothered by the cold, he had on a soft felt hat and light topcoat, his customary bow tie visible beneath. Bracken, the Trade and Commerce Minister, a wealthy westerner who had joined the Cabinet only a few months earlier, was being taken along for appearance's sake, since trade was supposed to be a main topic in the Washington talks.

Harvey Warrender was in the cabinet line-up. "A profitable journey." His manner was carefully correct, containing no hint of their previous clash. He added, "And you too, Margaret."

"Thank you," the Prime Minister answered. His response was notably less courteous than to the others.

Unexpectedly Margaret said, "Haven't you a Latin tag for us, Harvey?"

Warrender's eyes flickered between the two. "Sometimes I have the impression your husband dislikes my little gambits."

"Never mind that," Margaret said. "I think it's rather fun."

The Immigration Minister smiled slightly. "In that case, may it be true: *vectatio, interque, et mutata regio vigorem dant.*"

"I dig the *vigorem* bit," Stuart Cawston said. "What's the rest, Harvey?"

"An observation of Seneca," Warrender responded. "Voyage, travel, and a change of place impart vigor."

"I'm quite vigorous, with or without travel," James Howden declared curtly. The exchange had annoyed him and he took Margaret's arm firmly, steering her towards the U.S. Ambassador who moved forward, doffing his hat. As if instinctively the others held back.

"Angry, this is an unexpected pleasure," Howden said.

"On the contrary, Prime Minister—my privilege and honor." The ambassador bowed slightly to Margaret. Phillip Angrove, a grizzled career diplomat with friends in many countries of the world, had a way of making protocol courtesies seem personally meant, as perhaps, at times, they were. We tend too much, Howden thought, to discount everything that is said politely as surface dressing only. He noticed the ambassador was stooped at the shoulders rather more than usual.

Margaret had observed too. "I hope your arthritis hasn't bothered you again, Mr. Angrove."

"It has, I'm afraid." A rueful smile. "The Canadian winter

has many delights, Mrs. Howden, but also penalties for us arthritics."

"For heaven's sake don't be polite about our winter!" Margaret exclaimed. "My husband and I were born here and still dislike it."

"I hope not entirely." The ambassador spoke quietly, his seamed face meditative. "I have often considered, Mrs. Howden, that Canadians have much to thank their climate for: stalwart character and hardihood, but with great warmth seldom far away."

"If true, it's another reason we've so much in common." James Howden offered his hand. "You'll be joining us in Washington, I understand."

The ambassador nodded assent. "My own flight leaves a few minutes after yours." As their hands clasped, "A safe journey, sir, and a return with honor."

As Howden and Margaret turned away, toward the waiting aircraft, the press group closed in. There were a dozen reporters from the parliamentary press gallery and wire services, along with a self-important TV interviewer and accompanying film crew. Brian Richardson had stationed himself where he could hear and be seen by Howden, and the Prime Minister gave a grin and friendly nod, to which Richardson responded. The two of them had already discussed press arrangements for the trip and agreed that the principal official statement—though still not revealing the major issues involved—should be made on arrival in Washington. All the same, Howden knew he must provide something for use by the Ottawa press corps. He spoke briefly, employing some of the regular platitudes concerning Canada-U.S. relations. He then awaited questions.

The first was from the TV interviewer. "There have been rumors, Mr. Prime Minister, that this trip of yours may involve more than just trade talks."

"Well, that's true," Howden said with apparent seriousness. "If there's time the President and I may play a little handball." There was a ripple of laughter; he had touched the right note, being good-natured without scoring off the interviewer.

"But besides the sporting side, sir"—the TV man smiled dutifully, exposing a double moon of faultless white teeth— "hasn't there been some talk of major military decisions being taken at this time?"

So there had been leakage, after all, though obviously just in a general way. It was not surprising really, Howden thought; he had once heard someone say that when a secret went beyond a single person it was a secret no longer. All the same it was a reminder that vital information could not be stoppered up too long, and after Washington he must act quickly if he hoped to control release of the major news himself.

Now he answered, speaking carefully and remembering that what he said could be quoted later on, "Naturally the subject of our joint defense will be discussed in Washington, as it always is on these occasions, along with other subjects of mutual concern. But as to decisions, any decisions will, of course, be taken in Ottawa with the full knowledge of Parliament and, if necessary, parliamentary approval."

There was a small outburst of hand clapping from spectators.

"Can you say, Mr. Howden," the TV interviewer asked, "whether the recent submarine incident will be discussed and, if so, what the Canadian attitude will be?"

"I am quite sure it will be discussed," Howden answered, his long, beaked face serious, "and naturally we share the deep United States concern at the tragic loss of the *Defiant* and its crew. But beyond that, at present, I have no further statement to make."

"In that case, sir . . ." the TV man began, but another reporter cut in impatiently, "Do you mind if someone else has a turn, chum? Newspapers haven't been abolished yet, you know."

There was a murmur of assent from others in the press group and James Howden smiled inwardly. He saw the TV interviewer flush, then nod to the camera crew. That particular portion of film, the Prime Minister guessed, would be edited out later.

The interrupter, a brisk, middle-aged journalist named George Haskins who worked for the Winnipeg *Free Press*, now proclaimed, "Mr. Prime Minister, I'd like to ask a question, not about Washington, but about the Government's stand on this man-without-a-country issue."

James Howden frowned. Puzzled, he asked, "How's that again, George?"

"I'm talking about this young fellow Henri Duval, sir—the one in Vancouver that the Immigration Department won't let in. Can you tell us why the Government is taking the stand it is?"

Howden caught Brian Richardson's eye and the party director shoved forward to the front. "Gentlemen," Richardson said, "surely this is not the time . . ."

"Like hell it isn't, Brian!" the reporter Haskins flared. "It's the hottest news story in the country, that's all." Someone else added grumblingly, "What with TV and public relations you can't hardly ask questions any more."

Good-humoredly James Howden interposed, "I'll answer any question that I can. I always have, haven't I?"

Haskins said, "Yes, sir, you sure have. It's just other people who try to do the blocking." He glared accusingly at Brian Richardson, who stared back, his face impassive.

"My only doubt—" the Prime Minister said, "and obviously Mr. Richardson's—is whether the subject matter is appropriate at this particular time." He hoped he could lead the questioning away; if not, he supposed he would have to make the best of it. Sometimes he thought, there must be advantages in having a press secretary—as the U.S. President did—who could handle this kind of thing. But he had always avoided appointing one for fear of becoming too remote.

Tomkins of the Toronto *Star*, a mild, scholarly Englishman who was greatly respected in the capital, said courteously, "The fact is, sir, most of us here have had telegrams from our editors asking for a quote from you about this man Duval. A lot of people, it seems, are interested in what's going to happen to him."

"I see." There was to be no avoidance of the subject then. Even a Prime Minister, if he were wise, could not bypass that kind of appeal. It was infuriating, however, to realize that some of the attention to his own Washington journey might be taken away as a result. Howden considered carefully. He could see Harvey Warrender edging nearer but ignored him, remembering angrily the other's obstinate stupidity which had caused this to happen. He caught Richardson's eye. The party director's expression seemed to say: "I warned you there could be trouble if we didn't keep Warrender in line." Or perhaps by now Richardson had guessed there was an additional factor involved; he was shrewd enough for that. But either way, with Harvey Warrender's threat still poised like a guillotine, James Howden himself would have to deal with the situation as competently as he could. One thing was certain, he reasoned: the incident, while briefly embarrassing, was the type of thing which would undoubtedly blow over in a few days and be forgotten. He noticed the TV film camera was in action again; perhaps, after all, this was a good time to explain the official position forcefully and thereby silence criticism.

"All right, gentlemen," the Prime Minister declared briskly, "here is what I have to say." In front of him pencils poised, then scribbled as he began.

"It has been pointed out to me that there has been considerable newspaper coverage concerning the individual whose name Mr. Haskins mentioned a moment ago. Some of the reports, I must say quite frankly, have been of a somewhat sensational nature, tending to ignore certain facts— facts which the Government, because of its responsibilities, cannot ignore."

"Will you tell us what these are, sir?" This time, the Montreal *Gazette*.

"If you'll be patient I'm coming to that." Howden's voice held a touch of sharpness. He disliked interruptions and it did no harm occasionally to remind these men that they were not interviewing some junior minister. "I was about to remark that there are many individual cases receiving no publicity but which, nevertheless, come regularly before the Department of Citizenship and Immigration. And dealing with such cases, fairly and humanely, yet on the basis of law, is not a new experience either for this Government or its Immigration officers."

The Ottawa *Journal* asked, "Isn't this case a little different, Mr. Prime Minister? I mean, the man having no country and all that."

James Howden said soberly, "When you are dealing with human beings, Mr. Chase, every case is different. That is why—to provide a measure of fairness and consistency— we have an Immigration Act, approved by Parliament and the Canadian people. The Government, as it must by law, operates within the framework of that act and, in the instance we are speaking of, this is exactly what has been done." He paused, waiting for the note takers to catch up with his words, then continued. "I have, of course, none of the details immediately before me. But I have been assured that the application of the young man in question has been considered carefully on its merits and that he is in no way admissible to Canada under the Immigration Act."

A young reporter, whom Howden failed to recognize, asked, "Wouldn't you say, sir, there are times when human considerations are more important than technicalities?"

Howden smiled. "If you are asking me a rhetorical question, my answer is that human considerations are always important, and this Government has frequently demonstrated its awareness of them. But if your question is specifically about the case we are speaking of, let me repeat that human factors *have* been taken into account as far as is possible. However, I must remind you again that the Government is bound—as it must, and should be—by what it can accomplish legally."

The wind blew bitingly and James Howden felt Margaret shiver beside him. This was enough, he decided; the next question would be the last. It came from the mild-mannered Tomkins who began, almost apologetically, "The Leader of the Opposition made a statement earlier this morning, sir." The reporter shuffled copy paper, consulting his notes, then went on, "Mr. Deitz said, 'The Government should resolve the case of Henri Duval on broad human principles, rather than stubborn adherence to the letter of the law. The Minister of Citizenship and Immigration has power, if he chooses to use it, to enact an order in council permitting this tragically unfortunate young man to enter Canada as an immigrant.'"

"The Minister has no such power," James Howden snapped. "The power is vested in the Crown in the person of the Governor General. Mr. Bonar Deitz is equally aware of that as anyone else."

There was a moment's silence, then with bland innocence the reporter asked, "But doesn't the Governor General always do exactly what you yourself recommend, sir, including waiving the Immigration Act, which has happened quite a few times, I believe?" For all his seeming mildness, Tomkins had one of the sharpest minds in the Ottawa press corps, and Howden realized he had walked into a verbal trap.

"I have always understood that the Opposition object to government by order in council," he said sharply. But it was a weak answer and he knew it. He caught sight of Brian Richardson's face suffused with anger—and with good reason, Howden thought. Not only had the focus of attention shifted from the important Washington mission to this trivial affair, but he himself had not come out of the questioning well.

He decided to recover as best he could, "I am sorry to learn from the reference to Mr. Deitz that the matter we are speaking of could become an issue, perhaps, between political parties. My own conviction is that it should not." He paused for effect, then continued earnestly, "As I indicated earlier, there are no grounds for admitting this man Duval to Canada under our present laws and, from what I am told, many other countries have taken a similar stand. Nor do I see any obligation upon Canada to take such action when other countries will not. As to the facts, both known and alleged, let me assure you again that these have been examined thoroughly by the Department of Citizenship and Immigration before a decision was reached. And now, gentlemen, if you please, that is all."

He had been tempted to add something about newspapers maintaining a sense of news proportion, but decided not; the press, while every brother's keeper, could be savagely resentful when criticized itself. Instead, smiling outwardly but seething with inner fury at Harvey Warrender, the Prime Minister took Margaret's arm and walked toward the waiting aircraft. Applause and cheers from his supporters followed them.

2

The V.I.P. turbo-prop *Vanguard*, maintained by the Government for official flights, was partitioned into three compartments—a conventional section forward for non-ministerial staff who had been boarded before the Prime Minister's arrival; a more comfortable center cabin, now occupied by the three ministers and several deputies; and, aft, a comfortably upholstered drawing room, decorated in pastel shades of blue, with a cozily compact bedroom adjoining.

The rearmost suite, which had been designed originally for use by the Queen and her husband on state visits, was to be used now by the Prime Minister and Margaret. The steward, an R.C.A.F. flight sergeant, helped strap them into two of the deep soft seats, then discreetly disappeared. Outside, the deep, muted throb of the four Rolls Royce motors increased in tempo as they began to taxi toward the airport perimeter.

When the steward had gone James Howden said sharply, "Was it really necessary to encourage Warrender in that absurd conceit of his about Latin doggerel?"

Margaret answered calmly, "Not really, I suppose. But if you must know, I thought you were being extremely rude and I wanted to make amends."

"Goddammit Margaret!" His voice rose. "I had good reason to be rude with Harvey Warrender."

His wife removed her hat carefully and placed it on a small table beside her seat. The hat was a wispy affair of black velvet and net which she had bought in Montreal. She said levelly, "Kindly don't snap at me, Jamie. You may have had reason, but I didn't, and I've said before I'm not a carbon copy of your moods."

"That isn't the point at all . . ."

"Yes, it is the point!" Now there was a flush of red in Margaret's cheeks. She was always slow to anger, which was the reason their quarrels were comparatively rare. "Judging by the way you behaved with the reporters just now, I'd say that Harvey Warrender isn't the only one to be accused of vanity."

He asked abruptly, "What do you mean?"

"You were angry with that Mr. Tomkins just because he wasn't silly enough to be taken in by all your pompous nonsense about fairness and humanity. If you want to know, I wasn't either."

He expostulated, "Surely, at least here, I'm entitled to some loyalty."

"Oh, don't be ridiculous," Margaret flared. "And for goodness' sake stop talking to me as if I were a political meeting. I'm your wife, remember?—I've seen you undressed. It's perfectly obvious what's happened. Harvey Warrender has put you in a difficult position . . ."

He interjected, "It's an impossible position."

"Very well, impossible. And for some reason you feel you must back him up, but because you don't like it you're taking your bad temper out on everyone else, including me." Unusually, with the last words there was a catch in Margaret's voice.

There was a silence between them. Outside the engines' tempo increased for take-off; the runway slid by and they were airborne, climbing. He reached for Margaret's hand. "You were quite right. I *was* being bad-tempered."

This was the way most of their arguments ended, even the serious ones, and there had been a few in their married life. Invariably one of them saw the other's point of view and then conceded. James Howden wondered if there really were married couples who lived together without quarreling. If so, he thought, they must be dull and spiritless people.

Margaret's head was averted but she returned the pressure of his hand.

After a while he said, "It isn't important about Warrender —not to us, I mean. It's hampering in some ways, that's all. But things will work out."

"I expect I was being a bit silly too. Perhaps because I haven't seen much of you lately." Margaret had taken a tiny square of cambric from her bag and delicately touched the corners of both eyes. She went on slowly, "Sometimes I get a terrible feeling of jealousy about politics, a sort of help-lessness in a way. I think I'd prefer it if you had another woman hidden somewhere. At least I'd know how to compete."

"You don't have to compete," he said. "You never did." For an instant he had a pang of guilt, remembering Milly Freedeman.

Abruptly Margaret said, "If Harvey Warrender is so difficult, why give him the Immigration Department? Couldn't you put him somewhere where he'd be harmless—like Fisheries?"

James Howden sighed. "Unfortunately Harvey wants to be Immigration Minister and he still has influence enough to make his wishes count." He wondered if Margaret really believed the second statement, but she gave no sign of questioning.

The *Vanguard* was turning south on to course, still climbing, but less steeply now. The midmorning sun shone brightly through the port side windows and, to the right, visible from both seats, Ottawa lay spread like a miniature city three thousand feet below. The Ottawa River was a slash of silver between snow-clad banks. To the west, near the narrows of Chaudière Falls, faint white streamers pointed like fingers to the Supreme Court and Parliament, dwarfed and puny from above.

The capital slid out of sight below, leaving flat open country ahead. In ten minutes or so they would cross the St. Lawrence and be over New York State. A guided missile, Howden thought, would cover the same ground, not in minutes but seconds.

Turning from the window Margaret asked, "Do you think

that people outside have any idea of all the things that go on in government? The political deals, favors for favors, and all the rest."

Momentarily James Howden was startled. Not for the first time he had the feeling that Margaret had dipped into his thoughts. Then he answered, "Some do, of course—those close to the inside. But I imagine that most of the people don't really, or at least don't want to know. And there are others who wouldn't believe it if you produced documented proof and swore out affidavits."

Reflectively Margaret said, "We're always so quick to criticize American politics."

"I know," he agreed. "It's quite illogical, of course, because in proportion we have as much patronage and graft as the Americans, perhaps even more. It's just that most times we're a good deal more discreet and every now and then we offer up a public sacrifice of somebody who became too greedy."

The seat-belt sign above their heads had gone out. James Howden unsnapped his own belt and reached across to help Margaret release hers. "Of course, my dear," he said, "You must realize that one of our greatest national assets is our sense of self-righteousness. It's something we inherited from the British. You remember Shaw?—'There is nothing so bad or so good that you will not find Englishmen doing it; but you will never find an Englishman in the wrong.' That kind of conviction helps the national conscience quite a lot."

"Sometimes," Margaret said, "you sound positively gleeful about the things which are wrong."

Her husband paused, considering. "I don't mean it to seem that way. It's just that when we're alone I try to drop pretenses." He smiled faintly. "There aren't many places left nowadays where I'm not on show."

"I'm sorry." There was concern in Margaret's voice. "I shouldn't have said that."

"No! I wouldn't want either of us to feel there was something we couldn't say to each other, no matter what it was." Fleetingly he thought of Harvey Warrender and the deal between them. Why had he never told Margaret? Perhaps he would someday. Now he continued, "A good deal of what I know about politics saddens me. It always has. But then I get to thinking of our mortality and human weakness, remembering there has never been power with purity—anywhere. If you want to be pure, you must stand alone. If you seek to do positive things, achieve something, leave the world a mite better than you found it, then you must choose power and throw some of your purity away. There's no other choice." He went on thoughtfully, "It's as if we're all together in a strong-flowing river; and though you'd like to, you can't change its course suddenly. You can only go along, and try to ease it slowly in one direction or the other."

A white intercom telephone near the Prime Minister's seat *pinged* musically and he answered it. The aircraft captain's voice announced, "This is Galbraith, sir."

"Yes, Wing Commander?" Galbraith, a veteran pilot with a reputation for solidity, was usually in command on V.I.P. missions out of Ottawa. He had flown the Howdens many times before.

"We're at cruising height, twenty thousand, and estimating Washington in one hour ten minutes. Weather there is sunny and clear, temperature sixty-five."

"That's good news," Howden said. "It'll be a taste of summer." He told Margaret about the Washington weather, then said into the phone, "I understand there'll be a luncheon at the embassy tomorrow, Wing Commander. We shall expect to see you."

"Thank you, sir."

James Howden replaced the telephone. While he had been speaking the R.C.A.F. steward had reappeared, this time with coffee trays and sandwiches. There was also a single glass of grape juice. Margaret pointed to it. "If you really like that so much, I'll order some at home."

He waited until the steward had gone, then lowered his voice. "I'm beginning to loathe the stuff. I once said I liked it and word seems to have passed around. Now I understand why Disraeli hated primroses."

"But I always thought he loved primroses," Margaret said. "Weren't they his favorite flower?"

Her husband shook his head emphatically. "Disraeli said so just on one occasion, out of politeness to Queen Victoria, who had sent him some. But afterwards, people showered primroses on him until the mere sight of one could drive him to distraction. So you see, political myths die hard." Smiling, he took the grape juice, opened a door of the rear of the cabin and poured it down the toilet.

Margaret said thoughtfully, "You know, I sometimes think

you're rather like Disraeli, though a little fiercer perhaps."
She smiled. "At least you have the nose for it."

"Yes," he agreed, "and this old craggy face of mine has
been a trade mark." He fondled his eagle-beak nose, then
said reminiscently, "It used to surprise me when people said I
appeared fierce, but after a while, when I learned to switch
it on and off, it became quite useful."

"This is nice," Margaret said, "being by ourselves for a
while. How long do we have before Washington?"

He grimaced. "No longer than this, I'm afraid. I have to
talk to Nesbitson before we land."

"Do you really, Jamie?" It was more an entreaty than a
question.

He said regretfully, "I'm sorry, my dear."

Margaret sighed. "I thought it was too good to last. Well,
I'll lie down so you can be private." She got up, gathering
her bag and hat. At the doorway of the little bedroom she
turned. "Are you going to bully him?"

"Probably not—unless I have to."

"I hope you don't," Margaret said seriously. "He's such a
sad old man. I always think he should be in a wheel chair
with a blanket, and another old soldier pushing."

The Prime Minister smiled broadly. "All retired generals
should be like that. Unfortunately they either want to write
books or get into politics."

When Margaret had gone he buzzed for the steward and
sent a courteous message asking General Nesbitson to join
him.

3

"You're looking extremely fit, Adrian," James Howden
said.

From the depths of the soft chair which Margaret had vacated earlier, his pink pudgy hands nursing a scotch and
soda, Adrian Nesbitson nodded in pleased agreement. "I've
been feeling first class these past few days, Prime Minister.
Seem to have thrown off that damn catarrh at last."

"I'm delighted to hear it. I think you were overdoing things
for a while. In fact we all were. It made us impatient with
each other." Howden studied his Defense Minister carefully.
The old man really did look healthier, distinguished even,
despite increasing baldness and the trace of resemblance to

Mr. Five-by-Five. The thick white mustache helped; carefully trimmed, it added an aura of dignity to the square-jawed face which still retained a hint of soldierly authority. Perhaps, Howden thought, the course he had been considering might work. But he remembered Brian Richardson's warning: "Go easy on the bargaining; the old boy has a reputation for straightness."

"Impatient or not," Nesbitson said, "I still can't share your views on this Act of Union idea. I'm sure we can get what we want from the Yanks without giving so much away."

James Howden willed himself to calmness, ignoring, in his mind, a ground swell of anger and frustration. Nothing, he knew, would be achieved by loss of control, by shouting aloud as impulse urged: "For God's sake wake up! Wake up and acknowledge the obvious: that it's desperately late and there isn't time for ancient weary nostrums." Instead he said placatingly, "I'd like you to do something for me, Adrian, if you will."

There was a trace of hesitancy before the old man asked, "What is it?"

"Go over everything in your mind: what the situation is likely to be; the time we have available; what was said the other day; then the alternatives, and your own conscience."

"I've already done it." The answer was determined.

"But once again?" Howden was at his most persuasive. "As a personal favor to me?"

The old man had finished his scotch. It had warmed him and he put the glass down. "Well," he conceded, "I don't mind doing that. But I warn you my answer will still be the same: we must keep our national independence—all of it."

"Thank you," James Howden said. He rang for the steward and when he appeared, "Another scotch and soda, please, for General Nesbitson."

When the second drink came Nesbitson sipped it, then leaned back, surveying the private cabin. He said approvingly, with something of the old military bark in his voice, "This is a damn fine setup, P.M., if I may say so."

It was the opening James Howden had hoped for.

"It isn't bad," he acknowledged, his fingers toying with the fresh glass of grape juice which the steward had brought, along with the Defense Minister's scotch. "I don't use it a great deal, though. This is more the Governor General's airplane than mine."

"Is that so?" Nesbitson seemed surprised. "You mean that Sheldon Griffiths gets to ride around like this?"

"Oh yes, whenever he wants." Howden's voice was elaborately casual. "After all, the G.G. *is* Her Majesty's representative. He's entitled to rather special treatment, don't you think?"

"I suppose so." The old man's expression was bemused.

Again casually, as if their conversation had reminded him, Howden said, "I expect you'd heard that Shel Griffiths is retiring this summer. He's had seven years at Government House and feels he'd like to step down."

"I'd heard something of the sort," Nesbitson said.

The Prime Minister sighed. "It's always a problem when a Governor General retires—finding the best man to succeed him: someone with the right kind of experience who is willing to serve. One has to remember that it's the highest honor the country can award."

As Howden watched, the older man took a generous sip of scotch. "Yes," he said carefully, "it certainly is."

"Of course," Howden said, "the job has disadvantages. There's a good deal of ceremonial—guards of honor everywhere, cheering crowds, artillery salutes, and so on." He added lightly, "The G.G. rates twenty-one guns, you know—as many as the Queen."

"Yes," Nesbitson said softly, "I know."

"Naturally," Howden continued, as if thinking aloud, "it needs a special brand of experience to handle that kind of thing well. Someone with a military background usually does it best."

The old warrior's lips were slightly parted. He moistened them with his tongue. "Yes," he said, "I expect that's true."

"Frankly," Howden said, "I'd always hoped that you might take it on someday."

The old man's eyes were wide. "Me?" His voice was barely audible. "Me?"

"Well," Howden said, as if dismissing the thought. "It's come at the wrong time, I know. You wouldn't want to leave the Cabinet and I certainly wouldn't want to lose you."

Nesbitson made a half-movement as if to rise from the cabin seat, then subsided. The hand which held the glass was trembling. He swallowed in an attempt to keep his voice under control and succeeded partially. "Matter of fact, been think-

ing for some time of getting out of politics. Sometimes a bit
trying at my age."

"Really, Adrian?" The Prime Minister allowed himself to
sound surprised. "I'd always assumed you'd be working with
us for a long time to come." He stopped to consider. "Of
course, if you did accept, it would solve a lot of problems. I
don't mind telling you that as I see it, after the Act of Union
there'll be a difficult time for the country. We shall need a
sense of unity and a continuance of national feeling. Personally, I see the office of Governor General—assuming it's en-
trusted to the right hands—as contributing a great deal towards that."

For a moment he wondered if he had gone too far. As he
had spoken, the old man's eyes had risen, meeting his own
directly. It was hard to read what they contained. Was it contempt; or unbelief; or even both, with a mingling of ambition? One thing could be counted on. Though in some ways
Adrian Nesbitson was a fool, he was not so obtuse that he
could fail to grasp what was being offered: a deal, with the
highest possible price for his own political support.

It was the old man's assessment of the prize that James
Howden counted on. Some men, he knew, would never covet
the Governor Generalship on any terms; for them it would
be a penalty rather than reward. But to a military mind, lov-
ing ceremony and pomp, it was the glistering ultimate ideal.

James Howden had never believed the cynic's dictum that
all men have their price. In his lifetime he had known individuals who could not be bought, either with wealth or
honors, or even the temptation—to which so many succumbed
—to do good for their fellow men. But most who were in
politics had a price of one kind or another; they had to have
in order to survive. Some people preferred to use euphemisms
like "expediency" or "compromise," but in the end it amounted to the same thing. The question was: had he gauged cor-
rectly the price of Adrian Nesbitson's support.

The inner struggle was written on the old man's face: a
sequence of expressions, swift-changing like a child's kaleido-
scope in which doubt, pride, shame, and longing were con-
joined . . .

*He could hear the guns in memory . . . the bark of German
88's and answering fire . . . a sunstreaked morning; Antwerp*

behind, the Scheldt ahead . . . the Canadian Division clamber-
ing, clawing, moving forward; then slowing, wavering, ready
to turn away . . .

It was the pivot point of battle and he had commandeered
the jeep, beckoned the piper, and ordered the driver forward.
To the skirl of pipes from the back seat he had stood, facing
the German guns, leading, cajoling, and the wavering ranks
had reassembled. He had urged stragglers on, cursing with
foul oaths, and the men had cursed him back and followed.

Din, dust, motors gunned, the smell of cordite and oil,
cries of wounded . . . The movement forward, slow at first,
then faster . . . The wonderment in men's eyes—at himself,
upstanding, proud, a target no enemy gunner could miss . . .

It was the ultimate moment of glory. It had been hopeless
but they had snatched back victory. It had been suicidal but
wondrously he had survived . . .

They called him the Mad General and the Fighting Fool,
and afterwards a slim frail man with a stutter, whom he re-
vered, had pinned on a medal at Buckingham Palace.

But now the years had gone, and memories with them; and
few remembered the moment of glory, and fewer cared. No
one called him, any more, the Fighting Fool. If they called
him anything they omitted the 'Fighting.'

Sometimes, however briefly, he longed for the taste of
glory again.

With a trace of hesitancy Adrian Nesbitson said, "You
seem very sure about this Act of Union, Prime Minister. Are
you certain it will go through?"

"Yes, I am. It will go through because it has to." Howden
kept his face and voice serious.

"But there'll be opposition." The old man frowned in concentration.

"Naturally. But in the end, when need and urgency are
seen, it will make no difference." Howden's voice took on a
note of persuasion. "I know your first feeling has been to
oppose this plan, Adrian, and we all respect you for it. I
suppose, too, that if you felt you must continue to oppose,
we would be obliged to part company politically."

Nesbitson said gruffly, "I don't see the need for that."

"There is no need," Howden said. "Particularly when, as
Governor General, you could do far more to serve the
country than you ever could from the political wilderness."

"Well," Nesbitson said; he was studying his hands. "I suppose when you look at it like that . . ."

It's all so simple, Howden thought. Patronage, the power of bestowal, brings most things within reach. Aloud he said, "If you're agreeable I'd like to notify the Queen as soon as possible. I'm sure Her Majesty will be delighted with the news."

With dignity Adrian Nesbitson inclined his head. "As you wish, Prime Minister."

They had risen to their feet and shook hands solemnly. "I'm glad; very glad," James Howden said. He added informally, "Your appointment as Governor General will be announced in June. At least we shall have you in the Cabinet until then, and your campaigning with us through the election will mean a great deal." He was summing up, making clear without any shadow of misunderstanding what they had agreed upon. For Adrian Nesbitson there would be no bolting from the Government, no criticism of the Act of Union. Instead, Nesbitson would fight the election with the remainder of the party—supporting, endorsing, sharing responsibility . . .

James Howden waited for dissent, if any. There was none.

A moment or two earlier the note of the aircraft engines had changed. Now they were descending evenly and the land below was no longer snow covered, but a patchwork quilt of browns and greens. The intercom phone gave its gentle *ping* and the Prime Minister answered.

Wing Commander Galbraith's voice announced, "We'll be landing in Washington in ten minutes, sir. We have priority clearance right on down and I've been asked to tell you that the President is on his way to the airport."

4

After take-off of the Prime Minister's flight Brian Richardson and Milly drove back from Uplands Airport in Richardson's Jaguar. Through most of the journey into Ottawa the party director was silent, his face set grimly, his body tense with anger. He handled the Jaguar—which normally he gentled lovingly—as though it were responsible for the abortive press conference on the airport ramp. More than others, perhaps, he could already visualize the hollowness of James Howden's statements about Immigration and Henri Duval as they would appear in print. Even more unfortunate, Richardson fumed, the Government—in the person of the Prime Minister—had taken a stand from which it would be exceedingly difficult to retreat.

Once or twice after leaving the airport Milly had glanced sideways but, sensing what was in her companion's mind, she refrained from comment. But nearing the city limits after a particularly savage cornering, she touched Richardson's arm. No words were necessary.

The party director slowed, turned his head and grinned. "Sorry, Milly. I was letting off steam."

"I know." The reporters' questioning at the airport had distressed Milly too, aware as she was of the secret restraint upon James Howden.

"I could use a drink, Milly," Richardson said. "How about going to your place?"

"All right." It was almost noon and for an hour or two there was little urgency for Milly to return to the Prime Minister's office. They crossed the Rideau River at Dunbar Bridge and swung west on Queen Elizabeth Drive toward the city. The sun, which had been shining earlier, had retreated under sullen clouds and the day was graying, the drab stone buildings of the capital merging with it. The wind whistled in gusts, stirring eddies of dust and leaves and paper, cavorting in gutters and around week-old snow piles, defiled and ugly now from sludge and soot. Pedestrians hurried, coat collars upturned, holding their hats and hugging buildings closely. Despite the Jaguar's warmth, Milly shivered. This was the time of year when winter seemed endless and she longed for spring.

They parked the Jaguar at Milly's apartment building and rode up in the elevator together. Inside the apartment, out of habit, Milly began to fix drinks. Brian Richardson put a hand around her shoulder and kissed her quickly on the cheek. For an instant he looked directly into Milly's face, then abruptly released her. The effect within himself had startled him; it was as if, for an instant, he had floated into some other megacosm, dreamlike, airy . . . More practically he said, "Let me do the drinks. A man's place is at the bar."

He took glasses and, as she watched, poured even measures of gin, then sliced a lemon, squeezing part into each drink. He added ice cubes, efficiently opened a bottle of Schweppes tonic and divided it neatly between the two glasses. It was simple and effortless but Milly thought: how wonderful to share things—even a simple thing like mixing drinks—with someone you genuinely cared for.

Milly took her glass to the settee, sipped, and put it down. Leaning back she let her head fall comfortably against the cushions, savoring the welcome luxury of rest at midday. She had a sense of moments stolen from time. Stretching, she extended her nyloned legs, heels against the rug, shoes kicked free.

Richardson was pacing the small, snug living room, his glass clenched tightly, his face absorbed and frowning. "I don't get it, Milly. I just plain don't get it. Why is the chief behaving this way when he never has before? Why, of all things, is he backing Harvey Warrender? He doesn't believe in what he's doing; you could tell that today. Then what's the reason? Why, why, why?"

"Oh, Brian!" Milly said. "Couldn't we forget it for a while?"

"Forget it, hell!" The words rapped out in frustration and anger. "I tell you we're being stupid goddam morons by not giving in and letting that bastard stowaway off the ship. This whole affair could build and keep on building until it costs us an election."

Illogically Milly was tempted to ask: Would it matter if it did? It was wrong, she knew, to think that way, and earlier her anxiety had been as great as Richardson's own. But suddenly she was overwhelmed with a weariness for political concerns: the tactics, maneuvering, petty scoring over opponents, the self-implanted certainties of right. In the end what did it all amount to? Today's seeming crisis would be a forgotten trifle next week or next year. In ten years, or a hundred, all the tiny causes and people who espoused them, would be lost in oblivion. It was individuals, not politics, that mattered most. And not just other people . . . but themselves.

"Brian," Milly said softly, steadily, "please make love to me now."

The pacing had stopped. There was a silence.

"Don't say anything," Milly whispered. She had closed her eyes. It was as if someone else was speaking for her, another voice inhabiting her body. It had to be that way since she herself could never have said the words of a moment or two ago. In a way, she supposed, she ought to speak in denial of the stranger's voice, canceling what had been said, resuming her own identity. But a sense of delicious languor held her back.

She heard a glass set down, feet moving softly, drapes drawn, then Brian was beside her. Their arms went around each other, lips meeting ardently, their bodies demanding. "Oh God, Milly!" he breathed. His voice was trembling, "Milly, I want you and I love you."

5

In the quietness of the apartment the telephone bell purred softly. Brian Richardson propped himself on an elbow. "Well," he said, "I'm glad it didn't ring ten minutes ago." He had a sense of speaking for speaking's sake; as if using commonplace words as a shield to his own uncertainty.

"I wouldn't have answered it," Milly said. The languor had gone. She had a sense of quickening and expectation. This time and last it had been different, so different, from other times she remembered . . .

Brian Richardson kissed her forehead. How much difference there was, he thought, between the Milly the outside world saw, and Milly as he had come to know her here. At this moment she seemed sleepy, her hair disordered, warm . . .

"I'd better answer it," Milly said. Pushing herself upright she padded to the phone.

It was the Prime Minister's office, one of the assistant stenographers. "I thought I ought to call you, Miss Freedeman. There've been a lot of telegrams. They started coming in this morning and there are seventy-two now, all addressed to Mr. Howden."

Milly ran a hand through her hair. She asked, "What about?"

"They're all about that man on the ship, the one that Immigration won't let in. There was some more about him in this morning's paper. Did you see it?"

"Yes," Milly said, "I saw it. What do the telegrams say?"

"Mostly the same thing in different ways, Miss Freedeman: that he should be let in and given a chance. I thought you'd want to know."

"You were right to call," Milly said. "Start listing where

the telegrams come from and summarizing what they say.
I'll be in very soon."

Milly replaced the phone. She would have to notify Elliot
Prowse, the executive assistant; he would be in Washington
by now. Then it would be up to him whether or not to tell
the Prime Minister. He probably would; James Howden regarded mail and telegrams very seriously, insisting on daily
and monthly tabulations of their contents and source, which
were studied carefully by himself and the party director.

"What was it?" Brian Richardson asked, and Milly told
him.

Like gears engaging, his mind swung back to practical
concerns. He was immediately concerned, as she had known
he would be. "It's being organized by somebody, otherwise
there wouldn't be that many telegrams together. All the same,
I don't like it any more than I like the rest." He added
gloomily, "I wish I knew what the hell to do."

"Perhaps there isn't anything that can be done," Milly
said.

He looked at her sharply. Then, turning, he took both her
shoulders gently in his hands. "Milly, darling," he said,
"there's something going on I don't know about, but I think
you do."

She shook her head.

"Listen, Milly," he insisted. "We're both on the same side,
aren't we? If I'm to do anything, I have to know."

Their eyes met.

"You can trust me, can't you?" he said softly. "Especially
now."

She was aware of conflicting emotions and loyalties. She
wanted to protect James Howden; she always had . . .

And yet, suddenly, her relationship with Brian had
changed. He had told her that he loved her. Surely, between
them now, there was no place for secrets. In a way it would
be a relief . . .

His grip on her shoulders tightened. "Milly, I have to
know."

"Very well." Releasing herself from his hands, she took
keys from her bag and unlocked the bottom drawer of a
small bureau beside the bedroom door. The copy photostat
was in a sealed envelope which she opened and gave to him.
As he began to read she was aware that the mood of a few

minutes earlier was dissolved and lost, like mist before a morning breeze. Once more it was business as usual: politics.

Brian Richardson had whistled softly as he read. Now he looked up, his expression stunned, his eyes showing disbelief.

"Jesus!" he breathed; "Jesus Christ!"

Ten   The Order *Nisi*

The Supreme Court of the Province of British Columbia closed the ponderous oak doors of its Vancouver Registry office promptly each day at 4 P.M.

At ten minutes to four on the day following his second shipboard interview with Captain Jaabeck and Henri Duval (and at approximately the same time—ten to seven in Washington, D.C.—that the Prime Minister and Margaret Howden were dressing for the White House state dinner) Alan Maitland entered the courthouse Registry, brief case in hand.

Inside the Registry, Alan hesitated, surveying the long, high-ceilinged room with one wall occupied entirely by file cabinets, and a polished wood counter top running most of its length. Then he approached the counter, opened the brief case, and removed the papers inside. As he did, he was aware that the palms of his hands were more than usually moist.

An elderly clerk, the Registry's only occupant, came forward. He was a frail gnomelike man, stooped as though years of closeness to the law had set a weight upon his shoulders. He inquired courteously, "Yes, Mr. . . . ?"

"Maitland," Alan said. He passed across a set of the papers he had prepared. "I've these for filing, and I'd like to be taken to the chamber judge, please."

The clerk said patiently, "Judge's chambers are at 10.30 A.M. and today's list is finished, Mr. Maitland."

"If you'll excuse me"—Alan pointed to the documents he had handed over—"this is a matter of the liberty of the subject. I believe I'm entitled to have it brought on immediately." On this point at least, he was sure of his ground. In any proceedings involving human liberty and illegal detention the law brooked no delay and, if necessary, a judge would be summoned from his bed in dead of night.

The clerk took rimless glasses from a case, adjusted them, and bent to read. He had an attitude of incuriosity, as if nothing surprised him. After a moment he lifted his head. "I beg your pardon, Mr. Maitland. You're quite right, of course." He pulled a cloth-bound ledger towards him. "It isn't every day we get an application for habeas corpus."

When he had completed the ledger entry the clerk took a black gown from a peg and shrugged it around his shoulders. "Come this way, please."

He preceded Alan out of the Registry, along a paneled corridor, through double swing doors, and into the courthouse hallway where a wide stone staircase led to the upper floor. The building was quiet, their footsteps echoing. At this time of day most of the courts had risen and some of the building's lights were already turned out.

As they climbed the stairs, treading sedately one step at a time, an unaccustomed nervousness gripped Alan tautly. He subdued a childish impulse to turn and run. Earlier, in considering the arguments he intended to present, they had appeared plausible, even if some of the legal ground was shaky. But now, abruptly, the structure of his case seemed witless and naive. Was he about to make a fool of himself in the august presence of a Supreme Court judge? And if he did, what of the consequences? Judges were not to be trifled with, or special hearings demanded without good reason.

In a way he wished he had chosen another time of day, with the courthouse busy, as it usually was in the morning and early afternoon. The sight of other people might have been reassuring. But he had chosen this time carefully, to avoid attention and any more publicity which at this point might prove harmful. Most of the newspaper court reporters would have gone home by now, he hoped, and he had been careful to give other newspapermen who had phoned him several times today no hint of what was planned.

"It's Mr. Justice Willis in chambers today," the clerk said. "Do you know him, Mr. Maitland?"

"I've heard his name," Alan said, "but that's all." He was aware that the roster of chamber judges changed regularly, each justice of the Supreme Court taking his turn to be available in chambers outside regular court hours. Therefore whichever judge one drew was mainly a matter of chance.

The clerk appeared about to speak, then changed his mind.

Alan prompted him, "Was there something you were going to tell me?"

"Well, sir, just a suggestion—if it isn't presumptuous."

"Please go ahead," Alan urged.

They had come to the head of the stairway and turned down a darkened corridor. "Well, Mr. Maitland"—the clerk lowered his voice—"his lordship is a fine gentleman. But he's very strict about procedure and especially interruptions. Take as long as you like over your argument and he'll give you all the time you need. But once he's begun to talk himself he doesn't like anyone to speak, not even to ask questions, until he's finished. He can get very annoyed when that happens."

"Thanks," Alan said gratefully, "I'll remember."

Stopping at a heavy door, marked with the one word PRIVATE, the clerk rapped twice, his head cocked forward to listen. Faintly from inside a voice called "Come!" The clerk opened the door, ushering Alan in.

It was a large, paneled room, Alan saw, carpeted, and with a tiled fireplace. In front of the fireplace a portable electric fire had two of its elements turned on. A mahogany desk, piled with files and books, occupied the room's center, with more books and papers on a table behind. Brown velvet draperies were drawn back from leaded windows, revealing dusk outside, with lights of the city and harbor beginning to wink on. Within the room a single desk lamp burned, providing a pool of light. Outside the lamp's radius an erect lean figure had been putting on an overcoat and hat, preparing to leave, as the clerk and Alan entered.

"My lord," the clerk said, "Mr. Maitland has an application for habeas corpus."

"Indeed." The one word, gruffly spoken, was the sole response. As the clerk and Alan waited, Mr. Justice Stanley Willis carefully removed the coat and hat, replacing both on a stand behind him. Then, moving into the circle of light by the desk, and seating himself, he instructed sharply, "Come forward, Mr. Maitland."

His lordship, Alan judged, was a man of sixty or sixty-two, white-haired and sparely built, but with wide bony shoulders and a ramrod posture which made him seem taller than he was. His face was long and angular with a dominant jutting chin, bushy white eyebrows, and mouth set firmly in an even line. His eyes were penetrating and alert, yet unrevealing of themselves. The habit of authority set naturally upon him.

Still nervously, despite his own inner reasoning, Alan Maitland approached the desk, the clerk remaining in the room as protocol required. From the brief case Alan produced typed ribbon copies of the application and affidavit he had filed in Registry. Clearing his throat, he announced, "My lord, here is my material and these are my submissions."

Mr. Justice Willis accepted the documents with a curt nod, moved closer to the light, and began to read. As the other two stood silently, the only sound was the rustle of pages turning.

When he had completed reading, the judge looked up, his expression noncommittal. Gruffly as before he asked, "Do you intend to make an oral submission?"

"If Your Lordship pleases."

Again a nod. "Proceed."

"The facts of the matter, my lord, are these." In sequence, as he had memorized earlier, Alan described the situation of Henri Duval aboard the *Vastervik*, the refusal of the ship's captain on two occasions to bring the stowaway before immigration authorities ashore, and Alan's own submission—supported by his personal affidavit—that Duval was being illegally imprisoned in violation of basic human rights.

The crux of the situation, as Alan well knew, lay in establishing that the present detention of Henri Duval was procedurally wrong under the law, and therefore illegal. If this could be proven, the Court—in the person of Mr. Justice Willis—must automatically issue a writ of habeas corpus, ordering the stowaway's release from the ship and his appearance before the court for consideration of his case.

Marshaling the arguments, and quoting statutes in support, Alan felt some of his confidence return. He was careful to confine himself to legal points only, leaving the emotional aspect of the stowaway's plight unspoken. Law, not sentiment, was what counted here. As he spoke the judge listened impassively, his expression unchanging.

Turning from the question of illegal detention to the present status of Henri Duval, Alan declared, "It is argued by the Department of Immigration, my lord, that since my client is a stowaway and allegedly without documents, he has no legal rights and therefore cannot demand—as others may do at any Canadian port of entry—a special inquiry into his

immigrant status. But it is my contention that the fact of
his being a stowaway and apparently uncertain of his birthplace in no way detracts from this right.

"If Your Lordship will consider certain possibilities: a
Canadian citizen by birth, traveling abroad and held unlaw-
fully in custody, with papers taken from him, might find his
only means of escape by stowing aboard a ship he knows
to be destined to this country. Would he, in such case, because of his description as a stowaway and the absence of
papers, be relegated to apparent non-existence, unable to
prove his lawful right to enter Canada because an inquiry
by the Department of Immigration had been denied him? I
suggest, my lord, that this absurd situation could, in fact,
exist if the department's present ruling were carried to its
logical conclusion."

The judge's bushy eyebrows went up. "You're not suggesting, are you, that your client Henri Duval is a Canadian
citizen?"

Alan hesitated, then replied carefully, "That is not my suggestion, my lord. On the other hand, an immigration inquiry
might reveal him as a Canadian, a fact which could not be
established without the inquiry first." When you had a weak
case and knew it, Alan thought, even straws should be
grasped at firmly.

"Well," Mr. Justice Willis said, and for the first time his
face had the ghost of a smile, "it's an ingenious argument,
if a little thin. Is that all, Mr. Maitland?"

Instinct told Alan: *quit when you're ahead*. He gave the
slightest of bows. "With respect, my lord, that is my submission."

In the desk lamp's glow Mr. Justice Willis sat meditatively
silent. The momentary smile had gone, his face once more
a stern immobile mask. The fingers of his right hand
drummed the desk top softly. After a while he began,
"There is, of course, a time element involved—the question
of the ship's sailing . . ."

Alan interjected, "If Your Lordship pleases: in the matter
of the ship . . ." He was about to explain the *Vastervik's* delay
in Vancouver for repairs but stopped abruptly. At the interruption the judge's face had clouded angrily, his eyes beneath the bushy eyebrows bleak. Across the room Alan could
sense the clerk's reproach. He swallowed. "I beg Your Lordship's pardon."

Briefly Mr. Justice Willis stared coldly at the young lawyer. Then he continued, "As I was about to observe, although there is a time limit involved, namely the question of the ship's departure, this must not interfere in any way with a matter of individual justice."

Alan's heart leaped. Did this mean that the writ of habeas corpus was to be granted? . . . that afterwards he could take his time about procedure, moving slowly through successive legal steps while the *Vastervik* sailed, leaving Henri Duval behind?

"On the other hand," the judge's voice proceeded evenly, "as a matter of public policy, and in fairness to the shipping company concerned, which is somewhat an innocent bystander in this affair, it is equally pertinent that everything possible should be done to expedite procedure so as to render a final decision before the ship's normal sailing."

So the optimism had been premature. Gloomily Alan reflected that not only Edgar Kramer, but now this judge, had seen through his ruse of a delaying action.

"I consider the matter of illegal detention not proven." His lordship drew the submissions toward him and made a penciled notation. "But neither is it disproven and I am prepared to hear further argument. I shall therefore allow an order *nisi*."

It was not defeat then, but partial victory, and a wave of relief swept over Alan. True he had achieved less than hoped for, but at least he had not made a fool of himself. The order *nisi*—the old English legal procedure—meant "unless." The *nisi* writ alone would not free Henri Duval from his shipboard prison and bring him before the Court. But it did mean that Edgar Kramer and Captain Jaabeck were to be summoned here to explain their stand. And *unless* their arguments—or those of legal counsel—prevailed, the habeas corpus writ, releasing Duval, would follow.

"In the course of events, Mr. Maitland, when will the ship sail?"

The eyes of Mr. Justice Willis were upon him. Alan paused, wary before speaking, then realized the question was addressed directly.

"As far as I can learn, my lord, the ship will be here another two weeks."

The judge nodded. "It should be sufficient."

"And the hearing on the writ, my lord?"

Mr. Justice Willis pulled a desk calendar toward him. "We should set the date, I think, for three days' time. If that is convenient." It was the traditional courteous exchange between judge and lawyer, no matter how junior the latter might be.

Alan inclined his head. "Yes, my lord."

"You will have the papers drawn, of course."

"If Your Lordship pleases, I have them ready." Alan opened the brief case.

"An order *nisi*?"

"Yes, my lord. I foresaw that possibility."

The moment the words were out Alan regretted them as youthful and brash. In the ordinary way the writ would have been typed and submitted for the judge's signature next day. It had been Alan's idea to prepare a final order for signing promptly, and Tom Lewis had suggested the addition of an order *nisi*. Now, with slightly less assurance, Alan laid the typed pages, clipped together, on the judge's desk.

Mr. Justice Willis's expression had not changed, except for a slight crinkling around the eyes. He said impassively, "In that event, Mr. Maitland, there will be a time saving and I suggest we bring on the hearing sooner. Shall we say the day after tomorrow?"

Mentally Alan Maitland denounced his own stupidity. Instead of furthering the delay he sought, he had succeeded merely in speeding things up. He wondered if he should request more time, pleading the need for preparation. He caught the eye of the clerk who shook his head imperceptibly.

With inward resignation Alan said, "Very well, my lord. The day after tomorrow."

Mr. Justice Willis read the order, then carefully signed it, the clerk blotting and gathering the page. As he watched, Alan remembered the arrangements he had made earlier for service of the document if his plan succeeded. Tom Lewis would go to the *Vastervik*, tonight, with Captain Jaabeck's copy and explain its contents. Tom, in any case, had been keen to see the ship and meet both the captain and Henri Duval.

For himself Alan had reserved what he thought of as a particular pleasure: attendance at the Department of Immigration and service of the order personally upon Edgar S. Kramer.

Darkness, which had spread damply across the harbor and city of Vancouver, still found lights burning in the superintendent's office of the water-front Immigration Building.

Edgar S. Kramer, though punctilious about beginning each day precisely on time, rarely bothered to end his own working day at prescribed office hours. Whether in Ottawa, Vancouver, or elsewhere, he usually remained for at least an hour after the rest of the staff had gone, partly to disassociate himself from the usual eager exodus, and partly to avoid any accumulation of paper on his desk. A habit of getting things done and prompt handling of paper work were two reasons Edgar Kramer had been a conspicuous success as a career civil servant. Over the years of his progress upward there had been plenty of people who disliked him personally and a few whose antagonisms went deeper. But no one, even in enmity, could reasonably accuse him either of laziness or procrastination.

A good example of Kramer promptitude had been the decision taken today and described in a memorandum with the unlikely subject heading "Pigeon Guano." Edgar Kramer had dictated the memo earlier and now, reading over the typed copies which tomorrow would go to the building supervisor and others concerned, he nodded approvingly at his own resourcefulness.

The problem had come to his attention yesterday. Examining the proposed annual budget of the Immigration Department's West Coast Headquarters, he had queried a number of expenses for building maintenance, including an item of $750—apparently recurring each year—for "cleaning eaves-trough and downpipes."

Edgar Kramer had summoned the building supervisor—a bull-necked, loud-spoken man, happier behind a broom than a desk—who responded forcefully. "Hell, Mr. Kramer, sure it's too much money to spend, but it's all that pigeon shit." Prompted further he had crossed to the office window and gestured. "Look at the bastards!" Outside, as they watched, the air was thick with thousands of pigeons which nested, flew and scavenged in the water-front area.

"Shittin', shittin' twenty-four hours a day, like they got the permanent runs," the supervisor grumbled. "And if one of 'em wants the can, they fly up to our roof. That's why we have

to steam out the eavestroughs and downpipes six times a year
—they're full of pigeon shit. Costs money, Mr. Kramer."

"I understand the problem," Kramer said. "Has anything
been done to reduce the number of pigeons—by killing some?"

"Tried shootin' the bastards once," the building supervisor
answered gloomily, "and there was all hell to pay. Humane
Society people down here an' all. They say there's a bylaw in
Vancouver says you can't. Tell you what, though: we could
try putting poison on the roof. Then when they go there for
a . . ."

Edgar Kramer said sharply, "The word is guano—pigeon
guano."

The supervisor said, "In my book it's all . . ."

"And furthermore," Kramer interjected firmly, "if the
pigeons are protected by law, then the law will be observed."
He mused. "We must find some other way."

He had dismissed the other man and, once alone, considered the problem carefully. One thing was certain: the
wasteful $750 expense each year must be eliminated.

Eventually, after several false starts and a number of
sketches, he had devised a scheme based on a half-remem-
bered idea. In essence the plan was to string piano wires at
six inch intervals across the Immigration Building roof, with
each strand supported on several short poles six inches high.
The theory was that a pigeon could pass its feet through the
strands of wire, but not its wings. Therefore, when a bird
alighted, the wire would prevent folding of its wings and it
would fly off at once.

This morning Edgar Kramer had had a small experimental
section made and installed on the roof. The device worked
perfectly. Now the memorandum he had approved was an
instruction to put the full scheme into effect. Although the
initial cost would be a thousand dollars, it should eliminate
permanently the annual $750 expense—a saving to the coun-
try's taxpayers, although few would ever know about it.

The thought pleased Edgar Kramer, as his own conscien-
tiousness always did. There was another satisfaction too: the
local bylaw had been observed, with even the pigeons treated
justly and according to regulations.

It had been (Edgar Kramer decided) a most satisfactory
day. Not least among the matters pleasing him was that his
frequency of urination seemed definitely less. He checked his
watch. It had been close to an hour since the last occasion

and he was confident he could wait longer, even though a slight warning pressure . . .

There was a tap on the door and Alan Maitland walked in. "Good evening," he said coolly, and laid a folded paper on the table.

The young lawyer's appearance had been sudden and startling. Edgar Kramer asked abruptly, "What's all this about?"

"It's an order *nisi*, Mr. Kramer," Alan announced calmly. "I believe you'll find it self-explanatory."

Opening the folded page Kramer read quickly. His face flushed angrily. He spluttered, "What the devil do you mean by this?" At the same time he was aware that the mild pressure on his bladder of a moment before had suddenly become intense.

Alan was tempted to reply caustically, then decided not. After all, he had merely gained a partial victory and the next round might easily go the other way. Therefore, politely enough, he answered, "You did turn me down, you know, when I asked for a special inquiry into the case of Henri Duval."

Momentarily Edgar Kramer wondered at his own fierce resentment of this callow youthful lawyer. "Of course I turned you down," he snapped. "There was no earthly reason one should be held."

"It just happens that I don't share your opinion," Alan observed mildly. He pointed to the order *nisi*. "This is to see which view—yours or mine—a court of law will take."

The pressure was becoming agonizing. Holding himself in, Kramer fumed, "This is solely a matter for department ruling. No court has any business interfering."

Alan Maitland's face was serious. "If you care for some advice," he said quietly, "if I were you I wouldn't tell that to the judge."

Eleven   The White House

From the window of Blair House library James Howden examined the view across Pennsylvania Avenue. It was 10 A.M. on the second day in Washington, and the meeting between himself, the President, Arthur Lexington, and the President's chief of staff was scheduled to begin in an hour's time.

A fresh soft breeze stirred the filmy curtains beside him at the open window. Outside, the weather was Washington at its best: balmy and springlike with warm bright sunshine. Across the avenue the Prime Minister could see the trim White House lawns and glimpse the Executive Mansion, sun-streaked, beyond.

Turning toward Arthur Lexington, Howden asked, "What's your feeling about everything so far?"

The External Affairs Minister, wearing a comfortable Harris tweed jacket instead of the suit coat he would put on later, straightened up from the color TV with which he had been experimenting. Turning the set off, he paused considering.

"Put in its crudest terms," Lexington said, "I'd say we're in a seller's market. The concessions we have to offer, the United States needs, and needs desperately. What's more, they're very much aware of it here."

The two had breakfasted separately, the Prime Minister with Margaret in their private suite, Arthur Lexington with others of the delegation downstairs. The Canadians were the only guests in the President's spacious guest house, to which they had returned last night after the White House state dinner.

Now Howden nodded slowly. "That's been my impression too."

The Prime Minister surveyed the long, gracious library. With its overstuffed sofas and chairs, big Chippendale table, and the book-lined walls, it seemed a gentle backwater of coolness and quiet. It was here in this room, he thought, that Lincoln had once rested and talked; that in later years the Trumans spent their leisure during the White House remodeling; here, in the library, that King Saud of Arabia slept guarded by his own soldiers, scimitar-armed; here that de Gaulle had prepared to huff, Adenauer to charm, and Khrushchev to bluster . . . and so many others. He wondered if he himself would be remembered in that long procession. And if so, with what verdict.

"Small things add up," Lexington mused. "The kind of reception you were given yesterday, for instance. I've never known the President to come out to the airport for Canadians. We're usually met by smaller fry and treated like country cousins—even Prime Ministers. Once, when John Diefenbaker

was down for a White House dinner, they put him in line
with a bunch of Presbyterian ministers."

Howden chuckled reminiscently. "Yes, I remember. He
hated it and I can't say I blame him. Wasn't that the time
Eisenhower made a speech and kept talking about the 'Re-
public' of Canada?"

Lexington nodded, smiling.

James Howden dropped into an upholstered wing chair.
"They certainly did us brown last night," he remarked. "You'd
think if they *are* making a switch, being considerate and so
on, they'd be a bit more subtle."

Arthur Lexington's eyes twinkled in the round, ruddy face
above the inevitable neatly knotted bow tie. At times, Howden thought, the External Affairs Minister resembled a benev-
olent schoolmaster accustomed to dealing firmly but patiently
with small, obstreperous boys. Perhaps it was that which always made him seem young, and always would, even though
the years were advancing upon him like all the rest of them.

"Subtlety and the State Department keep separate houses,"
Lexington said. "I've always considered, you know, that
American diplomacy comes two ways—either contemplating
rape or ready to receive it. There's seldom any in between."

The Prime Minister laughed. "How about now?" He invariably enjoyed the moments which the two of them had
alone. They had long been staunch friends who trusted each
other firmly. One reason, possibly, was that there was no
sense of competition between them. While others in the Cabinet openly or covertly aspired to the Prime Ministership,
Arthur Lexington, as Howden knew full well, had no ambitions in that direction.

Lexington, in fact, would probably still have been an ambassador, happy in his spare time with the twin hobbies of
stamp collecting and ornithology, had not Howden persuaded
him years earlier to resign from the diplomatic corps and
enter the party and later the Cabinet. Loyalty and a strong
sense of duty had kept him there since, but he made no secret
of looking forward with pleasure to the day when he would
return from public to private life.

Lexington had paced the long garnet-colored rug before
answering the Prime Minister's question. Now he stopped and
said, "Like you, I don't care to get violated."

"But there'll be plenty who'll say we have been."

"Some will say that whichever line we take. There'll be

sincere people among them too—not just the rabble-rousers."

"Yes, I've thought of that," Howden said. "The act of Union will cost us some of our own party, I'm afraid. But I'm still convinced there's no other choice."

The External Affairs Minister sank into a facing chair. He hooked a footstool close and stretched out, resting both feet.

"I wish I were as sure as you, Prime Minister." As Howden eyed him sharply Lexington shook his head. "Oh, don't misunderstand me; I'm with you the whole way. But the speed of it all disturbs me. The trouble is, we're living in a time of compressed history, yet so few realize it. Changes which used to take fifty years take five or less, and we can't help it because communications have made it that way. The one thing I hope is that we can keep a sense of national unity, but it won't be easy."

"It was never easy," Howden said. He glanced at his watch. They would have to leave Blair House in thirty minutes, to allow for a session with the White House press corps before the official talks began. But he supposed there was time to discuss with Lexington a subject which had been on his own mind for some time. This seemed a good moment to bring it up.

"On the subject of identity," he announced thoughtfully, "there's something the Queen mentioned not long ago—the last time I was in London."

"Yes?"

"The lady has suggested—in fact I may say urged—that we reinstate titles. She made what I thought was an interesting point."

James Howden half-closed his eyes, recalling the scene as it had been, four and a half months earlier: a mellow September afternoon in London; himself at Buckingham Palace for a courtesy call. He had been received with appropriate respect and escorted promptly to the royal presence . . .

". . . Do please have some more tea," the Queen had said, and he had passed the fragile gold-rimmed cup and saucer, unable to resist the thought—though knowing it naive—that the British monarch was pouring tea in her palace for the orphan boy from Medicine Hat.

"And bread and butter, Prime Minister!" He took some. There was brown and white, cut paper-thin. He declined the jam—three kinds in a gold server. As it was, you needed a juggler's skill to balance everything at English teatime.

They were alone in the drawing room of the Private Apartments—a large airy place, overlooking the palace gardens, formal by North American standards but less overpowering with gilt and crystal than most of the other state rooms. The Queen was dressed simply in a silk cornflower-blue dress, her neat ankles crossed casually above matching kid leather pumps. No women, Howden thought with admiration, have quite so much poise as upper-class Englishwomen not consciously trying.

The Queen spread strawberry jam thickly for herself, then observed in her precise, high-pitched voice, "My husband and I have frequently considered that for Canada's own sake there should be more to distinguish it."

James Howden had been tempted to reply that there was a good deal to distinguish Canada, compared with current British achievements, but decided that perhaps he had misinterpreted the meaning. A moment later showed he had.

The Queen added: "To distinguish it in the sense of difference, that is, from the United States."

"The trouble is, ma'am," Howden responded carefully, "it's hard to maintain a separate appearance when two countries live so close and similarly. From time to time we try to emphasize our separateness, though not always succeeding."

"Scotland has succeeded quite well in keeping its identity," the Queen remarked. She stirred her tea, her expression guileless. "Perhaps you should take a lesson or two from them."

"Well . . ." Howden smiled. It was true, he thought. Scotland, which had lost its independence two and a half centuries earlier, still possessed more nationhood and character than Canada ever had or would.

The Queen continued thoughtfully: "One reason, perhaps, is that Scotland has never yielded its traditions. Canada, if you will forgive me for saying so, has seemed in rather a hurry to shed them. I remember my father saying much the same thing." The Queen smiled disarmingly, her manner robbing the words of any offense. "Will you have tea?"

"Thank you, no." Howden surrendered his cup and saucer to a uniformed manservant who had come in quietly with more hot water for the teapot. He had a sense of relief at having balanced everything without mishap.

"I do hope you haven't minded my saying that, Prime Minister." The Queen replenished her own cup as the servant disappeared.

"Not in the least," Howden replied. It was his own turn to smile. "It does us good to be told our failings sometimes, even if one isn't sure what to do about them."

"There is, perhaps, a thing which might be done," the Queen said deliberately. "My husband and I have often regretted the absence of a Canadian honors list. It would give me considerable pleasure if New Year's and Birthday honors were to be established again."

James Howden pursed his lips. "Titles of nobility are delicate ground in North America, ma'am."

"A part of North America, possibly, but are we not speaking of our Dominion of Canada?" Though spoken gently, it was a rebuke and despite himself Howden flushed. "Actually," the Queen observed with the faintest of smiles, "I had gained the impression that in the United States, the British with titles are somewhat sought after."

Touché! Howden thought. How true it was!—Americans loved a lord.

"Our award of honors has worked remarkably well in Australia, I am informed," the Queen went on calmly, "and here in Britain, of course, it continues to do so. Perhaps in Canada it might help you towards separateness from the United States."

James Howden wondered: how were you supposed to handle this kind of thing? As Prime Minister of an independent Commonwealth country his own power was a thousand times greater than the Queen's, yet custom obliged him to assume a fictional role of dutiful deference. Titles, nowadays— "Sirs" and "Lords" and "Ladies"—were nonsense, of course. Canada had had no part of them since the 1930s, and the few residual titles remaining among elderly Canadians were usually referred to with discreet smiles.

With a sense of annoyance the Prime Minister wished the monarchy would content itself with being ornamental, the way it was generally assumed to be, instead of spinning royal spider webs. Behind the Queen's suggestion, he suspected, was the fear one always sensed in London—that Canada was slipping away as other Commonwealth nations had done and that anything, anything—even a silken skein—should be tried in an attempt to delay the drifting.

"I shall inform the Cabinet of your feelings, ma'am," James Howden said. It was a polite lie; he had no intention of doing anything of the kind.

"As you see fit." The Queen inclined her head graciously, then added, "On a related subject, one of our happier prerogatives in awarding honors is to confer an earldom upon Prime Ministers at their retirement from office. It is a custom we should be most happy to extend to Canada." Her innocent eyes met Howden's directly.

An earldom. Despite his own conviction, imagination stirred. It was almost the loftiest rank in British nobility; only marquesses and dukes ranked higher. Of course, he could never accept, but if he did, what title would he take? The Earl of Medicine Hat? No—too outlandish; people would laugh. The Earl of Ottawa? Oh yes! It had a rolling sound, and with deep meaning.

The Queen took a linen napkin, wiped a trace of jam delicately from a manicured finger tip, then rose, James Howden following suit. The intimate tea party was at an end and considerately, as she often did on informal occasions, the Queen strolled with him.

They were halfway across the room when the Queen's husband entered breezily. The Prince came in through a narrow private doorway camouflaged by a long gilt-framed mirror. "Is there any tea left?" he asked cheerfully. Then seeing Howden, "What!—leaving us already?"

"Good afternoon, Your Royal Highness." Howden bowed. He knew better than to reciprocate the informality. The Prince had been responsible for clearing away a good deal of stuffiness around the throne, but he still demanded deference and his eyes could flash and his tone become icy if he sensed it lacking.

"If you really must go, I'll walk with you," the Prince announced. Howden leaned over the Queen's hand which she offered, then with momentary formality retreated the rest of the way out. "Careful!" the Prince warned. "Chair astern to port!" He made a half-hearted attempt at backing out himself.

The Queen's face was stony as they left. Howden surmised that sometimes she felt her husband's breeziness went a little far.

Outside, in an ornate anteroom, the two men shook hands as a liveried footman waited to escort the Prime Minister to his car. "Cheeerio then," the Prince said, unabashed. "Before you go back to Canada try to pop in again."

Ten minutes later, driving down the Mall, away from Buckingham Palace and toward Canada House, James Howden had smiled, remembering. He admired the Prince's determination to be informal, though when you had a permanent rank like the Queen's husband you could turn informality on and off as you pleased. It was permanence of that sort which made a difference to a man, inside as well as out, and politicians like himself always knew that someday soon their tenure of rank would end. Of course, in England most retired cabinet ministers were given titles as a reminder that they had served their country well. But nowadays the system was out of date . . . an absurd charade. It would be even more ridiculous in Canada . . . the Earl of Ottawa, no less. How amused his colleagues would be!

And yet, in fairness, he supposed he ought to examine the Queen's proposal carefully before dismissing it. The lady had a point when she spoke of the need for distinction between Canada and the United States. Perhaps, after all, he should sound out the Cabinet as he had promised. If it was for the country's good . . .

The Earl of Ottawa . . .

But he had not sounded out the Cabinet, nor mentioned the subject to anyone until this moment in Washington with Arthur Lexington. Now, though omitting the Queen's reference to himself, he explained, with touches of humor, the conversation as it had taken place.

At the end, glancing at his watch, he saw that only fifteen minutes remained before they must cross Pennsylvania Avenue to the White House. Rising, he strolled once more to the open library window. Over his shoulder he asked, "Well, what do you think?"

The External Affairs Minister swung down his legs from the footstool and stood upright, stretching. His expression was amused. "It would make us different from the U.S. all right, but I'm not so sure it would be in the right direction."

"I thought much the same thing," Howden said, "but I must say it has since occurred to me that Her Majesty's point about separateness may be well taken. In the future, you know, anything which can help make Canada distinctive and an entity is going to be important." He felt Lexington glance at him curiously and added, "If you feel strongly we'll forget the whole thing, but in view of the lady's request I felt all of us should discuss it."

"Discussion won't do any harm, I suppose," Lexington conceded. He began to pace the rug again.

"The thing is," Howden said, "I wonder if you'd be the one to bring the matter up in Cabinet. I believe it might come better from you, and, that way, I could reserve my judgment until we got some other opinions."

Arthur Lexington said dubiously, "I'd like to think about that, Prime Minister, if you don't mind."

"Of course, Arthur; whatever you decide." Obviously, Howden thought, the subject must be handled cautiously, if at all.

Lexington paused beside a telephone on the polished center table. Half-smiling, he inquired, "Shall we call for coffee before our date with destiny?"

2

Across the swathe of White House lawn dividing them, the President called out cheerfully in his strong, bluff voice to the group of focusing, jostling photographers.

"You men must have shot enough film for a double feature." Then to the Prime Minister at his side: "What do you think, Jim? Shall we go inside and begin work?"

"It's a pity, Mr. President," James Howden said. After the chill Ottawa winter, he had enjoyed the warmth and sunshine. "But I suppose we'd better." He nodded agreeably to the short, broad-shouldered man with the angular, bony features and sharp, determined jaw. The outdoor session which both of them had just had with the White House press corps had pleased Howden greatly. Throughout, the President had deferred courteously to the Prime Minister, saying little, and turning reporters' questions toward Howden so that the latter would be the one quoted today and tomorrow in press, TV, and radio. And afterwards, when they had strolled together on the south lawn of the White House for the benefit of photographers and TV cameras, the President had carefully maneuvered James Howden nearest the battery of lenses. The result of such consideration, Howden thought—a rare experience for a Canadian in Washington—could contribute a good deal to his own status back home.

He felt the President's massive, big-fingered hand grasp his arm, steering, and the two of them moved towards the Executive Mansion steps. The other man's face, under the untidy thatch of gray-flecked hair with its abbreviated cowlick, was relaxed and agreeable. "How'd it be, Jim . . ."—it was the easy Midwestern twang used so effectively in the televised Fireside Talks—"How'd it be if we dropped the Mr. President business?" A deep chuckle. "You know my first name, I imagine."

Genuinely pleased, Howden replied, "I'd be honored, Tyler." In a segment of his mind he wondered if it would be possible to leak this intimate relationship to the press. In Canada it would give the lie to some of his critics who were always carping that the Howden government lacked influence in Washington. Of course, he recognized that most of the courtesies today and yesterday had stemmed from Canada's strong bargaining position—which he intended to uphold. But that was no reason for not being pleased, or making political hay whenever one could.

As they stolled across the lawn, the ground soft beneath their feet, James Howden said, "There hasn't been an opportunity before to congratulate you personally on your reelection."

"Why, thank you, Jim!" Again the pawlike hand, this time clapped firmly on the Prime Minister's shoulder. "Yes, it was a wonderful election. I'm proud to say I have the largest popular vote a United States President has ever received. And we swept Congress, as you know. That's something else again—no President has ever enjoyed stronger support than I have right at this moment in the House and Senate. I can tell you confidentially there isn't any legislation I want that I can't get passed. Oh, I make few concessions here and there for the sake of it, but nothing to matter. It's a unique situation."

"Unique for you, perhaps," Howden said. He decided some good-natured needling would do no harm. "But, of course, with our own parliamentary system the party in power can always have the legislation it wants."

"True! True! And don't think there haven't been times when I—and some of my predecessors—have envied you. The miracle about our constitution, you know, is that it works at all." The President's voice ranged lustily on. "The trouble was, the Founding Fathers were so damned anxious to cut loose from everything British that they threw out the best things along with the bad. But one makes the best of what one has, whether it's the body politic or the body personal."

With the last words they had reached the wide, balustraded steps leading under the curved and colonnaded South Portico. Preceding his guest, the President leaped upward two steps at a time and, not to be outdone, James Howden followed at the same pace.

But at the halfway mark the Prime Minister stopped, short of breath and perspiring. His dark blue worsted suit, ideal in Ottawa, was uncomfortably heavy in the warm Washington sunshine. He wished he had brought one of his lightweight suits, but on looking them over none had seemed quite good enough for this occasion. The President was reported to be meticulous about dress and sometimes changed suits several times a day. But then, the U.S. Chief Executive was not subject to the personal money worries of a Canadian Prime Minister.

The thought reminded Howden briefly that he had not yet broken the news to Margaret of just how serious their own financial position had become. The man from Montreal Trust had made it clear: unless they stopped eroding the few thousands of capital remaining, his resources on retirement would be equal to the wages of a minor artisan. Of course, it would never really come to that: the Rockefeller Foundation and others could be appealed to—Rockefeller had granted Mackenzie King a hundred thousand dollars on the day of the veteran Prime Minister's retirement—but the thought of actively seeking an American handout, however generous, was still humiliating.

A few steps up the President had stopped. He said contritely, "Do forgive me. I'm always forgetting, and doing that to people."

"I should have known better." James Howden's heart was pounding; his heavy breathing punctuated the words. "I expect it was your remark about the body personal." Like everyone else he was aware of the President's lifelong passion for physical fitness in himself and those around him. A succession of White House aides, including dispirited generals and admirals, staggered exhausted from daily presidential sessions of handball, tennis, or badminton. A frequent complaint from the President's lips was that "This generation has the bellies of Buddhas and shoulders like bloodhounds' ears." It was the President, too, who had revived the Theodore Roosevelt pastime of taking country walks in straight lines, going over objects—trees, barns, haystacks—instead of around them. He had even attempted something of the kind in Washington and, remembering, Howden asked, "How did those local forays of yours go— the A to B idea?"

The other man chortled as they moved together, leisurely, up the stairs. "I had to quit in the end; got into a few problems. We couldn't scramble over buildings here, except some small ones, so we started going through them wherever a straight line led. Got in some strange places too, including a toilet in the Pentagon—in the door and out the window." He chuckled reminiscently. "But one day my brother and I wound up in the Statler Hotel kitchens—walked in the cold room and short of blasting there was no way out."

Howden laughed. "Perhaps we'll try it in Ottawa. There are some of the Opposition I'd like to see depart in straight lines—especially if they'd keep on going."

"Our opponents are sent to try us, Jim."

"I suppose so," Howden said. "But some try harder than others. By the way, I've brought some new rock samples for your collection. Our Mines and Resources people tell me they're unique."

"Well, thank you," the President said. "I'm really most grateful. And please thank your people too."

From the South Portico's shade they passed into the cool White House interior, then threaded a hallway and corridors to the presidential office on the building's southeast corner. Opening the white-painted single door, the President ushered Howden in.

As usual, on the several occasions he had been here, the Prime Minister was conscious of the room's simplicity. Oval-shaped, with waist-high paneling and plain gray carpeting, its principal furnishings comprised a wide flat-topped desk, set center, a padded swivel chair in the rear and, behind the chair, twin gold-trimmed banners—the Stars and Stripes and the President's personal flag. Floor-to-ceiling casement windows and a french door to a terrace outside faced a satin-damask sofa occupying most of one wall to the desk's right. At present the sofa was occupied by Arthur Lexington and

Admiral Levin Rapoport, the latter a small, scrawny man in a neat brown suit, his hawklike face and incongruously large head seeming to dwarf the remainder of his body. The two men rose as the President and Prime Minister came in.

"Good morning, Arthur," the President said warmly, offering his hand to Lexington. "Jim, you know Levin, of course."

"Yes," Howden said, "we've met. How are you, Admiral?"

"Good morning." Admiral Rapoport nodded curtly and coolly. He seldom did more, notoriously having no patience either for small talk or social functions. The admiral—presidential assistant *extraordinaire*—had been a notable absentee from the previous evening's state banquet.

As the four men sat down, a tray of drinks was whisked in by a Filipino manservant. Arthur Lexington chose scotch and water, the President a dry sherry. Admiral Rapoport shook his head in refusal and, before James Howden, the man smilingly placed a glass of iced grape juice.

While the drinks were being served Howden watched the admiral covertly, recalling what he had heard of this man who (some said) was now virtually as powerful as the President himself.

Four years earlier Captain Levin Rapoport, U.S.N., had been a regular navy officer on the point of compulsory retirement—compulsory because his superior admirals had twice passed him over for promotion despite a brilliant, highly-publicized career in pioneering underwater firing of intercontinental missiles. The trouble was that almost no one liked Levin Rapoport personally and a surprising number of influential superiors harbored feelings of active hatred. Mostly, the latter stemmed from a long-standing Rapoport habit of being dead right on every major issue affecting naval defense, and afterwards never hesitating to say "I told you so," singling out by name those who had disagreed with him.

Coupled with this was a massive personal conceit (entirely justified, but unpleasant nonetheless), grossly bad manners, impatience with "channels" and red tape, and open contempt for those whom Captain Rapoport considered his intellectual inferiors, as most were.

But what the higher navy brass had not foreseen in deciding to retire its controversial genius was the fierce outcry —from Congress and the public—at the prospect of the nation's loss if the Rapoport brain were no longer brooding actively upon its affairs. As one congressman put it succinctly, "Goddam, we *need* the bastard."

Thereupon, prodded sharply both from the Senate and White House, the Navy had climbed down and promoted Captain Rapoport to rear admiral, thus avoiding his retirement. Two years and two ranks later, following a series of fresh brilliancies, Rapoport (a full admiral by now and pricklier than ever) had been whisked by the President from the Navy's orbit to be presidential chief of staff. Within a few weeks, through zeal, speed, and sheer ability, the new appointee was exercising more direct power than predecessors like Harry Hopkins, Sherman Adams, or Ted Sorenson had ever enjoyed.

Since then the list of directed achievements, known and unknown, had been formidable; a self-help overseas aid program which, though late, was gaining America respect instead of contempt; at home, an agriculture policy which farmers fought savagely, claiming it wouldn't work, but (as Rapoport had said from the beginning would happen) it did; a crash research effort and, for long term, realignment of scientific education and pure research; and in law enforcement a crackdown on industrial fraud at one end of the scale and, at the other, a housecleaning of labor, with Lufto, the once supreme labor hoodlum, ousted and jailed.

Someone (James Howden recalled) had asked in a moment of intimacy with the President, "If Rapoport's that good, why doesn't he have your job?"

The President (it was said) had smiled benignly and answered, "It's simply that I can get elected. Levin wouldn't receive six votes for dog catcher."

Along the way, while the President had been acclaimed for his shrewdness in choosing talent, Admiral Rapoport continued to attract animosity and hate in much the same proportion as before.

James Howden wondered how this austere and harsh-minded man would affect Canada's destiny.

"Before we go on," the President said, "I'd like to ask: have you been getting everything you need at Blair House?"

Arthur Lexington replied smilingly, "We're being cosseted with kindness."

"Well, I'm glad of that." The President had settled himself

comfortably behind the big desk. "Sometimes we have a little trouble over the road there—like when the Arabs burned incense, and part of the house along with it. Though I guess you won't check under the paneling the way the Russians did, looking for concealed microphones."

"We'll promise not to," Howden said, "if you'll tell us where they are."

The President gave his deep throaty chuckle. "You'd better cable the Kremlin. Anyway, I shouldn't be surprised if they slipped their own transmitter in while they were about it."

"That might not be such a bad arrangement," Howden said easily. "At least we'd get through to them. We don't seem to be doing much of a job by other means."

"No," the President agreed quietly, "I'm afraid we don't."

There was a sudden silence. Through a partially opened window the sound of traffic on B Street and children's cries from the White House playground, drifted in faintly. From somewhere close by, muted by intervening walls, a clack of typewriter keys could be sensed rather than heard. Subtly, Howden realized, the atmosphere had changed from flippancy to deadly seriousness. Now he asked, "For the record, Tyler, do you still hold the opinion that open major conflict, within a comparatively short time, has become inevitable?"

"With all my heart and soul," the President answered, "I wish that I could say no. I can only tell you—yes."

"And we're not ready, are we?" It was Arthur Lexington, his cherubic face pensive.

The President leaned forward. Behind him a breeze stirred the curtains and twin flags. "No, gentlemen," he said softly, "we are not ready, and shall not be, until the United States and Canada, acting in the name of freedom and the hope of a better world we cling to, have manned, together, our single border and our common fortress."

Well, Howden thought, we've come to the point quickly. The eyes of the others upon him, he said matter-of-factly, "I've given your proposal for an Act of Union a great deal of consideration, Tyler."

There was a ghost of a smile on the President's face. "Yes, Jim; I imagined you would."

"There are many objections," Howden said.

"When something of this magnitude is involved"—the voice came quietly across the desk—"it would be surprising if there were not."

"On the other hand," Howden declared, "I may tell you that my senior colleagues and I are aware of substantial advantages in what is proposed, but only if certain considerations are met and specific guarantees given."

"You talk of considerations and guarantees." It was Admiral Rapoport, head thrust forward, speaking for the first time. His voice was taut and crisp. "No doubt you, and the colleagues you refer to, have taken into account that any guarantee, from whatever source, would be useless without survival."

"Yes," Arthur Lexington said, "we've considered that."

The President interjected quickly, "A point I'd like us to hold in mind, Jim—you too, Arthur—is that time is against us. That's the reason I want us to move swiftly. It's also why we must speak plainly, even if we ruffle some feathers in the doing of it."

Howden smiled grimly. "There'll be no ruffled feathers, unless they're on your eagle. What do you suggest first?"

"I'd like to cover the ground again, Jim; that's what I'd like to do. Go over what we talked of last week by telephone. Let's be sure we understand each other. Then we'll see which way the compass points from there."

The Prime Minister glanced at Lexington who gave the slightest of nods. "Very well," Howden said. "I'm agreeable to that. Will you be the one to begin?"

"Yes, I will." The President settled his broad-shouldered body in the swivel chair, half-turning from the others and toward the sunlight outside. Then he swung back, his eyes meeting Howden's.

"I spoke of time," the President said slowly. "Time in which to prepare for the attack which we know inevitably must come."

From the sidelines Arthur Lexington asked quietly, "How long do you think we have?"

"There is no time," the President answered. "By reckoning, reason, logic, we've used it all. And if we do have time— for anything—it will be by God's good grace alone." Softly: "Are you a believer in God's good grace, Arthur?"

"Well," Lexington smiled, "it's a nebulous kind of thing."

"But it's there, believe me." Above the desk a hand rose,

pawlike, fingers spread as if in benediction. "It saved the British once when they stood alone, and it may yet save us. I'm praying that it will, and I'm praying for the gift of a year. There can't be any more."

Howden interjected, "Three hundred days is what I'd hoped for myself."

The President nodded. "If we get it, it will be from God. And whatever we get, tomorrow will be a day less, and an hour from now, an hour less." The voice, with its Midwestern tone, quickened. "So let us consider the picture as we in Washington see it now."

Point by point, with a master's instinct for order and summary, the brush strokes filled in. First the factors which Howden had described for his own Defense Committee: the primary protection of U.S. food-producing areas—key to survival after nuclear attack; the bristling missile bases on the U.S.-Canada border; the inevitability of missile intercept over Canadian territory; Canada the battleground, defenseless, destroyed by explosion and fallout; its food areas poisoned . . .

Then the alternative: missile bases to the North, greater U.S. striking power, early intercept with reduction of fallout over both countries, avoidance of the battleground, and a chance for survival. But the desperate need of speed, and authority for America to move quickly . . . The Act of Union as proposed; total assumption of Canadian defense by the United States, and joint conduct of foreign affairs; disbandment of all Canadian armed forces and immediate re-recruitment under a joint Oath of Allegiance; abolition of border restrictions; customs union; the twenty-five-year term; a guarantee of Canadian sovereignty in all matters not proscribed . . .

The President declared simply: "In face of our common peril, which knows no border and respects no sovereignty, we offer the Act of Union in friendship, esteem, and honor."

Now there was a pause, the gaze of the small sturdy figure behind the desk ranging quizzically over the other three men. A hand went up to push back the familiar graying cowlick. The eyes beneath were wise and alert, James Howden thought, but behind them was an unmistakable sadness, the sadness perhaps of a man who has achieved so little of his lifetime's dream.

It was Arthur Lexington who interposed quietly, "Whatever the motives, Mr. President, it isn't a slight matter to abandon independence and change the course of history overnight."

"Nevertheless," the President observed, "the course of history will change whether we direct its course or not. Borders are not immutable, Arthur; nor have they ever been in human history. Every border that we know will change or disappear in time, and so will our own and Canada's, whether we hasten the process or not. Nations may last a century or two, or even more; but in the end there's no forever."

"I agree with you there." Lexington smiled faintly. He put down the drink he had been holding. "But will everyone else?"

"No, not everyone." The President shook his head. "Patriots—the ardent ones, at least—have short-term minds. But others—if it's put to them plainly—will face facts when they have to."

"Perhaps they may in time," James Howden said. "But as you point out, Tyler—and I agree—time is the one commodity we lack."

"In that case, Jim, I'd like to hear what you suggest."

The moment had come. This was the time, Howden thought, for plain, hard dealing. Here was the crucial point at which Canada's future—if one existed—would be determined. True, even if broad agreement were reached now, there would be more negotiating later on, and specifics—many specifics and infinite detail—would have to be hammered out by experts on both sides. But that would come afterwards. The big broad issues, the major concessions—if any were to be wrung—would be determined here and now between the President and himself.

It was quiet in the oval room. There were no longer noises of traffic or children from outside—perhaps the wind had changed; and the typewriter had stopped. Arthur Lexington shifted position on the sofa; beside him Admiral Rapoport remained still—as he had from the beginning—as if lashed in place. The President's chair creaked as he swung it slightly, his eyes troubled and questioning across the desk, fixed on the Prime Minister's hawklike, brooding face. *We are merely four men,* Howden thought . . . *ordinary mortal men, of flesh and blood, who will die soon and be forgotten . . . and yet, what we decide today will affect the world for centuries to come.*

For a moment, as the silence hung, James Howden's mind was torn with indecision. Now that reality had come, doubt —as earlier—assailed him. A sense of history wrestled with a sane appraisal of known facts. Was his presence here, by its very nature, a betrayal of his own country? Was practicality—which had brought him to Washington—a matter for shame and not a virtue? These were specters he had already faced, fears he had allayed. But now they arose, fresh and challenging again.

Then he reasoned, as he had in the days past, that the course of human history had shown national pride—the inflexible kind—to be mankind's worst enemy, and ordinary people paid the price in suffering. Nations had gone down because of vainglory, when moderation might have civilized and saved them. Canada, he was determined, should not go down.

"If this is to be done," James Howden said, "I shall need a mandate from our own voters. That means I must fight an election—and win."

"I'd expected that," the President said. "Will it be soon?"

"Tentatively I'd say early June."

The other nodded. "I don't see how you could do it faster."

"It will be a short campaign," Howden pointed out, "and we'll have strong opposition. Therefore I must have specific things to offer."

Arthur Lexington put in, "I'm sure, Mr. President, that as a practical politician yourself, you'll see how necessary that is."

The President grinned broadly. "I'm almost afraid to agree for fear you fellows will hold me to ransom. So let me say: yes, I'm sure you'll get hell from your Opposition, but after all that's no novelty for any of us here. You'll win, though, Jim; I'm sure of it. But as to the other—yes, I do see."

"There are a number of points," Howden said.

The President leaned back in his swivel chair. "Shoot!"

"Canadian industry and employment must be safeguarded after the Act of Union." Howden's voice was clear, his tone emphatic. He was no supplicant, he took pains to make clear, but an equal discussing equalities. "United States investment and manufacturing in Canada must continue and expand. We don't want General Motors moving out because of customs union, consolidating with Detroit; or Ford with Dearborn. The same thing goes for smaller industry."

"I agree," the President said. He toyed with a pencil upon the desk. "Industrial weakness would be a disadvantage all around. Something can be worked out, and I'd say you'll get more industry, not less."

"A specific guarantee?"

The President nodded. "A specific guarantee. Our Commerce Department and your Trade and Finance people can devise a tax incentive formula." Both Admiral Rapoport and Arthur Lexington were making notes on pads beside them.

Howden got up from the chair facing the President's, took a turn away, then back. "Raw materials," he announced; "Canada will control withdrawal permits and we want a guarantee against plundering. There's to be no bonanza for Americans—taking everything out for processing elsewhere."

Admiral Rapoport said sharply, "You've been ready enough to sell your raw resources in the past—if the price was high."

"That's the past," Howden snapped. "We're discussing the future." He was beginning to understand why dislike of the presidential assistant was so widespread.

"Never mind," the President interceded. "There *should* be more secondary manufacturing on the spot and it will help both countries. Next!"

"Defense contracts and foreign-aid buying," Howden said. "Canada will want some major manufacturing—aircraft and missiles, not just screws and bolts."

The President sighed. "There'll be hell to pay from our own lobbies. But somehow we'll do it." More notes.

"I'll want one of my own cabinet ministers here in the White House," Howden said. He had seated himself again. "Someone who can be close to you to interpret both our points of view."

"I'd planned to offer you something of the kind," the President observed. "What else do you have?"

"Wheat!" the Prime Minister announced. "Your own exports and giveaways have taken over what were once our markets. What's more, Canada can't compete with production subsidized on your scale."

The President glanced at Admiral Rapoport who thought briefly, then stated, "We could give a no-interference guarantee, I suppose, affecting Canadian commercial sales, and insure that the Canadian surplus—up to last year's figures—is sold first."

THE WHITE HOUSE 217

"Well?" The President cocked a quizzical eyebrow at Howden.

The Prime Minister took his time about answering. Then he said carefully, "I'd prefer to accept the first part of the deal and leave the second to negotiation. If your production increases, so should ours, with matching guarantees."

With a trace of coolness the President asked, "Aren't you pressing a little, Jim?"

"I don't think so." Howden met the other's eyes directly. He had no intention of conceding yet. Besides, his biggest demand was still to come.

There was a pause, then the President nodded. "Very well —negotiation."

They continued to talk—of trade, industry, employment, foreign relations, consular activities, foreign exchange, domestic economics, authority of Canadian civil courts over U.S. forces . . . In each instance the concessions the Prime Minister sought were granted, sometimes with minor modifications, in some cases after discussion, but mostly with none. It was not surprising really, Howden thought. Obviously there had been anticipation of most of the things he asked and the President had entered their parley prepared for speed and action.

If times had been ordinary—as much as any time in history is ordinary, James Howden reasoned—the concessions he had already wrested would remove obstacles to Canadian development which previous governments had sought to change for generations. But—he was forced to remind himself—the times were not ordinary or any future certain.

Lunchtime came and went. Absorbed, they had cold roast beef, a salad, and coffee on trays in the presidential office.

For dessert the Prime Minister nibbled on a chocolate bar which he had pocketed before leaving Blair House. It was one of a supply which the Canadian Ambassador had sent around the previous day, the Prime Minister's sweet tooth being well known among intimates and friends.

And afterwards there arrived the moment for which James Howden had waited.

He had asked for a map of North America and, during lunch, one had been hung on the wall facing the President's desk. It was a large-scale political map with Canadian territory colored pink, the United States sepia, and Mexico green. The U.S.-Canadian border—a long black line—ran clear across the center. Beside the map a pointer had been propped against the wall.

Now James Howden addressed the President directly. "As you observed an hour or two ago, Tyler, borders are not immutable. We of Canada—if the Act of Union becomes law in both our countries—are prepared to accept a change of border as a fact of life. The point is: are you?"

The President leaned forward across the desk, his brow furrowed. "I'm not sure I follow you, Jim."

Admiral Rapoport's face was expressionless.

"When the nuclear firing begins," the Prime Minister said, speaking carefully, "anything can happen. We may gain victory of a sort; or we may be routed and invaded, in which case no present plan will help. Or, in a short time, we may reach stalemate, with the enemy as reduced and helpless as ourselves."

The President sighed. "All our so-called experts tell me we shall virtually destroy each other in a matter of days. God knows how much or little they really know, but one has to predicate plans on something."

Howden smiled as a passing thought struck him. "I know what you mean about experts. My barber has a theory that after a nuclear war the earth will split down the middle and break into pieces. Sometimes I wonder if I shouldn't put him in the Defense Department."

"The real thing that stops us," Arthur Lexington added, "is that he's a damn good barber."

The President laughed. Admiral Rapoport's face creased slightly in what might have been a smile.

Seriously once more, the Prime Minister went on, "For our present purpose I believe we must consider the postwar situation on the assumption that we will not be defeated."

The President nodded. "I agree."

"In that case," Howden said, "it seems to me there are two main possibilities. First, that both our governments— Canada and the U.S.—may have ceased to function entirely, so that law and order are non-existent. In that event, nothing we say or do here can be of usefulness at that time; and I suppose, in any case, none of us in this room would be around as observers."

How casually we talk of it all, he thought: life and death; survival and annihilation; the candle burning, the candle snuffed. And yet in our hearts we never really accept the

truth. Always we assume that something, somehow, will
impede the ultimate ending.

The President had risen silently from behind the desk.
Turning his back to the others, he drew aside a curtain so
that he was looking out across the White House lawn. The
sun had gone in, Howden noticed; gray stratus cloud was
filling the sky. Without turning the President intoned, "You
said two possibilities, Jim."

"Yes," Howden assented. "The second possibility is the one
I believe most likely." The President left the window, returning to his chair. His face, Howden thought, seemed wearier
than before.

Admiral Rapoport inquired, "What about your second
point?" His tone said: Get on with it!

"It is the possibility," Howden said evenly, "that both our
governments will survive to some extent, but that Canada,
by reason of our closeness to the enemy, will have taken the
severest blow."

The President said softly, "Jim, I swear to you before God
that we shall do the best we can . . . before and afterwards."

"I know," Howden said, "and it's the 'afterwards' I'm considering. If there's a future for Canada, you must give us
the key."

"Key?"

"Alaska," James Howden said quietly. "Alaska is the key."

He was conscious of the rhythm of his own breathing,
aware from outside of a sudden minuet of melding sounds:
the muted, distant note of an automobile horn; a patter of
first raindrops; a bird's soft chirruping. Arthur Lexington, he
reasoned inconsequentially, could name what breed of bird
it was . . . Arthur Lexington, ornithologist . . . The Right
Honorable Arthur Edward Lexington, P.C., M.A., LL.D.,
Secretary of State for External Affairs, his command on each
Canadian passport: "In the name of Her Majesty the Queen
. . . allow the bearer to pass freely without let or hindrance
. . . afford assistance and protection." Arthur Lexington . . .
now poker faced, challenging with himself, James Howden,
the might and union of the United States.

You must give us Alaska, he repeated in his mind. *Alaska
is the key.*

Silence. Immobility.

Admiral Rapoport, beside Lexington on the sofa: still. No
warmth, no message, on the crinkled parchment face, the

outsize head. Only steely eyes, coldly staring. Hurry . . . come to the point . . . don't waste my time . ! . how dare you . . . !

How dare he . . . How dare he face, across that flag-flanked desk, the incumbent of the mightiest office in the world . . . with himself—leader of a smaller, weaker power—outwardly calm, inwardly tense, his absurd, preposterous demand already spoken.

He remembered the exchange between himself and Arthur Lexington eleven days earlier, the day before the cabinet committee. "The Americans would never agree, never," Lexington had said. And he had answered: "If they are desperate enough, I think perhaps they might."

Alaska. Alaska is the key.

The President's eyes were staring. They mirrored disbelief. And still the silence.

After time which seemed endless, the President swiveled in his chair. He said evenly, "Unless I have misunderstood you, I cannot believe that you are serious."

"I have never been more serious," James Howden said, "in all my political life."

Now, standing himself, he said forcefully and clearly, "You were the one, Tyler, who spoke today of our 'common fortress'; it was you who declared that our policies must concern themselves with 'how' rather than 'if'; you who affirm urgency, the absence of time. Well, I tell you now, and speaking for the Government of Canada, that there is agreement with all you say. But I tell you too, that for our own survival —and this we are determined upon if the Act of Union is to be accomplished—Alaska must become Canadian."

The President spoke earnestly, pleadingly, "Jim, it could never be done, believe me."

"You're mad!" It was Admiral Rapoport, his face flushed.

"It *can* be done!" Howden hurled the words across the room. "And I'm not mad, but sane. Sane enough to want survival of my own country; sane enough to fight for it—as, by God, I will!"

"But not this way . . . !"

"Listen to me!" Howden crossed swiftly to the map and took the pointer resolutely. He swung the tip in an arc, from east to west, the line he followed tracing the 49th parallel. "Between here and here"—he traced a second line across the 60th parallel—"your experts and ours tell us there will be devastation and fallout, perhaps—if we are lucky—in great patches across the country; perhaps overall, if we are not. Therefore our only chance of rebuilding afterwards, our sole hope for consolidating whatever is left of Canada, is to establish a new focal point, a new national center away from devastation and until such time as we can regroup and move back, if ever we do."

The Prime Minister paused, surveying the others grimly. The President's eyes were riveted upon the map. Admiral Rapoport opened his mouth as if to interject once more, then closed it. Arthur Lexington was covertly watching the admiral's profile.

"The Canadian regrouping territory," Howden continued, "must meet three main needs. It must be south of the tree line and the subarctic zone; if it were not, communications and support of life would be beyond our means. Second, the area must be west of our combined northern missile line; and, third, it must be a place where fallout is likely to be negative or light. North of the 49th parallel there is only one such area meeting all requirements—Alaska."

The President asked softly, "How can you be sure about fallout?"

Howden replaced the pointer against the wall. "If, at this moment, I had to pick the safest place in the Northern Hemisphere during a nuclear war," he said, "it would be Alaska. It is fortified against invasion. Vladivostok, the nearest major target, is three thousand miles away. Fallout, either from Soviet attacks or our own, will be unlikely. As certain as anything can be—Alaska will come through."

"Yes," the President said, "I think I agree with you—about that at least." He sighed. "But as to the other . . . its an ingenious idea—and I must admit in honesty that a good deal of it makes sense. But surely you must see that neither I nor Congress can barter away a state of the Union."

"In that case," James Howden replied coldly, "there is even less reason for my own Government to barter away a country."

Admiral Rapoport snorted angrily, "The Act of Union would involve no bartering away."

"That scarcely seems true," Arthur Lexington interceded sharply. "Canada would pay a heavy price."

"No!" The admiral's voice took on a cutting edge. "Far from paying a price, it would be an act of amazing generosity to a greedy, vacillating country which has made a national pastime of timidity, fence-straddling, and hypocrisy. You talk of rebuilding Canada, but why bother? America did it for you once before; we'll probably do it again."

James Howden had resumed his chair. Now, his face suffused with anger, he sprang to his feet. He said icily, "I don't believe I have to listen to this, Tyler."

"No, Jim," the President said calmly, "I don't believe you do. Except that we agreed to speak plainly, and sometimes there are things better said, and out in the open."

Tense with resentment, Howden fumed, "Am I to assume that you subscribe to this vicious libel?"

"Well, Jim, I grant that what was said could have been put more tactfully, but then that isn't Levin's way, though if you like I apologize for his choice of words." The voice drawled easily across the desk to the Prime Minister, still standing erect. "But I'd also say he has a point about Canada always wanting a great deal. Even now, with all that we are offering in the Act of Union, you're demanding more."

Arthur Lexington had risen along with Howden. Now he walked to the window and, turning, his eyes were on Admiral Rapoport. "Perhaps," he observed, "it's because we're entitled to more."

"No!" The word snapped back from the admiral as though a needle had been jabbed. "I said you were a greedy nation and so you are." His thin voice rose. "Thirty years ago you wanted an American standard of living, but you wanted it overnight. You chose to ignore that American standards took a century of sweat and belt-tightening to build. So you opened up your raw wealth that you might have husbanded instead; and you let Americans move in, develop your birthright, take the risks, and run the show. That way you bought your standard of living—then you sneered at the things we had in common."

"Levin . . ." the President remonstrated.

"Hypocrisy, I said!" As if he had not heard, the admiral stormed on, "You sold your birthright, then went searching for it with talk about distinctive Canadianism. Well, there was a Canadianism once, but you got soft and lost it, and not all your Royal Commissions piled on end will ever find it now."

Hating the other man, his own voice tight with anger, James Howden exclaimed, "It hasn't all been softness. There's a list from two world wars you may have heard of: St. Eloi,

Vimy, Dieppe, Sicily, Ortona, Normandy, Caen, Falaise . . ."

"There are always exceptions!" the admiral snapped. "But I also recall that while U.S. Marines were dying in the Coral Sea, the Parliament of Canada was debating conscription—which you never had."

Wrathfully Howden said, "There were other factors—Quebec, compromise . . ."

"Compromise, fence-straddling, timidity . . . what in hell's the difference when it's a national pastime? And you'll still be fence-straddling on the day the United States defends Canada with nuclear weapons—weapons you're glad we have, but are too self-righteous to employ yourselves."

The admiral had risen and was standing facing Howden. The Prime Minister resisted an urgent impulse to strike out, raining blows on the face before him. Instead the President broke the hostile silence. "I tell you what," he suggested. "Why don't you two fellows get together tomorrow morning at dawn by the Potomac. Arthur and I will be seconds, and we'll have the Smithsonian lend us pistols and swords."

Lexington inquired dryly, "Which of the two would you recommend?"

"Oh, if I were Jim, I'd take pistols," the President said. "The only ship Levin ever commanded missed everything it fired on."

"We had poor ammunition," the admiral remarked. For the first time the ghost of a smile creased his leathery face. "Weren't you Secretary of the Navy then?"

"I've been so many things," the President said. "It's hard to remember."

Despite the lessened tension, the heat of indignation still gripped Howden. He wanted to retaliate; to return words in kind, countering what had been said; attacking, as he could so readily: An accusation of greed came ill from a nation grown fat and opulent from riches . . . Timidity was hardly a charge to be laid by the United States which had practiced selfish isolationism until forced at gun point to abandon it . . . Even Canadian vacillation was better than the blundering, naive ineptness of American diplomacy, with its crude belief in the dollar as an answer to all problems . . . America with its insufferably virtuous air of always being right; its refusal to believe that other concepts, alien systems of government, might sometimes have their virtues; its obstinate support of puppet, discredited regimes abroad . . . And at home

slick, glib talk of freedom through the same mouth which
smeared dissenters . . . and more, much more . . .

About to speak . . . fiercely, wildly . . . James Howden
checked himself.

At times, he thought, there was statesmanship in silence.
No catalogue of faults could ever be one-sided, and most of
what Admiral Rapoport had said was uncomfortably true.

Besides, whatever else Rapoport might be, he was no fool.
Subtly the Prime Minister had an instinct that a performance
had been staged with himself as a participant. Had there been
a deliberate attempt, he wondered, adroitly managed by the
admiral, to throw him off balance? Perhaps; perhaps not; but
brawling would achieve nothing. He was determined not to
lose sight of the original issue.

Ignoring the others, he faced the President. "I must make it
perfectly clear, Tyler," he announced evenly, "that failing a
concession on the issue of Alaska there can be no agreement
between our respective governments."

"Jim, you *must* see that the entire situation is impossible."
The President seemed calm and controlled, unshakable as
ever. But the fingers of his right hand, Howden noticed,
were drumming urgently upon the desk top. Now he went on,
"Couldn't we go back?—let's talk about the other conditions.
Maybe there are more points we can cover, things we can
spell out to Canada's advantage."

"No." Howden shook his head firmly. "First, I don't see
the situation as impossible and, second, we'll talk of Alaska
or nothing." He was convinced now—there *had* been an
attempt to make him lose control. Of course, even if it
had succeeded, the other side might have gained no advantage. But on the other hand he might just have tipped his
hand on how far he was prepared to compromise if forced.
The President was a seasoned, wily negotiator who would
never miss a hint like that if given.

The Prime Minister rubbed the tip of his long nose gently.
"I'd like to tell you," he said, "of the conditions we have in
mind. Foremost, there would be a free election in Alaska,
jointly supervised, and with a 'yes' or 'no' vote."

The President said, "You'd never win." But the deep-
pitched voice was a shade less dogmatic than before. Howden
had a sense that subtly, in some undefinable way, dominance
of the negotiations had shifted to himself. He recalled Arthur
Lexington's words earlier in the morning: "Put in its crudest

terms I'd say we're in a seller's market. The concessions we have to offer, the United States needs, and needs badly."

"Frankly, I think we *would* win," Howden said, "and we'd go into the campaign intending to. There has always been a good deal of pro-Canadian feeling in Alaska, and lately it's intensified. What's more, whether you know it or not, the bloom has worn off statehood. You haven't done as much for them as they expected, and they're lonely up there. If we took over, we'd create a duplicate center of government. We'd make Juneau—or maybe Anchorage—a secondary capital of Canada. We'd concentrate on Alaskan development ahead of all other provinces. We'd give Alaskans a sense of no longer being apart."

"I'm sorry," the President said flatly. "I can't accept all that."

This was the moment, Howden knew, to play his ace. "Perhaps you will believe more readily," he announced quietly, "if I tell you that the first approach in this matter has come, not from Canada, but from Alaska itself."

The President stood up. His eyes were riveted on Howden's. He said sharply, "Please explain yourself."

"Two months ago," the Prime Minister declared, "I was approached in secrecy by a single spokesman for a group of prominent Alaskans. The proposal I have made to you today is the proposal made to me at that time."

The President moved from behind the desk. His face was close to Howden's. "The names," he said. His voice was unbelieving. "I would have to know the names."

Arthur Lexington produced a single sheet of paper. Taking it, the Prime Minister passed it to the President. "These are the names."

As he read, incredulity spread over the President's face. At the end he passed the list to Admiral Rapoport.

"I will not attempt . . ." For once the words came haltingly. "I will not attempt, I say, to hide from you that these names and information are a considerable shock."

Howden was silent, waiting.

"Assuming," the President said slowly, "just assuming there was a plebiscite, and you lost."

"As I say, we wouldn't expect to. We'd make the specific terms attractive, just as you've made the Act of Union attractive. And you yourself would urge a 'yes' vote on the grounds of North American unity and defense."

"Would I?" Eyebrows shot up.

"Yes, Tyler," Howden said firmly; "that would be a part of our agreement."

"But even with that, you might lose," the President persisted. "The vote might go 'no.'"

"Obviously, if that happened, we would accept the decision. Canadians believe in self-determination too."

"In that event, what about the Act of Union?"

"It would be unaffected," James Howden said. "With the promise of Alaska—or at least the plebiscite—I can win an election in Canada, and a mandate for the Act of Union. The plebiscite would come afterwards and, whatever the result, there could be no going back on what was already done."

"Well . . ." The President glanced at Admiral Rapoport, whose face was inscrutable. Then, half in thought, half-aloud: "It would mean a constitutional convention in the State . . . If I took it to Congress, I suppose those conditions would make it discussable . . ."

Howden remarked quietly, "May I remind you of your own statement about congressional support. I believe your words were: 'There isn't any legislation I want that I can't have passed.'"

The President slammed a fist into his palm. "Goddam, Jim! You're adroit at turning a man's own words against him."

"I should warn you, Mr. President," Arthur Lexington said easily, "the gentleman has a tape-recorder memory for spoken words. At times, back home, we find it disconcerting."

"By God, I should think so! Jim, let me ask you a question."

"Please do."

"Why is it that you believe you can hold out for what you're demanding? You need the Act of Union and you know it."

"Yes," James Howden said, "I think we do. But frankly I believe you need it more, and, as you said, time is what counts."

There was a silence in the small room. The President drew a deep breath. Admiral Rapoport shrugged and turned away.

"Supposing, just supposing," the President said softly, "that I agreed to your terms, subject of course to congressional approval, how would you plan to make this known?"

"An announcement to the House of Commons eleven days from now."

Again a pause.

"You understand . . . I'm only supposing . . ." The words were reluctant, labored. "But if it happened, I would be obliged to make an identical statement before a joint session of Congress. You realize that our two statements would have to be coincided to the second."

"Yes," Howden said.

He had succeeded, he knew. In his mouth was the taste of victory.

3

In the private cabin of the *Vanguard,* Margaret Howden, smartly dressed in a new gray-blue suit, a velour hat perched neatly on her attractive gray hair, had emptied the contents of her handbag onto a small reading table in front of her seat. Sorting crumpled U.S. and Canadian bills—mostly small denominations—she glanced at her husband who was absorbed with the editorial page of a day-old Toronto *Daily Star.* Fifteen minutes earlier, after a ceremonial farewell by the Vice President, supported by an honor guard of U.S. Marines, their special flight had taken off from Washington airport. Now, in midmorning sunshine, above broken cumulus cloud, they were flying smoothly northward toward Ottawa and home.

"You know," Howden said, turning pages, "I've often wondered why we don't let editorial writers take over and run the country. They've a solution for everything. Though, of course," he mused, "if they did run the country there's always the problem of who'd write the editorials."

"Why not you?" Margaret said. She put the bills beside a small pile of silver already counted. "Perhaps that way you and I could have more time together and I wouldn't have to go shopping to fill in time on trips. Oh dear!—I'm afraid I've been quite extravagant."

Howden grinned involuntarily. Putting down the newspaper, he asked, "How much?"

Margaret checked the money she had counted against a penciled list with receipts attached. She answered ruefully, "Almost two hundred dollars."

He was tempted to protest mildly, then remembered he had not revealed to Margaret their latest financial problem. Well, the money was spent; what was the point in worrying now?

Besides, a discussion about their own finances—which always made Margaret anxious—would consume more energy than he was willing to expend at the moment. Instead he said, "I'm not due for a customs exemption, but you are. So you can take in a hundred dollars' worth, duty-free, but declare the rest and you'll have to pay some tax."

"No, I won't!" Margaret exclaimed. "It's the most absurd thing I ever heard of. You know perfectly well the customs men would never come near us if you didn't insist on it. You're entitled to privileges; why not use them?" As if instinctively, her hand covered the small remaining pile of dollars.

"Dear," he said patiently—they had been over this same ground on other occasions—"you know how I feel about this sort of thing. I happen to believe that I should act like any ordinary citizen is expected to by law."

A flush of color in her cheeks, Margaret said, "All I can say is, you're being absolutely childish."

"Perhaps so," he insisted gently. "All the same, that's the way I'd like it done."

Again he felt a reluctance to involve himself in deeper explanations; to point out the political wisdom of being painstakingly honest about small things, even to avoiding the mild smuggling which most Canadians indulged in at one time or another when they returned across the border. Besides, he had always been aware how easy it was for people like himself in public life to be tripped up by small, and sometimes innocent, transgressions. There were petty minds, especially among rival parties, always at watch for the slightest slip which afterwards the newspapers would gleefully record. He had seen politicians hounded out of public life, disgraced, through small offenses which in other circles would draw no more than a mild rebuke. And then there were others who for years had lined their pockets with huge sums of public money but were caught out—through carelessness usually—on some minor issue.

He folded the newspaper and put it down.

"Don't be too upset, dear, about paying duty just this once. There may not be any duty—or customs procedure— soon." He had already told Margaret, the previous evening, the broad outline of the Act of Union.

"Well," his wife said, "I'm certainly not sorry about that. I've always thought it silly to go through so much perform-

THE WHITE HOUSE   229

ance—opening bags, declaring things—between two countries
so close together in every way."

Howden smiled, but decided not to lecture Margaret on
the history of Canadian tariffs which had made possible the
extremely favorable terms of the Act of Union. And they
were favorable terms, he thought, leaning back in the comfortable upholstered seat. Once more, as he had several
times in the past twenty-four hours, James Howden reflected
on the undoubted success of his negotiations in Washington.

Of course, even at the end the President had given no
firm commitment on the demand about Alaska. But there
would be a commitment for the Alaskan plebiscite; of that,
Howden was convinced. The idea, naturally, needed time to
accept. At first the whole proposal—as it had originally in
the Prime Minister's own mind—would seem outrageous and
impossible in Washington. But considered carefully it was
a sane and logical extension of the Act of Union, in which
Canada was to concede so much.

And as for the plebiscite in Alaska, coupled with the support he already had, Canada could make the terms for a
"yes" vote so attractive that they would not be refused.
Moreover, in advance, he would declare generous compensa-
tion for Alaskan residents who chose not to stay under a new
regime, though he hoped most would. In any case, with the
Act of Union in force, the borders between Alaska, Canada,
and the remainder of the continental U.S. would be merely
imaginary. The difference in Alaska would simply be one
of Canadian civil law and administration taking over.

The one major factor which he had not discussed with the
President was the possibility that Canada, despite expected
devastation, might emerge, postwar, the stronger and senior
partner in the Act of Union. But as to that, and its practical
effect, only time could determine.

The prop-jet motors whined on as the *Vanguard* winged
northward. Glancing from the cabin window, he saw there
were still green fields beneath them.

"Where are we, Jamie?" Margaret asked.

He glanced at his watch. "We'll have left Maryland by
now, so I expect we're over Pennsylvania. After that, just
New York State, then a few minutes to home."

"I hope it isn't snowing in Ottawa," Margaret said, putting
her receipts and money away. "I'd like to get cold again
gradually."

He thought amusedly: there are things I'd like to do gradually, too. Ideally, there should be a slow, painstaking buildup of influential support for the Act of Union. But, as always, time was short and he would have to take chances and move swiftly.

Fortunately, he now had a great deal to offer. The arrangement about Alaska, plus the other substantial concessions, would be ample to place before Parliament and the voters. Coupled with the gravity of the times, which required no emphasis, he was convinced he could win an election, thereby providing a mandate for the Act of Union.

And even apart from crisis, the time was ripe. Ten or even five years ago, when the search for a so-called Canadian identity, with all its attendant chauvinism, was at its height, any Act of Union would have been rejected out of hand. But the national mood since then had changed.

Naturally, the Opposition, led by Bonar Deitz, would fight with every weapon they could employ. But he could beat them, he was sure. Extreme nationalism nowadays was seen for what it was—a dangerous self-indulgence; and dangerous because, for a while, it had alienated Canada from its strongest friend in a hostile world. Now, ties of culture, idealism, fellow feeling, and sometimes even love, ran frankly north and south in increasing measure. It was not that people had ceased to be critical of the United States; on the contrary, the U.S. could frequently be the despair of friends and admirers alike. But at least underneath, with all faults allowed for, there was a common basic decency—in contrast to the festering, malevolent evil elsewhere in the world.

Margaret had picked up the *Star* and turned its pages.

"Oh, here are the horoscopes, Jamie. Did you read yours?"

Turning his head, he answered testily, "No, and I wish you wouldn't keep bringing that up." He wondered if Margaret were trying to bait him in retaliation for their argument earlier. Just lately their relationship had been a trifle strained, he thought, perhaps because they had spent too little time alone. Their last long talk had been when? . . . oh yes, the evening of the affair at Government House. He supposed he ought to be more considerate of Margaret, but the trouble was, there were so few hours in a day and so many things that were important and could be done only by himself. Perhaps, when some of the preparation he now faced was over, there would be more time . . .

"What awful gibberish this is!" Margaret rustled the news-paper indignantly. "Really!—the *Star* is so self-righteous with its exposés of this and that, and then they print this kind of dishonesty every day."

"They're probably ashamed of it," her husband said. "But it helps sell papers. So they put it near the back hoping no one will notice except those who want to read."

"Listen! This is your prediction for today, Jamie—Sagit-tarius." Margaret read carefully, holding the page toward the light. " 'Important and favorable Venus vibrations. Do not worry about your efforts; they have been good and will materialize further. Carry on, and don't lose faith in your-self. But look out for clouds which are becoming bigger.' " She put the paper down. "What rubbish! What appalling rub-bish!"

"Yes," James Howden said, "isn't it?" It was strange, though, he thought: the reference to the cloud once more. What had it been the time before, just a week and a half ago: *beware the cloud no larger than a man's hand.* The phrase was from the Old Testament, wasn't it? The story of Elijah, who had seen a little cloud arise from the sea . . . and afterwards he had been touched by the angel, and had anointed kings; and later still he had divided the waters of Jordan and risen to heaven in a fiery chariot. But to Elijah the cloud had been an omen of strength. Was it that for him-self; or an omen of warning? Which? Suddenly the words of old Mrs. Zeeder came back . . . the day in court at Medicine Hat . . . *I'm a child born under Sagittarius, dear. You'll see!*

"Jamie!" Margaret said sharply.

"What is it?" Abruptly he refocused his thoughts.

"What were you thinking then?"

"I wasn't," he lied. "I'd switched my mind off."

A few minutes later Margaret announced, "Wing Com-mander Galbraith invited me to the flight deck. I suppose I'd better go."

Her husband nodded. "I wish you would; and apologize for me this trip." He glanced across the cabin at a wall clock. "While you're gone I suppose I'd better see young Prowse. He's been bursting with something or other for the past two days."

Despite the presence of an entourage—the three cabinet ministers and his own senior staff, now in the forward cabin

—the Prime Minister had spent little time in Washington with anyone except Arthur Lexington.

"All right," Margaret said. "I'll send him in."

Elliot Prowse, who entered from the forward cabin after Margaret had left, was one of the Prime Minister's two executive assistants. Young, athletically handsome, independently wealthy, and an honors graduate of McGill University, he was serving a political apprenticeship in a manner quite usual nowadays for young men whose ambitions lay toward higher political office. In a few years' time he would resign his present job and seek election to the House of Commons. Meanwhile, the party made good use of his brains and scholarship, while he himself acquired a unique insight into administrative government, which eventually could be a short cut to cabinet rank.

James Howden was never quite certain how much he liked Prowse, who, at times, could be uncomfortably earnest. But now the Prime Minister's glowing satisfaction about the Washington talks prompted him to be expansive. Waving the assistant to a facing chair, he inquired, "Well, Elliot, I believe you've something on your mind."

"Yes, sir." Prowse sat down carefully, his expression serious as usual. "If you remember, I started to tell you yesterday . . ."

"I know you did," Howden said, "and I'm sorry I cut you off. But there were special problems—some of them you know—and I couldn't take time out."

He thought he detected a trace of impatience in the younger man. Well, that was something else you had to learn in politics: to become used to talk, a great deal of it unnecessary, but it was the coinage of the business.

"Mr. Richardson and Miss Freedeman have both been in touch with me," Elliot Prowse said. "It's about that immigration case in Vancouver."

"For God's sake, no!" James Howden exploded. "I've already heard enough of that to last a lifetime."

"It seems they've been hearing a good deal more in Ottawa." Prowse consulted a sheet of paper in a file he had brought in.

Howden fumed, "Haven't people anything else to occupy their damn fool minds? Don't they know there are other things—more important issues—going on in the world?" An-

nouncement of the Act of Union, he thought, would effectively
wipe anything about immigration out of the news; when
word came, the newspapers would have room for nothing
else. But it was too soon yet . . .

"I can't answer that, sir." Prowse had a habit of always
taking questions literally, rhetorical or not. "But I do have
figures on telegrams and mail received on the subject so
far."

"Tell me," Howden grunted.

"Since you left Ottawa, and up to this morning, there've
been two hundred and forty telegrams and three hundred
and thirty-two letters addressed to you. All but two telegrams and eighteen of the letters are in favor of the man
on the ship and critical of the Government."

"Well," Howden growled, "at least there are twenty people
with sense."

"There have also been some new developments." Elliot
Prowse consulted his notes again. "The man on the ship
apparently has a lawyer who, the day before yesterday, obtained an order *nisi* for habeas corpus. The application is
down for hearing in Vancouver this afternoon."

"The court will throw it out," Howden said wearily. "It's
an old legal dodge. I've used it myself."

"Yes, sir; I understand they hold that opinion in Ottawa.
But Mr. Richardson is very concerned about newspaper coverage. It seems there's been a good deal. He asked me to report that the news stories are increasing in size and most
of them are on page one. Some of the Eastern dailies now
have their own reporters in Vancouver covering the case.
There were fourteen critical editorials following your own
remarks before leaving for Washington. Mr. Bonar Deitz is
also making statements attacking the Government at every
opportunity. In Mr. Richardson's words, 'the Opposition is
making hay.' "

"What the hell did he think they'd do?" the Prime Minister said angrily. "Come out to cheer for us?"

"I really don't know what he thought about that."

Howden snapped irritably, "And why the hell do *you* have
to answer every question?"

"I always assumed you expected an answer," Prowse said.

The young man's tone expressed polite surprise and despite his own anger Howden released a smile. "It isn't your

fault. It isn't anybody's fault, except . . ." His thoughts were on Harvey Warrender.

"There's one other thing," Elliot Prowse was saying. "Mr. Richardson asked me to warn you there'll be more press questioning at the airport on landing. He says he doesn't see how you can avoid it."

"I won't do any avoiding," James Howden said grimly. He looked at his assistant directly. "You're supposed to be a bright young man. What do you suggest?"

"Well . . ." Prowse hesitated.

"Go on."

"If I may say so, sir, you're quite effective when you lose your temper."

Howden smiled again, then shook his head. "Let me warn you: never, never lose your temper with the press."

But later, forgetting his own advice, he had.

It happened after landing at Ottawa airport. They had taxied, as incoming V.I.P. flights usually did, to the public side of the airport instead of the R.C.A.F. side from which the *Vanguard* had taken off. In the private cabin, with Elliot Prowse gone and his own recent anger shelved for the time being, James Howden basked contentedly in the mental glow of a triumphal homecoming, even though, for the moment, his success in Washington could be shared only with an inner few.

Peering from a window, Margaret observed, "There seems quite a crowd on the observation deck. Do you think they're waiting for us?"

Releasing his own seat belt, he leaned forward across Margaret. It was true, he saw at once; several hundred people, most with heavy overcoats and scarves protecting them from the cold, were tightly packed against the guard rail and behind. Even while they watched, others arrived to swell the numbers.

"It's entirely possible," he said expansively. "After all, the Prime Minister of Canada does have a certain status, you know."

Margaret's expression was non-committal. "I hope we can get through it all quickly," she said. "I'm a little tired."

"Well, it shouldn't be too long, but I expect I'll have to say a few words." His mind toyed with phrases: . . . extremely successful talks (he could say that much without being premature) . . . an announcement on practical achievements within the next few weeks . . . striving for closer, cordial (better not say intimate) relations between our two countries . . . happy to renew my own long-standing friendship with the President . . .

Something on those lines, he decided, should suit the occasion well.

The engines were stopped, fuselage door opened, and a stairway wheeled in. As the others aboard waited politely, James Howden and Margaret were the first out.

The sun was shining patchily and a chilling north wind gusted across the airport.

As they paused, sheltered partially from the wind, on the platform above the stairs it occurred to Howden that the crowd, no more than a hundred yards away, was strangely quiet.

Stuart Cawston trotted up to meet them, his hand outstretched. "Greetings!" he beamed, "and welcome home on behalf of us all."

"Goodness!" Margaret exclaimed. "We were only away three days."

"It's just that it seemed longer," Cawston assured her. "We missed you."

As Smiling Stu's hand clasped Howden's he murmured, "A wonderful, wonderful outcome. You've done a great service for the country."

Moving down the stairway, with Margaret ahead, Howden inquired softly, "You've talked with Lucien Perrault?"

The Finance Minister nodded. "Just as you instructed by phone. I informed Perrault, but no one else."

"Good!" Howden said approvingly. They began to walk toward the airport buildings. "We'll hold a full Cabinet tomorrow, and meanwhile I'd like to talk with you, Perrault, and one or two others tonight. It had better be in my office."

Margaret protested, "Must it really be tonight, Jamie? We're both tired and I did so hope it could be a quiet evening."

"There'll be other quiet evenings," her husband replied with a trace of impatience.

"Perhaps you could drop over to our place, Margaret," Cawston suggested. "I'm sure Daisy would be pleased."

"Thank you, Stu," Margaret shook her head. "I think not tonight."

Now they were halfway to the terminal building. Behind them, others were descending from the airplane.

Once more the Prime Minister was conscious of the silent, watching crowd. He observed curiously, "They're unusually quiet, aren't they?"

A frown crossed Cawston's face. "I'm told the natives aren't friendly." He added: "It's an organized demonstration, it seems. They came in buses."

At that, as if the words were a signal, the storm broke.

The catcalls and boos came first, intensely fierce, as if pent up and suddenly released. Then there were shouts, with words audible like "Scrooge!" "Dictator!" "Heartless Bastard!" "We'll get you out!" "You won't be Prime Minister long!" "Wait until the next election!"

At the same time, with a kind of ragged precision, the placards went up. Until this moment they had been concealed, but now Howden could read:

IMMIGRATION DEPT:
CANADA'S GESTAPO

LET DUVAL IN, HE
DESERVES A BREAK

CHANGE FIENDISH
IMMIGRATION LAWS

JESUS CHRIST WOULD BE
TURNED AWAY HERE

CANADA NEEDS DUVAL,
NOT HOWDEN

THIS HEARTLESS GOVERNMENT
MUST GO

Tight-lipped he asked Cawston, "You knew of this?"

"Brian Richardson warned me," the Finance Minister said unhappily. "According to him, the whole thing has been bought and paid for by the Opposition. But, frankly, I didn't think it would be this bad."

The Prime Minister saw television cameras swing towards the placards and the booing crowd. This scene would be going across the country tonight.

There was nothing else to do but continue on to the terminal doorway as the angry shouts and booing grew louder. James Howden took Margaret's arm and forced a smile. "Just act as if nothing is happening," he urged, "and don't hurry."

"I'm trying," Margaret said. "But it's a bit hard."

The sound of shouting diminished as they entered the terminal building. A group of reporters was waiting, Brian Richardson hovering behind. More TV cameras were focused upon the Prime Minister and Margaret.

As the Howdens halted, a young reporter asked, "Mr. Prime Minister, have you changed your views at all on the Duval immigration case?"

After Washington . . . the parley in high places, the President's respect, his own success . . . to have this the first question was a final indignity. Experience, wisdom, caution fled as the Prime Minister declared wrathfully, "No, I have not changed my views, nor is there any likelihood that I shall. What occurred just now—in case you are unaware— was a calculated political demonstration, staged by irresponsible elements." The reporters' pencils raced as Howden continued, "These elements—and I need not name them—are using this minor issue in an attempt to divert public attention from the real achievements of the Government in more important areas. Furthermore, I say to you that the press, by its continued emphasis on this insignificant affair, at a time when grave and great decisions confront our country, is being duped or is irresponsible, and perhaps both."

He saw Brian Richardson shake his head urgently. Well, Howden thought, the newspapers had things their own way often enough, and sometimes attack was the best defense. But more moderately, his temper cooling, he continued, "You gentlemen should remember that I answered questions on this subject, patiently and at length, three days ago. But if you have forgotten, I will emphasize again that the Government intends to abide by the law as embodied in the Immigration Act."

Someone said quietly, "You mean you'd leave Duval to rot on the ship?"

The Prime Minister snapped: "The question does not concern me."

It was an unfortunate choice of phrase: he had meant that the matter was outside his own jurisdiction. But obstinacy prevented him from changing what was already said.

By evening the quotation had gone from coast to coast.

Radio and TV repeated it, and morning paper editors, with minor variations, slugged the story:

Duval: P.M. "Unconcerned"
Press, Public "Irresponsible"

Twelve   Vancouver, January 4

The Prime Minister's flight had landed at Ottawa airport a few minutes before 1.30 in the afternoon, Eastern Standard Time. In Vancouver at the same moment—four provinces and three time zones to the west—it was still morning and nearing 10.30 A.M., at which hour the order *nisi* affecting the future and freedom of Henri Duval was due to be heard in judge's chambers.

"Why judge's chambers?" Dan Orliffe asked Alan Maitland, whom he had intercepted in the bustling upper floor corridor of the B. C. Supreme Court Building. "Why not in a courtroom?" Alan had come in a moment earlier from outside where, overnight, a bitter blustering wind had set the city shivering. Now, in the warm building, a press of human traffic swirled around them: hurrying lawyers, gowns billowing; others with litigants in last-minute conclaves; court officials; news reporters—more of the latter than usual today because of interest the Duval case had aroused.

"The hearing *will* be in a courtroom," Alan said hurriedly. "Look, I can't stop; we'll be heard in a few minutes." He was uncomfortably aware of Dan Orliffe's poised pencil and open notebook. He had faced so many in the past few days: ever since Orliffe's original news story; then yesterday again, after the news had broken of his application for a habeas corpus writ. There had been a spate of interviews and questions: Did he really have a case? What did he expect would happen? If the full writ was granted, what next? . . .

He had sidestepped most of the questions, excusing himself on professional grounds; and in any event, he had said, he could not discuss a case which was now *sub judice*. He had been conscious too of the disfavor with which judges looked on publicity-seeking lawyers, and the press attention so far had made him acutely uncomfortable on this score.

But none of this concern had stopped the headlines, yesterday and today; or the news reports on radio and television . . .

Then, starting yesterday afternoon, there had been the phone calls and telegrams, pouring in from across the country; from strangers—most of them people he had never heard of, though a few big names among them that he had. All had wished him well, a few had offered money, and he found himself moved that the plight of a single hapless man should, after all, cause such genuine concern.

Now, in the moment or so during which Alan had stopped to speak with Dan Orliffe, other reporters were surrounding him. One of the out-of-town men whom Alan remembered from yesterday—from the Montreal *Gazette*, he thought—asked, "Yes, what's with this 'chambers' business?"

Alan supposed he had better take a minute to spell things out. These were not regular court reporters, and the press had helped him when he needed help . . .

"All matters, other than formal trials," he explained quickly, "are dealt with in judge's chambers instead of in court. But usually there are so many items to be heard, with a lot of people involved, that the judge moves into a courtroom which, for the time being, becomes his chambers."

"Hell!" a derisive voice said from the rear. "What's that old line about the law being an ass?"

Alan grinned. "If I agreed with you, you might quote me."

A small man at the front asked, "Will Duval be here today?"

"No," Alan answered. "He's still on the ship. We can only get him off the ship if the order *nisi* is made absolute—that is, a habeas corpus writ. That's what today's hearing is about."

Tom Lewis pushed his short chunky figure through the group. Taking Alan's arm he urged, "Let's go, man!"

Alan glanced at his watch; it was almost 10.30. "That's all," he told the reporters. "We'd all better get inside."

"Good luck, chum!" one of the wire service men said. "We're pulling for you."

As the outer door swung closed behind the last to enter, the court clerk called "Order!" At the front of the small, square courtroom, preceded by a clerk, the spare, bony figure of Mr. Justice Willis entered briskly. He mounted the judge's dais, bowed formally to counsel—the twenty or so who would appear briefly before him within the next half-hour—and, without turning, dropped smartly into the seat which the clerk had placed behind him.

Leaning towards Alan beside him, Tom Lewis whispered, "If that guy is ever late with the chair it'll be Humpty Dumpty all over."

For an instant the judge glanced in their direction, his sharp angular face, austere beneath the bushy gray eyebrows and brooding eyes which Alan had been so aware of two days earlier. Alan wondered if he had heard, then decided it was impossible. Now, with a tight, formal nod to the clerk, the judge indicated that chambers procedure could begin.

Glancing around the mahogany-paneled courtroom, Alan saw that the press had occupied two full rows of seats, near the front, on the opposite side of the center aisle. On his own side, behind and in front, were fellow lawyers, most clasping or reading legal documents, ready for the moment their business would be called. Then, while his head was turned toward the rear, five men came in.

The first was Captain Jaabeck in a blue serge suit with a trench coat over his arm, moving uncertainly in the unfamiliar surroundings. He was accompanied by an older, well-dressed man whom Alan recognized as a partner in a downtown legal firm specializing in marine law. Presumably this was the shipping company's lawyer. The two took seats behind the reporters, the lawyer—whom Alan had met once—looking across and nodding agreeably and Captain Jaabeck inclining his head with a slight smile.

Immediately following was a trio—Edgar Kramer, as usual neatly attired in a well-pressed pin-stripe suit with white pocket handkerchief carefully folded; a second, stockily built man with a trim, toothbrush mustache, who deferred to Kramer as they entered—probably an assistant in the Immigration Department, Alan reasoned; and, ushering the other two, a heavy-set distinguished figure who, from his air of confidence in the court, was almost certainly another lawyer.

At the front of the courtroom the day's crop of applications had begun, called one after another by the clerk. As each was named, a lawyer would stand up, stating his business briefly. Usually there was a casual question or two from the judge, then a nod, signifying approval of the application.

Tom Lewis nudged Alan. "Is that your friend Kramer—the one with the acid-jar face?"

Alan nodded.

Tom swiveled his head to examine the others, then a moment later turned back, his lips pursed in a silent whistle. He whispered: "Have you seen who's with him?"

"The fashion plate in the gray suit?" Alan whispered back. "I don't recognize him. Do you?"

Tom put a hand to his mouth, speaking behind it. "I sure do. A. R. Butler, Q.C., no less. They're firing the big guns at you, boy! Feel like running?"

"Frankly," Alan murmured, "yes."

A. R. Butler was a name to conjure with. One of the city's most successful trial lawyers, he had a reputation for consummate legal skill and his examinations and argument could be deadly. Normally he interested himself in major cases only. It must have taken some persuasion, Alan thought, plus a fat fee, for the Department of Immigration to have secured his services. Already, Alan noticed, there was a stirring of interest among the press.

The clerk called: "In the matter of Henri Duval—application for habeas corpus."

Alan stood. He said quickly, "My lord, may this stand until second reading?" It was a normal courtesy to other lawyers present. Those behind him on the list, and with application requiring no argument could transact it speedily and go. Afterwards the residue of names—those anticipating lengthier proceedings—would be called again.

As the judge nodded, the clerk intoned the next name.

Resuming his seat, Alan felt a hand touch his shoulder. It was A. R. Butler. The older lawyer had moved across during Alan's interjection, taking the seat behind. He brought with him a waft of perfumed after-shave lotion.

"Good morning," he whispered. "I'm appearing in your case—for the department. My name is Butler." Smiling courteously, as became a senior approaching a junior member of the bar, he offered his hand.

Alan shook the soft, well manicured hand. "Yes," he murmured, "I know."

"Harry Tolland is representing Nordic Shipping." Still whispering, the other gestured to the lawyer who had accompanied Captain Jaabeck. "They're the owners of the ship; I expect you knew."

"No," Alan breathed, "I didn't. Thank you."

"That's all right, old chap; just thought you'd like the information." Again A. R. Butler put a hand on Alan's shoulder. "Interesting point you've raised; we'll have a good go at it." With a friendly nod he moved back to the other side of the courtroom.

Alan glanced across, intending to return courtesy for courtesy by greeting Edgar Kramer. For a moment he caught Kramer watching him. Then, his expression bleak, the civil servant turned away.

A hand covering his mouth, Tom said, "Ease round and rub your coat against me—right where the great man touched you."

Alan grinned. "Very friendly, I thought." But the outward confidence was a pose. Tension and a growing nervousness were creeping over him.

"One of the nice things about our profession," Tom murmured, "everybody smiles before they plunge the knife in."

The second reading had begun.

Normally by now the courtroom would have been almost empty, but so far only one or two of the other lawyers had left. It was obvious they were staying because of the interest the Duval case had aroused.

A divorce matter immediately ahead had been dealt with. Now there was an air of expectancy.

As he had before, the clerk called: "In the matter of Henri Duval."

Alan rose. When he spoke, unexpectedly, his voice was strained. "My lord . . ." He hesitated, coughed, then stopped. There was silence in the courtroom. Reporters turned their heads. The appraising gray eyes of Mr. Justice Willis were upon him. Now he began again.

"My lord, I am appearing on behalf of the applicant Henri Duval. My name is Alan Maitland, and my learned friend Mr. Butler"—Alan glanced across the court as A. R. Butler rose and bowed—"is appearing on behalf of the Department of Citizenship and Immigration, and my learned friend Mr. Tolland"—Alan consulted a note he had made a moment ago—"represents the Nordic Shipping Company." The lawyer beside Captain Jaabeck rose and bowed to the judge.

"All right," Mr. Justice Willis said gruffly, "what's all this about?"

For all its gruffness, the question had a quiet irony. It was unlikely that even the remote figure of a Supreme Court judge—who presumably read newspapers—could have remained unaware during the past eleven days of the existence of Henri Duval. But it was a reminder also that the Court would concern itself solely with facts and submissions properly presented. Moreover, Alan was aware that the arguments he had outlined two days earlier must be restated here in full.

Still nervously, at times his voice halting, he began.

"If it please Your Lordship, the facts of the matter are these." Once more Alan Maitland described the status of Henri Duval aboard the *Vastervik*, coupled with Captain Jaabeck's "refusal" on two occasions to bring the stowaway before immigration authorities ashore. Again he submitted the argument that this constituted an illegal imprisonment of Duval, violating, in turn, a principle of individual human rights.

Even while speaking Alan was aware of the flimsy structure he was building. But though his fluency and confidence were less than on the previous occasion, a dogged obstinacy kept him pounding on. To his right, as he spoke, he was aware of A. R. Butler Q.C., listening politely, one ear cocked, and occasionally making a note on a pad of paper. Only once, as Alan glanced sideways, did the senior lawyer's expression betray a faint indulgent smile. Captain Jaabeck, he could see, was following his words intently.

Again, as he knew he must in these surroundings, Alan was careful to avoid reference to the emotional aspects of the case. But throughout, in a crevice of his mind, he remembered the young stowaway's haunting face with its strange admixture of hope and resignation. In an hour or two from now, which would dominate—the hope or resignation?

He ended with his own closing argument of two days ago: Even a stowaway, he claimed, had the right to demand a special Department of Immigration inquiry into his immigration status. If such an inquiry were denied to all comers, perhaps even a bona fide Canadian citizen—temporarily without proof of identity—might be refused access to his own country. It was the same argument which had elicited a smile from Mr. Justice Willis when presented before.

There was no smile now. Only, from the white-haired erect figure on the bench, a bleakness of impassivity.

Miserably conscious of what he thought of as his own inadequacy, after an address of ten minutes, Alan sat down.

Now the confident, broad-shouldered figure of A. R. Butler rose. With effortless dignity—like a Roman senator, Alan
thought—he faced the bench.

"My lord"—the urbane, deep voice filled the courtroom—
"I have listened with both interest and admiration to the
argument of my distinguished colleague, Mr. Maitland."

There was a studied pause in which Tom Lewis whispered,
"The bastard managed to say you were inexperienced without
ever using the word."

Alan nodded. He had thought the same thing.

The voice continued: "Interest because Mr. Maitland has
presented a most novel inversion of a somewhat simple point
of law; admiration because of a remarkable ability to make
bricks—or seem to make them—from the merest handful of
legal straw."

From anyone else it would have been crude and brutal.
From A. R. Butler, delivered with a cordial smile, the words
seemed a good-natured homily with the merest edge of gentle ribbing.

Behind Alan someone tittered.

A. R. Butler continued, "The plain truth of the matter, as
I shall seek to show, my lord, is that my friend's client, Mr.
Duval, of whose peculiar problem we are all aware and to
which, I may say, the Department of Immigration is extremely
sympathetic . . . The truth of the matter is that Duval is detained, not illegally, but *legally*, pursuant to a detention order,
issued with due and proper process under the Immigration
Act of Canada. Furthermore, I shall submit to Your Lordship
that the captain of the vessel *Vastervik* has acted with entire
legality in detaining Duval, as my learned friend reports is
being done. In fact, if the ship's captain had failed to do
this . . ."

Smoothly the skillful, polished phrases marched on. Where
Alan had stumbled, seeking words, A. R. Butler delivered
them with flowing, rhythmic precision. Where Alan had
reached points of argument circuitously, sometimes returning
again to nibble, A. R. Butler dealt effectively with each item
in turn, then moved swiftly to the next.

His arguments were convincing: that the detention was
legal; that everything necessary by law had been done; that
the ship's captain had not erred nor, in its procedures, had
the Department of Immigration; that, as a stowaway, Henri

Duval had no legal rights and therefore a special immigration inquiry could not be demanded; that Alan's argument about a hypothetical Canadian citizen being denied entry was so flimsy as to be laughable. And laugh—good-naturedly, of course—A. R. Butler did.

It was, Alan admitted to himself, a superb performance.

A. R. Butler concluded: "My lord, I ask for dismissal of the application and discharge of the order *nisi.*" After bowing ceremoniously, he resumed his seat.

As though a star had been on stage and gone, there was a stillness in the small courtroom. Since his original words—"What's this all about?"—Mr. Justice Willis had not spoken. Even though emotion had no place here, Alan had expected at least some show of judicial concern, but there had been none. As far as the bench was concerned they might, he thought, have been discussing bricks or cement, and not a living, human being. Now the judge moved, changing his ramrodlike position in the high-backed judicial chair, studying his notes, reaching out for ice water which he sipped. The reporters were becoming restive, Alan observed; he noticed several checking their watches. For some, he supposed, a deadline was approaching. Although it was after eleven o'clock, the room was still unusually full. Only a few of the lawyers with other business had left and now, turning his head, he noticed that more seats behind had filled.

For the first time Alan was conscious of the sounds of the city from outside: the wind, rising and falling; traffic; a reverberating rumble that sounded like pneumatic drills; distantly a bell; and from the water front a tugboat's bass horn; perhaps a ship was leaving, as the *Vastervik* would leave soon, with or without Henri Duval. Well, in a moment they would know.

In the quiet, a chair scraped back. It was Tolland, the shipping-company lawyer. In a voice which rasped oddly in contrast to the mellifluous tones of A. R. Butler, he began, "If Your Lordship pleases . . ."

Mr. Justice Willis looked up sharply from his notes and across the courtroom. "No, Mr. Tolland," he said, "I need not trouble you."

The lawyer bowed and sat down.

So that was it.

The judge's interjection meant one thing only. Alan's case

had collapsed and no additional argument was needed to
help demolish it.

"Well," Tom whispered. "At least we tried."

Alan nodded. He supposed that all along he had expected
defeat. After all, he had known from the beginning that his
strategy was no more than a long shot. But now that
defeat had come, there was a taste of bitterness. He wondered how much to blame was his own inexperience, his
verbal awkwardness in court. If he had been more assured
—as convincing, say, as A. R. Butler, Q.C.—might he have
succeeded instead of failed?

Or if he had had the better fortune to appear before
another judge—more sympathetic than the austere, forbid-
ding figure upon the bench—would the result be different
now?

As it happened, it would not.

In the mind of Mr. Justice Stanley Willis the decision he
was about to render had appeared inevitable before either
lawyer had begun to speak. He had, in fact, recognized the
glaring weakness of Alan Maitland's case, despite its equally
obvious ingenuity, within seconds of its presentation two
days earlier.

But at that time there had been sufficient grounds to
grant the order *nisi*. Now, however—to the judge's keen
regret—there were no grounds for issuance of a habeas
corpus writ.

Mr. Justice Willis considered A. R. Butler, Q.C., an exhibitionist and a poseur. The rhetoric and flowing speech,
the show of affable benevolence, were histrionic tricks in the
bag which might, and did, influence juries, but judges were
often less impressed. Nevertheless there was nothing wrong
with A. R. Butler's legal knowledge, and the arguments he
had just concluded were virtually unanswerable.

Mr. Justice Willis must—and in a moment would—reject
the habeas corpus application. But he wished fervently that
there were some way in which he could help the young
lawyer Alan Maitland and, thereby, Henri Duval.

The wish had two origins. First, as an avid newspaper
reader, Mr. Justice Willis had been convinced that the
homeless stowaway should be given a chance to land and
live in Canada. From the first report he had believed that
the Immigration Department should waive regulations as had

been done, he knew, for countless others. It had astounded and angered him to learn that not only would this not be done, but that the Government—through its immigration officials—had taken what he considered to be an inflexible and arbitrary stand.

The second reason was that Mr. Justice Willis liked what he had seen of Alan Maitland. The awkwardness, an occasional stumbling, mattered not in the least in the judge's mind; a sound lawyer, as he well knew, need be no Demosthenes.

When the Duval case had broken in the newspapers Mr. Justice Willis had assumed that one of the senior members of the bar, out of compassion for the stowaway, would promptly volunteer legal aid. At first it had saddened him that no one had done so, then, at the news that a single young lawyer had filled the breech, he had been secretly pleased. Now, watching Alan Maitland, the pleasure had extended into pride.

His own involvement in the case had, of course, been entirely coincidental. And naturally no personal prejudice must influence his judicial function. All the same, sometimes there were small things a judge could do . . .

It all depended, Mr. Justice Willis thought, on how astute the youthful counsel for Henri Duval turned out to be.

Briefly the judge announced his reasons for upholding the argument of A. R. Butler. The captain's detention of Duval conformed to the Immigration Department's lawful detention order, the judge ruled. Therefore it was not an illegal detention for which habeas corpus could be issued. He added gruffly: "The application is dismissed."

Preparing to leave, Alan was gloomily putting papers into a brief case when the same voice said distinctly, "Mr. Maitland!"

Alan rose. "Yes, my lord."

The bushy eyebrows seemed even more formidable. Alan wondered what was coming. A sharply worded reprimand, perhaps. Others, who had stood up to leave, resumed their seats.

"You stated in argument," the judge proclaimed sternly, "that your client has a right to an immigration hearing. The logical course, I suggest, is for you to apply for that hearing to the Department of Citizenship and Immigration whose

officials"—Mr. Justice Willis glanced at the group of which
Edgar Kramer was the center—"will undoubtedly facilitate
what you are seeking."

"But, my lord . . ." Alan began impatiently. He stopped,
frustrated, seething. Even with legal circumlocutions there
was no way you could say to a judge of the province's Supreme Court: "What you are telling me is nonsense. Haven't
you heard?—the Immigration Department refuses to grant
a hearing, which is the reason we have been arguing here
today. Didn't you listen to what was said? Or understand?
Or were you just asleep?"

It was bad enough, Alan thought, to have drawn a hard,
unfeeling judge. To be obliged to suffer a fool into the bargain was a crowning mockery.

"Of course," Mr. Justice Willis observed, "if the Immigration Department proved adamant, you could always apply
for a writ of mandamus, couldn't you?"

Heated words sprang to Alan's tongue. This was too much
to endure. Wasn't it enough to have lost without . . .

A darting thought stopped him. Alongside he could see
Tom Lewis, his expression a mixture of impatience and disgust. Obviously, Tom also had shared his feelings about the
absurd suggestion of the judge.

And yet . . .

Alan Maitland's mind raced back . . . through half-remem-
bered law-school lectures . . . dusty law books, opened and
forgotten . . . Somewhere he was sure there was a key, if
he could turn it . . . Then memory stirred; pieces fell in
place.

Alan's tongue touched his lips. Facing the bench he said
slowly, "If it please Your Lordship . . ."

The eyes impaled him. "Yes, Mr. Maitland?"

A moment ago Alan had heard quiet footsteps going toward the outer door. Now they were returning. A chair
creaked as the owner of the feet sat down. The others in
the courtroom waited.

A. R. Butler had his eyes on Alan's face. They shifted
to the judge. And back.

Edgar Kramer was frankly puzzled. Alan observed that
Kramer was also strangely restless. Several times he shifted
around uneasily in his seat as if physically uncomfortable.

"Would Your Lordship be kind enough," Alan asked, "to
repeat the last statement?"

The eyebrows beetled. Was there the faintest of smiles beneath them? It was hard to decide.

"I stated," Mr. Justice Willis answered, "that if the Immigration Department was adamant, you could always apply for a writ of mandamus."

A dawning comprehension—and anger—were mirrored in A. R. Butler's face.

In Alan's mind two words drummed out like starter's pistols: obiter dictum.

Obiter dictum: that which is said by the way . . . a judge's opinion, off the cuff, on a point of law not material to his immediate decision . . . Obiter dictum, without binding authority . . . intended for guidance . . . Guidance.

Mr. Justice Willis had spoken casually, as if an offhand thought had come and gone. But there was nothing casual, Alan now realized, about the mind of this shrewd judge whom he had so falsely suspected of indifference and dozing.

"Thank you, my lord," Alan said. "I shall apply for mandamus immediately."

A writ of mandamus was not material today. But it could be, if applied for. Mandamus, the ancient "we command!" . . . instructing a public officer to do his public duty . . . prerogative of English kings since the Reformation, and nowadays of judges, though seldom invoked.

Such a writ, directed to Edgar Kramer with all the power of the court behind it, would compel him to hold the hearing Alan sought without delay or further questioning. And by obiter dictum Mr. Justice Willis had made clear that a mandamus writ, if sought, would now be granted.

"Look at them huddling," Tom Lewis whispered. "They're in a real sweat."

Across the courtroom, heads together, A. R. Butler, Edgar Kramer and the shipping-company lawyer were engaged in urgent, low-voiced discussion.

After a moment A. R. Butler, red-faced and no longer affable, rose and faced the bench. With barely controlled politeness, he said, "I request Your Lordship's permission for a few moments' discussion with my client."

"Very well." His finger tips together, the judge surveyed the ceiling as he waited. Counsel for the stowaway Duval had been as alert and astute as he had hoped.

Alan sat down.

"Bless his old gray hairs!" Tom Lewis murmured.

"Did you get it?" Alan asked.

"I didn't at first," Tom whispered, "I do now. Good for you!"

Alan nodded. Inwardly beaming, he was careful not to show it.

The judge's seemingly casual words had, he knew, placed the other side in an impossible position. The Immigration Department, in the person of Edgar Kramer, must choose immediately between one of two courses: either continue to refuse the special inquiry which Alan sought, or change its mind and grant it. If the first choice were made, Alan could apply for the writ of mandamus which would force Kramer's hand. Moreover, by taking his time about obtaining the writ and serving it, Alan could make certain that Henri Duval was ashore, enmeshed in legal proceedings, when the *Vastervik* sailed.

On the other hand—as Edgar Kramer had shrewdly pointed out at their first meeting—if the department granted the hearing it would have recognized Henri Duval officially, thus opening the way to further legal steps, including avenues of appeal. And this way too, chances were good that procedures could be extended until the *Vastervik* had gone, leaving Henri Duval in Canada as a *fait accompli*.

A. R. Butler was on his feet again. Some, though not all, of the apparent good humor had returned. But behind him Edgar Kramer was scowling.

"My lord, I wish to announce that the Department of Citizenship and Immigration, having regard to your Lordship's wishes—though not, I would point out, legally bound to do so—has decided to hold a special inquiry into the case of my friend's client, Mr. Duval."

Leaning forward, Mr. Justice Willis said sharply, "I expressed no wish."

"If Your Lordship pleases . . ."

"I expressed no wish," the judge repeated firmly. "If the department chooses to hold a hearing, it is its own decision. But there has been no pressure from this source. Is that clearly understood, Mr. Butler?"

A. R. Butler appeared to swallow. "Yes, my lord, it is understood."

Facing Alan, the judge asked sternly, "Are you satisfied, Mr. Maitland?"

Alan rose. "Yes, my lord," he answered. "Entirely satisfied."

There was a second hurried consultation between A. R.
Butler and Edgar Kramer. The latter appeared to be making
an emphatic point. The lawyer nodded several times and, at
the end, was smiling. Now he faced the judge again.

"There is one further point, my lord."

"Yes?"

Glancing sideways toward Alan, A. R. Butler asked,
"Would Mr. Maitland be free for further consultation on this
matter later today?"

Mr. Justice Willis frowned. This was time wasting. Private
meetings between opposing counsel were no business of the
court's.

With a sense of embarrassment for Butler, Alan nodded
and answered, "Yes." Now that he had gained his objective
there was no point, he thought, in being unco-operative.

Ignoring the judge's frown, A. R. Butler said blandly, "I
am glad of Mr. Maitland's assurance on that point because in
view of the special circumstances it would seem expedient
to bring on this matter promptly. Therefore the Department
of Citizenship and Immigration proposes to hold the special
inquiry later today at a time convenient to Mr. Maitland and
his client."

He had, Alan realized glumly, been neatly hooked by an
expert angler. Except for his own too eager assent of a moment earlier, he could have objected to the short notice,
pleaded other business . . .

The score, if you thought of it that way, was even.

The austere gaze of Mr. Justice Willis was upon him. "We
may as well settle this. Is that agreeable, Mr. Maitland?"

Alan hesitated, then glanced at Tom Lewis who shrugged.
They shared the same thought, Alan knew: that once more
Edgar Kramer had foreseen and forestalled their plan of
delaying tactics—the only real resource they had. Now, with
the special inquiry this afternoon, even the legal steps to
follow might not last long enough to keep Henri Duval ashore
until the *Vastervik* sailed. Victory, which a moment ago had
seemed within reach, had now receded.

Reluctantly Alan said, "Yes, my lord—agreeable."

As A. R. Butler smiled benignly, the reporters scrambled
for the door. Only one figure was ahead of them—Edgar

Kramer, his face strained and body tense, was hurrying, almost running, from the courtroom.

2

As Alan Maitland left the courtroom he was surrounded by a half-dozen reporters who had returned from telephoning their stories.

"Mr. Maitland, what are the chances now?" . . . "When do we get to see Duval?" . . . "Hey, Maitland!—what's with this special inquiry?" . . . "Yeah, what's so special about it?" . . . "Tell us about that writ business. Did you get the wrong one?"

"No," Alan snapped. "I didn't."

More reporters were joining the group, partially blocking the already busy corridor.

"Then what the . . ."

"Look," Alan protested, "I can't talk about a case that's still under way. You all know that."

"Explain that to my editor, chum . . ."

"For crying out loud, give us something!"

"All right," Alan said. There was an immediate quietening. The group pressed in as people from other courts pushed by.

"The situation is simply that the Department of Immigration has agreed to hold a special inquiry into my client's case."

Some of the passers-by looked at Alan curiously.

"Who does the inquiring?"

"Usually a senior immigration officer."

"Will young Duval be present?"

"Of course," Alan said. "He has to answer questions."

"How about you?"

"Yes, I'll be there."

"Where is it held—this hearing?"

"At the Immigration Building."

"Can we get in?"

"No. It's a departmental inquiry and it isn't open to the public or the press."

"Will there be a statement afterwards?"

"You'll have to ask Mr. Kramer about that."

Someone murmured: "That stiff-necked sod!"

"What good will a hearing do if you couldn't get Duval in the country already?"

"Sometimes at a proper inquiry new facts come out which are important." But it was only a slender hope, Alan knew. Any real chance for the youthful stowaway lay in legal delay, which now had been circumvented.

"What's your feeling about what happened this morning?"

"Sorry. I can't discuss that."

Tom Lewis appeared quietly beside Alan.

"Hi," Alan greeted him. "Where'd you disappear to?"

His partner replied softly, "I was curious about Kramer, so I followed him out. Well, did you fix a time with your buddy, Butler?"

"I talked to him. We agreed on four o'clock."

A reporter asked, "What was that?"

Alan answered, "The special inquiry is to be held at four o'clock. Now, if you'll excuse me, I've a lot to do before then."

Disengaging himself from the group, he moved away with Tom Lewis.

Out of the reporters' hearing Alan asked, "What was that about Kramer?"

"Nothing really. He was just in a hurry to get to the can. While I was there I hung out beside him and for a minute or two he seemed almost in pain. I figured the poor bastard has some kind of prostate trouble."

It explained Edgar Kramer's restlessness in court, the obvious distress towards the end. The fact was insignificant; all the same, Alan filed it away mentally.

Walking along, they had come to the wide stone stairway leading to the main floor below.

A soft voice behind said, "Mr. Maitland, could you answer one more question?"

"I already explained . . ." Alan turned, then stopped.

"All I wanted to know," Sharon Deveraux said, her deep eyes innocent, "was where are you going to lunch?"

Startled and pleased, Alan asked, "Where did you spring from?"

"Spring is the word," Tom said. He was looking at Sharon's hat, a wispy affair of velvet and net veiling. "You remind me of it."

"I was in court," Sharon smiled. "I snuck in at the back.

I didn't understand it all, but I thought Alan was wonderful, didn't you?"

"Oh, sure," Tom Lewis said. "Of course, he just happened to have the judge in his pocket, but he was wonderful, all right."

"Aren't lawyers supposed to be responsive?" Sharon said. "No one's answered my question about lunch."

"I hadn't planned anything," Alan said, then brightened. "Right by our office we could offer you a nice line in pizza pie."

Together they began walking down the stairs, Sharon between them.

"Or steaming, creamy spaghetti," Tom urged. "With oozy hot meat sauce—the kind that trickles out both corners of your mouth and meets in rivulets at the chin."

Sharon laughed. "Some day I'd love to. What I really came to say, though, is that Granddaddy wondered if you could join him. He'd very much like to hear from you directly how things are going."

The prospect of accompanying Sharon anywhere was enticing. All the same, Alan looked doubtfully at his watch.

"It needn't take long," Sharon assured him. "Granddaddy has a suite in the Georgia. He keeps it for when he's downtown, and he's there now."

"You mean," Tom asked curiously, "he rents a suite there all the time?"

"I know." Sharon nodded. "It's dreadfully extravagant and I'm always telling him so. Sometimes it goes for weeks without being used."

"Oh, I wouldn't worry about that," Tom told her airily. "I'm just sorry I've never thought of it myself. Only the day before yesterday I was caught in a shower downtown with just a drugstore to go into."

Sharon laughed again. At the foot of the stairs they halted.

For an instant Tom Lewis switched his glance between the faces of the other two: Sharon, lighthearted, unself-conscious; Alan, at the moment serious, thoughtful, with a part of his mind still back in the courtroom where this morning's hearing had been held. And yet for all the outward difference, Tom Lewis thought, there was a warm affinity between the two. He suspected they could care about the same things. He wondered if they were aware of it yet.

Remembering his wife at home, pregnant, Tom gave an inward nostalgic sigh for carefree, single days.

"I'd love to come," Alan said, meaning it. He took Sharon's arm. "But do you mind if we hurry a bit? I have to be at that inquiry this afternoon." There was just enough time, he decided—as a matter of courtesy—to fill Senator Deveraux in on the background of events so far.

Sharon asked, "You'll join us as well, Mr. Lewis, won't you?"

Tom shook his head. "Thanks all the same, but this isn't my show. I'll walk to the hotel with you, though."

With Alan and Tom on either side of the Senator's grand-daughter, they left the echoing lobby of the Supreme Court Building by the Hornby Street side door. The cold of the narrow cavernous street outside was a sharp, biting contrast to the building's warm interior. A bitter blast of wind caught, and for a moment held them, and Sharon pulled her sable-trimmed coat tightly around her. She had a sense of pleasure at Alan's nearness.

"The weather's from the sea," Tom said. There was a side-walk excavation ahead and he led the way, jaywalking through traffic, to the northwest side of Hornby, turning toward West Georgia. "It must be the coldest day of winter."

With one hand Sharon was holding her impractical hat tightly. She told Alan, "Every time I think of the sea I think of your stowaway, and what it must be like never going ashore. Is the ship as bad as the newspapers say?"

He answered curtly, "Worse, if anything."

"Shall you mind very much—I mean really mind—if you don't win?"

With a vehemence that surprised himself Alan answered, "I shall mind like hell. I shall wonder what kind of rotten, stinking country I belong to which can turn away someone homeless like this: a good man, young, who'd be an asset . . ."

Tom Lewis asked quietly, "Are you sure about being an asset?"

"Yes." Alan sounded surprised. "Aren't you?"

"No," Tom said. "I don't think I am."

"Why?" It was Sharon's question.

They had come to West Georgia Street, waited for the lights, then crossed on green.

"Tell me why," Sharon insisted.

"I don't know," Tom said. They recrossed Hornby, reached

the Georgia Hotel and stopped, sheltering a little from the wind by the front entrance door. There was a dampness in the air which spoke of rain to come. "I don't know," Tom repeated. "It isn't something you can put a finger on. A sort of instinct, I guess."

Alan asked abruptly, "What makes you feel that way?"

"When I served the captain's order *nisi* I talked to Duval. I asked you if I could meet him, remember?"

Alan nodded.

"Well, I did, and I tried to like him. But I had a feeling there was a flaw somewhere; a weakness. It was almost as if he had a crack down the middle—maybe not his own fault, maybe something his background put there."

"What kind of a crack?" Alan frowned.

"I told you it wasn't something I could be specific about. But I had a feeling that if we get him ashore and make him an immigrant, he'll come apart in pieces."

Sharon said, "Isn't that all rather vague?" She had a feeling of defensiveness, as if something Alan cared about were being assailed.

"Yes," Tom answered. "It's why I haven't mentioned it till now."

"I don't think you're right," Alan said shortly. "But even if you are it doesn't change the legal situation—his rights and all the rest."

"I know," Tom Lewis said. "That's what I keep telling myself." He pulled his coat collar tighter, preparing to turn away. "Anyhow, good luck this afternoon!"

3

The substantial double doors of the twelfth-floor hotel suite were open as Alan and Sharon approached, along a carpeted corridor, from the elevator. All the way up, from the moment they had left Tom Lewis on the street below, he had had an exciting awareness of their closeness to each other. It still persisted as, through the doorway of the suite, Alan could see an elderly uniformed waiter transferring the contents of a room-service trolley—apparently a buffet luncheon—to a white-clothed table in the room's center.

Senator Deveraux was seated in an upholstered wing chair, his back to the doorway, facing the harbor view which the center window of the suite's living room commanded. At the sound of Sharon's and Alan's entry he turned his head without rising.

"Well, Sharon my dear, my compliments to you for successfully ensnaring the hero of the hour." The Senator offered Alan his hand. "Allow me to congratulate you, my boy, on a most remarkable success."

Alan took the proffered hand. Momentarily he was shocked to see how much frailer and aged the Senator appeared than at their last meeting. The old man's face had a marked pallor, its earlier ruddiness gone, and his voice, by comparison, was weak.

"There hasn't been a success by any means," Alan said uncomfortably. "Not even much of a dent, I'm afraid."

"Nonsense, my boy!—even though your modesty becomes you. Why, a moment ago I was listening to a paen of praise about you on the radio news."

"What did they say?" Sharon asked.

"It was described as a clear-cut victory for the forces of humanity against the monstrous tyranny of our existing Government."

Alan asked doubtfully, "Did they actually use those words?"

The Senator waved a hand airily. "I may have paraphrased a little, but that was the gist of it all. And Alan Maitland, that young upstanding lawyer, justly armed, was described as having routed the opposing forces."

"If someone really said that, they may have some fancy backtracking to do." The elderly waiter was hovering beside them and Alan slipped off his overcoat, handing it to the man, who hung it in a closet, then discreetly left. Sharon disappeared through an adjoining door. Alan's eyes followed her, then he moved to a window seat and sat facing the Senator. "We gained a temporary advantage, it's true. But through a piece of stupidity I managed to lose part of it." He related what happened at judge's chambers and his own final outwitting by A. R. Butler.

Senator Deveraux nodded sagely. "Even so, I would say your efforts have produced a splendid outcome."

"So they did," Sharon said, returning to join them. She had taken off her outdoor clothes, revealing a soft woolen dress. "Alan was simply magnificent."

Alan smiled resignedly. It seemed useless to protest. "All the same," he said, "we're a long way from getting Henri Duval admitted here as a landed immigrant."

The older man made no immediate answer, his eyes returning to the water front and harbor spread beneath them. Turning his head, Alan could see Burrard Inlet, spume flecked from the streaming wind, the North Shore whipped by spray. A ship was leaving port—a grain boat, low in the water, laden; from the markings it looked Japanese. A Vancouver Island ferry headed in, cutting white water through the First Narrows, beginning a wide starboard turn toward the C.P.R. pier. Elsewhere were other arrivals, departures: of ships and men, cargoes, commerce, the weft and warp of a busy deep-sea port.

At length the Senator said, "Well, of course, in the end we may not achieve that final objective of landing your stowaway. One can win battles and lose a war. But never underestimate the importance of the battles, my boy, particularly in political affairs."

"I think we've gone over that, Senator," Alan rejoined. "I'm not concerned about the politics, just in doing the best I can for my client!"

"Indeed! Indeed!" The old man's voice, for the first time held a trace of testiness. "And I think you'll allow that you lose no opportunity to point it out. Sometimes, if I may say so, there is nothing quite so tedious as the self-righteousness of the very young."

Alan flushed at the rebuke.

"But you'll forgive an old campaigner," the Senator said, "if I rejoice in the discomfiture which, in certain quarters, your resourceful actions have aroused."

"I guess there's no harm in that." Alan tried to make the remark sound light. He had an uncomfortable feeling of having been boorish without need.

Behind them a telephone bell rang. The room-service waiter, who had quietly reappeared, answered. The man moved familiarly around, Alan noticed, as if he were used to the habits of this private suite and had served the Senator many times before.

To Alan and Sharon the Senator said, "Why don't you two young people have lunch? It's there behind you. I think you'll find whatever you need."

"All right," Sharon said. "But aren't you having something, Granddaddy?"

The Senator shook his head. "Perhaps later, my dear; not now."

The waiter put down the telephone and came forward. He announced, "It's your call to Ottawa, Senator, and they have Mr. Bonar Deitz on the line. Will you take it here?"

"No, I'll go in the bedroom." The old man eased upward in the chair, then, as if the effort were too much for him, fell back. "Dear me, I seem to be a little heavy today."

Concernedly, Sharon came to his side. "Granddaddy, you shouldn't try to do so much!"

"Stuff and nonsense!" The Senator reached out, taking Sharon's hands, and she helped him to his feet.

"May I, sir?" Alan offered his arm.

"No, thank you, my boy. I'm not ready for cripplehood yet. It's merely to overcome gravity that I need some trifling help. Perambulation I've always managed myself and always shall, I hope."

With the words he entered the doorway Sharon had used earlier, closing it partially behind him.

"Is he all right?" Alan asked doubtfully.

"I don't know." Sharon's eyes were on the doorway. Turning back to Alan, she added, "Even if he isn't, there's nothing he'll let me do. Why is it that some men are so obstinate?"

"I'm not obstinate."

"Not much!" Sharon laughed. "From you it comes in waves. Anyway, let's have lunch."

There was vichyssoise, shrimp casserole, curried turkey's wings, and jellied tongue on the buffet table. The elderly waiter hurried forward.

"Thank you," Sharon said. "We'll serve ourselves."

"Very well, Miss Deveraux." Inclining his head respectfully, the man closed the double doors behind him, leaving them alone.

Alan ladled two cups of vichyssoise and gave one to Sharon. They sipped, standing.

Alan's heart was pounding. "When all this is over," he asked slowly, "shall I see you sometimes?"

"I hope so." Sharon smiled. "Otherwise I might have to stay around the law courts all the time."

He was conscious of the faint perfume he had detected at their meeting in the house on the Drive. And of Sharon's eyes, mirroring amusement and perhaps something else.

Alan put down his soup cup. He said decisively, "Give me yours."

Sharon protested, "I haven't finished yet."

"Never mind that." He reached out, taking it, and returned it to the table.

He held out his hands to Sharon and she came to him. Their faces were close. His arms went around her and their lips met softly. He had a blissful, breathless sense of floating on air.

After a moment, shyly, he touched her hair and whispered, "I've wanted to do this ever since Christmas morning."

"So have I," Sharon said happily. "Why ever did you take so long?"

They kissed again. As if from some other unreal world the sound of Senator Deveraux's voice came, muffled, through the partly open door. ". . . so this is the time to strike, Bonar . . . naturally you will lead in the House . . . Howden on the defensive . . . splendid, my boy, splendid! . . ." To Alan, the words seemed unimportant, unconnected with himself.

"Don't worry about Granddaddy," Sharon whispered. "He's always ages on the phone to Ottawa."

"Stop talking," Alan said. "You're wasting time."

Ten minutes later the voice stopped and they broke away. After an interval Senator Deveraux came out, walking slowly. He lowered himself carefully onto a sofa facing the buffet table. If he noticed that the luncheon was virtually untouched, he made no comment.

After pausing for breath, the Senator announced, "I have some excellent news."

With a sense of returning to earth, hoping his voice sounded normal, Alan asked, "Has the Government given in? Will they let Duval stay?"

"Not that." The old man shook his head. "In fact, if that happened it might upset our present strategy."

"What then?" Alan had both feet on the ground now. He contained his irritation that politics, apparently, still came first.

"Come on, Granddaddy," Sharon said; "give!"

"Tomorrow in Ottawa," the Senator declared grandly, "the

Parliamentary Opposition will stage a full-dress House of Commons debate in support of our young friend, Henri Duval."

"Do you think it will do any good?" Alan asked.

The Senator replied sharply, "It won't do any harm, will it? And it will keep your client's name very much in the news."

"Yes," Alan acknowledged. He nodded thoughtfully. "It will certainly help us that way."

"I'm sure it will, my boy. So at your special inquiry this afternoon remember that others are working with you in the same good cause."

"Thank you, Senator. I will." Alan glanced at his watch and realized he had better be moving. Acutely conscious of Sharon close by, he walked to the closet where the waiter had put his coat.

"Concerning this afternoon," Senator Deveraux said softly, "I have a single small suggestion."

Slipping into his coat, Alan turned. "Yes, sir?"

There was a glint of amusement of the old man's eyes. "It might be better," he said, "if sometime before the hearing you removed the lipstick."

4

At five minutes to four a Department of Immigration clerk politely ushered Alan Maitland into a board room of the water-front Immigration Building, where the special inquiry affecting Henri Duval was due to be held.

It was a strictly utilitarian room, Alan observed—about fifteen feet wide and twice as long, with varnished plywood panels topped by pebbled glass on all four sides, extending to the ceiling. A plain office table, also varnished, occupied the center, and around the table five wooden chairs were set neatly in place. On the table before each chair were a pad of paper and a sharpened pencil. Four ash trays, symmetrically in line, were spaced evenly down the table's length. On a smaller side table were glasses and a jug of ice water. There was no other furniture.

Three people had preceded Alan. One was a red-haired girl stenographer, already seated, with her notebook open at a blank page, now languidly inspecting her manicured nails. The second was A. R. Butler, perched with dignified casualness on a corner of the table. Chatting with Butler was the stockily built man with the trim toothbrush mustache who had accompanied Edgar Kramer to the morning hearing.

A. R. Butler observed Alan first.

"Welcome and congratulations!" Standing, his smile broad and warm, the older lawyer offered his hand. "Judging by the afternoon papers, we are in the presence of a public hero. I suppose you've seen them."

Embarrassed, Alan nodded. "Yes, I'm afraid I have." He had bought copies of the early editions of the *Post* and *Colonist* soon after leaving Sharon and the Senator. In both papers the hearing in judge's chambers had been the top story on page one, with pictures of Alan prominently featured. Dan Orliffe's report in the *Post* had used phrases like "shrewd legal moves," "a successful Maitland coup," and "tactical victory." The *Colonist*, still not quite as heated as the *Post* about Henri Duval, had been less laudatory, though most of the facts were reasonably correct.

"Well," A. R. Butler said good-humoredly, "where would we lawyers be without the press. Even with inaccuracies, it's the only advertising we're allowed. Oh, by the way, do you know Mr. Tamkynhil?"

"No," Alan said, "I don't think I do."

"George Tamkynhil," the mustached man said. They shook hands. "I'm with the department, Mr. Maitland. I'll be conducting the inquiry."

"Mr. Tamkynhil has had a good deal of experience in this kind of thing," A. R. Butler said. "You'll find him extremely fair."

"Thank you." He would wait and see, Alan decided. But at least he was glad the inquiry officer would not be Edgar Kramer.

There was a light tap and the door opened. A uniformed immigration officer ushered in Henri Duval.

On the previous occasion on which Alan Maitland had seen the young stowaway, Duval had been grimed and grease-stained, his hair matted from laboring in the *Vastervik's* bilges. Today, in contrast, he was clean and scrubbed, his face freshly shaven, and his long black hair combed tidily in place. His clothing was simple: as before, patched denims, a darned blue seaman's jersey, and old cloth shoes—probably rejected, Alan thought, by some other member of the ship's crew.

But as usual it was the face and eyes which held attention: the face with its round, strong, boyish features; the deep set eyes appealing and intelligent, yet with wariness never far behind.

At a nod from Tamkynhil the uniformed officer withdrew.

Standing by the door, Henri Duval's gaze moved quickly from one face to the next. He saw Alan last and, as he did, gave a warm smile of recognition.

"How are you, Henri?" Alan moved forward so that they were close. He placed a hand reassuringly on the young stowaway's arm.

"I good, real good." Henri Duval nodded, then, looking into Alan's face, asked hopefully, "Now I work Canada—stay?"

"No, Henri," Alan shook his head. "Not yet, I'm afraid. But these gentlemen are here to ask you questions. This is an inquiry."

The young man glanced around him. With a trace of nervousness he asked, "You stay with me?"

"Yes, I shall stay."

"Mr. Maitland," Tamkynhil interjected.

"Yes."

"If you'd care for a few minutes alone with this young man," the inquiry officer announced courteously, "the rest of us will gladly withdraw."

"Thank you," Alan acknowledged. "I don't believe that's necessary. If I can just explain to him, though . . ."

"By all means."

"Henri, this is Mr. Tamkynhil from Canadian Immigration, and Mr. Butler, who is a lawyer." As Alan spoke, Duval turned his head inquiringly from one man to the other and each rejoined with an amiable nod. "They are going to ask you questions and you must answer them honestly. If you do not understand anything that is said, you must say so and I will try to explain. But you must hold nothing back. Do you understand?"

The stowaway nodded vigorously. "I tell truth. All time, truth."

Speaking to Alan, A. R. Butler said, "There won't be any questioning from me, by the way. I'm just here with a watch-

ing brief." He smiled blandly. "You might say that my
business is to insure the law is carefully observed."

"For that matter," Alan said pointedly, "so is mine."

George Tamkynhil had taken the chair at the head of the
table. "Well, gentlemen," he announced firmly, "if you're
ready I think we can begin."

Alan Maitland and Henri Duval sat together on one side
of the table, the stenographer and A. R. Butler facing them.

Tamkynhil opened a file before him, selected a paper on
top and passed a carbon copy to the stenographer. In a
careful, precise voice he read, "This is an inquiry held under
the provision of the Immigration Act at the Canadian Immigration Building, Vancouver, B. C., on January 4, by me,
George Tamkynhil, a special inquiry officer, duly nominated
by the Minister of Citizenship and Immigration under Sub-
section 1 of Section 11 of the Immigration Act."

Through the rest of the official wording the voice droned
on. It was all so pretentiously correct, Alan thought. He had
little hope about the outcome of this inquiry; it was
unlikely in the extreme that the department would reverse
its own firm stand as a result of a procedure it controlled
itself, especially since no new facts were likely to emerge.
And yet, because he had demanded that this be done, the
formalities—all of them—were to be observed. Even now
he wondered if anything had been gained by his own efforts
so far. And yet in law, so often, you could only take one
step at a time, hoping that something would turn up before
the next step was due.

The promulgation finished, Tamkynhil asked Henri Duval,
"Do you understand why this inquiry is being held?"

The young stowaway nodded eagerly. "Yes, yes. I understand."

Consulting a note, Tamkynhil continued, "If you so desire, and at your own expense, you have the right to be represented by counsel at this hearing. Is Mr. Maitland, present
here, your counsel?"

A nod again. "Yes."

"Will you take an oath upon the Bible?"

"Yes."

With the familiar ritual Duval affirmed that he would tell
the truth. The stenographer wrote in longhand, her polished
fingernails gleaming, "Henry Duval duly sworn."

Now, putting his notes aside, Tamkynhil stroked his mustache meditatively. From now on, Alan knew, the questions would be unrehearsed.

Tamkynhil asked quietly, "What is your correct name?"

"My name, Henri Duval."

"Have you ever used any other name?"

"Never. That is the name my father give me. I never see him. My mother tell me."

"Where were you born?"

It was a repetition of the questioning which Duval had undergone—first from Dan Orliffe, then Alan Maitland—since his arrival twelve days earlier.

Steadily, eliciting a single short answer at a time, the queries and answers went on. Tamkynhil, Alan conceded mentally, was indeed a skilled and conscientious interrogator. His questions were simple, direct, and quietly spoken. As far as feasible, he dealt with events in correct chronology. Where, through difficulty of language, there seemed misunderstanding, he patiently went back to clear it up. There was no attempt at haste, no browbeating, no effort to score, nor any trickery. At no time did Tamkynhil raise his voice.

Each question and answer was dutifully recorded by the stenographer. The inquiry transcript Alan realized, would be a model of correct procedure to which, obviously, it would be difficult to object on grounds of error or unfairness. A. R. Butler, from his occasional approving nods, evidently thought so too.

The story, emerging point by point, was much as Alan had heard it before: The lonely birth of Henri Duval on the unknown ship; the return to Djibouti; early childhood —poverty and wandering, but with a mother's love at least . . . and then his mother's death when he was six years old. Afterwards, the frightening aloneness: an animal existence scavenging in the native quarter; the elderly Somali who gave him shelter. Then, wandering once more, but this time alone. Ethiopia to British Somaliland . . . Ethiopia again . . . attachment to a camel train; food for work; crossing borders with other children . . .

Then, a child no longer, his rejection at French Somaliland, which he had thought of as his home . . . The crushing realization of belonging nowhere, officially non-existent, without documents of any kind . . . The retreat to Massawa, stealing on the way; his detection in the market place; the sudden flight; terror . . . the pursuers . . . and the Italian ship.

The Italian shipmaster's anger; the boatswain's cruelties; near-starvation, and finally flight . . . The dockyard at Beirut; the guards; terror once more, and a shadow looming; in desperation—a stowaway again on the silent ship.

Discovery on the *Vastervik;* Captain Jaabeck; the first kindnesses; attempts to disembark him; refusals; the *Vastervik* a prison . . . The long two years; despair, rejection; . . . everywhere the tight-slammed doors: Europe; the Middle East; England and the United States, with all their vaunted freedom . . . Canada his final hope . . .

Listening once more, Alan Maitland wondered: could anyone hear this and not be moved? He had been watching Tamkynhil's face. There was sympathy there, he was sure. Twice the inquiry officer had hesitated in his questioning, looking doubtful, fingering his mustache. Could it have been emotion that made him pause?

A. R. Butler no longer wore a smile. For some time now he had been looking down at his hands.

But whether sympathy would do any good was another matter.

Almost two hours had gone by. The inquiry was nearing its end.

Tamkynhil asked, "If you were allowed to remain in Canada, what would you do?"

Eagerly—even after the long interrogation—the young stowaway answered, "I go school first, then work." He added: "I work good."

"Do you have any money?"

Proudly, Henri Duval said: "I have seven dollar, thirty cents."

It was the money, Alan knew, which the bus drivers had collected on Christmas Eve.

"Do you have any personal belongings?"

Once more eagerly, "Yes, sir—many: these clothes, a radio, a clock. People send me these, and fruit. They give me everything. I thank them very much, these nice people."

In the ensuing silence the stenographer turned a page.

Finally Tamkynhil said, "Has anyone offered you work?"

Alan interjected, "If I may answer that . . ."

"Yes, Mr. Maitland."

Riffling through papers in his brief case, Alan produced two. "There have been a good many letters in the past few days."

For a moment the smile returned to A. R. Butler. "Yes," he said, "I'm sure there must have been."

"These are two specific offers of employment," Alan explained. "One is from the Veterans Foundry Company, the other from Columbia Towing, who would take on Duval as a deck hand."

"Thank you." Tamkynhil read the letters which Alan offered, then passed them to the stenographer. "Record the names, please."

When the letters had been returned, the inquiry officer asked, "Mr. Maitland, do you wish to cross-examine Mr. Duval?"

"No," Alan said. Whatever might happen now, the proceedings had been as thorough as anyone could have wished.

Tamkynhil touched his mustache again, then shook his head. He opened his mouth as if to speak, then stopped. Instead he inspected the file before him and removed a printed form. While the others waited, he completed several portions of the form in ink.

Well, Alan thought—once more, here it comes.

Tamkynhil looked directly at the young stowaway. "Mr. Henri Duval," he said, then lowered his eyes to the printed form. He read quietly, "On the basis of the evidence adduced at this inquiry I have reached the decision that you may not come into or remain in Canada as of right, and that it has been proven that you are a member of the prohibited class described in paragraph (t) of Section 5 of the Immigration Act, in that you do not fulfil or comply with the conditions of requirements of Subsections 1, 3, and 8 of Section 18 of the Immigration Regulations."

Pausing, Tamkynhil looked again at Henri Duval. Then reading firmly, "I hereby order you to be detained and deported to the place whence you came to Canada, or to the country of which you are a national or citizen, or to such country as may be approved by the Minister . . ."

Detained and deported . . . paragraph (t) of Section 5 . . . Subsections 1, 3 and 8 of Section 18. Alan Maitland thought: we clothe our barbarisms in politenesses and call them civilized. We are Pontius Pilates who delude ourselves we are a Christian country. We allow in a hundred tubercular immigrants and beat our breast in smug self-righteousness, ignoring millions more, broken by a war from which Canada grew rich. By selective immigration, denying visas, we sentence families and children to misery and sometimes death, then avert our eyes and nostrils that we shall not see or smell. We break, turn down, a single human being, rationalizing our shame. And whatever we do, for whichever hypocrisy, there is a law or regulation . . . *paragraph (t) of Section 5 . . . Subsections 1, 3, and 8 of Section 18*.

Alan pushed back his chair and stood. He wanted to get out of this room, to taste the cold wind outside, the clean fresh air . . .

Henri Duval looked up, his young face troubled. He asked the single question, "No?"

"No, Henri." Alan shook his head slowly, then put a hand on the stowaway's shoulder under the darned blue jersey. "I'm sorry . . . I guess you knocked at the wrong door."

Thirteen   The House of Commons

"So you've told the Cabinet," Brian Richardson said. "How did they take it?" The party director rubbed a hand over his eyes to relieve their tiredness. Since the Prime Minister's return from Washington the previous day, Richardson had spent most of the intervening hours at his desk. He had left it ten minutes ago to come by taxi to Parliament Hill.

Hands thrust deeply into the pockets of his suit coat, James Howden continued to face the window where he had been looking down, from his Center Block office, on the steady afternoon stream of arrivals and departures. In the past few minutes an ambassador had come and gone; a trio of senators, like ancient pundits, had passed beneath and out of sight; there had been a black-habited cleric, stalking hawk-faced like a shade of doom; official messengers with monogrammed dispatch cases, self-important in their brief authority; a handful of press-gallery reporters; M.P.s. returning from lunch or a stroll, at home like members of a club; and the inevitable tourists, some standing to be photographed by friends beside sheepish, grinning Mounties.

What does it all mean, Howden thought? What does it

all amount to in the end? Everything around us seems so permanent: the long procession down the years; the statuary; the storied buildings; our systems of government; our enlightenment, or so we choose to think. And yet it is all so temporary, and we ourselves the most fragile, temporary part. Why do we struggle, strive, achieve, when the best we can do, in time, will amount to nothing?

There was no answer, he supposed. There was never any answer. The party director's voice recalled him to reality.

"How did they take it?" Brian Richardson repeated. A full meeting of Cabinet had been held early that morning.

Turning from the window, Howden asked, "Take what?"

"The Act of Union, of course. What else?"

James Howden considered before answering. The two men were in the Prime Minister's parliamentary office—Room 307S, a smaller and more intimate chamber than the regular suite of offices in the East Block, but only an elevator ride from the House of Commons.

"It's strange that you should ask what else. As far as the Act of Union was concerned, most of the Cabinet took it remarkably well. Of course, there'll be some dissension—perhaps strong dissension—when we discuss it again."

Brian Richardson said dryly, "That figures, doesn't it?"

"I suppose so," Howden took a turn around the room. "But then again, perhaps not. It's often true that big concepts can be accepted more readily than smaller ones."

"That's because most people have little minds."

"Not necessarily." There were times when Richardson's cynicism grated on Howden. "You were the one, I think, who pointed out that we've been moving toward the Act of Union for a long time. What's more, the terms as I have now negotiated them, are extremely favorable to Canada." The Prime Minister paused, tweaked his nose, then continued thoughtfully, "The extraordinary thing about this morning's Cabinet was that some people were much more anxious to talk about this wretched immigration affair."

"Isn't everybody? I suppose you saw today's papers?"

The Prime Minister nodded, then sat down, motioning Richardson to a facing chair. "This lawyer Maitland in Vancouver seems to be giving us a good deal of trouble. What do we know about him?"

"I checked. Seems to be just a young fellow, fairly bright, with no political connections that are known of."

"Not now, maybe. But this kind of case is a good way to start them. Is there any way we could approach Maitland indirectly; offer him a by-election seat if he'll take things easier?"

The party director shook his head. "Too risky. I made some inquiries and the advice I get is to stay away. If anything like that was said, Maitland would use it against us. He's that type."

In his own young days, Howden thought, he had been that type too. "All right," he said. "What else can you suggest?"

Richardson hesitated. For three days and nights, ever since Milly Freedeman had produced the fateful photostatic record of the deal between the Prime Minister and Harvey Warrender, his mind had explored possibilities.

Somewhere, Brian Richardson was convinced, a counter-lever against Harvey Warrender existed. There was always a counter-lever; even blackmailers had secrets they preferred to keep, though the problem was inevitably the same: how to wrest the secret out. There were many individuals in politics—inside and outside the party—whose secrets Richardson had been told or had stumbled on over the years. And in a locked safe in his own office a slim brown book contained them all, written in a private shorthand that only he could read.

But under "Warrender" in the private brown book there was nothing save a new entry made a day or two ago.

Yet . . . somehow . . . the counter-lever must be found; and if anyone found it, Richardson knew, it would be himself.

Over the three days and nights he had turned his memory inside out . . . probing recesses . . . recalling chance words, incidents, asides . . . juggling faces, places, phrases. It was a process which had worked before, but this time it had not.

Except that for the past twenty-four hours he had had a nagging sense of being close. There was something, he knew; and it was near the surface of his mind. A face, a memory, a word might trigger it. But not yet. The question was: how long?

He was tempted to reveal to Howden his knowledge about the nine-year-old agreement; to have a full and frank discussion. It might clear the air, perhaps produce a plan for countering Harvey Warrender, possibly even release whatever was locked in his own mind. But to do so would involve Milly, at this moment, in the office outside, guarding their privacy. And Milly must not be involved, now or later. The Prime Minister had asked: "What else can you suggest?"

"There's a fairly simple remedy, chief, which I've urged before."

Howden said sharply, "If you mean, let the stowaway in as an immigrant, that's out of the question now. We've taken a stand and we must maintain it. To back down would be an admission of weakness."

"If Maitland has his way, the courts may overrule you."

"No! Not if things are handled properly. I intend to talk to Warrender about that civil servant who's in charge out there."

"Kramer," Richardson said. "He's a deputy director who was sent out temporarily."

"He may have to be recalled. An experienced man would never have allowed a special inquiry. According to the newspapers he offered it voluntarily after the habeas corpus writ had been refused." Howden added with a flash of anger, "Because of that stupidity, the whole issue has been reactivated."

"Maybe you should wait till you get out there. Then you can give him hell personally. Did you look over the schedule?"

"Yes." Howden rose from the chair he had been occupying and crossed to his paper-strewn desk near the window. Dropping into an armchair behind, he reached for an open file folder. "Considering the short notice," he said approvingly, "it's a good program you've arranged for me."

Howden's eye ran down the list. Allowing for a House of Commons announcement about the Act of Union in ten days' time, there were five days available for a whirlwind speaking tour across the country—the "conditioning" period they had planned. He would begin in Toronto the day after tomorrow —a joint meeting of the influential Canadian and Empire Clubs—and end, on the final day, in Quebec City and Montreal. In between would be Fort William, Winnipeg, Edmonton, Vancouver, Calgary, and Regina.

He observed dryly, "I see you've included the usual quota of honorary degrees."

"I always thought you collected them," Richardson said.

"I suppose you could call it that. I keep them in the basement of Number 24, along with the Indian headdresses. The two things are about as useful."

Richardson gave a broad grin. "Don't ever get quoted on that. We'd lose the Indian and intellectual votes together." He added: "You said the Cabinet kicked the Duval case around, as well as the Act of Union. Was there any new conclusion?"

"No. Except that if the Opposition forces a debate in the House this afternoon, Harvey Warrender will speak for the Government and I shall intervene if needed."

Richardson said with a grin, "More discreetly than yesterday, I hope."

The Prime Minister flushed brick red. He answered angrily, "That kind of remark is not required. What I said yesterday at the airport was an error, which I admit. But everyone has lapses occasionally. Even you, from time to time, have made a few mistakes."

"I know." The party director rubbed the tip of his nose ruefully. "And I guess I just made another. Sorry."

Slightly mollified, Howden said, "Possibly Harvey Warrender can handle the whole thing himself."

Actually, Howden thought, if Harvey spoke as well and convincingly as he had in Cabinet, he might very well retrieve some lost ground for the Government and the party. This morning under sharp attack from other ministers, Harvey had defended the Immigration Department's action, making it seem sane and logical. There had been nothing erratic about his manner, either; it was subdued and rational, though the trouble with Harvey was, you could never be sure when his mood might switch.

The Prime Minister stood up again and faced the window, his back to Brian Richardson. There were fewer people down below, he noticed. Most, he supposed, had gone inside the Center Block where the House of Commons would be convening in a few minutes' time.

"Will the rules allow a debate in the House?" Richardson questioned.

"Not in the ordinary way." Howden answered without turning. "But there's a supply motion coming up this afternoon, and the Opposition can pick any subject they choose. I hear a rumor that Bonar Deitz may make it immigration."

Richardson sighed. He could already imagine the radio

and television coverage tonight, the news stories tomorrow morning.

There was a light tap at the door. It opened to admit Milly. Howden turned, facing her.

"It's almost half past," Milly announced. "If you're going in for prayers . . ." She smiled at Richardson and nodded. On the way in the party director had handed her a folded note which read characteristically: "Expect me at seven tonight. Important."

"Yes," the Prime Minister said. "I'm going."

Above them the Westminster quarters of the Peace Tower carillon began to chime.

2

The sonorous, distinguished voice of the Speaker of the House was moving toward the end of prayers as James Howden entered the Government lobby. As always, the Prime Minister thought, Mr. Speaker was putting on an impressive show. Through the nearest doorway to the floor of the House he could hear the familiar daily words . . . *beseech Thee . . . particularly for the Governor General, the Senate and the House of Commons . . . that Thou wouldst be pleased to direct and prosper all their consultations . . . that peace and happiness, truth and justice, religion and piety may be established among us for all generatons . . .*

Such splendid sentiments, Howden thought—alternated daily in French and English for a presumably bilingual God. It was a pity that in a few minutes from now the words would be forgotten among the minutiae of petty political sparring.

From inside came a chorus of sonorous amens, led strongly by the Clerk of the House, as was his special privilege.

Now other ministers and members were moving in, the House filling as it usually did for question time at the opening of a daily session. Around the Prime Minister in the lobby, supporters of his own majority party filed to their seats. Howden stayed, chatting briefly with members of the Cabinet, nodding to others who acknowledged his presence respectfully as they passed.

He allowed time for the galleries to fill before making his own entrance.

As always, there was a stir and turning of heads as he appeared. As if unaware of the attention, he made his way leisurely to the front row double desk on the Government side of the House, which he shared with Stuart Cawston, already seated. Bowing to the Speaker, presiding from his canopied, thronelike chair at the north end of the high oblong chamber, James Howden took his own seat. A moment later he nodded urbanely to Bonar Deitz in the Opposition Leader's seat directly across the center aisle.

The routine barrage of questions to Government ministers had already begun.

A Newfoundland member was upset because of great numbers of dead codfish floating off the Atlantic coast, and what did the Government propose to do? The Minister of Fisheries began an involved and labored answer.

Beside the Prime Minister, Smiling Stu Cawston murmured, "I hear Deitz has chosen immigration for sure. I hope Harvey can carry the ball."

James Howden nodded, then glanced behind him at the second row of Government desks where Harvey Warrender sat, apparently imperturbable, except that now and then the muscles of his face were twitching.

As questioning continued, it was evident that the subject of immigration and Henri Duval—normally the kind of issue with which the Opposition would delight to bombard the Government at question time—was being omitted. It was added confirmation that Bonar Deitz and his supporters planned a full-dress debate when the supply motion was moved in a few minutes.

The press gallery was crowded, Howden noted gloomily. All the front row seats were occupied and other reporters had crowded in behind.

The questions had ended and Smiling Stu arose from beside the Prime Minister. He moved formally that the House go into Committee of Supply.

Gathering his silk Q.C.'s gown around his corpulent figure, the Speaker nodded. At once, the Leader of the Opposition was on his feet.

"Mr. Speaker," the Hon. Bonar Deitz enunciated crisply, then paused, his scholarly, gaunt face turned questioningly toward the presiding officer. Again a nod from the Speaker, like a black, watching beetle, in his chair under the carved oak canopy.

For a moment Deitz paused, looking up—an unconscious habit he sometimes had—toward the soaring ceiling of the chamber fifty feet above. It was almost, James Howden thought on the other side of the House, as if his principal opponent sought to draw, from the painted Irish linen surface and elaborate gold-leaf cornices, the words he needed for a moment's greatness.

"The sorry record of this Government," Bonar Deitz began, "is nowhere more depressingly exemplified than in its policies affecting immigration, and the day-to-day administration of immigration affairs. I suggest, Mr. Speaker, that the Government and its Department of Citizenship and Immigration have their collective feet firmly rooted in the nineteenth century, a period from which they will not be stirred by considerations of a changed world or by simple, everyday humanity."

It was an adequate opening, Howden thought, though whatever else Bonar Deitz had gathered from his survey of the ceiling, it had not been greatness. Most of the words, in one form or another, had been used before by successive oppositions in the House of Commons.

The thought prompted him to scribble a note to Harvey Warrender. "Quote instances where Opposition, when in power, followed exact same procedure as us now. If you've not details, instruct your Dept. rush them here." He folded the note, beckoned a page boy and indicated the Minister of Immigration.

A moment later Harvey Warrender turned his head toward the Prime Minister, nodded, and touched a file folder among several on the desk before him. Well, Howden thought, that was as it should be. A good executive assistant would brief his minister carefully on something like that.

Bonar Deitz was continuing, ". . . in this motion of 'no confidence' . . . a current example of a tragic case where humanitarian considerations, as well as human rights have been wantonly ignored."

As Deitz paused there was a thumping of desk tops on the Opposition side. On the Government side a back-bencher called out, "I wish we could ignore *you*."

For a second the Opposition Leader hesitated.

The rough and tumble of the House of Commons had

never appealed greatly to Bonar Deitz. Right from his own
first election as a Member of Parliament years before,
the House had always seemed to him remarkably like a
sports arena where competing teams attempted to score
points off each other at every opportunity. The rules of conduct, it seemed, were childishly simple: if some measure was
favored by your own party, it was naturally good; if favored
by another party, and not your own, it was just as automatically bad. There was seldom any in between. Similarly, to
doubt your own party's stand on any issue and wonder if,
for once, your opponents might be right and wiser, was
considered disaffecting and disloyal.

It had been a jolt, also, to Deitz the scholar and intellectual, to discover that effective party loyalty extended
to banging desk tops in support of other party members
and hurling gibes and counter-gibes across the House in
the manner of exuberant schoolboys, with sometimes a good
deal less erudition than schoolboys might show. In time—
long before he had become Opposition Leader—Bonar Deitz
had learned to do both, though seldom without a degree of
inward squirming.

The heckler had cried: "I wish we could ignore *you*."

His instinctive reaction was not to bother with a rude
and silly interruption. But his own supporters, he knew,
would expect some retaliation. Therefore he snapped back,
"The honorable member's wish is understandable since the
Government he supports has ignored so much for so long."
He wagged an accusing finger at the other side of the
House. "But there will come a time when the conscience
of this country can no longer be ignored."

Not very good, Bonar Deitz decided inwardly. He suspected that the Prime Minister, who excelled in repartee,
would probably have done better. But at least his attempt
at counter-attack had earned a volley of desk-top banging
from the members behind him.

Now, responding, there were jeers, and shouts of "Oh,
oh," and "Are you our conscience?" from the other side.

"Order, order." It was Mr. Speaker, standing, putting on
his tricorn hat. In a moment or two the hubbub died down.

"I referred to the conscience of our country," Bonar
Deitz proclaimed. "Let me tell you what that conscience
tells *me*. It tells me that we are one of the richest and
most underpopulated nations in the world. And yet we are

informed by the Government, through its Minister of Immigration, that there is not space here for this single unfortunate human being . . ."

In a separate compartment of his mind the Opposition Leader was aware that he was being verbally reckless. It was dangerous to put sentiments of that kind so unequivocally on record, because any party which came to power found speedily that political pressures for limiting immigration were too great to be ignored. Someday, Deitz knew, he might well regret his present ardent words.

But at moments—and this was one—the compromises of politics, the endless mealy-mouthed speeches, wearied and disgusted him. Today, for once, he would say what he believed forthrightly and hang the consequences!

In the press gallery, he noted, heads were down.

Pleading for Henri Duval, an insignificant man whom he had never met, Bonar Deitz continued to address the House.

Across the center aisle, James Howden was listening with half an ear. For the past few minutes he had been watching the clock at the south end of the chamber below the steeply-tiered ladies' gallery, three-quarters full today. He was aware that very soon a third of the reporters present would be leaving to file stories for their papers' late afternoon editions. With deadlines close, they would begin moving out at any moment. Listening carefully, he waited for an opening . . .

"Surely there are times," Bonar Deitz declaimed, "when humanitarian considerations should override stubborn adherence to the letter of the law?"

The Prime Minister was on his feet. "Mr. Speaker, will the Leader of the Opposition permit a question?"

Bonar Deitz hesitated. But it was a reasonable request he could hardly refuse. He said curtly, "Yes."

"Is the Leader of the Opposition suggesting," Howden asked with sudden rhetoric, "that the Government should ignore the law, the law of this country, enacted by Parliament . . ."

He was interrupted from the Opposition side by shouts of "Question, question!" "Get on with it!" "It's a speech!" And from his own supporters came retaliatory cries of "Order!" "Listen to the question!" "What are you afraid of?" Bonar Deitz, who had resumed his seat, was once more on his feet.

"I am coming to the crux of my question," the Prime Minister declared loudly, his voice rising above the others, "and it is simply this." He paused, waiting for relative silence, and when it came he continued, "Since it is plain that this unfortunate young man, Henri Duval, is in no way admissible to Canada under our own law, I ask the Leader of the Opposition if he is in favor of referring the case to the United Nations. And I may say that in any event it is the Government's intention to bring this matter immediately to United Nations attention . . ."

There was instant uproar. Once more, shouts, accusations and counteraccusations flew back and forth across the House. The Speaker was on his feet, his voice unheeded. Red-faced, his eyes blazing, Bonar Deitz faced the Prime Minister. He cried angrily, "This is a device——"

And so it was.

In the press gallery, reporters were hurrying out. The interruption, the announcement, had been perfectly timed . . .

James Howden could predict the one-sentence lead on most news stories now being telephoned or typed: *Henri Duval, the man-with-out-a-country, may have his case referred to the United Nations, the Prime Minister revealed to the House of Commons today.* CP and BUP had probably sent three-bell bulletins already. "DUVAL CASE GOES TO U.N.—PRIME MINISTER," the teletypes would clatter, and time-pressured editors, feverishly in search of a new angle, would use the words in headlines. The Opposition attack; Bonar Deitz's speech—these would be mentioned, of course, but in a secondary sense.

Inwardly glowing, the Prime Minister scribbled a one-line note to Arthur Lexington: "Write a letter." If questioned later, he must be able to state that the promise of an approach to U.N. had been properly fulfilled by External Affairs.

Bonar Deitz had resumed his interrupted speech. But there was a sense of lessened impact, of a head of steam dispersed. James Howden was aware of it; he suspected Deitz was too.

Once, long ago, there had been a time when the Prime Minister had liked and respected Bonar Deitz despite the gulf of party politics dividing them. There had seemed an integrity and depth of character about the Opposition Leader, an honest consistency to all his actions, which it was hard not to admire. But in time Howden's attitude had changed until nowadays he thought of Bonar Deitz with little more than tolerant contempt.

Mostly the change had come through Deitz's own performance as Opposition Leader. Many times, Howden had been aware, Bonar Deitz had failed to take full advantage of James Howden's own vulnerability on specific issues. That sometimes such action—or lack of it—argued a reasonable restraint, was (as Howden saw it) beside the point. A leader's role was to lead and, whenever advantage offered itself, to be tough and ruthless in taking it. Party politics was no cream-puff affair and inevitably the path to power was strewn with shattered hopes, and husks of other men's ambitions.

It was ruthlessness which Bonar Deitz had lacked.

He had other qualities: intellect and scholarship, perception and foresight, patience and personal charm. But overall these qualities had never made him a match—or at least had never seemed to—for James McCallum Howden.

It was next to impossible, Howden thought, to imagine Bonar Deitz as Prime Minister, commanding the Cabinet, dominating the House of Commons, maneuvering, feinting, acting swiftly—as he himself had done a moment ago— to gain tactical advantage in debate.

And what of Washington? Could the Leader of the Opposition have faced the U.S. President and his formidable aide, and have stood his ground, and come away from Washington with as much as Howden himself had gained. More than likely Deitz would have been reasonable, never as tough as James Howden and, in the end, have conceded more and gained less. And the same would be true in whatever was to happen in the months to come.

The thought was a reminder that in a mere ten days he, James Howden, would stand here in the House and announce the Act of Union and its terms. Then would be a time for greatness and great issues, with petty concerns— stowaways, immigration, and their like—forgotten or ignored. He had a sense of frustration and annoyance that the present debate was at this moment considered significant when, in fact, it was laughably trivial compared with the issues he would soon reveal.

And now, after a speech of almost an hour, Bonar Deitz was ending.

"Mr. Speaker, it is not too late," the Opposition Leader declared. "It is not too late for the Government, in charity and magnanimity, to allow this young man Henri Duval the Canadian domicile he seeks. It is not too late for the individual himself to escape the tragic prison to which an accident of birth has grimly sentenced him. It is not too late for Duval—with our help and in our midst—to become a useful, happy member of society. I plead with the Government for compassion. I urge them that we should not plead in vain."

After announcing the wording of the formal motion ". . . that this House regrets the refusal of the Government to accept and discharge its proper responsibility in the matter of Immigration . . ." Bonar Deitz sat down to a thunder of desk tops on the Opposition side.

Immediately, Harvey Warrender was on his feet.

"Mr. Speaker," the Immigration Minister began, in his bass, booming voice, "as usual the Leader of the Opposition has managed to flavor fact with fantasy, cloud a simple issue with excessive sentimentality, and has succeeded in making a normal lawful procedure of the Department of Immigration appear like a sadistic conspiracy against all mankind."

At once there were angry cries of protest and "Withdraw!" countered by cheers and desk thumping.

Ignoring the outcry, Harvey Warrender continued heatedly, "If this Government had been guilty of a breach of law we would deserve the contumely of the House. Or if the Department of Citizenship and Immigration had failed in its proper legal duty, ignoring the statutes enacted by Parliament, I would bow my head and accept its condemnation. But since we have done neither, I tell you I will accept neither."

James Howden found himself wishing that Harvey Warrender would moderate his aggressive tone. There were occasions in the House of Commons which called for a boisterous, free-swinging kind of tactic, but today was not one. Here and now quiet reasonableness would be more effective. Besides, the Prime Minister was uncomfortably aware of an undercurrent of hysteria in Warrender's voice. It persisted as he continued, "What is this charge of infamy and heartlessness which the Opposition Leader lays before you? It is simply that the Government has not broken the law; that its Department of Citizenship and Immigration has honored its obligations exactly according to the Immigration Act of Canada, with undeviating fairness."

Well, there was nothing wrong with that; in fact it was something which needed to be said. If only Harvey, personally, could be less intense . . .

"The Leader of the Opposition has spoken of the man Henri Duval. Let us ignore for the moment the question of whether this country should take on a burden which no one else wants, whether we should open our doors to the human garbage of the seas . . ."

From across the House a roar of protest eclipsed in volume all the earlier skirmishes of the day. Harvey Warrender had gone too far, Howden knew. Even on the Government side there were shocked faces, with only a few members responding halfheartedly to the opposition clamor.

Bonar Deitz was on his feet. "Mr. Speaker, on a question of privilege, I object . . ." Behind him were other heated, protesting cries.

Amid the growing din Harvey Warrender plowed determinedly on. "I say let us ignore the phony sentimentalities and consider the law alone. The law has been served . . ." His words were drowned out in a rising tide of angry shouts.

One voice persisted above the rest. "Mr. Speaker, will the Minister of Immigration define what he means by human garbage?" Uneasily, James Howden recognized the question's source. It had come from Arnold Geaney, a backbench Opposition member who represented one of the poorer districts of Montreal.

There were two notable things about Arnold Geaney. He was a cripple, only five feet tall, with a partially paralyzed and twisted body, and a face so uniquely ugly and misproportioned as to suggest that nature had conspired against him to produce a human freak. And yet, despite his incredible handicap, he had carved a notable career as a parliamentarian and champion of downtrodden causes. Personally, Howden had an intense dislike for the man, believing him to be an exhibitionist who traded shamelessly upon his physical deformity. At the same time, well aware that popular sympathy was all too ready to be on the side of a cripple, the Prime Minister was invariably wary of tangling with Arnold Geaney in debate.

Now Geaney demanded again, "Will the Minister define the words 'human garbage'?"

The muscles of Harvey Warrender's face were twitching once more. James Howden envisaged the answer which, in unconsidered haste, the Immigration Minister might make: "No one is in a better position than the honorable member to know exactly what I mean." At all costs, Howden decided, that kind of rejoinder must be prevented.

Rising, the Prime Minister declared above the shouts and countershouts, "The honorable member for Montreal East is placing an emphasis upon certain words which I am perfectly sure my colleague did not intend."

"Then let him say so!" Geaney, raising himself awkwardly on crutches, hurled the words across the center aisle. Around him there were supporting shouts and cries, "Withdraw! Withdraw!" In the galleries people were craning forward.

"Order! Order!" It was the Speaker, his voice barely heard above the din.

"I withdraw nothing!" Harvey Warrender was shouting wildly, his face flushed hotly, his bull neck bulging. "Nothing, do you hear!"

Again the clamor. Again the Speaker's cries for order. This was a rare parliamentary occasion, Howden realized. Only some deep-rooted division or a question of human rights could arouse the House in the way that had happened today.

"I demand that the minister be made to answer." It was still the persistent, penetrating voice of Arnold Geaney.

"Order! The question before the House . . ." At last the Speaker was succeeding in making himself heard. On the Government side the Prime Minister and Harvey Warrender resumed their seats in deference to the chair. Now from all quarters the shouts were dying. Only Arnold Geaney, swaying on his crutches, continued to defy the Speaker's authority.

"Mr. Speaker, the Minister of Immigration has spoken to this House of human garbage. I demand . . ."

"Order! I would ask the member to resume his seat."

"On a question of privilege . . ."

"If the member will not resume his seat, I shall be obliged to name him."

It was almost as if Geaney were courting censure. Standing

orders, the rules of the House, were definite that when
the Speaker stood, all others must give way. In this case
there had been reinforcement by a specific order. If Geaney
continued in defiance, some form of disciplining would become essential.

"I will give the honorable member one more opportunity,"
the Speaker warned sternly, "before I name him."

Arnold Geaney said defiantly, "Mr. Speaker, I am standing for a human being three thousand miles from here,
contemptuously referred to by this Government as 'garbage' . . ."

The pattern, James Howden suddenly perceived, was perfectly simple. Geaney the cripple was seeking to share the
martyrdom of Duval the stowaway. It was an adroit, if
cynical, political maneuver which Howden must prevent.

Standing, the Prime Minister interjected, "Mr. Speaker, I
believe this matter can be resolved . . ." He had already
decided that on behalf of the Government he would withdraw the offensive words, whatever Harvey Warrender might
feel . . .

Too late.

Ignoring the Prime Minister, the Speaker pronounced
firmly, "It is my unpleasant duty to name the honorable
member for Montreal East."

Infuriatingly aware that he had lost the gambit, James
Howden sat down.

The formalities followed swiftly. The Speaker's naming of
a member of the House was a measure rarely resorted to.
But when it occurred, disciplinary action by the remaining
members became automatic and inevitable. Authority of the
Speaker must, above all things, be upheld. It was the authority of Parliament itself, and of the people, won by centuries of struggle . . .

The Prime Minister passed a two-word note to Stuart
Cawston, leader of the House. The words were "minimum
penalty." The Finance Minister nodded.

After a hurried consultation with the Postmaster General
behind him, Cawston rose. He announced, "In view of your
decision, Mr. Speaker, I have no alternative but to move,
seconded by the Postmaster General, Mr. Gold: 'That
the honorable member for Montreal East be suspended for
the duration of this day's sitting.' "

Unhappily the Prime Minister observed that the press

gallery was once again crowded. Tonight's TV and radio news, as well as a headline for the morning papers, was in the making.

It took twenty minutes for a recorded vote on Cawston's motion. The balloting was 131 for, 55 against. The Speaker announced formally, "I declare the motion carried." There was silence in the House.

Carefully, wavering on his crutches, Arnold Geaney rose. Deliberately, step by awkward step, he swung his distorted body and misshapen features past the Opposition front benches into the center aisle. To James Howden, who had known Geaney in the House of Commons for many years, it seemed that the other man had never moved more slowly. Facing the Speaker, with a pathetic awkwardness, the cripple bowed and for a moment it seemed as if he might fall foward. Then, recovering, he turned, retreated slowly the length of the House, then turned and bowed again. As he disappeared through the chamber's outer doors, held wide by the sergeant at arms, there was an audible sigh of relief.

The Speaker said quietly, "The Minister of Citizenship and Immigration has the floor."

Harvey Warrender—a shade more subdued than before—continued where he had left off. But James Howden knew that whatever happened now could only be anticlimactic. Arnold Geaney had been justly expelled, for a few hours only, for a flagrant breach of House of Commons rules. But the press would make the most of the story, and the public, not knowing or caring about rules of debate, would see two underprivileged men—the cripple and the friendless stowaway—as victims of a harsh, despotic Government.

For the first time Howden wondered how much longer the Government could afford to lose popularity, as had happened since the coming of Henri Duval.

3

Brian Richardson's note had said: "Expect me at seven."

At five minutes to, Milly Freedeman, nowhere near ready and stepping drippily from her bath, hoped he would be late.

Milly often wondered with vague incuriosity why it was that she, who managed her office life—and James Howden's—with machine-like efficiency, almost never carried the same process through to her life at home. On Parliament Hill she was punctual to the second; at home, seldom so. The Prime Minister's office suite was a model of orderliness, including neatly arranged cupboards, and a file system from which, in seconds Milly could whisk a five-year-old hand-written letter from an obscure individual whose name had long since been forgotten. But at the moment, typically, she was rummaging through untidy bedroom drawers in search of an elusive fresh brassière.

She supposed—when she bothered thinking about it— that her own mild disorganization out of office time was an inner rebellion against having her private life affected by outside habits or pressures. She had always been rebellious, even perverse at times, about extraneous affairs, or the ideas of others which spilled over, embroiling her personally.

Nor had she ever liked others planning her own future, even when the planning was well-intentioned. Once, when Milly had been in college at Toronto, her father had urged her to follow him into the practice of law. "You'd be a big success, Mill," he had predicted. "You're clever and quick, and you've the kind of mind which can see straight to the heart of things. If you wanted to, you could run rings around men like me."

Afterwards she reasoned: if she had thought of it herself she just might have followed through. But she had resented —even from her own father, whom she loved—the implication that her personal, private decisions could be made by someone other than herself.

Of course, the whole idea was a contradiction. You could never live a wholly independent existence, any more than you could separate your private and your office lives completely. Otherwise, Milly thought, as she found the brassière and put it on, there would have been no love affair with James Howden, and no Brian Richardson coming here tonight.

But should there be? Should she have allowed Brian to come? Wouldn't it have been better if she had been firm at the beginning, insisting that her private life remain inviolate: the private life she had carefully created since the day she learned finally that there was no future for herself and James Howden together?

She stepped into a pair of panties, and again the questions troubled her.

A self-contained private life, reasonably happy, was worth

a good deal. With Brian Richardson was she running the risk of losing her hard won contentment and gaining nothing in return?

It had taken time—a good deal of time after the break with James Howden—to adjust her outlook and mode of living to the permanence of being alone. But because (Milly imagined) of her deep-rooted instinct for solving personal problems unaided, she *had* adjusted to the point where her life nowadays was content, balanced, and successful.

Quite genuinely, Milly no longer envied—as she once had—married girl friends with their protective pipe-smoking husbands and sprawling children. Sometimes, in fact, the more she saw of them all, the more boring and routine their lives appeared compared with her own independence and freedom.

The point was: were her feelings for Brian Richardson inclining her back towards thoughts of conventional involvement?

Opening the bedroom closet door, Milly wondered what she should wear. Well, on Christmas Eve, Brian had said she looked sexy in pants . . . She selected a pair of bright green slacks, then searched through the drawers again for a white, low-necked sweater. She left her feet bare, slipping them into slim white sandals. When she had the slacks and sweater on and the light make-up she always wore, day or evening, it was already ten past seven.

She ran her hands through her hair, then decided she had better brush it after all, and went hurrying to the bathroom.

Looking in the mirror, she told herself: There is nothing, absolutely nothing to be concerned about. Yes, if I am honest I could fall in love with Brian, and perhaps I have already. But Brian is unavailable, and he wants it that way. So no question arises.

But there *is* a question, her mind insisted. What will it be like afterwards? When he has moved on. When you are alone again.

For a moment Milly stopped. She remembered how it had been nine years earlier. The empty days, desolate nights, the long weeks creeping . . . She said aloud: "I don't think I could go through that again." And silently: Perhaps, after all, I should end it tonight.

She was still remembering when the downstairs buzzer sounded.

Brian kissed her before he took off his heavy overcoat. There was a slight stubble on his face and a smell of tobacco. Milly had a sense of weakness, of resolve vanishing. I want this man, she thought; on any terms. Then she remembered her thought of a few minutes earlier: Perhaps I should end it tonight.

"Milly, doll," he said quietly, "you look terrific."

She eased away, looking at him. Then, concernedly, "Brian, you're tired."

"I know." He nodded. "And I need a shave. And I just came from the House."

Not really caring at this moment, she asked, "How did it go?"

"You haven't heard?"

She shook her head. "I left the office early. I didn't turn on the radio. Should I have?"

"No," he said. "You'll hear about it soon enough."

"The debate went badly?"

He nodded gloomily. "I was in the gallery. I wished I hadn't been. They'll slay us in tomorrow's papers."

"Let's have a drink," Milly said. "You sound as if you need one."

She mixed martinis, going lightly on the vermouth. Bringing them from the kitchenette, she said almost gaily, "This will help. It usually does."

No ending tonight, she thought. Perhaps a week from now, a month. But not tonight.

Brian Richardson sipped his drink, then put it down. Without preliminary, almost abruptly, he announced, "Milly, I want you to marry me."

There was a silence of seconds which seemed like hours. Then, this time softly: "Milly, did you hear me?"

"For a minute," Milly said, "I could have sworn you asked me to marry you." The words as she spoke seemed airy, detached, her voice disembodied. She had a sense of lightheadedness.

"Don't make a joke of it," Richardson said gruffly. "I'm serious."

"Darling, Brian." Her voice was gentle. "I'm not making a joke. Really I'm not."

He put down his glass and came to her. When they had kissed again, long and passionately, she put her face against his shoulder. There was the tobacco smell still. "Hold me," she whispered. "Hold me."

"When you get around to it," he said into her hair, "you can give me some sort of an answer."

Every womanly instinct urged her to cry yes. The mood and the moment were made for swift consent. Wasn't this what she had wanted all along? Hadn't she told herself, just a few minutes ago, that she would accept Brian on any terms; and now unexpectedly, she could have the best terms of all—marriage, permanence . . .

It was all so easy. A murmured acceptance, and it would be done; with no turning back . . .

The finality frightened her. This was real, not dreaming. She was assailed by a tremor of uncertainty. A voice of caution whispered: Wait!

"I guess I'm not much of a catch." Brian's voice rumbled in her hair; a hand caressed her neck gently. "I'm a bit shop soiled, and I'll have to get a divorce, though there won't be any trouble over that. Eloise and I have a sort of understanding."

There was a pause, then the voice continued slowly. "I guess I love you, Milly. I guess I really do."

She lifted her face, her eyes full with tears, and kissed him. "Brian, darling, I know you do; and I think I love you too. But I have to be sure. Please give me a little time."

His face twisted to a rugged grin. "Well," he said, "I rehearsed all the way over. I guess I loused it up."

Maybe, he thought, I left it all too late. Or handled everything the wrong way. Or maybe it's a retribution for the way we started: with me not caring, cagey against involvements. Now I'm the one who wants to get involved and I'm left, like a joker, on the outside looking in. But at least, he consoled himself, the indecision had come to an end: the restless soul searching of the past few days; the knowledge that Milly was what counted most. Now, without her, there seemed only emptiness . . .

"Please, Brian." Milly was calmer now, her poise and self-control returning. She said earnestly, "I'm flattered and honored, darling, and I think the answer will be yes. But I want to be sure—for both our sakes. Please, dear, give me a little time."

He asked brusquely, "How long?"

They sat down together on the long settee, their heads close and hands held tightly. "Honestly, darling, I don't know, and I hope you won't insist on a definite time. I couldn't bear to have a sort of deadline hanging over. But I promise I'll tell you as soon as I know."

She thought: What's wrong with me? Am I afraid of living? Why hesitate; why not settle now? But still the cautionary voice urged: Wait!

Brian put out his arms and she went into them. Their lips met and he kissed her fiercely again and again. She felt herself responding, her heart pounding wildly. After a while his hands moved gently.

Toward the end of the evening Brian Richardson came into the living room carrying coffee for both of them. Behind him in the kitchenette Milly was cutting salami sandwiches. She noticed her breakfast dishes still piled in the sink, unwashed. Really, she thought, perhaps I *should* bring some of my office habits home.

Richardson crossed to Milly's portable television, on a low table facing one of the big armchairs. Switching the set on, he called over, "I don't know if I can stand it, but I guess we'd better know the worst." As Milly brought the plate of sandwiches and set it down, the CBC national news was beginning.

As happened most days now, the first report concerned the worsening international scene. Soviet-inspired revolts that flared again in Laos, and the Kremlin had replied belligerently to an American note in protest. In the Soviet satellites of Europe, troops were reported massing. An exchange of cordialities had taken place between the now-repaired Moscow-Peking axis.

"It's getting closer," Richardson muttered. "Closer every day."

The Henri Duval story was next.

The well-groomed news announcer read, "In Ottawa today the House of Commons was in uproar over Henri Duval, the man-without-a-country, now awaiting deportation in Vancouver. At the height of a clash between Government and Opposition, Arnold Geaney, member from Montreal East, was suspended from the House for the remainder of today's sitting . . ."

Behind the announcer a screen flashed a picture of Henri Duval, followed by a large, still shot of the crippled M.P. As Richardson—as well as James Howden—had feared, the expulsion incident and Harvey Warrender's "human garbage" phrase which had provoked it were the news story's highlight. And no matter how fairly the report was handled, inevitably the stowaway and the cripple would appear victims of a harsh, relentless Government.

"CBC correspondent Norman Deeping," the announcer said, "describes the scene in the House . . ."

Richardson reached to switch off the set. "I don't think I can take any more. Do you mind?"

"No," Milly shook her head. Tonight, though knowing the significance of what she had seen, she found it hard to maintain interest. The most important question was still undecided . . .

Brian Richardson pointed to the darkened TV screen. "Goddam, do you know what audience that has? It's network—coast to coast. Add to that all the others—radio, local TV, tomorrow's newspapers . . ." He gave a shrug of helplessness.

"I know," Milly said. She tried to bring her mind back to impersonal concerns. "I wish there were something I could do."

Richardson had risen and was pacing the room. "You have done something, Milly dear. At least you found . . ." He left the sentence unfinished.

Both of them, Milly knew, were remembering the photostat; the fateful, secret agreement between James Howden and Harvey Warrender. She asked tentatively, "Have you done . . ."

He shook his head. "Damn all! There's nothing . . . nothing . . ."

"You know," Milly said slowly, "I've always thought there was something strange about Mr. Warrender. The way he talks and acts; as if he were nervous all the time. And then that business of idolizing that son of his—the one killed in the war . . ."

She stopped, startled by Brian Richardson's expression. His eyes were riveted on her face, his mouth agape.

"Brian——"

He whispered, "Milly, doll, say that again."

She repeated uncomfortably, "Mr. Warrender—I said he's

strange about his son. I understand there's a sort of shrine in his home. People used to talk a lot."

"Yeah." Richardson nodded. He tried to conceal his excitement. "Yeah. Well, I guess there's nothing in that."

He wondered how fast he could get away. He wanted to use a telephone—but not Milly's telephone. There were certain things . . . things he might have to do . . . he would never want Milly to know.

Twenty minutes later he was phoning from an all-night drugstore. "I don't give a goddam how late it is," the party director told the object of his call. "I'm telling you to get downtown now and I'll be waiting for you in the Jasper Lounge."

4

The pale young man with tortoise-shell glasses who had been summoned from bed turned the stem of his glass nervously in his hand. He said, with a touch of plaintiveness, "I really don't know if I could do it."

"Why not?" Brian Richardson demanded. "You're right there in the Defense Department. All you have to do is ask."

"It isn't as simple as that," the young man said. "Besides, it's classified information."

"Hell!" Richardson argued. "Something *that* old—who cares about that any more?"

"Obviously you do," the young man said with a show of spirit. "That's half of what I'm worried about."

"I give you my word," Richardson said, "that whatever use I make of what you give me, it will never be traced back to you."

"But it would be hard even to find. Those old files are buried away at the back of buildings, in basements . . . It might take days or weeks."

"That's your problem," Richardson said bluntly. "Except, I can't wait weeks." He beckoned a waiter. "Let's have the same again."

"No thank you," the young man said. "This is enough for me."

"Have it your way." Richardson nodded to the waiter, "Make it one; that's all."

When the waiter had gone, "I'm sorry," the young man said, "but I'm afraid the answer is no."

"I'm sorry too," Richardson said, "because your name was getting near the top of the list." There was a pause. "You know what list I'm talking about, don't you?"

"Yes," the young man said. "I know."

"In my job," Richardson said, "I have a lot to do with selecting Parliamentary candidates. In fact, there are people who say that I pretty well pick all the new men in our party who finally get elected."

"Yes," the young man said, "I've heard that too."

"Of course, the local association has the final word. But they mostly do what the Prime Minister recommends. Or what I tell the Prime Minister to recommend."

The young man said nothing. The tip of his tongue touched his lips and ran along them.

Brian Richardson said softly, "I'll make a deal. Do this thing for me, and I'll put your name right at the top. And not just for any old seat, but one where you're sure to win."

There was a flush of color in the young man's cheeks as he asked, "And if I don't do what you want?"

"In that case," Richardson said softly, "I positively guarantee that so long as I am with the party you will never sit in the House of Commons, and never be a candidate for any seat you can hope to win. You'll stay an executive assistant until you rot, and all your father's money will never change it."

The young man said bitterly, "You're asking me to start my political career with something rotten."

"Actually, I'm doing you a favor," Richardson said. "I'm introducing you to some facts of life which other people take years to discover."

The waiter had returned and Richardson inquired, "You're sure you won't change your mind and have another drink."

The young man drained his glass. "All right," he said. "I will."

When the waiter had gone, Richardson asked, "Assuming I'm right, how long will it take you to get what I need?"

"Well . . ." The young man hesitated. "I should think a couple of days."

"Cheer up!" Brian Richardson reached over, clapping a

hand on the other's knee. "In two years from now you'll have forgotten this whole thing ever happened."

"Yes," the young man said unhappily. "That's what I'm afraid of."

Fourteen "Detained and Deported"

From the surface of his office desk, the deportation order against Henri Duval stared up at Alan Maitland.

> . . . hereby order you to be detained and deported to the place whence you came to Canada, or to the country of which you are a national or citizen, or to the country of your birth, or to such country as may be approved . . .

Since the edict at the special inquiry five days earlier, the order had etched itself into Alan's mind until, eyes closed, he could repeat the words from memory. And he *had* repeated them often, searching in the official phraseology for a minute loophole, some tiny weakness, a cavity into which the probing antennae of the law might go.

But there had been none.

He had read statutes and old law cases, first by the dozen and later by the hundred, laboring at their involved and stilted language far into each night until his eyes were red rimmed, his body aching for lack of sleep. Through most of the daytime hours Tom Lewis had joined him in the Supreme Court law library, where together they had explored indexes, reviewed abridgments, and scrutinized case reports in ancient, seldom opened tomes. "I don't need lunch," Tom said on the second day. "My stomach's full of dust."

What they sought was a legal precedent which would demonstrate that the Immigration Department's handling of the Duval case was in error and therefore illegal. As Tom put it: "We need something we can slap in front of a judge and say, 'Jack, the bums can't screw us, and here's why.'" And later, perched wearily atop a library ladder, Tom declared, "It isn't what you know that makes a lawyer;

it's knowing where to look, and we haven't found the right place."

Nor had they found the right place in the remaining days of the search, which was now ended. "There's just so much anyone can do," Alan had admitted finally. "I guess we might as well give up."

Now it was two in the afternoon, Tuesday, January 9. They had quit an hour ago.

There had been one brief interruption in their law library vigil—yesterday morning when a departmental board had considered Henri Duval's appeal against the outcome of the special inquiry. But it was a hollow, formal proceeding, the outcome predictable with Edgar Kramer as chairman of the board and two immigration officers the supporting members.

This was a part of the procedure which originally Alan had hoped to delay. After his own *gaffe* in court it had all been too swift . . .

Though knowing the effort wasted, Alan had presented argument as forcefully and thoroughly as if before a judge and jury. The board—including Edgar Kramer, punctiliously polite throughout—had listened attentively, then solemnly announced its decision in favor of the earlier verdict. Afterwards Alan had told Tom Lewis, "It was like arguing with the Queen in *Alice in Wonderland,* only a lot more dull."

Tilting his chair back in the tiny, cluttered office, stifling a yawn from tiredness, Alan found himself regretting that the case was almost over. It seemed that there was nothing more he could do. The *Vastervik*—its repairs completed and now loading fresh cargo—was due to sail in four days' time. Sometime before then, perhaps tomorrow, he must go down to the ship to break the final news to Henri Duval. But he knew that it would not be unexpected news; the young stowaway had learned too much about human indifference for one more disavowal to surprise him greatly.

Alan eased his six-foot length upright, scratched his crew-cut head, then wandered from his glass-paneled cubicle to the modest outer office. It was deserted. Tom Lewis was downtown, involved in some real estate work they had been fortunate in getting a day or two ago; and their grandmotherly widow typist, exhausted from the unwonted pressure of the past few days, had gone home at lunchtime, as she put it, "to sleep the clock round, Mr. Maitland, and if you take my advice you'll do the same." Maybe it'd be smart at that, Alan thought. He was tempted to go home to the cramped Gilford Street apartment, let down the landing-gear bed and forget everything, including stowaways, immigration, and the general disagreeableness of mankind. Except Sharon. That was it: he would concentrate his thoughts on Sharon exclusively. He wondered where she was at this moment; what she had been doing since their last meeting two days ago—a snatched few minutes over coffee in between sessions in the law library; what she was thinking about; how she looked; if she were smiling, or frowning in that quizzical way she did sometimes. . . .

He decided to telephone her. There was time on his hands; nothing further he could do for Henri Duval. Using the outer office phone, he dialed the Deveraux number. The butler answered. Yes, Miss Deveraux was in; would Mr. Maitland kindly wait?

A minute or two later he heard light footsteps coming to the phone.

"Alan!" Sharon's voice was excited. "You've found something!"

"I wish we had," he said. "I'm afraid we've quit."

"Oh, no!" The tone of regret was genuine.

He explained the fruitless search; the futility of going on.

"All the same," Sharon said, "I can't believe it's the end. You'll keep thinking and thinking, and come up with something the way you did before."

He was touched by her confidence but did not share it.

"I did have one idea," he said. "I thought I'd make a model of Edgar Kramer and stick pins in. It's the only bit we haven't tried."

Sharon laughed. "I used to model in clay."

"Let's do it tonight," he suggested, brightening. "We'll start with dinner and maybe get to the clay later."

"Oh, Alan; I'm sorry, but I can't."

Impulsively he asked, "Why not?"

There was a moment's hesitation, then Sharon said, "I already have a date."

Well, he thought; you ask questions, you get answers. He wondered who the date was with; if it was someone Sharon had known long; where they would go. He had a pang of jealousy, then told himself it was irrational. After all, Sharon must have had a social life, and a full one, long before he himself had appeared upon the scene. And a kiss in the hotel was no firm claim . . .

"I'm sorry, Alan; really I am. But it's something I couldn't break."

"I wouldn't want you to." With determined cheerfulness he told her, "Have fun; I'll call you if there's any news."

Sharon said uncertainly, "Goodbye."

When he had replaced the phone, the office seemed smaller and more depressing than before. Aimlessly, wishing he had not made the telephone call, he walked its length.

On the stenographer's desk a pile of opened telegrams caught his eye. He had never received as many telegrams in his life as in the past few days. Picking one from the top of the pile, he read:

CONGRATULATIONS ON SPLENDID FIGHT EVERY WARM HEARTED CITIZEN MUST BE CHEERING FOR YOU

K. R. BROWNE

Who was K. R. Browne, he wondered. Man or woman? Rich or poor? And what kind of a person? Did he or she really care about all injustice and oppression . . . or merely get caught up in sentimental fervor? He put the message down and selected another.

JESUS SAID INASMUCH AS YE HAVE DONE IT UNTO ONE OF THE LEAST OF THESE MY BRETHREN YE HAVE DONE IT UNTO ME AS MOTHER OF FOUR SONS AM PRAYING FOR YOU AND THAT POOR BOY

BERTHA MCLEISH

A third, longer than the rest, drew his attention.

THE TWENTYEIGHT MEMBERS OF STAPLETON AND DISTRICT MANITOBA KIWANIS CLUB HERE GATHERED SALUTE YOU AND WISH ALL SUCCESS IN FINE HUMANITARIAN EFFORT STOP WE ARE PROUD OF YOU AS FELLOW CANADIAN STOP WE HAVE PASSED AROUND HAT AND CHEQUE FOLLOWS STOP PLEASE USE MONEY ANY WAY YOU SEE FIT

GEORGE EARNDT, SECRETARY

The cheque, Alan remembered, had arrived this morning. It had been passed, with others, to a B.C. trust company which had offered to administer donations for Henri Duval. As of today, something like eleven hundred dollars had flowed in.

Thank you K. R. Browne, Mrs. McLeish, and the Stapleton Kiwanians, Alan thought. And all the others. He thumbed the thick sheaf of telegrams. I haven't managed to do any good, but thank you all the same.

There were two big heaps of newspapers on the floor in a corner, he observed, and another batch piled high upon a chair. A good many, in all three piles, were out-of-town papers—from Toronto, Montreal, Winnipeg, Regina, Ottawa, and other cities. There was one, he noticed, from as far away as Halifax, Nova Scotia. Some of the visiting reporters had dropped off copies which, they said, had stories about himself. And an office neighbor across the hall had added a couple of New York *Times*, presumably for the same reason. So far Alan had had no time to do more than glance at a few. Sometime soon he would go through them all, and he supposed he should make a scrapbook; he would probably never again be as prominent in the news. He wondered about a title for the scrapbook. Perhaps something like: "Testament to a Lost Cause."

"Aw, cut it out, Maitland," he said aloud. "You're getting sorrier for yourself than you are for Duval."

With the last word there was a short knock on the outer door, which opened. A head came around—the ruddy, broad-cheeked face of Dan Orliffe. The reporter followed the head with his burly farmer's body, then looked about him. He asked, "Are you alone?"

Alan nodded.

"I thought I heard someone talking."

"You did. It was me talking to myself." Alan grinned wryly. "That's the stage I've gotten to."

"You need help," Dan Orliffe said. "How'd it be if I set up a talk with someone more interesting."

"Who, for instance?"

Orliffe answered casually, "I thought we might start with the Prime Minister. He's due in Vancouver the day after tomorrow."

"Howden himself?"

"No less."

"Oh sure." Alan dropped into the stenographer's chair, leaning back and raising his feet alongside the battered typewriter. "Tell you what I'll do: I'll rent a put-you-up and invite him to stay in my apartment."

"Look," Dan pleaded, "I'm not kidding. This is for real. A meeting could be arranged, and it might do some good." He asked questioningly, "There's not much more you can do for Duval through the courts, is there?"

Alan shook his head. "We're at the end of the line."

"Well then, what is there to lose?"

"Nothing, I guess. But what's the point?"

"You can plead, can't you?" Dan urged. " 'The quality of mercy' and all that stuff. Isn't that what lawyers are for?"

"You're supposed to have a few solid arguments too." Alan grimaced. "I can just see the way it would be: me down on my knees and the P.M. wiping away tears. 'Alan, my boy,' he'd say. 'All these weeks I've been so terribly wrong. Now if you'll just sign here we'll forget the whole thing, and you can have everything you want.' "

"Okay," Dan Orliffe admitted, "so it won't be any pushover. But neither was any of the rest you've done. Why give up now?"

"One simple reason," Alan replied quietly. "Because there comes a time when it's sensible to admit you're licked."

"You disappoint me," Dan said. He extended a foot and scuffed a desk leg disconsolately.

"Sorry. I wish I could do more." There was a pause, then Alan asked curiously, "Why's the Prime Minister coming to Vancouver anyway?"

"It's some sort of nation-wide tour he's making. All very sudden; there's a lot of speculation about it." The reporter shrugged. "That's somebody else's business. My idea was to get the two of you together."

"He'd never see me," Alan declared.

"If he were asked, he couldn't afford not to." Dan Orliffe pointed to the pile of newspapers on the office chair. "D'you mind if I move these?"

"Go ahead."

Dan dumped the papers on to the floor, turned the chair around, and straddled the seat. He faced Alan, his elbows on the chair back. "Look, chum," he contended earnestly, "if you haven't figured it by now, let me lay this out. To ten million people, maybe more—to everyone who reads a newspaper, watches television or listens to a radio—you're Mr. Valiant-for-Truth."

"Mr. Valiant-for-Truth," Alan repeated. He inquired curiously, "That's from *Pilgrim's Progress*, isn't it?"

"I guess so." The tone of voice was indifferent.

"I remember I read it once," Alan said thoughtfully. "In Sunday school, I think."

"We're a long way from Sunday school," the reporter said. "But maybe some of yours rubbed off."

"Get on with it," Alan told him. "You were talking about ten million people."

"They've made you a national image," Orliffe insisted. "You're a sort of idol. Frankly I've never seen anything quite like it."

"It's a lot of sentiment," Alan said. "When all this is over I'll be a forgotten man in ten days."

"Maybe so," Dan conceded. "But while you *are* a public figure you have to be treated with respect. Even by Prime Ministers."

Alan grinned, as if the idea amused him. "If I did ask for an interview with the Prime Minister, how do you think it should be done?"

"Let the *Post* arrange it," Dan Orliffe urged. "Howden doesn't love us, but he can't ignore us either. Besides I'd like to run an exclusive story tomorrow. We'll say that you've asked for a meeting and are waiting for an answer."

"Now we're getting to it." Alan swung down his feet from beside the typewriter. "I figured there was an angle somewhere."

Dan Orliffe's face had a studied earnestness. "Everybody has an angle, but you and I would be helping each other, and Duval too. Besides, with that kind of advance publicity, Howden wouldn't dare refuse."

"I don't know. I just don't know." Standing up, Alan stretched tiredly. What was the point of it all, he thought. What could be gained by attempting any more?

Then, in his mind, he saw the face of Henri Duval, and behind Duval—smugly smiling and triumphant—the features of Edgar Kramer.

Suddenly Alan's face lighted, his voice strengthened. "What the hell!" he said. "Let's give it a whirl."

Fifteen The Party Director

The young man in the tortoise-shell glasses had said "a couple of days."

Actually, with a weekend in between, it had taken four.

Now, in party headquarters on Sparks Street, he faced Brian Richardson from the visitors' side of the party director's desk.

As always, Richardson's sparsely furnished office was stiflingly hot. On two walls, steam radiators, turned fully on, bubbled like simmering kettles. Although only midafternoon, the venetian blinds had been lowered and shabby drapes drawn to circumvent drafts through the leaky windows of the decrepit building. Unfortunately it also had the effect of blocking out fresh air.

Outside, where a bitter blanket of arctic air had gripped Ottawa and all Ontario since Sunday morning, the temperature was five below zero. Inside, according to a desk thermometer, it was seventy-eight.

There were beads of perspiration on the young man's forehead.

Richardson rearranged his heavy, broad-shouldered figure in the leather swivel chair. "Well?" he asked.

"I have what you wanted," the young man said quietly. He placed a large manila envelope in the center of the desk. The envelope was imprinted "Department of National Defence."

"Good work." Brian Richardson had a sense of rising excitement. Had a hunch, a long shot, paid off? Had he remembered accurately a chance remark—a fleeting innuendo, no more—uttered long ago at a cocktail party by a man whose name he had never known? It must have been all of fifteen years ago, perhaps even twenty . . . long before his own connection with the party . . . long before James Howden and Harvey Warrender were anything more to him than names in newspapers. That far back, people, places, meanings —all became distorted. And even if they were not, the original allegation might never have been true. He could, he thought, so easily be wrong.

"You'd better relax for a while," Richardson suggested. "Smoke if you like."

The young man took out a thin gold cigarette case, tapped both ends of a cigarette, and lit it with a tiny flame which sprang from a corner of the case. As an afterthought he reopened the case and offered it to the party director.

"No thanks." Richardson had already fumbled for a tobacco tin in a lower drawer of the desk. He filled his pipe and lit it before opening the envelope and removing a slim green file. When the pipe was drawing, he began to read.

He read silently for fifteen minutes. At the end of ten he knew he had what he needed. A hunch had been right; the long shot had paid off.

Closing the file, he told the young man with the tortoiseshell glasses, "I shall need this for twenty-four hours."

Without speaking, his lips tightly compressed, the other nodded.

Richardson touched the closed file. "I suppose you know what's in here."

"Yes, I read it." Two spots of color came into the young man's cheeks. "And I'd like to say that if you make use of any of it, in any way whatever, you're a lower and dirtier bastard even than I thought you were."

For an instant the party director's normally ruddy cheeks flushed deep red. His blue eyes went steely. Then, visibly, the anger passed. He said quietly, "I like your spirit. But I can only tell you that once in a while it becomes essential that someone get down in the dirt, much as he may dislike doing it."

There was no response.

"Now," Richardson said, "it's time to talk about you." He reached into a file tray, thumbed through some papers and selected two sheets clipped together. When he had glanced through them he asked, "You know where Fallingbrook is?"

"Yes, northwest Ontario."

Richardson nodded. "I suggest you start finding out all you can about it: the area, local people—I'll help you there —economics, history, all the rest. The riding's been represented by Hal Tedesco for twenty years. He's retiring at the next election, though it hasn't been announced yet. Fallingbrook is a good safe seat and the Prime Minister will be recommending you as a party candidate."

"Well," the young man said grudgingly, "you certainly don't waste any time."

Richardson said crisply, "We made a deal. You kept your part, so now I'm keeping mine." Pointing to the file on his desk, he added, "I'll get this back to you tomorrow."

The young man hesitated. He said uncertainly, "I don't quite know what to say."

"Don't say anything," Richardson advised. For the first time in their interview he grinned. "That's half the trouble with politics: too many people saying too much."

Half an hour later, when he had read the file again, this time more thoroughly, he picked up one of the two telephones on his desk. It was a direct outgoing line and he dialed the Government exchange, then asked for the Department of Immigration. After another operator and two secretaries, he reached the minister.

Harvey Warrender's voice boomed down the phone. "What can I do you for?"

"I'd like to see you, Mr. Minister." With most Cabinet members Brian Richardson was on first name terms. Warrender was one of the few exceptions.

"I'm free for an hour now," Harvey Warrender said, "if you want to come round."

Richardson hesitated. "I'd rather not do that if you don't mind. What I want to talk about is rather personal. Actually, I wondered if I could come to your house tonight. Say eight o'clock."

The minister insisted, "We can be plenty private in my office."

The party director replied patiently, "I'd still prefer to come to your house."

It was obvious that Harvey Warrender disliked being crossed. He announced grumblingly, "Can't say I like all the mysterioso. What's it all about?"

"As I said, it's rather personal. I think you'll agree tonight that we shouldn't discuss it on the phone."

"Look here, if it's about that son-of-a-bitch stowaway . . ."

Richardson cut in, "It isn't about that." At least, he thought, not directly. Only indirectly, through a vicious pattern of duplicity which, innocently enough, the stowaway had started.

"Very well, then," the Immigration Minister conceded

disagreeably. "If you must, come to my house. I'll expect you at eight o'clock."

There was a click as he hung up.

2

The residence of the Hon. Harvey Warrender was an impressive two-story house in Rockcliffe Park Village, northeast of Ottawa. A few minutes after eight the party director watched the headlights of his Jaguar pick out the winding, tree-lined boulevards of the Village, once known more prosaically as McKay's Bush, and now the elegant, exclusive habitat of the capital's elite.

The Warrender house, which Richardson reached after a few minutes more of driving, was built on a large landscaped and wooded lot, approached by a long crescent-shaped driveway. The house itself, strikingly fronted with cut stone, had white double entrance doors, flanked by two white pillars. To the west and east across abutting lawns, Richardson knew, were the homes of the French Ambassador and a Supreme Court Judge, with the Opposition Leader, Bonar Deitz, immediately across the street.

Parking the Jaguar in the crescent driveway, he passed between the pillars and pressed the glowing pinpoint of a bell button. Inside the house, door chimes reverberated softly.

The Minister of Citizenship and Immigration, wearing a smoking jacket and a red leather slippers, opened one of the double white doors himself and peered outward. "Oh," he said, "it's you. Well, you'd better come in."

The tone and manner were ungracious. There was also a slight slurring of speech, the result, Richardson presumed, of the tumbler of what appeared to be neat whisky in Harvey Warrender's hand, and probably several others preceding it. It was not a situation, he thought, likely to help what he had come to do. Or perhaps it might; with some people the effect of liquor was unpredictable.

The party director moved inside, stepping onto a deep Persian rug centered in a wide, oak-floored hallway. Harvey Warrender gestured to a straight-backed Queen Anne chair. "Leave your coat," he commanded, then, without waiting, walked down the hallway to a door already opened. Richardson slipped off his heavy overcoat and followed.

Warrender nodded to the room beyond the door, and Brian Richardson preceded him into a square, spacious study. Three of the walls, from floor to ceiling, were lined with books, many of them, Richardson noted, with expensive hand-tooled bindings. A massive stone fireplace centered the fourth mahogany-paneled wall. Earlier a fire had been burning, but now only a few charred logs smoldered in the grate. A darkly polished mahogany desk was set to one side, with leather armchairs arranged in groups around the room.

But the dominating feature was above the fireplace.

A recessed rectangle had been built into the paneling of the wall and within the rectangle, illuminated by skillfully concealed lighting, was a painting of a young man in air force uniform. It was a similar, but larger version, of the painting in Harvey Warrender's office.

The base of the rectangle, Richardson observed, formed a shelf and on it were three objects—a small-scale model of a World War II Mosquito bomber, a folded map in a pocket-size plastic case and, centered between the other two, an air force officer's cap, the cloth and cap badge faded and tarnished. With a mental shudder the party director remembered Milly's words: "a sort of shrine."

Harvey Warrender had come close behind him. "You're looking at my son, Howard," he said. The observation was more gracious than any other so far. It was also accompanied by a blast of whisky-laden breath.

"Yes," Richardson said, "I expected that's who it was." He had a sense of going through a ritual enforced upon all visitors. It was one which he wanted to get away from quickly.

But Harvey Warrender was not to be deterred. "You're wondering about the things beneath the picture, I expect," he said. "They were all Howard's. I had them sent back to me—everything he had when he was killed in action. I have a cupboardful and I change them every few days. Tomorrow I shall take away the little airplane and put a pocket compass there. Next week I have a wallet of Howard's which I shall substitute for the map. I leave the cap there most of the time. Sometimes I have the feeling he'll walk into this room and put it on."

What could you say in answer? Richardson thought. He

wondered how many others had suffered the same embarrassment. A goodly number, if rumor were true.

"He was fine," Warrender said. His speech was still slurred. "Fine in character through and through, and he died a hero. I expect you've heard that." Sharply: "You must have heard it."

"Well," Richardson began, then stopped. He had the feeling that whatever he said, there would be no stemming the other's flow of words.

"There was an air raid over France," the Immigration Minister declared. His voice warmed, as if he had told the story many times before. "They were flying Mosquitoes— two-seater bombers like the little model there. Howard didn't have to go. He'd already done more than his share of operations, but he volunteered. He was in command of the squadron."

"Look," Richardson interjected, "don't you think we should . . ." He wanted to stop this; stop it now, at once . . .

Warrender did not even hear the interruption. He boomed, "Thanks to Howard, the raid was a success. The target was heavily defended but they clobbered it. That's what they used to say, 'clobbered the target.' "

With a sense of helplessness the party director listened.

"Then, on the way back, Howard's airplane was hit, and Howard mortally wounded. But he went on flying . . . a crippled airplane . . . fighting it every mile of the way home; wanting to save his navigator . . . though dying himself . . ." Warrender's voice broke; he appeared, alcoholically, to be stifling a sob.

Oh God, Richardson thought; for God's sake let this end. But it went on.

"He made it home . . . and landed; the navigator safe . . . and Howard died." Now the voice changed and became querulous. "He should have been awarded a posthumous V.C. Or at least a D.F.C. Sometimes, even now, I think I should go after it . . . for Howard's sake."

"Don't!" The party director raised his voice, determined to make himself heard. "Let the past stay dead. Leave it alone."

The Immigration Minister raised his glass and drained it. He gestured at Richardson. "If you want a drink, mix it yourself."

"Thanks." Brian Richardson turned to the desk where there was a tray of glasses, ice, and bottles. I need this, he thought. He poured a generous rye, adding ice and ginger ale.

When he turned around, it was to find Harvey Warrender watching him intently. "I've never liked you," the Immigration Minister said. "Right from the beginning I never did."

Brian Richardson shrugged. "Well, I guess you're not the only one."

"You were Jim Howden's man, not mine," Warrender insisted. "When Jim wanted you to be party director I spoke out against it. I guess Jim's told you that, trying to set you against me."

"No, he never told me." Richardson shook his head. "And I don't think he'd want to set me against you either. There'd be no reason for it."

Abruptly Warrender asked, "What did *you* do in the war?"

"Oh, I was in the Army for a while. Nothing very spectacular." He forebore to mention three years in the desert —North Africa, then Italy, through some of the toughest wartime fighting. Ex-Sergeant Richardson seldom spoke of it now, even to close friends. War reminiscences, the parade of hollow victories, bored him.

"That's the trouble with you fellows who had soft billets. You all came through. Those that mattered most . . ." Harvey Warrender's eyes swung back to the portrait ". . . a good many of those didn't."

"Mr. Minister," the party director said, "couldn't we sit down? There's something I'd like to talk to you about." He wanted to have done with it all, and get out of this house. For the first time he wondered about Harvey Warrender's sanity.

"Go on then." The Immigration Minister pointed to two facing armchairs.

Richardson dropped into one of the chairs as Warrender crossed to the desk, splashing whisky into his glass. "All right," he said, returning and sitting down, "get on with it."

He might as well, Richardson decided, come directly to the point.

He said quietly, "I know about the agreement between you and the Prime Minister—the leadership, the television franchise, all the rest."

There was a startled silence. Then, his eyes narrowed, Harvey Warrender snarled, "Jim Howden told you. He's a double-crossing . . ."

"No." Richardson shook his head emphatically. "The chief didn't tell me, and he doesn't know that I'm aware of it. If he did, I think he'd be shocked."

"You lying son of a bitch!" Warrender jumped up, weaving unsteadily.

"You can think that if you like," Richardson said calmly. "But why would I bother lying? In any case, *how* I know doesn't make any difference. The fact is, I do."

"All right," Warrender stormed, "so you've come here to blackmail me. Well, let me tell you, Mr. Fancy-Pants Party Director, I don't *care* about that agreement being known. Instead of your threatening me with exposure, I'll get the last laugh yet. I'll beat you to it! I'll call the reporters and tell them—here, tonight!"

"Please sit down," Brian Richardson urged, "and shouldn't we lower our voices? We might disturb your wife."

"She's out," Harvey Warrender said shortly. "There's no one else in the house." But he resumed his seat.

"I haven't come here to threaten," the party director said. "I've come to plead." He would try the obvious way first, he thought. He had little hope of it succeeding. But the alternative must only be used when everything else had failed.

"Plead?" Warrender queried. "What do you mean by plead?"

"Exactly that. I'm pleading with you to give up your hold over the chief; to let the past be finished; to surrender that written agreement . . ."

"Oh yes," Warrender said sarcastically, "I imagined you'd get around to that."

Richardson tried to make his tone persuasive. "No good can come from it now, Mr. Minister. Don't you see that?"

"All I can see, suddenly, is why you're doing this. You're trying to protect yourself. If I expose Jim Howden, he's finished, and when he goes, so do you."

"I expect that would happen," Richardson said tiredly. "And you can believe it or not, but I hadn't thought too much about it."

It was true, he reasoned; that possibility had been least in his mind. He wondered: why *was* he doing this? Was it personal loyalty to James Howden? That was a part of it, he supposed; but surely the real answer should be more than that. Wasn't it that Howden, with all his faults, had been good for the country as Prime Minister; and whatever indulgences he had taken, as a means of retaining power, he had given more, far more, in return? He deserved better—and so did Canada—than defeat in disgrace and ignominy. Perhaps, Brian Richardson thought, what he himself was doing now was a kind of patriotism, twice removed.

"No," Harvey Warrender said. "My answer is positively and finally no."

So, after all, the weapon must be used.

There was a silence as the two surveyed each other.

"If I were to tell you," the party director said slowly, "that I possess certain knowledge which would force you to change your mind . . . knowledge which, even between ourselves I am reluctant to discuss . . . *would* you change your mind, change it even now?"

The Immigration Minister said firmly, "There is no knowledge in heaven or earth which would make me alter what I have already said."

"I think there is," Brian Richardson contended quietly. "You see, I know the truth about your son."

It seemed as if the quiet in the room would never end.

At length, his face pale, Harvey Warrender whispered, "What do you know?"

"For God's sake," Richardson urged, "isn't it enough that I know? Don't make me spell it out."

Still a whisper. "Tell me what it is you know."

There was to be nothing presumed, nothing unsaid, no avoidance of the grim and tragic truth.

"All right," Richardson said softly. "But I'm sorry you've insisted." He looked the other directly in the eye. "Your son Howard was never a hero. He was court-martialed for cowardice in the face of the enemy, for deserting and imperiling his companions, and for causing the death of his own aircraft navigator. The court martial found him guilty on all counts. He was awaiting sentence when he committed suicide by hanging."

Harvey Warrender's face was drained of color.

With grim reluctance, Richardson went on, "Yes, there *was* a raid to France. But your son wasn't in command, except of his own airplane with a single navigator. And he didn't volunteer. It was his first mission, the very first."

The party director's lips were dry. He moistened them with his tongue, then continued: "The squadron was flying defensive formation. Near the target they came under heavy attack. The other airplanes pressed on and bombed; some were lost. Your son—despite the pleas of his own navigator—broke formation and turned back, leaving his companions vulnerable."

Warrender's hands trembled as he put the whisky glass down.

"On the way back," Richardson said, "the airplane was struck by shellfire. The navigator was badly wounded, but your son was unhurt. Nevertheless your son left the pilot's seat and refused to fly. The navigator, despite his wounds and the fact that he was not a qualified pilot, took over in an attempt to bring the airplane home." . . . If he closed his eyes, he thought, he could visualize the scene: the tiny, crowded, noisy cockpit, bloody from the navigator's wounds; the motors deafening; the gaping hole where the shell had hit, the wind tearing through, outside the bark of gunfire. And within . . . fear over all, like a dank and evil-smelling cloud. And, in a corner of the cockpit, the cowering, broken figure . . .

You poor bastard, Richardson thought. You poor benighted bastard. You broke, that's all. You crossed the hairline a good many of us wavered over. You did what others wanted to do often enough, God knows. Who are we to criticize you now?

Tears were streaming down Harvey Warrender's face. Rising, he said brokenly, "I don't want to hear any more."

Richardson stopped. There was little more to tell: The crash landing in England—the best the navigator could do. The two of them pulled from the wreckage; Howard Warrender miraculously unhurt, the navigator dying . . . Afterwards the medics said he would have lived except for loss of blood through the exertion flying back . . . The court martial; the verdict—guilty . . . Suicide . . . And, in the end, reports hushed up; the subject closed.

But Harvey Warrender had known. Known, even as he built the false and foolish legend of a hero's death.

"What do you want?" he asked brokenly. "What do you want of me?"

Richardson told him evenly. "That written agreement between you and the chief."

Briefly a spark of resistance flared. "And if I won't give it up?"

"I was hoping," Richardson said, "you wouldn't ask me that."

"I *am* asking you."

The party director sighed deeply. "In that case I shall summarize the court-martial proceedings and have mimeo copies made. The copies will be mailed, anonymously in plain envelopes, to everyone who counts in Ottawa—M.P.s, ministers, the press gallery, civil servants, your own department heads . . ."

"You swine!" Warrender choked on the words. "You rotten evil swine."

Richardson shrugged. "I don't want to do it unless you force me."

"People would understand," Harvey Warrender said. The color was returning to his face. "I tell you they'd understand and sympathize. Howard was young; just a boy . . ."

"They'd always have sympathized," Richardson said. "And even now, they may feel sorry for your son. But not for you. They might have once, but not any more." He nodded to the portrait in its illuminated recess, the absurd and useless relics beneath. "They'll remember this charade, and you'll be the laughingstock of Ottawa."

In his mind he wondered if it were true. There would be curiosity in plenty, and speculation, but perhaps little laughter. People sometimes were capable of unexpected depths of understanding and compassion. Most, perhaps, would wonder what strange quirk of mind had led Harvey Warrender to the deception he had practiced. Had his own dreams of glory been reflected towards his son? Had the bitter disappointment, the tragedy of death, unhinged his mind? Richardson himself felt only an aching kind of pity.

But Warrender believed he would be laughed at. The muscles of his face were working. Suddenly he rushed to the fireplace and seized a poker from the stand beside it. Reaching up, he slashed savagely at the portrait, hacking, tearing, until only the frame and some shreds of canvas remained. With a single stroke he smashed the little airplane, then flung the map case and faded cap into the fireplace below.

Turning, his breath coming fast, he asked, "Well, are you satisfied?"

Richardson was standing too. He said quietly, "I'm sorry you did that. It wasn't necessary."

The tears were beginning again. The Immigration Minister went, almost docilely, to a chair. As if instinctively, he reached for the whisky glass he had put down earlier. "All right," he said softly, "I'll give you the agreement."

"And all copies, as well as your assurance that no more exist?"

Warrender nodded.

"When?"

"It will take two or three days. I have to go to Toronto. The paper is in a safety deposit box there."

"Very well," Richardson instructed. "When you get it I want you to give it directly to the chief. And he is not to know about what happened here tonight. That's part of our agreement, you understand?"

Again a nod.

That way he would be taking the arrangement on trust. But there would be no defection now. He was sure of that.

Harvey Warrender lifted his head and there was hatred in his eyes. It was amazing, Richardson thought, how the other man's moods and emotions could ebb and flow so swiftly.

"There was a time," Warrender said slowly, "when I could have broken you." With a touch of petulance, he added, "I'm still in the Cabinet, you know."

Richardson shrugged indifferently. "Maybe. But frankly, I don't think you count for anything any more." At the doorway he called over his shoulder, "Don't get up, I'll let myself out."

3

Driving away, the reaction set in: shame, disgust, an abyss of depression.

More than anything else, at this moment, Brian Richardson wanted warm, human companionship. Nearing the city center, he stopped by a pay phone and, leaving the Jaguar's motor running, dialed Milly's number. He prayed silently: Please be at home; tonight I need you. Please, please.

The ringing tone continued unanswered. Eventually he hung up.

There was no other place to go but his own apartment. He even found himself hoping that, just this once, Eloise might be there. She was not.

He walked through the empty, lonely rooms, then took a tumbler, an unopened bottle of rye, and proceeded methodically to get drunk.

Two hours later, shortly after 1 A.M., Eloise Richardson, cool, beautiful, and elegantly gowned, let herself in by the apartment front door. Entering the living room, with its ivory walls and Swedish walnut furniture, she found her husband prostrate and snoring drunkenly on the off-white broadloom. Beside him were an empty bottle and an overturned glass.

Wrinkling her nose in contemptuous disgust, Eloise proceeded to her own bedroom and, as usual, locked the door.

Sixteen Mr. Justice Willis

In the drawing room of his Hotel Vancouver suite, James Howden handed his executive assistant, Elliot Prowse, a one-dollar bill. "Go down to the lobby," he instructed, "and get me six chocolate bars."

If he ever wrote his memoirs, he decided, he would point out that one of the advantages of being Prime Minister was that you could send someone else to buy your candy. Surely that should prove a spur to any ambitious child!

When the young man—serious-faced, as always—had gone, James Howden closed the door to the room outside, shutting off the noise of telephones and clattering typewriters, manned by the temporary staff of party volunteers. Settling into an easy chair, he considered the progress of his whirlwind speaking tour so far.

Without any question it was proving a brilliant, personal success.

In all his political life James Howden had never risen to greater heights of oratory or wooed audiences with more effect. The speech writers who had been recruited by Brian Richardson—one from Montreal, the other a *Time*-and-*Lifer* from New York—had done their work well. But even better, at times, were Howden's own improvisations, when he discarded prepared scripts and spoke with conviction and a genuine emotion which conveyed itself to most who listened.

Principally he talked—prepared and unprepared—of the North American heritage and the pressures of rival ideologies which threatened its survival. It was a time for unity, he declared; a time to make an end of smallness and bickering; a time to rise above petty issues, putting the greater cause of human freedom first.

People reacted as if the words were what they had wanted to hear; a leadership they sought . . .

As planned, the Prime Minister had made no mention of the Act of Union. Constitutionally, that must be revealed to Parliament first.

But there was a sense of timeliness; as if the nation was ready for closer union with the United States. James Howden sensed it, and his political instinct for the winds of change had seldom been wrong.

In Toronto his audience had stood, cheering, for minutes on end. In Fort William, Winnipeg, Regina, Calgary, Edmonton, his reception had been the same or similar. Now, as the final stop before returning East, he had come to Vancouver where tonight, in the Queen Elizabeth Civic Theatre, he would address an audience of three thousand.

Press coverage of his tour, as well as press reaction, had been remarkably good. In newspapers, as on TV and radio, his own speeches were first-featured items. It was outstanding good luck, Howden thought, that over the past several days there had been a remarkable absence of competing news, and that, so far, neither a major disaster, some lurid sex killing nor a localized outbreak of war had intervened to snatch the spotlight away.

It was true there had been minor annoyances. The incident of the would-be immigrant, Henri Duval, was still mentioned daily in the newspapers, and criticisms of the Government's stand on the matter had continued. There had also been the demonstrators, with placards supporting the stowaway at every stop, and some heckling on the subject at those of his meetings which had been open to the public. But he sensed the clamor was dying, weakening—perhaps because nothing was eclipsed faster than enthusiasm for a lost cause.

He wished young Prowse would hurry.

A moment later, his pockets bulging with chocolate, the subject of his thoughts came in.

"Would you like one?" the Prime Minister asked. He removed a wrapper himself and began contentedly chewing.

"No, thank you sir," the executive assistant responded. "To tell you the truth, I don't care much for sweet things."

You wouldn't, Howden thought. Aloud he said, "Have you talked to the local man here in charge of immigration?"

"Yes, he was in this morning. His name is Kramer."

"What's he say about this Duval business?"

"He assured me there is nothing further legally that the man's sponsors can do. It would appear that the case is virtually defunct."

Only Elliot Prowse, Howden thought, would use words like "virtually defunct" in conversation. "Well," he said, "this time I hope he's right. I don't mind telling you, though, I'll be glad when the corpse is removed. When does the ship sail?"

"The evening of the day after tomorrow."

The same day, Howden thought, on which he would announce the Act of Union in Ottawa.

"Mr. Kramer was most anxious to see you personally," the executive assistant said. "He seemed to want to explain his actions in the case. But I told him it was quite impossible."

Howden nodded approval. Plenty of civil servants would like to explain their actions to the Prime Minister, especially when they had mismanaged a situation. Obviously Kramer was no exception.

"You can relay a message to him," James Howden said. It would do no harm, he decided, to give the man a jolt. "Tell him that I was extremely dissatisfied with his handling of the case in judge's chambers. He should not have offered a special inquiry. It merely reopened the affair when it was almost closed."

"It was that, I think, he wanted to explain . . ."

"Inform him that I expect better performance in the future," Howden added firmly. His tone made it plain that the subject was closed.

The executive assistant hesitated, then said apologetically, "There's the other matter, also about Duval. The man's lawyer, Mr. Maitland, has arrived to see you. You remember you agreed . . ."

"For God's sake!" In a sudden burst of temper the Prime Minister slammed his hand on the table beside him. "Is there never to be an end . . . ?"

"I was wondering that myself, sir." A year or so ago, when Elliot Prowse had been new, one of James Howden's temper tantrums could leave him upset for days. More recently he had learned to take them in his stride.

The Prime Minister inquired angrily, "It was that damned interfering newspaper's idea, wasn't it?"

"Yes, the Vancouver *Post*. They suggested . . ."

"I know what they suggested, and it's typical." He stormed on, "Newspapers aren't content with reporting the news any more. They have to make it themselves."

"But you did agree . . ."

"I know damn well I agreed! Why do you keep telling me what I already know?"

Wooden-faced, Prowse answered, "Because I wasn't sure if you remembered."

Sometimes Howden wondered if his executive assistant was as completely humorless as he seemed.

The request had been made to him yesterday in Calgary, after the Vancouver *Post* had run a news story saying that the lawyer, Maitland, would seek an interview with the Prime Minister when he reached the West Coast. The wire services had picked up the item and broadcast it.

After a telephone discussion with Brian Richardson they had agreed there was only one answer he could give. Now Maitland was here.

"All right," James Howden instructed bleakly. "Send him in."

Alan Maitland had been waiting for three quarters of an hour in an outer room of the hotel suite and, with the passage of each few minutes, his nervousness and uncertainty had increased. Now, as he was ushered into the inner room, he wondered what he was doing here at all.

"Good morning," the Prime Minister said briskly. "I understand you wished to see me."

The two appraised each other warily. Interest overcoming nervousness, Alan saw a tall figure, slightly stooped, slumped into a comfortable upholstered chair. The features—heavy hawklike face, brooding eyes, and long-beaked nose—were familiar from a thousand newspaper pages and television screens. And yet the face was older, more seamed than pictures showed it. There was an air of tiredness he had not expected.

"Thank you for seeing me, Mr. Prime Minister," Alan said. "I wanted to appeal to you personally on behalf of Henri Duval."

Young lawyers were younger than ever nowadays, James Howden thought. Or was it simply that to older lawyers, becoming older still, they merely appeared that way? He wondered if, forty years ago, he himself had seemed as youthful and vigorous as the crew-cut, athletically built young man who stood, uncertainly, before him now.

"Well, sit down." The Prime Minister indicated a facing chair, which Alan took. "You will have to be brief, Mr. Maitland, because I can't spare more than a few minutes."

"I'd expected that, sir." Alan was careful to keep his tone respectful. "So I thought I'd omit the facts of the case. I imagine you've heard most of them already."

"Heard them!" Howden resisted a sudden craving for hysterical laughter. "Great heavens!—for weeks I seem to have heard nothing else."

Alan smiled—a warm, boyish smile, Howden observed, which quickly came and went. Then, immediately serious, he began, "There are a lot of things, Mr. Prime Minister, which the facts don't tell: the conditions on the ship; a man cooped up in a hole no better than an animal's cage; a human being with no freedom, no hope . . ."

"Has it occurred to you, Mr. Maitland," Howden injected, "that this is not a Canadian ship; that some of these conditions have existed for a considerable time; and that they are of no concern to this country?"

"Then whose concern are they? Sir, I ask you." Alan's eyes flashed fire, his initial nervousness forgotten. "Are we not to have concern for human beings who don't belong to our nice tight club?"

James Howden answered patiently, "You speak of a nice tight club. Are you aware that Canada's record on immigration is one of the best in the world?"

Alan Maitland leaned forward in his chair. "There really isn't much competition, is there?"

Touché, Howden thought. Aloud he replied sharply, "That's beside the point. The real thing is that there are laws and regulations covering this kind of thing and if they're to mean anything they must be observed."

"Some of the law is pretty arbitrary," Alan said, "especially where it concerns human rights."

"If that's your opinion, then you have legal recourse to the courts."

"Your immigration chief in Vancouver didn't think so. He told me that no court had any business interfering."

"Nevertheless," the Prime Minister insisted, "you *did* go to court, and you lost your case."

Alan admitted ruefully, "Yes, we lost. And that's why I'm here—to beg." The smile flashed again. "If necessary I'll get down on my knees."

"No." Howden smiled in response. "I don't want you to do that."

"I'd like to tell you, sir, about Henri Duval." If his time were short, Alan thought, he would at least make the most of it. "He's a good little man, sturdy, a hard worker; I'm convinced he'd make a good citizen. True, he doesn't speak English well; he's had no education . . ."

"Mr. Maitland," the Prime Minister interrupted firmly, "the reason this man cannot be admitted is quite simple. The world is full of people who, on the surface of things, are perhaps worth helping. But there must be some order to the help; some plan, some scheme of action. It's the reason we have an Immigration Act . . ."

Besides, he thought obstinately, he would *not* give way to this absurd and disproportionate public clamor. The indignity at Ottawa airport still rankled. And even if he ignored the threat of Harvey Warrender, a concession now would seem weak and ridiculous. As Prime Minister he had made his decision known; surely that should count for something.

Alan Maitland was arguing, "Henri Duval is in Vancouver, Mr. Prime Minister. He isn't in Hungary, or Ethiopia or China. He's here and now." He added, with a trace of bitterness, "In a country where the underprivileged are supposed to get a break."

The underprivileged. For an instant James Howden had a troubled memory of the orphanage; the outside, unexpected chance, won for himself through one man—his own Alan Maitland, long ago. But at least he had been born here. He decided the interview had gone on long enough.

"The Immigration Act is the law of this country, Mr. Maitland. No doubt it has its faults, but the way it is, is the way the people of Canada choose to have it. Under the law I regret the answer to you must be no."

The concluding, speedy civilities were observed. Standing, James Howden shook Alan's hand. "Allow me to wish you great success in your profession," he remarked. "Perhaps one day you'll enter political life. I've a notion you'd do well."

Alan answered quietly, "I don't think so, sir. There are too many things about it I don't like."

When Alan Maitland had gone, the Prime Minister selected a second chocolate bar and nibbled it thoughtfully. After a while he summoned his executive assistant and irritably demanded the draft of his evening speech.

2

In the Hotel Vancouver lobby Dan Orliffe was waiting for Alan Maitland. He asked expectantly, "Any change?"

Alan shook his head.

"Well," Orliffe said cheerfully, "you're keeping the case before the public, and that's worth something."

Alan asked dourly, "Is it? Just tell me what the public can do when the Government won't budge."

"Haven't you heard? The public can change the Government; that's what."

"Oh, great!" Alan said. "We'll wait for an election, then send Henri a postcard with the news. *If* we can find out where he is."

"Come on," Dan told him. "I'll drive you to your office. On the way you can tell me what Howden said."

Tom Lewis was working in his own small cubicle when Alan came in. Dan Orliffe had driven away after their session in the car, presumably to the *Post*. Once more, for Tom's benefit, Alan repeated what had transpired.

"I'll say this," Tom said. "You don't let go of a bone once your teeth are in."

Alan nodded. He wondered if he should call Sharon; or perhaps there was really no reason. They had not talked since their telephone conversation two days earlier.

"By the way," Tom said, "a parcel came for you—chauffeur-delivered and all. It's in your office."

Curiously Alan went in. A square, wrapped package was in the center of the desk. Untying it, he drew out a box and removed the lid. Under layers of tissue paper was a clay-molded figure—head and shoulders. A note beside it read: "I tried to make it like Mr. Kramer, but it kept coming out the way it is. So, *please*, no pins—ever! With love—Sharon."

He lifted the figure. It was, he saw glowingly, a passable imitation of himself.

3

Less than a quarter-mile from the Prime Minister's suite in the Hotel Vancouver, Mr. Justice Stanley Willis of the British Columbia Supreme Court paced restlessly, as he had for more than an hour, his private judge's chambers.

Mr. Justice Willis, stern-faced, severe, and outwardly imperturbable, was waging an inward mental battle.

The lines of battle were clearly drawn. On one side was his judicial integrity, on the other his personal conscience. Both were focused upon a single subject: Henri Duval.

Edgar Kramer had told the Prime Minister's executive assistant: "There is nothing further legally that the man's sponsors can do." Alan Maitland, after a week-long search for legal precedents, had reached the same opinion.

Mr. Justice Willis possessed knowledge demonstrating both to be wrong. The knowledge was such that, if used promptly, it would free Henri Duval from his shipboard prison, at least temporarily, and possibly for good.

The key to the situation lay in a heavy, bound volume—*B.C. Reports*, Vol. 34, 1921—on the judge's desk. It was open at a page headed *Rex* vs. *Ahmed Singh*.

The paper upon which the words—and those which followed—appeared was faded and yellow. But the proposition of law—*ratio decidendi*—was as binding as if enunciated yesterday.

A Canadian judge had ruled: Ahmed Singh in 1921 . . . and therefore Henri Duval today . . . *could not be deported solely to a ship*.

Any individual (the long dead judge had declared in 1921) must be deported to the country from whence he came, *and not to any other place*.

But the *Vastervik* was not destined to Lebanon . . . the county whence Henri Duval had come . . . where he had boarded the ship. The M.V. *Vastervik* was an ocean-going tramp, its next port of call Belfast, its routing beyond that point uncertain . . .

The deportation order against Henri Duval was therefore unlawful and invalid.

Rex vs. *Ahmed Singh* said so.

Mr. Justice Stanley Willis had elicited the facts about the *Vastervik* discreetly, as he had followed other details of the case discreetly.

He had received word of the search by Alan Maitland and Tom Lewis for legal precedents which would prevent the deportation of Henri Duval. He had learned also of their failure and it did not surprise him.

He had no criticism of the two young lawyers for failing to discover *Rex*. vs. *Ahmed Singh*. The case was wrongly summarized and indexed in *Canadian Abridgements*, a not unusual happening. The judge himself would not have known of it, except that years before he had stumbled across the old report by merest chance, and it had remained in mind.

Knowing what he did, Mr. Justice Willis reflected, if he were Henri Duval's lawyer he would apply at once—this afternoon—for a new writ of habeas corpus. And, as a judge, if confronted by the application he would immediately accede—not with the half-measure order *nisi*, as earlier, but with full habeas corpus which would free Henri Duval from the *Vastervik* at once.

But he *was* a judge; and he was *not* a lawyer. And no man could be both.

The business of a judge was to deal judicially with matters brought before him. It was no part of his function to meddle directly in legal cases or to initiate action favoring one litigant over another. Occasionally, to be sure, a judge might nudge counsel, hinting at steps to be followed which, in his opinion, would advance the cause of justice. He himself had done this with Alan Maitland at the *nisi* hearing affecting Henri Duval.

But beyond that point judicial interference was reprehensible. More, it was betrayal of a judge's role.

Once more Mr. Justice Willis paced the rug between the window and his desk. Today the wide, bony shoulders were stooped over the spare body, as if responsibility weighed heavily upon them. The long, angular face, tense with thought, was troubled.

If I were not what I am, Mr. Justice Willis thought, it would be so simple. I would pick up the telephone on the desk and ask for Alan Maitland. When he answered I would simply say: Look at *B.C. Reports*, Volume 34, 1921, page 191, *Rex* vs. *Ahmed Singh*. Nothing more would be needed. He is an astute young man and before the court Registry closes today he would be here with a habeas corpus writ.

It would prevent Henri Duval from sailing with the ship.

And I care, he thought. Alan Maitland cares. And so do I.

But because I am what I am, I cannot . . . directly or indirectly . . . do this thing.

And yet . . . there was the *inarticulate major premise*.

It was a phrase he remembered from law school long ago. It was still taught, though—in the presence of judges —seldom mentioned.

The inarticulate major premise was the doctrine that no judge, whatever his intention, could ever be impartial. A judge was human; therefore he could never hold the scales exactly even. Consciously or unconsciously his every thought and action were influenced by the events and background of his life.

Mr. Justice Stanley Willis accepted the postulation. He also knew that he himself possessed a major premise. It could be summarized in one word.

Belsen.

It had been 1945.

The law career of Stanley Willis, like that of many others of his generation, had been interrupted by the years of World War II. As an artillery officer he had served with the Canadians in Europe from 1940 until the war's end. And, near its end, Major Stanley Willis, M.C., liaison officer with the British Second Army, had accompanied the 63rd Anti-Tank Regiment in its liberation of the Nazi concentration camp of Bergen-Belsen.

He had remained at Belsen a month, and what he had seen had been the single most haunting experience of his life. For years afterward, and sometimes even now, the horror of those thirty days could return to him in feverish, vivid dreams. And Stanley Willis—a scholarly, sensitive man beneath an austere façade—had departed from Belsen with an avowed intention: that, in the years left to him, whatever he could personally do to relieve the wretchedness of mistreated and afflicted human beings, that much he would do.

As a judge, it had not been easy. There had been occasions when despite inner misgivings he had been obliged to pass sentence on the guilty where instinct told him that society, and not individuals, was the principal offender. But, sometimes, some hapless miserable felon, dismissed by most as beyond salvation, had received a light or mitigated sentence because a shadow of the past . . . the inarticulate major premise . . . had touched the mind of Mr. Justice Willis.

As now.

The plight of Henri Duval, as it had before the *nisi* hearing, continued to stir him deeply.

A man was incarcerated. A man could be justly freed.

Between the one and the other stood the judge's honorable pride.

With humbled pride the lesson just, he thought. And he crossed to the telephone.

He must not call Alan Maitland directly; that much, discretion demanded. But there was another way. He could speak to his own former law partner, a respected senior counsel who was astute and would understand the implications of a conversation. The information conveyed would be relayed promptly, without revelation of the source. But his former law partner was also a man who held strong views on judges' meddling . . .

Mr. Justice Willis sighed. In conspiracy, he thought, there was no perfect pattern.

The connection was made. He announced, "This is Stanley Willis."

A deep voice on the telephone said affably, "It's a pleasant surprise, Your Lordship."

The judge injected quickly, "An informal call, Ben."

A chuckle down the line. "How are you Stan? It's been a long time." There was a note of genuine affection.

"I know. We must get together sometime." But he doubted if they would. A judge, by reason of his office, was forced to tread a lonely path.

"Well, Stan, what can I do for you? Is there somebody you'd like to sue?"

"No," Mr. Justice Willis said. He was never very good at small talk. "I thought I'd have a word with you about this Duval case."

"Oh yes; the stowaway affair. I read your ruling. A pity, but I don't see what else you could have done."

"No," the judge acknowledged, "there was nothing else. All the same, young Maitland's a bright young lawyer."

"I agree," the voice said. "I think he'll do the profession a lot of credit."

"I hear there's been quite a search for precedents."

"The way it was told to me," the deep voice said with a chuckle, "Maitland and his partner have turned the law library inside out. But they haven't had any luck."

"I've been wondering," Mr. Justice Willis said slowly, "why they haven't gone to *Rex* vs. *Ahmed Singh, B.C. Reports*, Volume 34, 1921, page 191. I should think, on that, they could get habeas corpus without question."

There was a silence at the other end of the line. The judge could imagine eyebrows raised, a sense of disapproval. Then, more coolly than before, the voice said, "You'd better give me that reference again. I didn't get all of it."

When he had repeated the reference and shortly afterwards hung up, Mr. Justice Willis thought: there is a price we pay for all we do. But the information, he knew, would be passed on.

He glanced at his watch before returning to an accumulation of written judgments upon his desk.

Four and a half hours later, as darkness was descending on the city, the frail elderly Registry clerk, standing at the door, announced, "My lord, Mr. Maitland has an application for habeas corpus."

4

Under bright, rigged floodlights the *Vastervik* was loading lumber.

Confidently, exultantly, Alan Maitland raced up the rusty iron gangway to the cluttered, dilapidated main deck.

The fertilizer smell had gone. Any traces of it remaining were being dispelled by a freshening breeze blowing from the sea. The clean-scented aroma of fir and cedar were wafting through the ship.

The night was cold, but overhead stars twinkled in a clear sky.

The third officer, whom Alan had seen on Christmas morning, approached him from the ship's forecastle.

"I'm here to see Captain Jaabeck," Alan shouted along the deck, "and if he's in his cabin I can find my way."

The thin, wiry ship's officer came closer. "Then you will find your way," he said. "And even if you did not know, you have the mood to find your way tonight."

"Yes," Alan agreed, "I guess I have." Instinctively he touched the pocket of his suit to insure that the precious paper was still there.

Turning into the ship's interior, he called over his shoulder, "How's your cold?"

"It will be better," the third officer answered, "as soon as we have sailed." He added, "Forty-eight hours more, that is all."

Forty-eight hours. It had been close, Alan thought, but it looked as if they had made it in time. This afternoon he had been at his Gilford Street apartment when the message, relayed through Tom Lewis, had reached him: *Look at Rex vs. Ahmed Singh.*

Deciding he must leave no chance untaken, but without much hope, he had gone to the law library. There, when he read the 1921 ruling, his heart had leaped. Afterwards it had been a feverish rush of drafting, typing, checking and assembling the multiple affidavits and writs which the law required. Emergency or not, the monster's maw must be appeased with paper . . .

Then the race to the courthouse—to reach the Supreme Court Registry before closing. And he had made it, though barely, and a few minutes later had appeared before Mr. Justice Willis, once again, today, the chambers judge.

The judge, austere and remote as always, had listened carefully then, after a few short questions, authorized an order for habeas corpus—the order absolute and not the minor *nisi* writ. It was a rare and quietly dramatic moment. The original writ, and a copy, were in Alan's pocket now: *Elizabeth, by the Grace of God, of the United Kingdom, Canada and her other realms and territories, Defender of*

*the Faith . . . command you immediately after the receipt
of this our writ . . . to deliver the body of Henri Duval . . .*

Of course, there must still be a court hearing, and it was
set for the day after tomorrow. But the outcome was a
virtual certainty: The *Vastervik* would sail, but Henri Duval
would not be aboard.

Sometime tomorrow, Alan reminded himself, he must
telephone the lawyer who had tipped them off to the case
of Ahmed Singh. Tom Lewis had his name. It had been a
deliverance . . .

He came to the captain's door and knocked. A voice inside commanded, "Come!"

Captain Jaabeck, in shirt sleeves, wreathed in thick tobacco smoke, was making entries in a ledger under a shaded
desk lamp. Putting down the pen, he stood up, courteous
as ever, motioning his visitor to one of the green leather
armchairs.

Coughing slightly as the smoke reached his lungs, Alan
began, "I'm interrupting . . ."

"It is nothing. There is enough writing for one time."
The captain reached over and closed the ledger. He added
tiredly, "Future archaeologists digging up our world will
never understand it. We have left too many words for them
to read."

"Talking of words," Alan said, "I've brought some with
me." Smilingly, he produced the habeas corpus writ and
handed it to Captain Jaabeck.

The captain read slowly, his lips moving, pausing over
the legal jargon. Eventually, looking up, he asked incredulously, "You have succeeded—after all?"

"Yes," Alan said happily. "What the writ means is that
Henri is freed from the ship. He will not be sailing with
you."

"And now—at this moment . . ."

"At this moment, Captain," Alan replied decisively, "I'd
like him to pack his belongings and come with me. The
writ releases him to my custody." He added, "If you've
any doubt, we can call the Mounties . . ."

"No, no! It will not be needed." Captain Jaabeck put
down the writ, his face creasing in a warm engaging smile.
"I do not understand how you have done this, Mr. Maitland,
but you are to be congratulated. It is so sudden, that is all."

"I know," Alan said. "I'm a little breathless myself."

Ten minutes later, eyes sparkling and with a wide happy grin, Henri Duval appeared in the captain's cabin. He was wearing a seaman's duffel coat several sizes too large for him and carrying a battered cardboard suitcase tied with string. One of the first things to be done tomorrow, Alan decided, must be to use some of the accumulated money to buy new clothes for the appearance in court.

"Mr. Maitland is taking you away, Henri," the captain announced.

The young stowaway nodded, his face lighting with excitement and anticipation. "I ready now."

"You will not be returning to the ship," the captain said quietly. "Now I will say goodbye."

For a moment, excitement left the youthful face. It was as if the captain's words had revealed a reality which Henri Duval had not foreseen. He said uncertainly, "This good ship."

"Many things are as we make them for ourselves." The captain held out his hand. "It is my wish that you will be happy, Henri, and that God will bless you. Work hard, say your prayers, and do as Mr. Maitland tells you."

The stowaway nodded with dumb unhappiness. It was a strange scene, Alan thought; almost as if a father and son were taking leave. He sensed a reluctance of the other two to end it.

"We'd better go." Alan retrieved the original writ, leaving a copy for the captain's use. Shaking hands, he said, "It's been a pleasure, Captain Jaabeck. I hope we shall meet again."

"If I have more stowaways, Mr. Maitland"—the captain smiled—"I shall seek you as their friend."

Word had gone swiftly around the ship. As Alan and Henri Duval appeared, the crew had quit their loading and were assembled along the rail. There was a jabber of excited voices. Stubby Gates shambled forward. "So long matey," he said, "and lotsa luck. Here's something from me an' the boys." Alan saw a small roll of bills change hands. As they went down the gangway the crew gave a ragged cheer.

"Stay where you are!" It was a commanding voice from the darkness of the dock. As Alan paused, a barrage of flashbulbs went off.

"Hey!" he called. "What's this?"

"Press coverage," Dan Orliffe said. "What else?" Orliffe and other reporters crowded around.

"You got sneaky, Maitland," someone said cheerfully, "but we tracked you down."

Another voice called "Nice work!"

"Look," Alan protested, "there's nothing I can say tonight. Maybe we'll have a statement in the morning."

"How about a word from Henri?"

"Will you let Duval talk?"

"No," Alan said firmly. "Not now, anyway."

Dan Orliffe asked quietly, "How did you get down here?"

"I had a taxi," Alan said.

"My car's right here on the dock. I'll take you wherever you want."

"All right," Alan agreed. "Let's go."

Amid cries of protest from the other reporters they climbed into Dan Orliffe's station wagon. Flashbulbs continued to go off. Henri Duval was grinning broadly.

When they were clear of the dockyard, Dan asked, "Where are you taking him?"

There had been so much else; so many things to think of . . . "Now you mention it," Alan said, "I hadn't thought about that." His own apartment, he reasoned, was too small. But Tom and Lillian Lewis might be able to fix a temporary bed . . .

"That's what I figured," Dan said. "So the paper's taken a suite at the Hotel Vancouver. We'll pick up the tab."

Alan said doubtfully, "I guess it's all right. Though I imagined something a little simpler . . ."

"What the hell!" Dan accelerated to beat an amber light. "Let Henri live a little."

A few minutes later he added, "About that hotel suite. I forgot to tell you—the Prime Minister's suite is just down the hall." He gave a deep chuckle. "Won't Howden love *that!*"

Seventeen Margaret Howden

"My goodness!" Margaret Howden exclaimed. "I've never seen such a great big headline."

The issue of the Vancouver *Post* was spread out on a

table in the Howdens' living room. The page one banner line read:

HENRI STEPS ASHORE!

The remainder of the page was devoted entirely to large pictures of Henri Duval and Alan Maitland, and a bold-face news story concerning them.

"They call it 'Second-Coming-of-Christ' type," the party director informed Margaret. "It's used only on special occasions." He added dourly, "Like, for instance, the fall of a Government."

Pacing the room, James Howden snapped, "We'll postpone the humor if you don't mind."

"We need something to brighten the outlook," Richardson said.

It was late afternoon, snowing outside and growing dark. During the night, following his Vancouver speech, the Prime Minister had returned to eastern Canada by air. At midday he had spoken in Quebec City; in less than an hour he would be leaving Ottawa for an evening rally in Montreal. Tomorrow at 4 P.M. in the House of Commons he would announce the Act of Union. The strain of the past few days was beginning to show.

The Vancouver newspaper, only a few hours old, had been brought by air through a special arrangement Richardson had made. He had collected it personally at Ottawa airport and driven directly to the Prime Minister's house at 24 Sussex Drive. The news story treatment, he already knew, was typical of others throughout the country.

James Howden interrupted his pacing to ask sarcastically, "I suppose they did mention my speech somewhere." It had been his finest of the entire tour; in other circumstances it would have been the focus of attention in today's news.

"Here it is," Margaret announced, turning pages. "It's on page three." She appeared to stifle some amusement. "Oh dear, it *is* rather small."

"I'm glad you find something funny," her husband observed icily. "Personally, I don't."

"I'm sorry, Jamie," Margaret said. She tried to make her voice contrite, though hardly succeeding. "But really, I can't help thinking: all of you, the whole Government so determined; and then this one little man . . ."

Brian Richardson remarked quietly, "I agree with you, Mrs. Howden. We've had the pants licked off us by a smart young lawyer."

"Once and for all," James Howden declared angrily, "I am not interested in who has beaten whom."

"Please don't shout, Jamie," Margaret admonished.

"I'm interested," Richardson said. "It makes a difference on the day they count votes."

"Is it too much to ask," the Prime Minister insisted, "that we should confine ourselves to facts?"

"All right," Richardson said bluntly, "let's try this on for size." He produced a folded paper from an inside pocket. "A new Gallup poll this morning shows the Government's popularity down seven per cent in the past two weeks. And to a question: 'Do you favor a change of Government?' sixty-two per cent replied yes, thirty-one per cent no, and seven per cent were undecided."

"Do sit down, Jamie," Margaret urged. "You too, Brian. I'll send for tea and we can have it here quietly."

Howden dropped into a chair by the fireplace. "Light that, will you?" He pointed to the fire which was already laid.

Striking a match from a folder, Richardson cupped it in his hands and bent down. After a moment flames began to grow.

Margaret was speaking into a house telephone across the room.

Howden said quietly, "I didn't realize it was quite that bad."

"It's worse than bad; it's grim. The mail's pouring in; so are telegrams, and all against us." Matching the Prime Minister's tone of a moment earlier, Richardson asked, "How would you feel about postponing tomorrow's announcement?"

"It's out of the question."

"I warn you: we're not ready for an election."

"We have to be," Howden declared. "We have to take our chances."

"And lose?"

"The Act of Union is essential to Canadian survival. When it's explained to them, people will see that."

"Will they?" Richardson asked softly. "Or will they see Henri Duval?"

On the point of an impulsive answer, Howden stopped.

The question, after all, was reasonable, he thought. And the presumption which went with it could prove true.

A loss of prestige through the incident of Duval *could* cause the Government's defeat on the issue of the Act of Union. He saw that now—in unmistakable terms which had not been clear to him before.

And yet, he reasoned, if it happened, how strange and ironic that something so insignificant as a ship's stowaway could affect the destiny of nations.

Or was it strange? Or new? Or even ironic? Perhaps, through all the centuries, it had been individual human issues which had swayed the world, creating history, moving mankind forward to an enlightenment dimly perceived, yet always out of reach . . .

Perhaps it's a way of humbling us, he thought; the way we learn; the upward struggle . . .

But practical issues were nearer. He told Richardson, "There are good reasons for not postponing. We need every day of the Act of Union we can get. Defense and survival depend on it. Besides, if we waited, there'd be leaks. Politically we'd be worse off."

The party director nodded. "I thought you'd say that. I just wanted to be sure."

"I've sent for tea," Margaret announced, rejoining them. "You'll stay, Brian, won't you?"

"Thank you, Mrs. Howden." Brian Richardson had always liked Margaret. He envied Howden his successful marriage, the comfort and serenity it afforded him.

"I suppose it wouldn't do any good," the Prime Minister said thoughtfully, "if, even now, the Immigration Department admitted Duval."

Richardson shook his head emphatically. "Not the slightest. Besides, he's in the country already. Whatever happens at the court hearing tomorrow, the way I understand it, he can't be deported to the ship."

The fire's kindling had burned through, and now birch logs were blazing. The heat spread out toward them in the already warm room.

Richardson reasoned: perhaps his own agonizing session with Harvey Warrender had been a mistake. Certainly it had come too late to help this particular issue, though at least it had removed a shadow over James Howden for the future. If there *was* to be a future, he thought glumly.

A maidservant brought in tea things and disappeared.

Margaret Howden poured, and Brian Richardson accepted the tea in a delicate Royal Doulton cup, declining cake.

Margaret said tentatively, "I suppose you really have to go to Montreal tonight, Jamie."

Her husband rubbed a hand across his face in a gesture of tiredness. "I wish I hadn't. Any other time I'd send someone else. But tonight is something I must do myself."

The party director glanced toward the windows where drapes were still undrawn. The darkness was complete now, and snow still falling. "I checked the weather when I came in," he said. "There'll be no problem about your flight. Montreal is clear and staying that way, and they'll have a helicopter waiting to take you into the city."

James Howden nodded.

There was a light tap on the door and Milly Freedeman came in. Richardson looked up, surprised; he had not been aware that Milly was in the house. But it was not unusual; he knew that she often worked with Howden in the Prime Minister's study upstairs.

"Excuse me," Milly said. She smiled at Richardson and Margaret, then addressed Howden. "The White House is on the line and they wish to know if it's convenient for you to talk with the President."

"I'll come immediately," the Prime Minister said, and rose.

Brian Richardson put down his tea cup. "I guess I'd better leave too. Thank you for the tea, Mrs. Howden." He stopped courteously by Margaret's chair, then touched Milly lightly on the arm. As the two men left the room together, Richardson's voice came back, "I'll be at the airport when you leave, chief."

"Don't go away, Milly," Margaret said. "Stay and have tea."

"Thank you." Milly took the chair which Richardson had vacated.

Busying herself with the silver teapot and hot water jug, Margaret declared, "This is a turbulent household. Nothing ever stays calm for more than a few minutes at a time."

Milly said quietly, "Except for you."

"I've no choice, my dear." Margaret poured Milly's tea and replenished her own. "Everything passes me by. Somehow I can never seem to get excited about all these important events." She added thoughtfully, "I suppose I should, really."

"I don't see why," Milly replied. "They're all much the same when you get right down to it."

"I've always thought so." Margaret smiled. She moved the sugar and cream jug so that both were nearer Milly. "But I'm surprised to hear it from you. I've always thought of you as Jamie's enthusiastic right arm."

Milly said suddenly, surprising herself, "Enthusiasm wears thin and arms get tired."

Margaret laughed. "We're both being terribly disloyal, aren't we? But I must say it's a relief now and then."

There was a pause, the crackling of the burning logs the only sound in the big shadowy living room. Firelight danced upon the ceiling. Putting down her tea cup, Margaret said gently, "Have you ever regretted the way things turned out? Between you and Jamie, I mean."

For an instant Milly caught her breath, the stillness in the room alive with meaning. So Margaret had known. Known all these years, and never spoken. Milly had often wondered, at times half-suspected. Now she knew, and found herself relieved.

She answered with simple honestly, "I've never been quite sure. I don't think about it very much any more."

"No," Margaret said, "eventually one doesn't, of course. At the time you think the wound will never heal. But in the end it always does."

Milly hesitated, searching for the right words for what was in her mind. Finally she said softly, "You must have minded very much."

"Yes." Margaret nodded slowly. "I remember I was terribly hurt at the time. Any woman would be. But one gets over those things in the end. It's a case of having to, really."

Milly said gently, "I wonder if I could be as understanding." After a moment she added impulsively, "Brian Richardson wants me to marry him."

"And shall you?"

"I haven't decided." Milly shook her head perplexedly. "I think I love him; I know I do. But then, in another way, I'm not sure."

"I wish I could help you." There was a gentleness in Margaret's voice. "I learned a long time ago, though—you can't live other people's lives. We have to make our own decisions even if we're wrong."

Yes, Milly thought, as she wondered again—how long could her own decision be postponed?

2

James Howden carefully closed the double doors of the study before picking up the special red telephone—a duplicate of one upon his East Block office desk. It was a "scrambled" phone, with direct, safeguarded circuits.

"Prime Minister speaking," he announced.

An operator's voice responded, "The President is waiting, sir. One moment please."

There was a click and then a strong bluff voice. "Jim, is that you?"

Howden smiled at the familiar Midwestern twang. "Yes, Tyler," he said, "Howden speaking."

"How have you been, Jim?"

He admitted: "Somewhat tired. I've covered a lot of ground in a few days."

"I know. Your ambassador was in; he showed me your schedule." The President's voice took on concern. "Don't kill yourself, Jim. We all need you."

"I'm stopping short of that." Howden smiled. "But I'm glad to hear I'm needed. I hope the electorate feels the same way."

The voice became serious. "Do you think you can carry it, Jim? Do you think you can carry it through?"

"Yes." The seriousness was matched. "It won't be easy, but I can do it, providing all the conditions we discussed are met." He added meaningfully, "*All* the conditions."

"It's that I called about." The gruff voice paused. "By the way, what's your weather up there?"

"It's snowing."

"That's what I thought." The President chuckled. "Are you sure you want more of that stuff—Alaska for instance?"

"We want it," Howden said. "And we know how to handle snow and ice; we live with it." He forbore from adding what the Minister of Mines and Resources had observed enthusiastically at Cabinet ten days earlier: "Alaska's like a can that's had two holes punched in it and the lid left on. If we take the lid off there are great areas can be developed—for agriculture, housing, industry. In time, as we learn to beat the weather, we'd push even further . . ." It was hard to think all the time in terms of imminent war.

"Well," the President said, "we've decided to let the plebiscite go through. I may have a fight on my hands—our people don't like taking stars off the flag once they put them on. But, like you, I figure I can have my way."

"I'm glad," James Howden said. "Very glad."

"You received the draft of our joint statement?"

"Yes," Howden acknowledged. "Angry flew out West to meet me. I made some suggestions and left him to work out the details with Arthur Lexington."

"Then we'll have it settled by tomorrow morning, with Alaska in the text. After the statement, when it comes to our separate speeches, I shall emphasize self-determination for Alaska. I presume you'll do the same."

"Yes, I shall." The Prime Minister added dryly, "For Alaska *and* Canada."

"Four o'clock then, tomorrow afternoon." The President chuckled. "I suppose we should synchronize our watches."

"Four o'clock," Howden said. He had a sense of finality, as if somewhere a door were closing.

The President's voice came softly through the phone. "Jim."

"Yes, Tyler?"

"Things are no better internationally; you know that."

"If anything," Howden said, "I'd say they're worse."

"You remember what I said: that I'm praying for the gift of a year before the fighting starts. It's the best we can hope for."

"Yes," Howden said. "I remember."

There was a pause, with heavy breathing, as if a moment of emotion were being controlled. Then the voice said quietly, "This is a good thing we are doing, Jim. The very best . . . for the children . . . their children yet to come . . ."

For a moment there was silence. Then, with a click, the line went dead.

When he had replaced the red telephone James Howden stood meditatively in the silent, book-lined study. A portrait of Sir John A. Macdonald, founder of Canadian confederation, statesman, *bon vivant,* and tippler extraordinary, looked down upon him.

This was a moment of triumph, Howden supposed. A moment ago the President had been jocular in his concession of the Alaska plebiscite, but it must have been bitter medicine to take and, except for Howden's own toughness in negotiations, the concession would never have been won. Now, as well as the other benefits for Canada, there was a single big red apple in return for the loss of a large part of Canadian sovereignty. He thought inconsequentially: A is for apple; A is for Alaska.

There was a single tap upon the study's double doors. "Yes," he called.

It was Yarrow, the steward. The soft-footed, aging major domo of Number 24 announced, "Mr. Cawston is here, sir. He informs me it's very urgent." Behind Yarrow, in the upstairs hallway, Howden could see the Finance Minister, wearing a heavy overcoat and scarf, Homburg hat in hand.

He called, "Come in, Stu."

Entering the study, Cawston shook his head as Yarrow moved to take his outdoor clothing. "I'll only be a few minutes; I'll leave these here." He slipped off the overcoat, folding it over a chair, the hat and scarf beside it. Turning, he smiled automatically, rubbed a hand across his balding head, then, as the door closed behind the steward, his face became somber. "I've bad news," he announced tersely. "About as bad as it can be."

Howden waited.

Cawston said heavily, "The Cabinet is split—right down the middle."

James Howden allowed the words to sink in before replying.

"I don't understand," he said. "I was under the impression——"

"So was I," Cawston affirmed. "I thought you had them sold—all of us." He gestured deprecatingly. "Except for one or two who might have resigned after tomorrow."

Howden nodded. Since his return from Washington there had been two full cabinet sessions on the Act of Union. The first had followed the pattern of the Defense Committee on Christmas Eve. At the second, enthusiasm had started to generate as advantages to Canada had begun to be seen. There had, of course, been a few dissidents; that was to be expected. He had foreseen, too, the inevitability of one or two resignations—they would have to be accepted and the subsequent disturbance weathered. But not a major cabinet split . . .

He commanded crisply, "Give me the details."

"There are nine involved."

"Nine!" So Cawston had not exaggerated when he said "down the middle." It was more than a third of the Cabinet.

"It wouldn't have been as many, I'm sure," Smiling Stu stated apologetically, "if it hadn't been for the leadership . . ."

"Leadership!" Howden snapped. "What leadership?"

"This is going to surprise you." Cawston hesitated, as if anticipating the Prime Minister's anger. "The leader of the revolt is Adrian Nesbitson."

Stunned, incredulous, James Howden stared.

As if anticipating, Cawston said, "There's no mistake; it's Adrian Nesbitson. He began two days ago. He persuaded the others."

"The fool! That old, useless fool!"

"No." Cawston shook his head firmly. "That won't do. You can't dismiss him like that."

"But we had an agreement. We made a deal." The arrangement on the airplane had been clear. The Governor Generalship, and in return the aging Defense Minister's support . . .

Cawston declared decisively, "Whatever deal you had has gone by default."

The two men were still standing. Grimly, the Prime Minister asked, "Who are the others?"

"Borden Tayne, George Yhorkis, Aaron Gold, Rita Buchanan . . ." Smiling Stu ran quickly through the remaining names. "But Adrian is the one who counts. He's holding them together."

"Lucien Perrault is still with us?" He thought quickly of Quebec: the important French Canadian support.

Cawston nodded.

It was like a bad dream, Howden thought; a nightmare in which ridiculous things had ousted sanity. After a while he would wake up.

There was a knock at the hallway door and Yarrow entered. He announced, "Your car is waiting, sir. It's time to leave for the airport."

Cawston said urgently, "Adrian has become a changed man. It's almost as if . . ." He struggled for a metaphor ". . . as if a mummy had been given blood and come to life. He's talked with me and I can tell you——"

"Don't tell me!" This had gone far enough. "I'll talk to him myself."

James Howden calculated rapidly. Time was ebbing away; there were few remaining hours between now and four o'clock tomorrow afternoon.

"Adrian knows he has to see you," Cawston said. "He's holding himself available."

"Where?"

"The whole group is in Arthur Lexington's office. I came from there. Arthur's talking to them; not getting anywhere, I'm afraid."

The steward coughed discreetly. Tonight's schedule, Howden knew was exceptionally tight. He had a vision of the waiting car; the V.I.P. *Vanguard* warming at Uplands Airport; the helicopter standing by at Montreal; a packed expectant audience . . .

He said decisively, "Nesbitson must come with me to Montreal. If he leaves for the airport now, he can be on my airplane."

Cawston nodded swiftly. "I'll take care of it." He was already on the telephone as Howden left.

3

The Prime Minister's Oldsmobile drove directly to the waiting aircraft.

The *Vanguard's* navigation lights flashed rhythmically in the darkness as ground crew, wrapped in hooded parkas, surrounded it like busy moles. A battery cart—ready for starting motors—was plugged into the fuselage.

The chauffeur opened the car door and the Prime Minister alighted. At the foot of the loading ramp, his coat collar tightly clasped against the wind and drifting snow, Brian Richardson was waiting. He said, without preliminary, "The old boy just got here. He's in your cabin, strapped in, with a scotch and soda in his hand."

Howden stopped. He asked, "Stu told you?"

Richardson nodded.

"I'll try reasoning with him," Howden said grimly. "I don't know what else I can do."

"Have you considered throwing him out?" The party director grinned dourly. "Say, at five thousand feet."

Despite his own depression, Howden laughed. "That way we'd have two martyrs: one in Vancouver, one here." He started up the ramp steps, then called over his shoulder, "Besides, after today, the news can only get better."

"Good luck, chief!" the party director shouted. But his words were whipped away by the wind.

In the compact V.I.P. drawing room, its ordered luxury softly lighted, the short pudgy figure of General Nesbitson was strapped into one of the four deep reclining chairs. As Richardson had said, the Defense Minister was holding a drink which he put down as the Prime Minister entered.

Outside there was a whine as the turbo-prop motors came to life.

The flight-sergeant steward hovered behind Howden, who shook his head. "Leave everything," he ordered curtly. "There's nothing I need and we'd like to be alone." He threw his outdoor clothing over one of the spare chairs and sat down facing the older man. One of the cabin reading lights, he noticed, had been turned on. It shone down on Nesbitson's balding head and pink-cheeked face like an interrogation lamp above a prisoner. Well, Howden thought, perhaps it was an omen of the line he should take.

"This is a short flight," he said peremptorily, "and we have very little time. I believe you owe me an explanation."

The *Vanguard* was taxiing now and, judging by their motion, moving fast. There was to be little delay. Tonight, Howden knew, they would have priority over everything else in the air.

Momentarily the old man flushed at Howden's tone. Then he said with surprising firmness, "I should have thought the explanation would be clear, Prime Minister. I intend to resign in protest against what you are planning, and so do others."

James Howden inquired coolly, "Isn't there something you've forgotten?—a compact we made. Here, in this airplane, ten days ago?"

The old man's eyes were steadfast. He said evenly, "I am ashamed to remember it. I believe we both should be."

"Speak of your own shame," Howden flared, "not of mine. I am trying to save this country. You and your kind, looking backward, would destroy it."

"If you are saving Canada, why plan to give it away?" There was a hint of new strength behind the words. Howden remembered what Stu Cawston had said: "Adrian is a changed man." Physically he seemed less shrunken, to have more stature than before.

"If you are speaking of the Act of Union," the Prime Minister argued, "we shall gain far more than we shall give."

The old man replied bitterly, "Disbanding our armed

forces; having the Yanks move in without restraint; letting them run our foreign policy—you call that gaining?"

The airplane had stopped briefly, then moved forward, gathering speed for take-off. A pattern of runway lights raced by, then disappeared. Now, they were airborne; a moment later, with a thud, the landing gear came up. The Prime Minister calculated: there would be twenty minutes of flying, perhaps less. It was always the same: so little time.

He declared, "We're facing war, and you're looking at one side only!"

"I'm looking at the whole," Nesbitson insisted, "and I tell you that war or not, your Act of Union would be the beginning of the end. Americans would never stop at partial union; they'd want it complete, and we'd be swallowed whole. We'd lose the British flag, the Queen, traditions . . ."

"No," Howden argued. "Those are things we'd keep."

The old man snorted. "How could we?—with the border wide open and Americans, including Negroes, Puerto Ricans, flooding in. Our identity would disappear because we'd be outnumbered and people wouldn't care. What's more, we'd have racial problems we never knew before. You'd make Toronto another Chicago; Montreal a New Orleans. We have an Immigration Act which you just got through defending. Why throw it away with all the rest?"

"We'd throw nothing away!" Howden said fiercely. "We'd merely make adjustments. Oh yes, there'll be problems, I grant you. But none as great as if we stay helpless and alone."

"I don't believe that."

"In terms of defense," the Prime Minister insisted, "the Act of Union provides for our survival. And economically Canada will have tremendous opportunities. Have you considered the Alaskan plebiscite, which we shall win—Alaska as a Canadian province?"

Nesbitson said gruffly, "I've considered that every sellout has its thirty pieces of silver."

A blazing anger swept over Howden. Controlling it with an effort of will, he declared, "Despite what you say, we are not surrendering our sovereignty . . ."

"No?" The tone was withering. "What good is sovereignty without the power to maintain it?"

Howden declared angrily, "We have no such power now, and have never had, except to defend ourselves against small skirmishes. The United States holds the power. By transferring our military strength and opening the border, we increase American strength, which is our own."

"I am sorry, Prime Minister," General Nesbitson said with dignity. "I can never agree. What you're proposing is to abandon our history, all that Canada has stood for . . ."

"You're wrong! I'm trying to perpetuate it." Howden leaned forward, speaking earnestly, directly, to the other man. "I'm trying to preserve the things we care about before. it's too late: freedom, decency, justice under the law. Nothing else really matters." He pleaded: "Can't you understand?"

"All I can understand," the old man said doggedly, "is that there must be some other way."

It was no use, Howden knew. But still he tried. After a while he asked, "At least answer me this: How would you have Canada defend itself against guided-missile attack?"

Nesbitson began stiffly: "Initially we would deploy our conventional forces . . ."

"Never mind," Howden said. He added dourly, "I'm only surprised that while you've been Defense Minister you haven't revived the cavalry."

In the morning, James Howden decided, he would interview the other dissident ministers one at a time. Some of them, he was sure, he could persuade over once again. But there would be others—in Cabinet, Parliament, and elsewhere—who would think as Adrian Nesbitson thought, who would follow his lead, dreaming their wishful dreams . . . until the last gasp of radioactive dust . . .

But then, he had always expected a fight, right from the beginning. It would be a stiff fight, but if he could lead Nesbitson on, persuading him to expound his views, demonstrate their quaint absurdity . . .

It was sheer bad luck, though, that this and the immigration debacle had come together.

The twenty minutes had gone. The note of the motors was changing and they were losing height. Below were scattered lights, ahead a reflected halo in the sky from the lighted, shimmering city of Montreal.

Adrian Nesbitson had taken the drink he put down when Howden came in. Some of it had spilled, but he sipped from the residue in the glass.

"P.M.," he said, "personally I'm damn sorry about this split between us."

Indifferently now Howden nodded. "You realize of

course, I can't possibly recommend you as Governor General."

The old man flushed. "I thought I had made it clear——"

"Yes," Howden said brusquely, "you made a good deal clear."

Dismissing Nesbitson from his mind, he applied his thoughts to what must be done between now and tomorrow afternoon.

Eighteen Henri Duval

A few minutes after 7.30 A.M. the telephone rang in Alan Maitland's Gilford Street apartment. Alan, still sleepy and in pajama trousers only—he never used the tops and had a collection of them in their original wrappers—was preparing breakfast at his portable two-burner stove. Unplugging the toaster, which had a habit of reducing bread to a cinder if unwatched, he answered on the second ring.

"Good morning," Sharon's voice said brightly. "What are you doing?"

"I'm boiling an egg." Trailing the telephone cord, Alan inspected an hourglass timer on the kitchenette table. "It's been on three minutes; one to go."

"Give it another six," Sharon suggested cheerfully. "Then you can have it hard-boiled tomorrow. Granddaddy would like you to have breakfast with us."

Alan reflected swiftly. "I suppose I could." He corrected himself: "At least—thank you, I mean."

"Good."

He interjected, "I presume your grandfather knows the Duval hearing is this morning."

"I think that's what he wants to talk about," Sharon said. "How long will you be?"

"I'll be up in half an hour."

While dressing he ate the egg anyway.

At the South West Marine Drive mansion the butler, who still moved as if his feet hurt, showed Alan into a spacious dining room, its walls lined—like the main entrance hall —with polished linen-fold paneling. An oak refectory table,

Alan saw, was laid for three, with gleaming silver and white napery. On a carved oak sideboard several lidded chafing dishes, presumably containing breakfast, were arranged. The butler announced, "Senator and Miss Deveraux will join you in a moment, sir."

"Thank you," Alan said. Waiting, he strolled the room's width to damask-draped windows facing the broad Fraser River a hundred feet below. Looking downward he could see the great log booms, touched by sunlight breaking through the morning mist. The source of wealth, he thought: of this house and others like it.

"Good morning, my boy." It was Senator Deveraux, in the doorway, with Sharon. Alan turned.

As on the last occasion, the Senator's voice seemed weak. Today he was leaning heavily on a cane and, on the opposite side, Sharon supported his free arm. She smiled at Alan warmly. He felt his breath catch at the sight of her again.

"Good morning, sir," Alan said. He pulled out a chair as Sharon helped her grandfather into it. "I hope you're well."

"I'm perfectly splendid, thank you." Momentarily the voice had some of its earlier ring. "My only trouble, periodically, is a touch of anno Domini." He regarded Sharon and Alan who had joined him at the table. "Even you young people will suffer from it in the end."

The butler had silently reappeared and began to serve breakfast from the chafing dishes onto warmed plates. There were eggs Florentine and scrambled. Alan chose Florentine.

Sharon said solicitously, "We can do a boiled one if you like."

"No thanks!" Alan surveyed the generous portion placed before him. "Only reason I have them that way at home is that I'm a good water boiler."

"You are, indeed, an accomplished boiler," the Senator observed. "And not only with water." He added slowly, "I find that your boiling can have unexpected results."

When the butler had left, closing the door softly behind him, Sharon announced, "I'm going to court today. I hope you don't mind."

"I almost wish you hadn't told me." Alan smiled across the table. "I might be self-conscious."

Abruptly Senator Deveraux inquired, "Tell me, my boy: is your law practice prospering?"

"Frankly, no." Alan grinned ruefully. "We had a thin time to begin with, and most of our savings soon disappeared. Then we began to break even. This month, though, I'm afraid we won't."

Sharon frowned, as if puzzled. "But surely all the publicity will help. Won't that bring you clients?"

"I thought so at first," Alan answered frankly. "But now I believe it's keeping people away. Tom and I were talking about it last night." He explained to the Senator: "Tom Lewis is my partner."

"Yes, I'm aware of that," the older man acknowledged. He added: "I made some inquiries about you both."

"The thing is, I think," Alan expounded, "conservative clients, like businesses for instance, don't care for their lawyers being involved in a lot of publicity; and others, with small legal things to be done, have the idea we're too important or expensive."

The Senator nodded. "A remarkably shrewd assessment, I should say."

"If it's true," Sharon said, "it's horribly unfair."

"I understand," Senator Deveraux remarked, "that your Mr. Lewis is especially interested in corporation law."

Surprised, Alan answered, "That's right; Tom always has been. Eventually he hopes to specialize." Curiously, he wondered where this conversation was leading.

"It occurs to me," the Senator said ponderously, "that it might be of assistance to you if we settled two things this morning. First, there is the question of an advance on the final fee for your present services. I wonder if two thousand dollars would be agreeable."

Alan swallowed the mouthful of eggs Florentine he had been chewing. Dazedly he replied, "Frankly, sir, I hadn't considered that the final bill would be anywhere near that amount."

"Allow me to give you some sound advice." Senator Deveraux had finished the small portion of breakfast he had received. Now, pushing his plate away, he leaned forward across the table. "In this life never sell yourself cheaply. In professional services some of the highest fees—law, medicine, everything else—are commanded by sheer audacity. Have audacity, my boy! It will carry you a long way."

"Besides," Sharon said, "in Grandaddy's case it comes off taxes."

Alan grinned. "Thank you, sir. When you put it like that, I'll take your advice."

"Then there is the second subject." The Senator took a cigar from the pocket of his suit coat and clipped the end. When it was lighted he continued, "Culliner, Bryant, et cetera now handle most of my business affairs requiring legal attention. Lately, however, the quantity of work has increased and I have considered splitting it. I believe it might prove satisfactory if you and your Mr. Lewis took over Deveraux Forestry Limited. It is a substantial account and should form a solid basis for your legal practice." He added, "We can discuss a retaining fee later."

"I don't know what to say," Alan said. "Except that this seems to be my morning." He had a sense of wanting to cheer aloud; he must get to a telephone quickly and share the joyous news with Tom.

Sharon was smiling.

"I hoped you'd be pleased, my boy. Now there is one further matter I would like to speak of. But perhaps, while we are doing it"—he glanced at Sharon—"you would be good enough to prepare a check for two thousand dollars for me to sign." He considered, then added: "On the Consolidated Fund, I think."

When you had money, Alan thought amusedly, it must be a problem knowing which account to draw it from.

"All right," Sharon said brightly. She rose, taking her coffee cup with her.

When the door had closed, the Senator faced his guest across the table. "If I may inquire," he said directly, "what are your feelings about Sharon?"

"We haven't talked about it," Alan answered quietly. "But sometime soon I shall ask her to marry me."

The Senator nodded. He put down the cigar. "I suspected something of the kind. You realize, I suppose, that Sharon will be wealthy—in her own right."

"I'd assumed that," Alan said.

"Do you believe that that difference between you would impede a happy marriage?"

"No, I don't," Alan affirmed. "I intend to work hard and build my own career. If we love one another, it would be silly to let something like that stand in the way."

Senator Deveraux sighed. "You are a remarkably sane and competent young man." His hands were clasped in front of him; his eyes went down to them. He said slowly,

"I find myself wishing that my own son—Sharon's father —had been more like you. Unfortunately, he is an authority on fast motor boats, women of the same kind, and nothing more."

There was nothing to say, Alan thought; nothing at all. He sat, silently.

At length the Senator raised his eyes. "What is between you and Sharon will remain between you. Sharon will make her own decision, as she always has. But I may tell you that if it were in your favor I, for one, would not stand in your way."

"Thank you," Alan said. He felt grateful—and dazed. So much was happening in so short a time. He would ask Sharon soon; perhaps today.

"As a culmination to all that we have talked of," the older man said, "I have one request."

Alan answered, "If it's something I can do, sir, I will."

"Tell me: do you expect to win your case in court today?"

Surprised, Alan answered, "Yes, I'm sure I can."

"Is there a possibility that you might lose?"

"There's always that possibility," Alan admitted. "The Immigration Department won't give in without a struggle, and I shall have to counter their arguments. But we've a strong case; much stronger than before."

"Suppose, just suppose, you were slightly lax in countering the arguments. *Could* you lose . . . without it being obvious . . . lose deliberately . . . ?"

Alan flushed. "Yes, but——"

"I want you to lose," Senator Deveraux said softly. "I want you to lose and Henri Duval to be deported. That is my request."

It took a long, full minute for the implication to sink in.

Incredulously, his voice strained, Alan protested, "Have you any idea what you are asking?"

"Yes, my boy," the Senator replied carefully, "I believe I have. I'm aware of asking a great deal because I know how much this case has meant to you. But I'm also appealing to you to believe that there are good and valid reasons for my request."

"Tell me," Alan demanded. "Tell me what they are."

"You understand," the Senator intoned slowly, "that what we are saying now is between the two of us, within the confines of this room. If you agree, as I hope you will, no one, not even Sharon, need ever know what has taken place."

"The reasons," Alan insisted softly. "Give me the reasons."

"There are two," the Senator answered, "and I will name the least important first. Your stowaway will better serve our cause—and the cause of others like him—if he is expelled, despite the efforts made on his behalf. Some men among us achieve their greatest heights in martyrdom. He is one."

Alan said quietly, "What you really mean is that politically it would make Howden's party look worse—because they threw Duval out—and your own party better because you tried to save him, or at least appeared to."

The Senator gave the slightest of shrugs. "You have your words, my boy. I choose mine."

"And the second reason?"

"I have an old and reliable nose," Senator Deveraux said, "for political trouble. I smell it now."

"Trouble?"

"It is possible that sometime soon the reins of government will be transferred. The star of James Howden is dimming, our own ascending."

"*Your* own," Alan reminded him. "Not mine."

"Frankly, I had hoped it might soon become yours also. But for the time being let us say that the fortunes of the party of which I have the honor to be chairman are on the mend."

"You said trouble," Alan insisted. "What kind of trouble?"

The Senator met Alan's eyes directly. "Your stowaway—if he is allowed to remain here—could become a source of acute embarrassment to his sponsors. His kind never fits. I speak from long experience; there have been other incidents like this before. If that happened, if he went wrong, the matter could become an harassment to our own party—a perpetual thorn—just as we have made it one to the Government now."

"What makes you so sure," Alan asked, "that—as you put it—he'll go wrong?"

Senator Deveraux said firmly, "Because it is inevitable he should. With his background . . . in our North American society . . ."

"I disagree," Alan said heatedly. "I disagree just about as much as anyone could."

"Your law partner, Mr. Lewis, doesn't." The Senator said softly, "I understand his words were to the effect that there

is a flaw in the man—'a crack down the middle'—and that
if you got him ashore he would, to quote your partner,
'come apart in pieces.' "

Alan thought bitterly: so Sharon had reported their conversation the day of the chambers hearing. He wondered if
she had any idea it would be used against him in this way.
Perhaps so; he found himself beginning to doubt the motives
of everyone around him.

"It's a pity," he said bleakly, "that you didn't think of this
before the case was started."

"I give you my word, my boy, that if I had known it
would lead to this moment I would never have begun." There
was genuineness in the older man's voice. He went on, "I
confess I underrated you. I never dreamed you would succeed as remarkably as you have."

He had to move, Alan thought; change position, pace
. . . Perhaps moving the muscles of his body could help to
quell the turmoil of his mind. Pushing back his chair from
the breakfast table, he rose and crossed to the window
where he had stood earlier.

Looking down he could see the river again. The sun had
cleared the mist. On a slight swell the logs, in tethered
booms, were rising and falling gently.

"There are choices we are obliged to make," the Senator
was saying, "which give us pain, but afterwards we know
they were best and wisest . . ."

Swinging around, Alan said, "I'd like to be clear about
something, if you don't mind."

Senator Deveraux, too, had moved back from the table
but remained in his chair. He nodded. "Certainly."

"If I refuse to do what you ask, what of the things we
were discussing—the legal work, Deveraux Forestry . . . ?"

The Senator looked pained. "I'd rather not put it on that
basis, my boy."

"But I would," Alan said bluntly. He waited for an answer.

"I suppose . . . in certain circumstances . . . I might be
obliged to reconsider."

"Thank you," Alan said. "I just wanted to be clear."

With bitterness, he thought: he had been shown the promised land, and now . . .

For an instant he weakened; temptation beckoned him.
The Senator had said: *no one . . . not even Sharon . . . need
ever know*. It could be done so easily: an omission, a

laxity in argument, a concession to opposing counsel . . .
Professionally, he might be criticized, but he was young; inexperience could be a cloak. Such things were quickly forgotten.

Then he dismissed the thought, as if it had never been.
His words were clear and strong.

"Senator Deveraux," he declared, "I already intended to
go into court this morning and win. I would like you to
know that I shall still win, except that now I am ten times
more determined."

There was no answer. Only the eyes uplifted, the face
weary as if drained by effort.

"Just one more thing." Alan's voice took on a cutting edge.
"I wish to make it clear that you are no longer retaining me
in any capacity. My client is Henri Duval, and no one else."

The door to the dining room opened. Sharon appeared, a
slip of paper in her hand. She inquired uncertainly, "Is
something wrong?"

Alan gestured to the check. "You won't be needing that.
I suggest you put it back in the Consolidated Fund."

"Why, Alan? Why?" Sharon's lips were parted, her face
pale.

Suddenly, unreasonably, he wanted to hurt and wound.

"Your precious grandfather made me a proposition," he
answered savagely. "I suggest you ask him about it. After all,
you were included in the deal."

He brushed rudely by, not stopping until he had reached
his battered Chevrolet in the driveway. Turning it, he
drove swiftly towards town.

2

Alan Maitland knocked sharply at the outer entrance of
the Hotel Vancouver suite reserved for Henri Duval. After
a moment, the door opened partially, behind it the broad
bulky figure of Dan Orliffe. Opening the door fully, the reporter asked, "What kept you?"

"I had another engagement," Alan answered shortly. Entering, he glanced about him at the comfortably appointed
living room, unoccupied except for Orliffe. "It's time we
were moving. Is Henri ready?"

"Just about," the reporter acknowledged. "He's in there
dressing." He nodded towards a closed bedroom door.

"I'd like him to wear the dark suit," Alan said. "It'll look better in court." They had purchased two new suits for Duval the previous day, as well as shoes and other accessories, utilizing money from the small accumulated trust fund. The suits were ready-mades, hastily adjusted but well-fitting. They had been delivered late yesterday.

Dan Orliffe shook his head. "He can't wear the dark one. He gave it away."

Alan said irritably, "What do you mean—gave it away?"

"Exactly what I say. There was a room-service waiter about Henri's size. So Henri gave the suit to him. Just like that. Oh yes, and he threw in a couple of the new shirts and a pair of shoes."

"If this is a joke," Alan snapped, "I don't think it's very funny."

"Listen, chum," Orliffe cautioned, "whatever's biting you, don't take it out on me. And for the record, I don't think it's funny either."

Alan grimaced. "Sorry. I guess I've a sort of emotional hangover."

"It happened before I got here," Orliffe explained. "Apparently Henri took a shine to this guy, and that was it. I phoned downstairs to try and get the suit back, but the waiter's gone off duty."

"What did Henri say?"

"When I asked him about it, he sort of shrugged and told me there will be many more suits and he wants to give away a lot of things."

"We'll soon straighten him out on that," Alan said grimly. He crossed to the bedroom door and opened it. Inside, Henri Duval, in a light brown suit, white shirt, neatly knotted tie and polished shoes, was studying himself in a long mirror. He turned to Alan, beaming.

"I look pretty, no?"

It was impossible to ignore the infectious, boyish pleasure. Alan smiled. Henri's hair had been trimmed too; now it was neatly combed and parted. Yesterday had been a busy time: a medical exam; press and TV interviews; shopping; a fitting for the suits.

"Sure you look pretty." Alan tried to make his voice sound stern. "But that doesn't mean you can give away new suits, bought for you specially."

Henri's face took on an injured look. He said, "The man I give, my friend."

"As far as I can make out," Dan Orliffe put in from behind, "it was the first time they'd met. Henri makes friends pretty fast."

Alan instructed, "You don't give your own new clothes away, even to friends."

The young stowaway pouted like a child. Alan sighed. There were going to be problems, he could see, in adapting Henri Duval to his new environment. Aloud he announced, "We'd better go. We mustn't be late in court."

On the way out Alan stopped. Looking around the suite, he told Duval, "If we are successful in court, this afternoon we will find a room for you to live in."

The young stowaway looked puzzled. "Why not here? This place good."

Alan said sharply, "I don't doubt it. But we don't happen to have this kind of money."

Henri Duval asserted brightly, "The newspaper pay."

"Not after today," Dan Orliffe shook his head. "My editor's already beefing about the cost. Oh yes, and there's another thing." He told Alan: "Henri has decided that from now on we must pay him if we take his picture. He informed me this morning."

Alan felt a return of his earlier irritability. "He doesn't understand these things. And I hope you won't print that in the paper."

"I won't," Dan said quietly. "But others will if they hear it. Sometime soon, I suggest you have an earnest talk with our young friend."

Henri Duval beamed at them both.

3

There was a milling crowd of people outside the courtroom in which this morning's hearing would be held. The public seats were already full; politely but firmly, ushers were turning newcomers away. Pressing through the throng, ignoring questions from reporters close behind him, Alan steered Henri Duval through the center courtroom door.

Alan had already stopped to put on a counsel's gown with starched white tabs. Today's would be a full dress hearing with all protocol observed. Entering, he was aware of the spaciously impressive courtroom with its carved oak furnishings, rich red carpet, and matching crimson and gold drapes at the high arched windows. Through venetian blinds sunlight streamed in.

At one of the long counsel's tables, Edgar Kramer, A. R. Butler, Q.C., and the shipping-company lawyer, Tolland, were already seated in straight-backed leather chairs, facing the canopied judge's bench with its royal coat of arms above.

With Henri Duval, Alan moved to the second table. To his right the press table was crowded, Dan Orliffe, the latest arrival, squeezing in among the others. The clerk of the court and court reporter were seated below the judge's bench. From the packed spectators' seats, behind counsel, came a low-pitched buzz of conversation.

Glancing sideways, Alan observed that the other two lawyers had turned toward him. They smiled and nodded, and he returned their greeting. As on the earlier occasion, Edgar Kramer's eyes were studiedly averted. A moment later Tom Lewis, also gowned, dropped into the seat beside Alan. Looking around, he remarked irreverently, "Reminds me of our office, only bigger." He nodded to Duval. "Good morning, Henri."

Alan wondered when he should break the news to Tom that there would no longer be a fee for the work which they were doing; that through impetuous pride he had brushed aside payment to which they were properly entitled, whatever his quarrel with Senator Deveraux might be. Perhaps it might mean the end of their partnership; at the very least there would be hardship for them both.

He thought of Sharon. He was sure now that she had had no knowledge of what her grandfather proposed this morning, and that was the reason she had been sent from the room. If she had stayed, she would have protested as he himself had done. But instead of having faith, he had doubted her. Suddenly, miserably, he remembered the words he had used to Sharon: *You were included in the deal.* He wished desperately that he could call them back. He supposed that she would not wish to see him again.

A thought occurred to him. Sharon had said she would be in court this morning. He craned around, surveying the public seats. As he had feared, she was not there.

"Order!" It was the clerk of the court.

The officials, counsel and spectators rose as, robes rustling, Mr. Justice Stanley Willis entered and took his seat upon the bench.

When the court had settled, the clerk announced, "Supreme Court, January 13, in the matter of Henri Duval."

Alan Maitland was on his feet. Speedily he dealt with the preliminaries, then began, "My lord, for centuries, every individual who is subject to the jurisdiction of the Crown—whether in the country temporarily or not—has been entitled to seek redress from injustice at the foot of the throne. Expressed in essence, in this application of habeas corpus, that is my client's plea today."

In its correct sense, Alan knew, the hearing would be legally formalistic, with points of abstruse law being debated by himself and A. R. Butler. But he had decided in advance to introduce every ounce of humanity that he could. Now he continued, "I draw the Court's attention to the deportation order issued by the Department of Immigration." Alan quoted the words he knew by heart, ". . . detained and deported to the place whence you came to Canada, or to the country of which you are a national or citizen, or to the country of your birth, or to such country as may be approved . . ."

An individual, he argued, could not be deported to four places at the same time; therefore there must be some decision as to which of the four was to apply. "Who is to make this decision?" Alan inquired rhetorically, then answered his own question: "One would conclude—the authorities issuing the deportation order. And yet there has been no decision; only that my client, Henri Duval, shall be imprisoned on the ship."

By this action—or inaction—Alan claimed, the ship's captain was being forced to make an impossible choice of the four alternatives. Alan declared vehemently, "It is as if Your Lordship found an individual guilty of a crime and said, 'I sentence this man either to three years in the penitentiary, or to twelve strokes of the paddle, or six months in local jail, and I leave it to someone else outside this courtroom to determine which it shall be.'"

As Alan paused, sipping from a glass of ice water which Tom Lewis poured, there was a hint of a smile on the judge's face. At the other counsel's table, A. R. Butler, his distinguished features impassive, made a penciled note.

Alan continued: "I submit, my lord, that the deportation order affecting Henri Duval is defective because it cannot be carried out precisely."

Now—the strongest pillar of his case—he sketched in the history of *Rex* vs. *Ahmed Singh*, reading in detail from the volume of law reports he had brought to court, the sig-

nificant portion flagged. In the 1921 case, stripped of legal
verbiage, a Canadian judge had ruled: a rejected immigrant,
Ahmed Singh, could not be deported solely to a ship. Nor,
Alan insisted, could Henri Duval.

"Under the law," Alan declared, "the two situations are
identical. Thus, under habeas corpus proceedings, the order
should be quashed and my client freed."

A. R. Butler stirred and made another note; soon he would
have the opportunity of rebuttal and initiating argument
himself. Meanwhile, Alan's words and reasoning flowed confidently on. He had told Senator Deveraux: *I intend to
win* . . .

In the seat beside A. R. Butler, Edgar Kramer listened unhappily to the lengthening proceedings.

Edgar Kramer had a working knowledge of the law, and
knowledge plus instinct told him that, for the Immigration
Department, the hearing was not proceeding well. He also had
a secondary instinct: that, if the verdict was adverse, a scape-
goat might be found within the department. And there was an
obvious one: himself.

He had been aware of this ever since the curt and cutting
message two days earlier: "The Prime Minister . . . extremely
dissatisfied . . . handling of the case in judge's chambers . . .
should not have offered a special inquiry . . . expect better
performance in future." The executive assistant who had
relayed the censure by telephone had seemed to do so with
especial relish.

Edgar Kramer seethed anew at the bitter, gross injustice.
He had even been denied the elementary privilege of self-
defense; of explaining to the Prime Minister personally that
the special inquiry had been forced upon him by this judge,
and that, faced with two impossible situations, he had
chosen the least harmful and most expeditious.

It had been the correct thing to do, as everything he had
done had been correct from the moment he had reached
Vancouver.

In Ottawa, his instructions before departure had been
explicit. The deputy minister had told him personally: if the
stowaway Duval did not qualify for admittance as an immigrant under the law, then, under no circumstances would
he be admitted. Furthermore, Edgar Kramer was authorized
to take all necessary legal steps to prevent such admittance,
whatever they might be.

There had been another assurance: political pressure or a
public outcry would not be allowed to interfere with application of the law. The assurance, he was told, had come directly from the Minister, Mr. Warrender.

Edgar Kramer had followed instructions conscientiously,
as he had always done in the course of his career. Despite
what was happening here and now, he had observed the law
—the Immigration Act, as passed by Parliament. He had
been dutiful and loyal, and not neglectful. And it was not
his fault that an upstart lawyer and a misguided judge had
thrown his efforts out of joint.

His superiors, he supposed, would understand. And yet . . .
the Prime Minister's displeasure was something else again.

Censure from a Prime Minister could cut a civil servant
down; make him a marked man, with promotion barred.
And even when governments changed, such judgments had a
way of hanging over.

In his own case, of course, the censure had not been
major; and perhaps already the Prime Minister had erased it
from his mind. All the same, uneasily, Edgar Kramer had an
instinct that the brightness of his future, compared with a
week ago, was slightly dimmed.

What he must guard against was another controversial
step. If the Prime Minister were reminded of his name once
more . . .

Within the courtroom the words flowed on. The judge had
intervened with questions at several points, and now A. R.
Butler and Alan Maitland were politely disputing a minute
point of law. ". . . My learned friend says the order is in the
exact terms of Section 36. I submit that the addition of these
commas may be important. It is not in the exact terms of
Section 36. . . ."

Edgar Kramer hated Alan Maitland's guts. He also had an
urge to urinate: emotion, including anger, nowadays had this
effect. And there was no denying that lately his affliction had
been worse, the pain from delay greater. He tried to shield
his mind . . . to forget . . . to think of something else . . .

He turned his eyes to Henri Duval; the stowaway was
grinning, not understanding, his gaze roving the courtroom.
Every instinct Kramer possessed . . . his years of experience
. . . told him that this man would never make a settled immigrant. His background was against him. Despite any help
he might be given, such a man could not adapt and conform
to a country he would never understand. There was a pattern

of behavior for his type: short-lived industry, then idleness; the eager search for quick rewards; weakness; dissolution; trouble . . . the pattern always moving downward. There were many cases in department files: the harsh reality which starry-eyed idealists ignored.

". . . Surely, my lord, the sole issue on the return of a habeas corpus is the question of the validity of the custody . . ."

The thought . . . the urge to urinate, near physical pain . . . would no longer be subdued.

Edgar Kramer squirmed miserably in his chair. But he would not leave.

Anything, anything, rather than draw attention to himself. Closing his eyes, he prayed for a recess.

It was to be no pushover, Alan Maitland realized. A. R. Butler, Q.C., was fighting hard, contesting every argument, citing precedents in rebuttal against *Rex* vs. *Ahmed Singh*. The judge, too, seemed extremely querulous, questioning minutely as if, for some reason of his own; he wished Alan's presentation turned inside out.

At this moment A. R. Butler was defending the Immigration Department's actions. "No individual freedom has been abrogated," he declared. "Duval, in the case at bar, has had his rights and now they have run out."

The older lawyer's performance, Alan thought, was as impressive as ever. The deep, urbane voice continued, "I submit, my lord, that to admit such an individual, under such circumstances as described, would inevitably open the gates of Canada to a flood of immigrants. These would not be immigrants as we know them. They would be those demanding admittance merely because they cannot remember where they were born, possess no travel documents, or speak in monosyllables."

Instantly Alan was on his feet. "My lord, I object to counsel's remarks. The question of how any man speaks . . ."

Mr. Justice Willis waved him down. "Mr. Butler," the judge said mildly, "I don't suppose you or I can remember being born."

"The point I was making, my lord———"

"Furthermore," the judge said firmly, "I imagine that some of our most respected local families are descended from those who got off a boat without travel documents. I can think of several."

"If Your Lordship will permit——"

"And as for speaking in monosyllables, I find myself doing it in my own country—as, for instance, when I visit the Province of Quebec." The judge nodded equably. "Please proceed, Mr. Butler."

For an instant the lawyer's face flushed. Then he continued, "The point I was making, my lord—no doubt badly, as Your Lordship was generous enough to point out—is that the people of Canada are entitled to protection under the Immigration Act . . ."

Outwardly, the words were summoned and marshaled with the same easy assurance. But now, Alan realized, it was A. R. Butler who was clutching straws.

For a while, after the hearing had begun, misgiving had haunted Alan Maitland. He had feared that, despite everything, he might lose; that even at this late stage Henri Duval would be condemned to the *Vastervik* when it sailed tonight; that Senator Deveraux might believe, mistakenly, his blandishments had worked . . . But now a sense of assurance was returning.

Waiting for the present portion of argument to conclude, his thoughts switched to Henri Duval. Despite Alan's conviction that the young stowaway was a potentially good immigrant, the incident this morning in the hotel had left him disturbed. Uneasily he remembered Tom Lewis's doubts. "A flaw somewhere; a weakness . . . maybe not his fault; perhaps something his background put there."

It need not be true, Alan told himself fiercely; everyone, whatever his background, took time to adjust to new environments. Besides, the principle was what mattered most: personal liberty, the freedom of an individual. Once, glancing around the courtroom, he had found the eyes of Edgar Kramer upon him. Well, he would show this smug civil servant that there were processes of law more powerful than arbitrary administrative rulings.

The focus of argument before the court had switched. Temporarily, A. R. Butler had resumed his seat, and now Alan sought to reopen old ground: the matter of the Immigration Department appeal following the special inquiry. At once A. R. Butler objected, but the judge ruled that the subject could be raised, then added casually, "When convenient to counsel, I believe we might recess briefly."

About to agree politely with the judge's suggestion, Alan had seen an expression of intense relief cross Edgar Kramer's

face. He had noticed, too, that for the past several minutes
the civil servant had been moving, as if uncomfortably, in
his high-backed chair. A sudden memory . . . instinct . . .
made Alan hesitate.

He announced, "With Your Lordship's permission, before
recess I would appreciate completing this single portion of
my argument."

Mr. Justice Willis nodded.

Alan continued to address the court. He examined the appeal proceedings, criticizing the composition of the appeal
board with its three members—including Edgar Kramer—
fellow immigration officers of the special inquiry officer,
George Tamkynhil.

Rhetorically he asked, "Can it be anticipated that a group,
so constituted, would nullify the findings of a close official
colleague? Moreover, would such a group reverse a decision
already announced in the House of Commons by the Minister
of Immigration himself?"

A. R. Butler interjected heatedly, "My friend is deliberately misinterpreting. The board is a board of review . . ."

The judge leaned forward. Judges were always touchy
about administrative tribunals . . . it was something Alan had
known. Now, his eyes on Edgar Kramer, he realized why he
had delayed. It was a vicious impulse—a stroke of malice
which, until this moment, he had not admitted to himself.
Nor had it been necessary; he knew the case was won. Uneasily, he waited.

Through a tortured mental haze Edgar Kramer had heard
the last exchange. He waited, pleading silently for it to end,
praying for the recess the judge had promised.

Mr. Justice Willis observed acidly, "If I am to understand
it, this so-called appeal from a special inquiry is nothing
more than a department rubber stamp. Why in the world call
it an appeal at all?" Fixing his gaze on Kramer, the judge
continued austerely, "I say to the representative of the Department of Citizenship and Immigration that the Court
harbors grave doubts . . ."

But Edgar Kramer was no longer listening. The physical
pain . . . the urge begun earlier and now intensified, was all
consuming. His mind, his body could encompass nothing
else. Brokenly, with anguish, he pushed back his chair and
hurried from the courtroom.

"Stop!" It was the judge's voice, sharply commanding.

He paid no heed. In the corridor, still hastening, he could

hear Mr. Justice Willis bitingly addressing A. R. Butler.
". . . Warn this official . . . disrespect . . . any further oc-
casion . . . contempt of court . . ." And then, abruptly:
"Court recessed for fifteen minutes."

He could envisage the eager, crackling press stories which,
in a moment or two, would be telephoned or written: *Edgar
S. Kramer, senior Immigration Department official, today
was threatened with contempt of court proceedings during
the British Columbia Supreme Court hearing into the case
of Henri Duval. Kramer, while being addressed critically by
Mr. Justice Willis, walked out of court, ignoring an order
by the judge . . .*

It would appear everywhere. And it would be read by the
public, colleagues, subordinates, seniors, the Minister, the
Prime Minister . . .

He could never explain.

He knew that his career was over. There would be repri-
mands; and afterwards he would stay a civil servant, but
without advancement. Responsibilities would grow less, respect diminishing. It had happened to others. Perhaps in his
own case there would be medical inquiries, early retirement . . .

He leaned forward, putting his head against the cool toilet
wall, resisting an urge to weep bitter anguished tears.

4

Tom Lewis asked: "What comes next?"

"If you want to know," Alan Maitland answered, "I was
just wondering myself."

They were on the steps of the Supreme Court Building. It
was early afternoon, warm, with unseasonal sunshine. Fifteen minutes earlier a favorable verdict had been handed
down. Henri Duval, Mr. Justice Willis ruled, could not be
deported to a ship. Therefore Duval would not sail with the
Vastervik tonight. There had been spontaneous applause in
court, which the judge had subdued sternly.

Alan said thoughtfully, "Henri isn't a landed immigrant
yet, and I suppose eventually he could be sent directly to
Lebanon where he boarded the ship. But I don't think the
Government will do it."

"I guess not," Tom agreed. "Anyway, he doesn't seem to
be worrying."

They looked across the steps to where Henri Duval was

surrounded by a knot of reporters, photographers, and admirers. Several women were among the group. The former stowaway was posing for pictures, grinning broadly, his chest thrown out.

"Who's the sleazy character in the camel-hair coat?" Tom inquired.

He was watching a florid man with sharp, pock-marked features and oiled hair. He had a hand on Henri Duval's shoulders and was including himself in the pictures being taken.

"Some sort of night-club agent, I understand. He showed up a few minutes ago; says he wants to put Henri on show. I'm against it, but Henri likes the idea." Alan said slowly, "I don't quite see what I can do."

"Did you talk to Duval about the job offers we have? The tugboat thing sounds good."

Alan nodded. "He told me he doesn't want to start work for a few days."

Tom's eyebrows went up. "Getting a little independent, isn't he?"

Alan answered shortly, "Yes." It had already occurred to him that certain responsibilities concerning his protégé might prove an unexpected burden.

There was a pause, then Tom remarked. "I suppose you know why Kramer went out of court the way he did."

Alan nodded slowly. "I remembered from the other time —what you told me."

Tom said quietly, "You rigged it, didn't you?"

"I wasn't sure what would happen," Alan admitted. "But I could see he was ready to blow." He added miserably, "I wish I hadn't done it."

"I imagine Kramer does too," Tom said. "You fixed him, but good. I was talking to A. R. Butler after. By the way, Butler's not a bad guy when you get to know him. He told me Kramer is a good civil servant—hard-working, honest. If I may quote my learned friend, 'When you consider what we pay civil servants, the Kramers of this country are a whole lot better than we deserve.' "

Alan was silent.

Tom Lewis went on, "According to Butler, Kramer already had one reprimand over this business—from the Prime Minister, no less. I should think what happened would be good for another, so you can probably figure that you managed to break him."

Alan said slowly, "I feel ashamed about the whole thing!"

Tom nodded. "At least that's two of us."

Dan Orliffe had left the group around Henri Duval and came towards them. He had a folded newspaper under his arm. "We're going back to Henri's room," he announced. "Somebody has a bottle and there seems to be an urge to start a party. Coming?"

"No, thanks," Alan said. Tom shook his head.

"Okay." About to turn away, the reporter handed Alan the paper. "It's the noon edition. There's a little about you, there'll be more in the final."

As Tom and Alan watched, the group with Henri Duval moved away. The energetic center of it was the man in the camel-hair coat. One of the women had her arm through Henri's. The former stowaway was beaming happily, enjoying the attention. He did not look back.

"I'll give him his head for now," Alan said. "Later on today I'll sort him out. I can't just leave him, turn him loose."

Tom grinned sardonically. "Good luck."

"He may be all right," Alan argued. "He may turn out fine. You can never tell, and you can't prejudge—ever."

"No," Tom said. "You shouldn't prejudge."

"Even if he doesn't do well," Alan persisted, "the principle is more important than the man."

"Yeah." Tom followed Alan down the courthouse steps. "I guess there's always that."

Over steaming spaghetti, at the Italian restaurant near their office, Alan broke the news about their fee. Surprisingly, Tom seemed almost unconcerned.

"I'd probably have done the same," he said. "Don't worry; we'll get by."

Alan felt a surge of warmth and gratitude. To hide his own emotion, he opened the newspaper Dan Orliffe had given him.

On page one there was a story of the Duval hearing, but written before the verdict and the Edgar Kramer debacle. An Ottawa CP dispatch disclosed that the Prime Minister would make "a grave and significant announcement in the House of Commons this afternoon"; the nature of the announcement was not given, but speculation tied it to worsening in-

ternational affairs. The late news box contained race results
and another single item:

Senator Richard Deveraux died suddenly this morning,
reportedly of a heart attack, at his Vancouver home. He was
74.

5

The door to the house was open. Alan walked through.

He found Sharon in the drawing room, alone.

"Oh Alan!" She came to him. Her eyes were red from
crying.

He said softly, "I hurried as soon as I heard." He took
her hands gently, steering her to a settee. They sat down
side by side.

"Don't talk," he told her. "Unless you want to."

After a while Sharon said, "It happened . . . about an
hour after you left."

He started guiltily. "It wasn't because . . ."

"No." Her voice was low but firm. "He had two heart
attacks before. We'd known for a year that one more . . ."

"It seems inadequate," he said. "But I'd like to say I'm
sorry."

"I loved him, Alan. He took care of me from the time I
was a baby. He was kind, and generous." Sharon's voice
faltered, then went on, "Oh, I know all about politics—
there were mean things, as well as good. Sometimes it
seemed as if he couldn't help himself."

Alan said softly, "We're all like that. I guess it's the way
we're made." He was thinking of himself and Edgar Kramer.

Sharon raised her eyes. She said steadily, "I hadn't heard
. . . with everything else. Did you win your case?"

He nodded slowly. "Yes, we won." But he wondered
what he had won and what he had lost.

"After you'd gone this morning," Sharon said carefully,
"Granddaddy told me what had happened. He knew he
shouldn't have asked you what he did. He was going to tell
you so."

He said consolingly, "It doesn't matter now." He wished,
though, that this morning he had been more gentle.

"He would have wanted you to know." Her eyes were

brimming, her voice unsure. "He told me . . . that you were
the finest young man . . . he had ever known . . . and if I
didn't grab and marry you . . ."

The voice broke. Then she was in his arms.

Nineteen   The Act of Union

It was 3.20. Forty minutes left.

At 4 P.M., simultaneously in Ottawa and Washington, the
Act of Union would be announced.

In the House of Commons tension was growing. This
morning the Prime Minister's office had allowed it to be
known that a "grave and significant announcement of national import" would be made. No details had been given,
but on Parliament Hill speculation had been growing hourly.

Within the House, routine business was proceeding but
there was an undercurrent of expectation. The public galleries
were already filled, a line of luckless latecomers lining the
halls outside. In the diplomatic gallery several ambassadors
had already arrived. In an adjoining gallery, members' wives,
vying for the choicest seats, were filing in.

Immediately outside the House, lobbies, corridors, and
press rooms were abuzz with talk. News of a cabinet split
was widely rumored but, so far as James Howden knew,
there had been no leak as to the cause. A moment earlier,
conversations in the Government lobby had stilled as the
Prime Minister had entered, walking to his own House of
Commons seat.

Settling down, he glanced around, then opened the folder
he had carried in. Closing his ears to the current speaker—
a back-bench M.P. enjoying the unusual attention—Howden
read, once more, the agreed joint statement and the opening
text of his own speech to follow.

For days he had labored on the speech, in between commitments, completing it in the early hours of this morning
after returning from Montreal. He had had little sleep, but
excitement and a sense of destiny sustained him.

The speech which he would make today in the House—
unlike others of the past few days—was entirely his own.
Other than Milly Freedeman, who had typed the drafts, no
one else had seen or worked on it. He was aware that what

he had written, and would say, was from his heart. What he proposed would divert the course of history. For Canada, for a while at least, it would lessen nationhood. But in the end, he was convinced, the gain of union would outweigh a separate peril. There was courage in facing facts; greater, perhaps, than in empty insurrections with which the past abounded.

But would others see it too?

Some would, he knew. Many would trust him, as they had before. Others would be won by argument, a few by fear. A large section of the nation was American in thought already; to them, the Act of Union would seem logical and right.

But there would be opposition, and a bitter fight. It had begun already.

Early this morning he had interviewed separately the eight cabinet dissidents who were supporting Adrian Nesbitson. By strong persuasion and a personal appeal he had won back three, but five were adamant. Together with General Nesbitson they would resign and resist the Act of Union as an independent opposition group. Undoubtedly a few M.P.s, at least, would follow them, to form a rump within the House.

It was a serious blow, though not entirely unpredictable. He could have been more confident of surviving it, however, if the Government's popularity had not decreased in recent weeks. If only there had been no stowaway incident . . . Resolutely, to avoid rekindling his inner, burning anger, Howden switched his thoughts away. He had noticed, though, that Harvey Warrender was not yet in the House. Nor was Bonar Deitz, the Leader of the Opposition.

A hand touched his shoulder. Turning, he saw the shock of black curls and bristling mustache of Lucien Perrault. Jauntily, as he managed to do everything, the French Canadian bowed to the Speaker and dropped into the empty seat of Stuart Cawston, who had briefly left the floor.

Perrault leaned over, whispering, "It is true, I hear, that we have a fight before us."

"I'm afraid so," Howden murmured. He added warmly, "I can't tell you how much your support has meant to me."

Perrault gave a Gallic shrug, his eyes humorous. "Well, we shall stand together, and if we fall there will be a thunderous sound." After a moment, smiling, he moved away to his own seat.

A page boy laid an envelope upon the Prime Minister's

desk. Ripping it open, Howden read in Milly Freedeman's handwriting, "The President is preparing to leave the White House for the Capitol." In the Prime Minister's office, a minute or two away, Milly was monitoring an open line to Washington. It was for last minute contingencies. So far there had been none.

On the other side of the House, the Opposition Leader came in. Bonar Deitz looked paler than usual and preoccupied, Howden thought. He went straight to his front row desk and snapped his fingers for a page boy. As the boy waited, Deitz scribbled a note, then folded it. To Howden's surprise the note was delivered to himself. It read: "Essential we discuss urgent, personal matter re you and Harvey Warrender. Please meet me immediately, Room 16—B.D."

Alarmed and startled, Howden looked up. But the Opposition Leader had already gone.

2

At the same moment that Bonar Deitz had entered the House of Commons, Brian Richardson strode into the outer office of the Prime Minister's suite where Milly Freedeman waited. The party director's face was set grimly. In his hand was a sheet torn from a teletype. Without preliminary he told Milly, "Wherever the chief is, I need him—fast."

Milly gestured to the telephone she was holding. She mouthed silently the one word "Washington." Her eyes went up to the clock upon the wall.

"There's time," Richardson said shortly. "If he's in the House, get him out." He laid the teletype on the desk in front of her. "This is Vancouver. Right now it comes first."

Milly read quickly, then, putting the telephone down on its side, wrote a hasty note. Folding the note and teletype sheet together she sealed them in an envelope and pressed a buzzer. Almost at once a page boy knocked and entered. Milly instructed, "Please take this quickly and come straight back." When the boy had gone, she picked up the telephone again and listened.

After a moment, covering the mouthpiece, Milly asked, "It's pretty bad, isn't it—the way things came out in court?"

Richardson answered bitterly, "If there's another way of making the Government look stupid, vicious, and fumbling all at once, I haven't thought of it."

"Is there anything can be done—anything at all?"

"With luck—if the chief will agree to what I want—we can salvage about two per cent of what we've lost." The party director dropped into a chair. He added glumly, "The way things are, even two per cent is worth saving."

Milly was listening to the telephone. "Yes," she said. "I have that." With her free hand she wrote another note. Covering the mouthpiece again, she told Richardson, "The President has left the White House and is driving to the Capitol."

He answered sourly, "Hooray for him. I hope he knows the way."

Milly noted the time: 3.30.

Brian Richardson got up and came close beside her. "Milly," he said; "the hell with everything. Let's get married." He paused, then added, "I've started my divorce. Eloise is helping."

"Oh, Brian!" Suddenly her eyes were moist. "You pick the strangest times." Her hand still cupped the telephone.

"There is no time—no right time ever." He said roughly, "We have to take what we can get."

"I wish I were as sure as you," she told him. "I've thought about it; thought so much."

"Look," he urged, "there's going to be a war—everybody says so; and anything can happen. Let's grab whatever's left and make the most of it."

"If only it were that simple." Milly sighed.

He said defiantly, "We can make it that simple."

Unhappily she answered, "Brian darling, I don't know. Honestly, I don't know."

Or do I know? she thought. Is it that I want too much: independence and marriage—the best of both, surrendering neither one? It couldn't be done, she knew. Perhaps independence had been something she had had too long.

He said awkwardly, "I love you Milly. I guess I told you, and it hasn't changed." He wished he could express the deeper things he felt. For some things it was hard to find the words.

Milly pleaded: "Can't we, just for a while, go on as we are?"

Just for a while. That was the way, he thought, that it always was and would be. Just for a while, and sooner or later one of them would decide the time had come to end.

"I guess so," he said. He had a sense of losing something he had never really possessed.

3

In Room 16—the big luxurious sanctum adjoining the Speaker's chambers, which all parties shared—the Prime Minister faced Bonar Deitz. Except for the two of them, the room was empty.

Deitz said quietly, "Thank you for coming promptly."

Howden nodded. The apprehension he had felt before persisted. He asked uncertainly, "What is it you have to tell me about Harvey Warrender?"

Instead of answering, Deitz said obliquely, "You know that we're neighbors in Rockliffe?"

"Yes." The Warrenders and Deitzes, Howden knew, had facing properties.

"This morning Harvey's wife called me to their house." The Opposition Leader added, "Harvey's wife and mine are quite good friends."

Howden said impatiently, "Go on."

The other hesitated, his gaunt scholarly face troubled. Then he said, "Harvey had locked himself in his study. He wouldn't come out. When we called to him he threatened to kill himself."

Shocked, Howden said, "Did he . . ."

"No." Deitz shook his head. "People who threaten usually don't; at least, that's what I'm told."

"Then what . . ."

"Eventually we broke in. They have a manservant. We forced the door together."

The slowness was infuriating. Howden snapped, "What then?"

"It was like a nightmare. Harvey went berserk. We tried to subdue him. He was raving, foaming . . ."

As if they were speaking of something abstract, Howden said, "I used to think that sort of thing was fictional . . ."

"It isn't. Believe me, it isn't." Deitz took off his rimless glasses; he passed a hand across his face. "I hope I never see anything like it again."

There was an air of unreality. Howden asked, "What happened then?" His eyes took in the other man's frail figure— the figure which a cruel cartoonist had once compared to a string bean.

"Oh, God!" Deitz closed his eyes, then opened them. With an effort he composed himself. "Fortunately their man is strong. He held Harvey. We tied him to a chair. And all the while . . . struggling, raving . . ."

It was unbelievable, grotesque. "I can't believe it," Howden said. He found his hands were trembling. "I simply can't believe it."

"You will," Bonar Deitz said grimly. "You will, if you see Harvey."

"Where is he now?"

"In Eastview Hospital. Under restraint, I think they call it. After it happened, Harvey's wife knew whom to call."

The Prime Minister said sharply, "How did she know?"

"Apparently this isn't wholly a surprise," Deitz answered. "Harvey's been having treatment—psychiatric treatment—for a long time. Did you know?"

Aghast, Howden said, "I had no idea."

"Nor had anyone, I suppose. His wife told me afterwards; also that there's a history of insanity—on Harvey's side. I gather she found out after they were married. And there was some sort of trouble while he was teaching, but it was hushed up."

"My God!" Howden breathed. "My God!"

They had been standing. With a sense of weakness he lowered himself into a chair. Deitz sat down beside him.

The Opposition Leader said softly, "It's strange, isn't it, how little we know about one another until something like this?"

James Howden's mind was in turmoil. It was difficult to know what to think first. He and Harvey Warrender had never been close friends, but for years they had been colleagues . . .

He asked, "How has Harvey's wife taken it?"

Bonar Deitz had cleaned his glasses with a tissue. Now he replaced them. He answered, "Now that it's over she's surprisingly calm. In a way she almost seems relieved. I imagine it wasn't an easy situation to be living with."

"No," he answered slowly, "I don't suppose it was." Harvey Warrender had not been easy on anyone. He remembered Margaret's words: "I've sometimes thought Harvey is a little mad." At the time he had agreed, but never dreamed . . .

Bonar Deitz said quietly, "There isn't much doubt, I imagine, that Harvey will be certified insane. They don't rush these things, but in this case it seems mostly a formality."

Howden nodded dully. Out of habit his fingers caressed the curve of his nose.

Deitz went on, "Whatever is necessary, we'll make it easy for you in the House. I'll pass the word to my people and there need be very little said. The newspapers won't report it, of course."

No, Howden thought; there were certain decencies the newspapers observed.

A thought occurred to him. He moistened his lips with his tongue.

"When Harvey was . . . raving . . . was there anything, especially, he said?"

The Opposition Leader shook his head. "Mostly it was incoherent: jumbled words; some bits of Latin. I couldn't make them out."

"And . . . nothing else?"

"If you're thinking of this," Bonar Deitz said quietly, "perhaps you should take it now." From an inside pocket he produced an envelope. It was addressed *Rt. Hon. James M. Howden.* The handwriting, though sprawling and uneven, was recognizable as Harvey Warrender's.

As Howden took the envelope and opened it, his hands were shaking.

There were two enclosures. One was a single sheet of stationery, the writing upon it in the same disordered hand . . . as if in stress—Harvey Warrender's resignation from the Government. The other was a faded convention program, on the back, the fateful scribbled agreement of nine years earlier.

Bonar Deitz was watching Howden's face. "The envelope was open on Harvey's desk," he said. "I decided to seal it. It seemed better that way."

Slowly Howden's eyes came up. The muscles of his face were working. There was trembling through his body, like an ague he could not control. He whispered, "You . . . saw . . . what was there?"

Bonar Deitz answered, "I'd like to say no, but it wouldn't be true." He hesitated, then continued. "Yes, I looked. It isn't something I'm proud of, but curiosity, I'm afraid, proved strong."

Fear, icy fear, struck Howden's heart. Then resignation took its place.

So, in the end, a scrap of paper had destroyed him. He had been brought down by his own ambition, recklessness . . . a moment of ill-judgment long ago. Giving him the original document was a trick, of course; Bonar Deitz had made a copy; it would be produced and published, as exposés affecting others had been . . . bribes, indiscreet cheques, furtive agreements . . . The press would trumpet; opponents would wallow in self-righteousness; politically he could not survive. With a strange detachment he wondered what came next.

He asked, "What are you going to do?"

"Nothing."

Somewhere behind, a door opened and closed. Footsteps came toward them. Bonar Deitz said sharply, "The Prime Minister and I would like to be alone." The footsteps retreated; again the door closed.

"Nothing?" Howden said. His voice held unbelief. "Nothing at all?"

The Opposition Leader said carefully, "I've done a good deal of thinking since this morning. I suppose I should use the evidence that Harvey left. If some of my own people knew I'd withheld it, they would never forgive me."

Yes, Howden thought; there were plenty who would rejoice to destroy him, and never mind the means. In his mind a gleam of hope flickered; was there to be a reprieve after all—on Deitz's terms?

Deitz said softly, "Somehow, though, I can't see myself doing it. I'm not partial to stirring mud; too much of it rubs off."

But I would have done it to you, Howden thought. *Without hesitation, I would have done it to you.*

"I might have, though, if it hadn't been for something else. You see, I can beat you in another way." There was a pause, then, with quiet confidence, Deitz said, "Parliament and the country will never pass the Act of Union. You will go down to defeat and I shall win."

"You knew?"

"I've known for several days." For the first time the other smiled. "Your friend in the White House has his opposition too. There've been some leaks down there. Two senators and a congressman flew up to see me and they represented others who don't like the concept or its terms. The briefing, I may say, was fairly thorough."

Howden said seriously, "If we don't unite, it's national suicide for Canada—annihilation."

"It seems to me it's national suicide if we do." Calmly

Deitz said, "We've come through wars before. I'd sooner do it again—as an independent nation—and take our chances."

"I hope you'll reconsider," Howden said, "think gravely, carefully . . ."

"I already have. Our policy has been determined." The Opposition Leader smiled. "You'll forgive me if I save my arguments for debate and the election." He added, "You'll call an election, of course."

"Yes," Howden said.

Deitz nodded. "I assumed you would."

As if by consent, they stood. Howden said awkwardly, "I suppose I should thank you for this." He looked at the envelope in his hands.

"I'd rather you didn't. We might both become embarrassed." Bonar Deitz held out his hand. "We shall be combatants, I expect, quite soon. There'll be name calling; there always is. I'd like to feel, to some extent, it isn't personal."

James Howden took the proffered hand. "No," he said, "it won't be personal." Somehow, he thought, despite the other's frailty, Bonar Deitz had more stature than ever before.

4

Hurriedly, the minutes fleeting past, the Prime Minister entered his parliamentary office, a sheaf of papers in his hand. He had a mood of crisp incisiveness.

Four people were waiting: Richardson and Milly; Margaret Howden, who had just arrived; Elliot Prowse. The executive assistant was looking anxiously at his watch.

"There's time," Howden snapped; "but only just." He asked Margaret, "Would you wait for me inside, dear?" When she had gone into his inner office he selected from the papers the teletype Richardson had sent to him. It was the report of the Vancouver verdict: the liberation of Henri Duval, the judge's censure of Edgar Kramer. He had read it a moment ago on returning to the floor of the House.

"It's bad," Richardson began, "but we can salvage . . ."

"I'm aware of that," Howden interrupted. "It's what I intend."

He was conscious of a freedom of action he had not possessed before. Despite the tragedy of Harvey Warrender, the personal threat was gone. Warrender's resignation—

crudely written, but effective nonetheless—was in his hand.

He told the party director, "Issue a press statement this afternoon that Duval will be given a temporary immigrant visa at once. You may quote me as saying that there will be no appeal of the Vancouver judgment or any further attempts to deport him. Also, that on my personal recommendation, the Cabinet will consider an order in council allowing Duval full immigrant status as quickly as possible. You might add something about the Government respecting, as always, the prerogatives of the courts and the rights of individuals. Is all that clear?"

Richardson said approvingly, "You bet it's clear. Now you're talking."

"There's something else." The words came fast, the tone commanding. "You can't quote me directly on this, but I want it known that this man Kramer is being relieved of his duties and recalled for disciplining. What's more, if you can implant the idea that Kramer has misadvised the Government on this whole Duval business from beginning to end, so much the better."

"Good," Richardson said. "Very good indeed."

Turning sharply to the executive assistant, the Prime Minister ordered, "And see that it's done. Call the deputy minister and tell him those are my instructions. You may add that as far as I am concerned I consider Kramer unfit to hold a responsible post again."

"Yes, sir," Prowse said.

"You may also tell the deputy that Mr. Warrender is indisposed and I shall name an acting minister tomorrow. Remind me."

"Yes, sir." Prowse was writing rapidly.

The Prime Minister paused for breath.

"There's this," Milly interjected. Still monitoring the telephone, she passed him an External Affairs telegram which had come a moment earlier. From the Canadian High Commissioner in London, it began, "Her Majesty has graciously agreed to accept the invitation . . ."

The Queen was coming.

It would help, Howden realized; help a great deal. He calculated rapidly, then said, "I'll announce it in the House tomorrow." Today would be premature. But coming tomorrow, the day after the Act of Union announcement, there would be an implication of royal approval. And by tomorrow, even though news of the Act of Union would have reached London, Buckingham Palace would not have had time to reconsider . . .

"There are cabinet resignations," Milly told him seriously. "The six that you expected." She had letters clipped together. He could see Adrian Nesbitson's signature on top.

"I'll take them in the House and table them." He thought: there was no point in delaying; the situation must be met head on. He informed Milly, "There's one more resignation, but keep this here." From the papers in his hand he selected Harvey Warrender's letter, then instructed, "We'll hold it up for several days." There was no point in advertising additional disunity; besides, Warrender's resignation was not over the Act of Union. They would wait for a week, then announce reasons of health as the cause. Genuinely, for once, he thought.

An idea occurred to him. He turned to Brian Richardson. "There's some information I want you to obtain. Within the past few days the Leader of the Opposition has received an unofficial U.S. delegation—two senators and a congressman; they represented others. I want names, dates, places; where they met; who was there; anything else you can get."

The party director nodded. "I'll try. It shouldn't be difficult."

He could use the information in debate, James Howden decided, as a weapon against Bonar Deitz. His own meeting with the President had been publicized; Deitz's meeting could be shown as furtive. Enlarged on skillfully, it could have the odor of conspiracy. People wouldn't like it, and the revelation—coming from himself—would be a telling point. He dismissed a qualm of conscience. Bonar Deitz could afford the luxury of forbearance; as a leader fighting for his political life, the Prime Minister could not.

Elliot Prowse said nervously, "The time . . ."

Howden nodded. Entering the inner office, he closed the door behind him.

Margaret was by the window. She turned, smiling. A moment ago, when she had been banished from outside, she had suffered a feeling of exclusion, knowing there were things about to be said for the ears of others but not her own. In a way, she thought, it was the pattern of her life; beyond certain barriers—unlike Milly Freedeman—she had never been allowed to pass. But perhaps it was her own shortcoming—a lack of enthusiasm for politics; and, either way, the time for protest had gone by long ago. She said softly, "I came to wish you luck, Jamie."

He came toward her and kissed her upturned face. "Thank you, my dear. It looks as if we'll need it all."

She asked, "Is it really bad?"

"There'll be an election soon," he answered. "To be honest, there's a strong chance that the party might lose."

"I know it isn't what you want," she told him, "but even if it happens, at least there's still ourselves."

He nodded slowly. "Sometimes I think it's that that keeps me going." He added, "Though we might not have long; the Russians don't intend it."

He was conscious of the minutes passing. "If it should happen that I lose," he said, "you know we've very little money."

Margaret said gravely, "Yes, I know."

"There'll be gifts offered—perhaps large sums. I've decided I shall not accept." He wondered: would Margaret understand? Understand that near the end of his life—the long upward road, from the orphanage to his country's highest office—he could not return to charity again.

Margaret reached out, her hand clasping his. "It doesn't matter, Jamie." There was emotion in her voice. "Oh, I think it's a shame that Prime Ministers should be poor, when you've given all you have and done so much unselfishly. Perhaps, someday, someone will change it. But for us it doesn't matter."

He had a sense of gratitude and love. How far, he wondered, could generous faith extend? He said, "There's something else I should have told you years ago." He held out the old convention program—its written side uppermost—which Bonar Deitz had brought him.

Margaret read the writing carefully. "Wherever this came from," she said, "I think you should burn it now."

He asked curiously, "You don't mind?"

"Yes," she answered, "I do mind in one way. You could have trusted me, at least."

"I suppose I was ashamed."

"Well," Margaret said, "I can understand that."

As he hesitated, she went on, "If it makes you feel any better, though, I don't believe this changed anything, except for Harvey Warrender. I always felt you were meant to be

what you were; to do the things you did." She handed the
paper back, then added softly, "Everyone does bad as well
as good. Burn it, Jamie; you wiped it out long since."

Crossing to the fireplace, he lit a match and watched the
paper flare. He held it by a corner until flames approached
his hand. Dropping it, he saw the rest consumed, then ground
it into ashes with his heel.

Margaret was fumbling in her handbag. Producing a torn
square of newsprint, she told him, "I saw this in this morning's newspaper. I saved it for you."

He took it and read: "For those born under Sagittarius,
today is a day of achievement. The tide is turning . . ."

Without finishing, he crumpled the paper into a ball.

"We make our own fortunes," he said. "I made mine the
day I married you."

5

At three minutes to four, in the Government lobby, Arthur
Lexington was waiting.

The External Affairs Minister said, "You've cut it fine."

James Howden nodded. "There were things to be done."

"I've bad news." Lexington spoke quickly. "Immediately
after your speech, Nesbitson and the other five are planning
to cross the floor of the House."

It was the ultimate blow. A cabinet split, with six resignations, was grave enough. For the same ex-ministers to cross
the floor—the utter repudiation of Government and party—
had connotations of disaster. Once, perhaps, in a generation,
a single M.P. might cross the floor in a moment of high
drama. But for a quarter of the Cabinet . . .

Howden thought grimly: it would focus attention—as nothing else—upon opposition to the Act of Union and to himself.

"They've made an offer," Lexington said. "If you'll postpone the announcement, they'll withhold action until we've
met again."

For an instant, Howden hesitated. It would be close, but
he could still reach Washington in time. Milly had the open
line . . .

Then he remembered the President's words: *There is no
time. By reckoning, reason, logic, we've used it all . . . If
we do have time it will be by God's good grace . . . I'm*

*praying for the gift of a year . . . The very best for the chil-
dren; their children yet to come . . .*

He said decisively, "There will be no postponement."

"That's what I thought," Lexington said quietly. He added,
"I suppose we should go in."

The House of Commons was packed—not a vacant seat on
the floor of the House, and every gallery full. Public, press,
diplomats, distinguished visitors were crammed in every inch
of room. There was a stir as the Prime Minister, with Arthur
Lexington behind, came in. The back-bench M.P. on the
Government side, who had been speaking earlier, was winding up, his eye upon the clock, his orders from the party
whips explicit.

For the second time since earlier in the afternoon, James
Howden bowed to the Speaker of the House and took his
seat. He was conscious of the multitude of eyes upon him.
Soon, as press wires hummed and teletypes spewed out their
urgent news, it would be the eyes of North America, even of
the world.

Above him, in the diplomatic gallery, he could see the
Soviet Ambassador, stiffly unsmiling; the U.S. Ambassador,
Phillip Angrove; the British High Commissioner; the ambassadors of France, West Germany, Italy, India, Japan, Israel
. . . a dozen others. Reports would go, by telegraph and
courier, to every major capital tonight.

There was a rustle in the Speaker's gallery as Margaret
took the front row seat reserved for her. She looked down
and, as their eyes met, smiled. Across the center aisle, Bonar
Deitz was attentive, waiting. Hunched behind Deitz was the
crippled Arnold Geaney, his bright eyes gleaming. On the
Government side, to Howden's right, Adrian Nesbitson
stared stiffly ahead, a touch of color in his cheeks, his
shoulders squared.

Respectfully, a page boy placed a note upon the Prime
Minister's desk. From Milly Freedeman, it read: "The Joint
Session of Congress is assembled, and the President has
entered the Capitol. He was delayed by cheering crowds on
Pennsylvania Avenue, but will begin his speech on time."

Delayed by cheering crowds. James Howden felt a surge
of envy. The President's strength was firm and growing, his
own ebbing away.

And yet . . .

No cause was ever lost until the final hour. If he were

going down, he would make a fight until the end. Six cabinet
ministers were not the nation, and he would take his case
to the people, as he had before. Perhaps, after all, he could
survive and win. A sense of force and confidence spread
over him.

Ten seconds to four. The House of Commons stilled.

There were commonplaces here at times: dullness and
mediocrity and petty bickerings. But the House could rise,
when needed, to a sense of great occasion. It had done so
now. This was a moment which history would remember,
whatever years for history were left.

In a way, Howden thought, we are a mirror of life itself:
our weakness and our smallnesses; and yet, always beyond
them, the heights which human beings can attain. Freedom
was a height, in whatever form and by whichever measure.
If, to sustain the greater part, a little must be lost, it was a
sacrifice worth making.

As best he could, he would find words to point the way.

In the Peace Tower above, the quarters chimed. Now,
majestically, the great Bourdon Bell announced the hour.

The Speaker intoned: "The Prime Minister."

Deliberately, not knowing what the future held, he rose to
address the House.